THE FOURTH ANGEL

The FOURTH ANGEL

Robin Hunter

ARBOR HOUSE / NEW YORK

Designed by Richard Oriolo

Manufactured in the United States of America

10 9 8 7 6 5 4 3 2 1

Library of Congress Cataloging in Publication Data

Hunter, Robin.
The fourth angel.

I. Title.
PR6058.U54F6   1986   823'.914   86-17457
ISBN 0-87795-820-3

FOR PATSY

AUTHOR'S NOTE

This is a work of fiction. I would like to make this clear because, even in the course of writing it, and in the short time which has passed from first publication in England to the appearance of this American edition, events have occurred which duplicate the scenes in the following pages. This only reflects the fact that the world we all live in has not gotten any better, for horrors once hard to imagine have become almost commonplace. I take no pleasure in the fact that terrorist acts have pointed up the situations imagined in this book, and I only regret that calculating the swift decline of public abhorrence of such acts is all too easy in our present times. *The Fourth Angel* remains a work of fiction, and so any references, actual or implied, to real people or events is both accidental and coincidental.

I would like to record my thanks to Wendy Stephenson, Don Philpott of The Press Association, Alastair Cunningham, various friends in Fleet Street, London, and Tel Aviv, and as always, to Estelle Huxley, who keeps me laboring at the wordface and up to date on relevant events.

ROBIN HUNTER
Puerto Pollensa, Spain
1986

"And the fourth angel poured out his vial upon the sun: and power was given unto him to scorch men with fire."

REVELATION 16:8

THE FOURTH ANGEL

THE ATTACK

Andy Brice was fiddling his expenses when he first heard the shooting. He had tucked himself away at the back of the Athens departure hall, spread his bills in neat piles around the table and, unconscious of the racket from crowds and loudspeakers, settled down to his accounts. When the sound first came to his ears he was three hundred dollars ahead. A familiar tapping, then a short burst, then another. He raised his eyes slowly from the columns of figures and the piles of bills, and cocked his head, listening. There it was again. As if to underline the point, the air pulsed softly as an explosion dinned faintly above the noise inside.

Andy had heard these sounds before. They were his business and there was money in it. Glancing round at the throng packing the airport concourse, he saw no alarm, no consciousness on their faces that somewhere, something was going on. He opened his camera case, lifted out the Nikon, snapped on his longest lens, and with a swift movement of his arm swept the bills inside. He rose, slung the case over his shoulder, and, camera in hand, headed toward the stairs, pushing his way through the crowd, climbing over luggage and barging through queues, until he found the stairway, and ran hard up the steps, looking around for an exit to the outside, to somewhere up high with a view.

As Andy arrived on the first level a man burst out of an office and ran ahead of him along the gangway toward the far door. Andy followed, ignoring a shout behind, ducking under the arm of another man who shot out of a door and tried to detain him.

"Press," said Andy, over his shoulder. "What's up?" Then he was through the far door and out into the roaring sunlight. On the terrace, a flat roof overlooking the ramp, the sun beat down on him. There were two people already there, airport police, sheltering behind the low parapet wall on the far side, and Andy ran at a crouch to join them. He heard another crackle of gunfire above the engine noise, and dropped onto his knees beside the wall. The police stared at him.

"Press," he said again, in answer to their nervous glare, lifted his camera and, following their example, peeped slowly over the wall.

Out on the ramp, the big jet was on fire. He could see that clearly. The air was pulsing with heat above the open door, and the aluminum was beginning to peel back above the cockpit. As he watched, another burst of fire raked the airplane, pocking the skin above the windows, and, craning over, Andy saw the gunman, a dark figure clad in white airport overalls, crouched behind a moving stairway just below, the barrel of his machine-gun jerking slightly as he fired. There was another, leaping into view as Andy focused his camera on the ramp, lying under the food trolley by the airplane. As the camera whined, snapping off photo after photo, Andy saw this man rise and lob a grenade up through the black flame-flecked doorway of the airliner. There was a dull explosion inside, a gush of flame from the door, and then another one. Somewhere inside the plane the liquor trolley exploded, red flame threading the oily smoke. A door flew off at the back of the aircraft and the safety chute shot out, a tumble of bodies cascading after it, raked by gunfire, rolling, falling, collapsing across the concrete as the gunman poured shots at them and into the doorway. The noise was tremendous, a blast of sound, of engines, of gunfire, and piercing yells and screams.

Then it happened, quite quickly. Above the wing the escape hatch window fell out. A woman appeared, crawling out of the airplane, wreathed in black smoke. The escape hatch slid off the wing, crashing down onto the concrete, but Andy concentrated on the woman, twisting his lens fast, jumping her into sharp focus. She reached inside, back into the flames, and lifted a child out onto the wing as, clearly in the camera's eye, bright blood leaped and spread across her smoldering dress. The gunman just below the wall was firing up at her.

Wild with elation, Andy stood up, careless of the gunfire, aiming his camera at the gunman who stood out clearly, shooting up at the woman. She fell over sideways against the fuselage, sliding down the wing, and then the child ran, clambering over her mother, moving out along the wing, running, running. Andy swore and swung his lens to bring her into focus again to catch that contorted face, the hair burning brightly in the sun, her clothes on fire. And he caught her too, just at the end of the wing, still running on, screaming, out into space as she fell, down to the concrete below. He heard the thud of her body hitting the concrete, saw the smoke puff out from her clothes, noticed that he was out of film and that the shooting had stopped.

Andy was breathless. He looked down and saw the gunmen standing up, kicking their weapons away from them, turning, hands in the air, toward the slowly advancing police. He saw the burning aircraft, the ragged, smoking escape chute, the huddled bodies, and began to load more film into his camera. Under the wing the child's body continued to smolder, but Andy's thoughts were already elsewhere.

"You beauty," he said aloud, pressing his lips to the barrel of the lens. "We've just made a bloody fortune."

ONE

 On the day his family died, Simon Quarry was sitting in his London office, teaching an author the facts of life. His office was a large, comfortable, friendly room, lined with books, thickly carpeted. The broad leather-topped desk at which he sat was well appointed with all the usual paraphernalia of office life, an angle-lamp, telephones, a bowl of flowers. The whole effect was balanced by the buff-colored files and stacks of folded galleys, several manuscripts sagging from their folders in a slight but comfortable disarray. More manuscripts rested on an adjoining side table, in front of a leather-framed photograph of his wife and two young daughters. The overall impression was one of relaxed affluence, of a man who enjoyed the good things of life without worrying unduly about them, and Quarry himself gave the same impression.

Quarry was tall, slim, slightly rumpled, his jacket slung behind his chair. He sat sideways to the desk, his long legs stretched out before him, ankles crossed. One elbow rested on the desk, the fingers of one hand playing with a pencil while he ran the other hand through his hair from time to time, head turned attentively toward his guest. The atmosphere, however, was tense. Quarry eventually put down his pencil and sat upright in his chair, holding up a document before the eyes of his author. The snapping voice slowed.

"I take it," said Quarry, "that you have actually read this contract? Because that is what it is, a contract, a legal, binding agreement. I do hope you realize that, and realized it before you signed."

James Dugdale, author, biographer and enraged visitor, slapped the document aside, the cup rattling in the saucer he held in his other hand. He was a small man, red of face, sandy-haired, wearing what Quarry thought of privately as "author kit," baggy flannels, a Fair-Isle pullover, a jacket with leather at the cuffs and elbows. Dugdale fumed.

"I've seen more contracts than you've ever signed, Quarry."

Quarry nodded and settled back in his chair, waving his hand to indicate in turn the files, the papers and the manuscript on his desk.

"Good," he said smoothly, smiling at Dugdale. "So let us look at what we contracted for. Here we have your original manuscript, readers' reports, amendments, edited copy, more edited copy, re-typed pages and various sections. And here," he held up a sheaf of folded sheets, "here we have the galleys. But one moment," he went on, as Dugdale opened his mouth to speak, "the largest amount of paper we have here is this file." He tapped a thick brown folder. "This file," he continued, "is full of rude letters, various inaccuracies and carping comments from you, plus replies, more or less soothing, from half my staff."

"I'm not happy with what your firm is doing to my book," retorted Dugdale. "I won't have my work cut to ribbons by those incompetent clowns you choose to employ."

Quarry smiled. It was not really a nice smile. "Opinions of what they are doing will vary," he conceded lightly. "My incompetents, as you call them, have done you a service. Can I refer you back to the contract, to specifics this time, not opinions? This manuscript was delivered eight months late and, may I point out, fifteen thousand words short of the length we originally commissioned. That's short weight, Mr. Dugdale. It contained five distinct areas steeped in plagiarism and two highly libelous statements about members of Her Majesty's present government. From an esteemed political biographer, that can hardly be described as a professional job. It needs work, Mr. Dugdale, work! As it is, it won't do. Not for the Quarry Press, not for your reputation."

Dugdale's complexion had deepened to a further shade of red. "If you aren't happy with my book," he cried, "then don't publish it. I've been published by the best publishers in the country. I don't need any lessons from you, Quarry. So, I say it again, if you don't want it, I'll take it somewhere else."

If anything, Quarry's smile broadened. "Ah! I thought you'd say that. Let us be honest, Mr. Dugdale. You have been carping about what we are doing to your manuscript. What we are doing is to turn it into a book. Incidentally, the book will be *ours* also, not just yours, with the Quarry Press imprint on it as well as your name. Your manuscript was just not good enough. I know it, and you know it. You've been published by a lot of people because, good as you are when published, you are notoriously difficult to work with, and most people are relieved, if not actually glad, when you take your work elsewhere. Smokescreens won't work here, Dugdale. I only hire people who can do their jobs, and when complaints like yours filter onto my desk, it means we take them seriously. So, I have examined your complaints. I have read the manuscript, checked the sources, read all your letters and our replies, and in my opinion you are ninety-nine percent wrong. Wait . . ." He held up his hand as Dugdale's mouth opened. "We won't publish your book if . . ." Quarry continued, "if you refund the advance, plus the sum paid over for expenses, plus the costs incurred by us on the book to date, not counting the delays, a sum which, as of this morning, we calculated as . . ." he picked up a coil of paper from the desk and smoothed it out, "£6,832, plus a few pence."

Dugdale's eyes blinked hurriedly. "I don't have anything like that sum," he said sharply, "and you damned well know it."

"Of course I know it," replied Quarry firmly, "which is why I raised the point about the contract." He picked up the contract and handed it across the desk. "Look, Dugdale, if we hadn't wanted the book we wouldn't have commissioned it. We respect your work, and when you are good, you are very good. But we are good, too, and a little mutual respect goes a long way in this business. So, let me tell you where we both stand. I have a simple rule for this company, Mr. Dugdale. We make a deal and we stick to it. Just in case our authors think differently, and some of them do, I must refer you to clause nine of that famous contract. In simple terms it means that we can turn your biography into a blue movie if we want to, and there is not much you can do about it. The rule in business, Mr. Dugdale, any business, is that the man who pays—says. Now, let us discuss how we are going to solve our problem."

It was not a happy meeting. When Dugdale had at last capitulated and shuffled out, the annotated manuscript under his arm, Quarry sat on for a while, idly putting order into the papers on his desk, stacking the files neatly again, slipping a rubber band around a bundle of loose papers. Although he was well into his forties, Quarry looked, and most of the time felt, at least ten years younger. When he had restored order to his desk, he stretched his arms high over his head, linking his fingers and stretching until his back creaked. Then he loosened his tie, rose from his chair, walked swiftly toward the office door and flung it open.

"Ruth!" he called out. "Is there any chance of some more tea? I have slain my daily dragon and deserve a biscuit. What a brute! That man works on the theory that there is no point in being difficult when, with a little extra effort, you can be completely impossible."

Ruth Frazer, Quarry's secretary, partner and confidante, looked up from her typewriter and smiled at him. She was an amiable, competent lady, a few years younger than Quarry, and they spoke like very old friends.

"Yes," she replied. "I know. He was ranting at me while we waited for you. Told me he was furious and not used to being kept waiting. What did you do to him? He flung out through the door in what some of our other authors would describe as a fair tizz."

"Not if they want to get published by us they wouldn't," grunted Quarry. "Bring in the tea and I'll tell you all about it."

When Ruth returned with large mugs of tea and the remains of a packet of biscuits, Quarry was back behind his desk, his chair pushed back against the wall, his feet resting on a pile of books. He looked, as usual, cheerful.

"It's typical," he remarked as Ruth put down the mugs. "When we have guests, even professional pains-in-the-A like that one, out comes the bone china, and when we're alone, it's the mugs. Is there no respect for authority in this company?"

"We must make a good impression, and Mr. Dugdale, as he himself will readily tell you," said Ruth primly, the corners of her mouth twitching in a smile, "is a very well-known author. When he's feeling modest, that is."

"Mr. Dugdale is a pain in the arse," replied Quarry shortly, dunking a biscuit into his tea. "Do you know, he began by...." They spent ten minutes or so discussing Dugdale and his ilk, before Ruth looked at her watch and stood up.

"It's getting on," she said, "and I have lots to do before the post goes, even if you haven't. There are several contracts for you to sign, and you ought to at least read the minutes of last month's editorial meeting before the next one tomorrow. What time does the family get back?"

"Their flight is due in around six, but I want to leave early to miss the traffic out to Heathrow. I might ring and check that it's on time, but if there is nothing much to do here, I'd rather wait at the airport."

"I expect you'll be glad to see them. It's been over a month since they left."

"You can say that again," said Quarry. "I'm too old to be left like this, but I can't go gallivanting off for a month at a time like Eleana and the kids can. Anyway, enough gallivanting for them, they can stay home and look after the master of the house for a while, or at least until the Christmas holidays. Then I think we might all go skiing. But the kids will want to stay at home now, I expect. They like it at home. I suppose it's having their own toys and friends around."

"It might be an idea to ring first and see if the flight is on time," agreed Ruth. "Do you want me to do it, or shall I give you a line?"

The first intimation that something might be wrong came on the five o'clock news. Quarry was cutting his way through the early evening traffic driving forcefully out west onto the M4 highway, when the announcer said simply, "Reports are coming in of a terrorist attack on an Israeli airliner at Athens Airport. Athens has been the scene of terrorist incidents in the past, notably when an Air France jet was hijacked to Entebbe some years ago. No details are yet to hand but we will bring you more news as it reaches the studio."

Quarry frowned and leaned forward to turn up the radio, a little concerned but still unworried. He pushed the BMW a little harder through the traffic, moving into the outside lane and increasing his speed to the limit as he reached the highway. Ten minutes later he had parked the car and was crossing the walkway toward Terminal 2. There had been no further news about the plane.

As he reached the concourse and turned through the crowds toward the arrival gate, a man and a woman came toward him. Preoccupied, Quarry had passed them before he realized that the man was supporting the woman and that both were crying. He hesitated, looking back, and noticed for the first time that a crowd of people were milling and shouting around the El Al counter. He looked up at the Arrival monitor, and waited until the screen rippled and announced, *Flight 841: Await Information.*

Quite suddenly, Quarry found it difficult to breathe. He went across toward the crowd, his heart pounding heavily, and gently but firmly pushed his way through to the counter. The desk was lined with people shouting questions at the harassed white-faced staff. Quarry reached across the counter and grasped a hostess by the sleeve.

"What has happened to 841?" asked Quarry. His voice sounded unreal, too loud, but she hardly seemed to hear him. The girl shook her head and snatched her arm away.

"You must wait for information. We have no details yet. We don't know anything . . . please! We have no information. As soon as we have something we will tell you."

"My wife and family are on that flight," said Quarry urgently. "What in the name of God has happened?"

The man at Quarry's elbow turned toward him roughly. "Wait your turn," he shouted into Quarry's face. "I have family on that flight, too. Wait your turn. Miss . . . Miss . . ."

The crowd surged forward again, their weight pressing at Quarry's back. There were screams now, the sound of sobbing, a clamor of voices rising up, beating on his ears. Quarry stared back at the man, his eyes wide, hostile, and then nodded quietly.

"I'm sorry," he said, "please excuse me, but we are all concerned." He turned to the girl again. "Can't you see what's happening here? Please phone your office and get the manager down here. You must give us some news or there will be a riot here. Can't you see that?" His plea worked. The manager appeared, a lounge was opened and the crowd ushered into it, security guards fending off the rapidly growing numbers of newsmen who attempted to follow them, and closing the doors.

Expressionless stewards moved about offering coffee and drinks, until the door opened again and several men came into the room. One was a uniformed policeman and at the sight a further tremor swept through the crowd, but it was an older man who spoke, looking around the room, his eyes everywhere but on the faces before him.

"Ladies and gentlemen," he began, "I must ask you all to be calm. There has been some very, very bad news . . . about our Flight 841 . . . at Athens."

"For God's sake!" a woman's voice shrieked from the crowd. "Tell us what's happened." The crowd roared and rose to their feet, falling back as the spokesman raised his arms again for silence.

"There has been an attack on 841. The plane has been set on fire . . . and there are many casualties."

A great, almost breathless wail went up from the crowd. People sat down suddenly, clasped hands to their faces, clung together or turned away from the group, but the majority surged forward, to surround the spokesman, yelling for news, calling out for more information, wanting names, names . . .

Quarry pushed his way back through the crowd. He asked no questions, caught no eyes. He sat down at the back of the room, waved away a girl offering coffee, but took a whisky from a passing tray. As he raised it to his lips, his hands started to shake.

Quarry let himself into his house a little after midnight, and closed the door quietly behind him, dropping the car keys onto a tray they kept by the door. Another set of keys, those to his wife's car, was already on the tray. Quarry picked up her keys and examined them carefully. With the keys dangling from his fingers, he walked slowly around the house, switching on the lights as he moved from room to room, so that the windows, one by one, blazed out into the night. He stopped in the kitchen, opened the door of the fridge and gazed for a while at the newly stocked shelves, the bottles of milk, the cartons of orange juice.

"Children should drink lots of milk," he said aloud. "It helps them grow well. Yes. Lots of milk. Lots of vitamins, things like that."

He returned to the hall and plodded up the stairs, turning along the landing into their bedroom. The lights from the floor below seeped up through the bedroom windows, lighting the room, and he made no move toward the light switch. He walked over to the bed, pulled back the coverlet and took a small wrapped package from under a pillow, before opening the closet doors. A light came on inside, flooding the row of dresses on their hangers, and he leaned his face into them, smelling the familiar perfume. He stayed like that for some time, his throat tight, his eyes closed.

Then, still holding the package, he went down the corridor into the girls' bedroom, switching on the lights as he went. He sat down on a chair close to the door, and looked around the room slowly, at the dolls and toys ranged along the window ledge, the shelves of books, the pop posters on the walls. There were two beds, each pillow piled with presents. Quarry rose and sat down again on the nearest bed, turning the presents over slowly with one hand.

"Welcome home, kids," he said slowly. "Welcome home."

Somewhere in the house a telephone began to ring, but Quarry just sat there, beside the presents he had bought to welcome home his dead children. After a while the phone stopped ringing, but in a short while it rang again, and continued to ring, on and off, for most of the night.

TWO

 Pausing in the corridor, Martin Clissold tugged gently at the hem of his jacket, smoothed a stray hair carefully back down over one ear, and smiled contentedly at the effect. Then, turning, he tapped lightly on the door and without waiting to be asked, slid inside.

"And how is my favorite secretary today?" he asked, resting his back against the door and letting the handle turn inside his fingers.

Sitting behind her desk, Ruth looked up from her typewriter, regarded him steadily for a moment and sighed audibly. She was wearing a grey silk blouse, a black scarf tied neatly at the neck. She looked tired. The skin beneath her eyes was a little puffy, and as she looked at Clissold her mouth was firm and unsmiling.

"Martin," she said, "if there ever was a time when I could well do without your shop-worn charm, today is the day. To be quite frank, I can do without it at any time. Don't you *ever* get tired of oiling your way around the office? Aren't you getting a little old for it? Since I've started, may I add that but for the fact that you are good at your job, I'd ask Simon to fire you. To be frank, Martin, you're a pain. I think I dislike you intensely. No, I don't *think*, I'm sure of it."

Martin Clissold had the sense to look slightly taken aback, but long habit carried him along. "My, my," he said lightly, "we are prickly today, but that's not surprising, I suppose. My humble apologies, Madam. What I really wanted to know is how is he today?" He nodded at the closed door of Quarry's office. "And how did it go?"

Ruth looked past Clissold, out of the window. "Considering that Simon has just returned from burying his wife and his children, he is quite remarkably calm. But for God's sake, how would you feel? How do you think funerals go? They aren't usually very jolly."

Martin raised his hands defensively. "OK, I'm sorry. I would have liked to have been there, but what can one say?"

"Nothing," replied Ruth. "There's nothing anyone can say, so say nothing. The funeral was close friends only but the mob was provided by the press, a charming bunch of morons. They've been hanging round Simon's neck like vultures for the last month, ever since it happened."

"But I am one of the directors," put in Martin. "I know we all sent wreaths and so on, but I still think . . . I think I should have been there."

"Look," said Ruth, "what has happened is *personal.* Simon's family are dead. Today was the funeral. The man has enough troubles. What has your damn directorship got to do with it? It's not a business matter. There's no profit in it. Can't you grasp that?"

"*You* went," pointed out Martin, "and I think I should have been there, that's all I said. Why are you being so difficult? Can't you see my point of view?"

Ruth ignored him, pushing her chair back hard against the wall. "Do you know, it's actually true what they say about the press. Journalists really do ring up and say, 'How did he feel when he saw the picture in the papers?' Did you see that picture of little Sarah running along the wing with her hair on fire? That awful picture."

"Yes, I did. Who didn't? It must have been on every front page in the country, even abroad. I saw it in *Paris Match* anyway, just last week. A double-page inside spread."

"Well, they want to know his reactions. You know the sort of thing . . . 'Tell me, Mrs. Jones, how did you feel when you saw young Johnny fall under the steamroller?' What do they think he felt, for God's sake?"

"What did you say?" asked Martin Clissold curiously.

"I'm afraid I forgot I was a lady. Several times in fact. Now I've told young Maureen to block all press calls at the switchboard, but what's the use? I expect they are picketing his house as well. They won't leave the poor man alone."

Clissold eased himself away from the door, walked over to the window and looked down into the square. "There are a few hanging about outside now," he said, "and photographers, even a TV crew."

"Bloody bunch of vultures," said Ruth viciously. She got up and moved across to join him, glaring down from the window at the little knot of newsmen clustered by the railings outside the office.

"I hardly like to ask," began Clissold, "but, just out of curiosity, how did he react? I bow to none in my admiration of Simon, but he is a curious fellow at times. A trifle unpredictable, dare I say it."

Ruth looked at him again, closely, that hint of contempt back in her eyes. "If you *really* want to know, he asked me to call the papers for a print of that photograph."

Clissold's astonishment was genuine. "He what! I can't believe it. That's incredible."

"He wants a full-plate, half-tone print of that terrible photograph. Glossy and bled, if possible. He was quite specific."

"But Good God!" said Clissold, shaking his head. "What sort of man would want a picture of his kid burning alive? Why? Did you ask him?"

"I didn't ask, and unless you feel like becoming rapidly unemployed, neither should you," said Ruth briefly. "He's not too predictable at the moment. If I were you, I'd leave Simon severely alone."

"He must be cracking up. It's not surprising after all. Perhaps he'd be better off going away for a while. You know, Ruth, I've been wanting to say this for some time, though perhaps this isn't the moment but, well, let's face it, he's been slacking off over the last year or so. Everyone has noticed it."

Ruth frowned at him. "He spent twelve years building up this firm, and as his children are . . . were . . . growing up, I expect he wanted to spend a little more time with them. That's why he cut down a seventy-hour week to a mere sixty-hour week. He even stopped working on weekends. That's hardly dereliction of duty."

"Even so," said Clissold. "Look, you and I could run things here. Perhaps he'll want to sell up. There really isn't any point in all this now. I've had lunch with one or two people in the last couple of weeks, and I think there would be offers around if he was interested in selling. With the existing management . . . " He stopped as Ruth looked hard at him, shaking her head slowly from side to side.

"You're another of the vultures, aren't you?" she said, wonderingly. "Just like those others outside. You've decided to look after number one and see if there are any pickings for you in this affair. You'll go far, Martin Clissold, if no one steps on you. Have you been crawling round the City suggesting that someone tries to pick up Simon's firm for a knock-down price while he's down on his knees? So that you can run it once he's been eased out."

Martin Clissold looked pained. "Face facts, Ruth. I like Simon, God knows. But he's well into his forties and you know how he doted on those kids. Anyway, everyone always said Eleana was the real driving force behind him. He's so easy-going, not a keen businessman like this company really needs, especially now. And, well, there's that photograph. That's not normal. Anyway, Simon didn't do it on his own. We all helped to make this company one of the best publishing houses in the country. And if Quarry can't hack if any more—not that anyone would blame him for that, after what happened—then we ought to think of managing without him. He'd probably be glad to get clear of it anyway. It must have knocked all the stuffing out of him."

Ruth laughed out loud. It was a short, unamused and far from pleasant laugh. She moved away from Clissold to take another look out of the window, before returning to face him again.

"I've misjudged you. You aren't just an irritating smoothie with the gift of the gab, are you?" she said. "You really are a first-class, self-seeking swine. Let me remind you that the Quarry Press has been going for over sixteen years, and it took Eleana, Simon and me, plus one or two others, a good few years before we needed overpaid mouthpieces like you. You joined us—and I have your file over there—about three years ago."

"As a director," interrupted Clissold. "I came in at the top because that's where help was needed. And I don't like your tone."

"As an executive director," stressed Ruth. "No shares. Simon and I now own all the shares. And now you think the time is right to move in, his wife hardly cold in her grave, elbow the old man aside and be sitting pretty. Amazing!"

"He'll sell," said Clissold confidently. "He doesn't care any more, you'll see. I'm sure of it. A good offer and he'd pack this company in tomorrow."

"You don't know Simon," said Ruth. "He keeps you because you're good at your job. That's his only criterion, as I told you. I think you would be wise to keep your ambitions to yourself until Simon decides what, if anything, he wants to do. If you cross him, you'll regret it. And that's my last warning."

"Oh yes?" said Clissold sharply. "Do I hear undertones there? Echoes of a threat? If it goes as I think it will, I'd like to think we could work together. I'm not going to stay on unless we have some changes. So don't you forget that either."

"Now, that is a threat," said Ruth, unworried. "I'm trying to tell you something about your employer. He's a very nice man. I like him. He's kind, very fair, but no fool. He's been hurt, but he'll get up again. He also has excellent connections and very long ears. I expect your little lunch parties are not unknown to him and, as I say, he isn't a good man to cross."

"Well, you know what I think," said Martin abruptly, walking across the room to leave. He stopped at the door and turned toward Ruth. "Incidentally, perhaps you could keep this conversation to yourself. All right?"

"Just go away," said Ruth. "Please . . . go away, and don't hurry back."

Clissold glanced toward the door of Quarry's office and left, shaking his head. When he had gone, Ruth got out a handkerchief, blew

her nose hard and reached for the telephone. "Maureen," she said
when switchboard answered, "get me the Press Association please. I
want a private word with the picture editor."

Quarry was sitting in his usual position behind the desk, his feet up
among the litter of files and papers, a glass of Scotch in his hand,
when Ruth came into the room and sat down opposite him. She
looked quickly at the glass, and at the half-empty bottle on the desk.

"Panic not," said Simon, catching her glance. "I am not taking to
the bottle. In fact it tastes awful at this hour, but if you fancy a belt
of booze, you know where the glasses are."

"Maybe I will."

Ruth went over to the open cupboard among the bookshelves, and
Simon heard the chink of ice and the scrape of glass and bottle. Presently she came back, sat down again, and raised the glass towards
him.

"Cheers," she said.

"Cheers," said Simon, lifting his glass in response. "By the way,
thanks a lot for coming along this morning . . . and for keeping those
bloody press people away from me. It hasn't been much fun for you
either, this last month. I'm very grateful to you."

"I've been glad to help," said Ruth. "It's nice to have something
to do and we all . . . all the staff . . . we all feel so useless. Well, almost all of us," she added reflectively.

They sat on for a while, companionably, until Ruth had to break
the silence, putting her glass on the desk and looking directly into
Simon's face.

"Tell me," she said, "where do we go from here?"

"You tell me," said Simon. "At this moment I feel a little, well,
spent, is the word that comes to mind."

"We go on, of course," said Ruth firmly. "What else can we do?
Life goes on."

Simon swung his feet down off the desk and leaned across the top
toward her, his elbows on the top, his chin resting on clasped hands.
"And that's it, is it?" he said curiously. "Someone comes along, blots
out my life, but life itself goes on? That's show business, et cetera, et

cetera. Correct me if I'm wrong, but I think I have experienced a fundamental change recently. Go on to what? Tell me what we go on for."

"Life does go on, Simon, " Ruth pointed out softly. "You are still here. So am I. So is this firm. We go on because that's all there is to do. I don't like clichés, God knows, but as I said, life goes on, with or without . . . people. They come, they go, life goes on. There isn't any choice."

"But not as before," said Simon bleakly. He looked suddenly tired and shaded his eyes with his hand for a moment before looking at her again.

"Hardly," agreed Ruth.

"Very hardly, indeed. So . . . ?"

"Simon, I don't know what to say. Sarah was my godchild, sort of, at least I thought of her as one, and Eleana and I were close friends. Don't think I don't care, but what can we *do?* Surely the best thing for you is to pick up the pieces and . . . Oh Lord, whatever I say is a cliché!" Her voice shook a little. "What can I do?"

"You can get me another drink. As small as you wish. That will help for a start, but easy on the hard stuff. Believe it or not I'm trying to think, honest I am."

Ruth rose, picked up his glass, added a little whisky and a lot of water and ice, and returned it to Simon. He was playing again with a pencil, tapping it softly on the leather top of the desk, not looking at her, as the silence deepened.

"That creep Clissold came round to offer his condolences," she said presently. "The phone hasn't stopped and what are laughingly described as the gentlemen of the press are outside to record your grief. You have become a circulation booster on the 'it's an ill wind' theory. And Clissold thinks you should sell out."

"I know," said Simon broodingly. "He's hinted as much from time to time. He had lunch last week at the L'Ecu de France and discussed the matter with MacAllistair. He's also been chatting to some City money but they aren't interested. Only publishers buy publishers, he ought to know that. Clissold is very ambitious but not very bright."

Ruth laughed, almost happily. "How do you know all this?" she asked, shaking her head at him.

"MacAllistair told me," said Simon. "He rang up when I got back from Athens to offer his sympathy. Telling me about Clissold's ideas gave him something else to say. He was quite embarrassed. Felt the timing was inopportune and so on."

"Will you sell?" asked Ruth.

"Well . . . why not?" said Quarry abruptly. "Let 'em all have a piece of me, the press, my competitors, even those within these walls. Why not? I'd hate to think my family died and nobody benefited at all. Now that would be a waste."

"Oh, for God's sake!" Ruth snapped sharply. "Don't get bitter. I've just been telling Clissold that when you've done your Sir Patrick Spens act, you'll rise up roaring. So don't start to whine and prove me wrong. I couldn't bear it, Simon."

"The allusion escapes me," Simon admitted. "Who is this Patrick Spens character?"

"I *think* it's Sir Patrick Spens. It's a poem, probably Walter Scott, or maybe not," said Ruth. "Don't you remember? He's the one who said, 'I'll just lie here and bleed awhile, and then I'll rise and fight again.' You must remember it from school."

"Vaguely," said Simon. "School was a fair while ago, but the fighting bit appeals to me. It's just *putting up* with the situation that's so hard. I know I can't mope about, but I can't get very worked up over manuscripts and contracts, not at the moment. I want something done about the death of my family and, let us not forget, over two hundred other passengers. How can a thing like that happen? Who did it? Who stood by? Why has nothing been done? Something must be done about this kind of thing. It's . . . criminal," he finished lamely.

"But what?" asked Ruth. "The people who did it are in prison. All the usual expressions of disgust, shock, horror and so on, have come from the authorities. There have been a lot of editorials. I think everyone is absolutely disgusted, but what can one do?"

"I don't know," said Simon wearily, putting the glass down slowly on his desk. "But something has to be done about this, just to prove it matters, that someone at least cares. It's not enough to say I'm sorry—too bad—tough luck."

"Look, Simon," said Ruth gently, "the last few weeks have been ghastly, and today was the worst. None of us is thinking straight at the moment, and frankly you look terrible. Why don't you go away for a few days, at least until the press lose interest and leave you alone? Go away and stay with Liz and Roger. Do some walking in the hills and clear your head. They have already asked me to try and persuade you, and I think you ought to go. You can talk it all out with Roger. He must be your oldest friend. Do it for me."

Quarry brooded on the idea. "All right," he said at last, "you're probably right. You usually are anyway, and you're more than capable of looking after this lot for a bit. Will you do something else for me while I'm away? Something difficult, I'm afraid."

"Of course," she said, pleased to have got her way so quickly. "I'll do anything I can, you know that."

"Go down to the house, clear it out, give the lot away or sell it if you like. Then put the house on the market. Then find me somewhere to live, a small flat somewhere near here. I don't care where, you choose."

"But Simon . . ." she protested, rising.

"No buts, Ruth, please," he said firmly. "Just clear it out. Have all the jewelry and anything that looks useful sent to Eleana's sister. Get someone in the secondhand furniture business to take the furniture and then put the place in the hands of the nearest real estate agent. Take the first offer on everything. Sell the lot. Type a letter giving yourself power of attorney and I'll sign it before I leave."

"Simon, you're crazy," cried Ruth. "The house, the contents, and everything, it must be worth a small fortune. You can't just give it away to the first bidder. Don't be silly. Think it over . . . you can't be serious?"

"Yes, I can," said Quarry, "and I'm not being silly. Think about it. How can I live there now? If you don't want to do it I'll get someone who does."

"No, I'll do it, if that's what you want. Leave it to me. You'll phone Roger and tell him you'll come? You'll call straight away?"

"Yes, I'll call him," agreed Quarry. "One other thing. Have you done anything about that photograph?"

"You know what I feel about that photograph, Simon. What good can that possibly do, and what do you want it for, anyway?"

"Ruth, don't argue with me. I don't know what I'm doing, not quite. I do know that something has to be done. I mustn't forget. Everybody else soon will, and then they will want me to. That's the way it is, I know, and that's why I need that photo. So, have you done anything about it?"

"I rang your pal down at the PA," said Ruth heavily. "He was amazed, and no wonder, but he said he will get you a print and keep his mouth shut as well. You realize what the press would make of this if they ever found out? It would be a scandal."

"I can't care about that," said Simon. "To hell with the press. Now, could you ask Maureen to get Roger on the line, and if he'll have me I'll sneak out of here through the mail room and leave you in peace."

"It's up to you, of course," said Roger, handing Simon the glass and dropping heavily into the next armchair. Roger was a big man, florid and fifty-ish, his waistline straining at the buttons of his shirt, his ruddy face full, his present manner paternal.

Simon had known Roger for over twenty years, for so long that he couldn't really remember how or where they had first met. They had spent a lot of time together in their twenties, sharing a flat, swapping girlfriends, walking in the Alps, skiing in Austria. Even marriage or, in Roger's case, marriage, divorce, re-marriage, divorce again, and now Liz, had failed to split them up. Simon was godfather to two of Roger's children and Roger was—had been—like an uncle to Simon's daughters. Looking into the fireplace, Simon reflected that Roger was probably the closest thing he had to a brother. Roger was an architect with a practice which seemed profitable enough to provide a fairly extravagant lifestyle, and if he had aged a little and was thickening perceptibly around the middle, the old, lively spark was still there. For the first time in over a month, since that dreadful nightmare at the airport, Simon felt the tension begin to ooze out of his body.

"Well," went on Roger, "we, well, Liz actually, thinks it might be a good idea if we got about, just a little. It won't do any good to sit and brood, my old mate, so lots of activity, that's the best thing. On Sunday I thought we might go out for a good tramp in the woods. Take a picnic. Have a good full day's bash."

"I'd like that," agreed Simon. "I haven't been for a good stiff walk in some months. There's nothing like a day on the hill to blow the clouds away, and, Lord, do I have clouds."

"Exactly," said Roger. "We really must do some hill walking this summer. Maybe Liz will let me off the leash and we could go over to France, or maybe even further. We never got to the Tatras, remember. You've kept it up, I know, but, well, we can't do much about that here in Sussex. There are the Downs, of course, but no real hills. Anyway, the point is, when we get back on Sunday, Liz has invited this girl round for dinner. Well, supper, actually. A casserole, a couple of bottles of claret, that sort of thing. Nothing complicated, just the four of us. A cozy evening. All right?" He shot a quick, anxious, sideways glance at Simon, who was still leaning forward, his glass clasped in both hands, staring into the fireplace.

"She's a nice girl, you'll like her," Roger continued. "Her husband ran off with one of her neighbors, left her flat. They are divorced now, but there she is, stuck at home with not much money and three kids."

Simon pulled his gaze away from the fireplace and slowly turned his eyes on Roger. There was something in his look that Roger didn't like. "Correct me if I'm wrong," said Simon quietly, "but do I gather that with my wife barely cold in the ground, you are fixing me up with the village divorcee?"

Roger flushed. "Of course not," he said quickly. "It's just to make up the numbers. For heaven's sake, Simon, don't be so touchy. This girl's had her own troubles, and Liz has told her all about you. You'll be company for each other. Besides, with her children . . ." He stopped abruptly.

Simon continued to look at him, that same expression deep behind his eyes, a look on his face that Roger couldn't fathom, and hadn't seen before.

"I get it," said Simon, tightening his lips. "Please don't explain, I get it. Misery needs company. Of course. Why not? Life goes on, doesn't it? Would you excuse me, I'll just take a turn in the garden." He got up and left the room without a backward glance. A few seconds later the back door closed behind him with a slam.

"Damn!" said Roger.

"Hello, how did it go?" asked Ruth, looking up in surprise as Simon came through her office door two days later, shrugging off his jacket and hurling it onto his peg.

"Don't ask. Any chance of coffee?" he said, picking up a pile of mail from her desk and disappearing into his own office, leaving the door open. As Ruth set out the cups she could hear the steady sound of crumpled paper dropping into his wastepaper basket.

"Well," she said, putting down the tray and slipping into a chair, "tell all. You look tired, Simon. The result of the break is not quite what I had hoped for. On the other hand, you have sorted out your mail with all your former speed. That's just the nonsense stuff by the way. I've already dealt with anything important."

Simon stirred his coffee moodily. "It's amazing," he said, his lips pursed. "Everyone sees what has happened only in relation to themselves. It's as if they say: 'One—Quarry's family is dead; two—Quarry is alive; three—how will the new widower-type Quarry affect me?' To which they answer as quickly as possible, 'Not at all if I can help it,' and rush to restore the status quo. I don't understand it."

"Well, what happened?" demanded Ruth, sitting down. "I gather that sending you off for Rest and Recreation didn't work out. What went wrong? It isn't easy for anyone, you know. But it didn't help?"

Simon laughed. "Hardly!" he said. "The day after I arrived I was supplied with the local easy lay. No, that's unkind. She was . . . is, a nice girl, thirty-ish, blonde, three kids, divorced and just the thing to put a twinkle back in any widower's eye. Poor woman. I'm afraid the evening was not a success."

"You're joking!" said Ruth shortly. "Surely Roger wouldn't have been so insensitive. Why, it's barely a month since . . . well, just over a month."

"Oh, they meant well," sighed Simon. "Roger got the message, but Liz thinks that everything can be forgotten if you can just get laid. She had dredged up two more women by the end of my visit. I think I'm in her black books for not getting their phone numbers. On the other hand, I didn't burst into tears over the soup and embarrass everyone. I think we can call it a draw."

Ruth poured more coffee into his cup, handed it back to him and picked up her shorthand pad. "So," she said, "we will have to try something else to keep you occupied. A little stirring up is what you need. How about a little work. I'm sure we have plenty here."

"No thanks," said Simon. "You handle it. I am going to do something about it."

"About what?"

"About those bastards who murdered my wife and children. That's what's been eating me up. Time ticks by and nothing gets done. Two hundred people were burned to death five weeks ago and there hasn't been so much as a line in the papers about it for the last ten days." Simon picked up a pencil and twiddled it between his fingers. "I don't want revenge or anything like that, but I want some justice done. I want someone to notice that something terrible has happened and do something about it. Just some acknowledgement that their deaths disturb those who are supposed to protect us, and can't be ignored. Fortunately we have some clout and good connections, so let's use them. Let's make the buggers jump."

"But how?"

"We'll start with the usual channels. Letters to the press, the Prime Minister, even the Queen, why not? Get me a list of all our authors, especially those in the House. One advantage of publishing political biographies is that it improves your contacts. Get hold of Alec Yates at the Foreign Office. He's a high-powered spook of some sort. Don't tell him what I want, but invite him to lunch. Say it's about his book. Strafe that useless MP of mine and get some questions asked in the House. Stir things up."

"Right," said Ruth excitedly, opening her notebook. "Where do we start?"

"Dear Prime Minister," began Simon. "Six weeks ago, on the morning of. . . ."

"An excellent lunch, Simon," said Alec Yates, twirling the wine in his glass, "and a really excellent wine. I've always liked this place. Isn't that Bernard Levin over there? I've seen that woman on the television, but I can't recall her name. A good place for you media folk with large expense accounts to mix and mingle, see and be seen. Very enjoyable."

Simon put down his fork, took a sip of wine, dabbed his mouth with a napkin, and looked directly across the table at his guest. "I'm glad you like it," he said. "We aim to keep our leading authors happy at the Quarry Press, but on this occasion, Alec, you are here to help me. I think it's only fair to tell you that I'm after something."

A slight frown, a shadow, a look of caution, passed over Alec Yates' face. He smoothed his hair back over his ears, the signet ring glinting on his little finger, and decided to prevaricate.

"Yes, that girl of yours indicated as much. Discreetly, of course. What a nice person she is. That marvelous telephone voice must be worth a fortune to you . . ."

"Alec," interrupted Simon gently, "I know that mixing with politicians has made you an expert at beating about the bush, but could you try, just this once, to give a direct answer to a direct question?"

Under his distinguished veneer, Yates looked actually uncomfortable. "That goes rather against the grain, old boy," he said, "and it would depend very much on the question."

Simon's glass went down a shade too firmly, spilling a dull red splash of wine onto the white cloth. He dabbed at it briefly with his napkin and looked directly at his guest. "Let me just remind you of a few facts," he said acidly. "About two months ago, some Middle East terrorists got onto the airfield at Athens, God knows how, and set an airplane alight, burning to death eleven crew members and two hundred and sixty-nine passengers. Among them were my wife and children." Simon's voice grew slightly louder. "The direct question is this. What are those idle bastards in that government you serve doing about it?"

Heads turned at nearby tables. The head waiter, hovering on the far side of the room, looked up and advanced a few steps toward Simon's table, before hesitating and turning back again.

"All right, Quarry, keep it down, please. I *know* all that. Dammit man, I've been to your home and met them. I'm very sorry, of course I am, we all are, but what do you expect Her Majesty's Government to do?"

"Act," snapped Simon. "Do something. Send a gunboat."

Yates leaned back, sighed, picked up his glass, thought better of it, and put it down again. He reached into his jacket pocket, took out and unfolded a piece of paper onto the table. Then he produced a pair of spectacles, put them on, read the paper carefully, and looked up at his host.

"I am not a fool, Quarry, and I'm not entirely unaware of your distress. Your letters are receiving attention. I put a note through to my minister yesterday morning, and this is the gist of the reply." He adjusted the spectacles and read aloud. " 'The airliner was an Israeli jet, attacked by Arabs on Greek territory. It was a disgraceful act of international terrorism, and resulted in the deaths of 269 innocent people, eleven of them British nationals. Her Majesty's Government has registered a strong protest with the Greek Government regretting the lack of security at the airport, pressing for the strongest measures against the alleged guerrillas as a deterrent to further acts, and requesting details of any improvements in airport security.' "

Yates looked at Simon over the top of his glasses. "They surrendered, you know. The terrorists—guerrillas is a diplomatic word—they put down their weapons and surrendered after the attack."

"I know," said Quarry, nodding at the paper. "So, is that all?"

"Not quite," said Yates. He continued reading from the piece of paper. " 'Her Majesty's Government and all sides of the House deplore such acts, which can only inhibit the search for a peaceful solution to the Middle East problem, a task in which the government is actively engaged, and on behalf of both Houses of Parliament, send condolences to the relatives of the victims.' "

An uneasy silence fell across their table, which the clatter of cutlery and the buzz of conversation from the surrounding tables hardly penetrated. Simon watched carefully while Yates refolded the note and placed it in his waistcoat pocket, removed his spectacles, put them in a case, closed it with a snap, and put the case inside his jacket. Their eyes met.

"So that's it?" asked Simon. "That's all. My family, my children, the purpose of my whole life blotted out, and you expect me to settle for a duplicated answer. The text of that message has been used so often in the last few years, it's a wonder the duplicating machine hasn't worn out, never mind the stencil."

Yates twirled the stem of his glass between his fingers, watching the wine swirl around in the bowl, and said nothing.

"That answer is rubbish, Alec, complete rubbish and you know it. In effect the government are shrugging their shoulders and passing a mild rebuke to the Greeks. Life goes on, too bad! That's it, isn't it?"

"But what do you expect the government to do, Quarry? Be realistic, man, it was in Greece, it was another flag carrier, and we are only involved peripherally, with eleven of our people out of nearly three hundred. Well, I'm sorry, Quarry, but you must see the position. What can we do?"

"I do see the position," exploded Quarry. "I just don't accept it. Why not apply for extradition and try those swine for mass murder?"

"I've explained why. Besides, it's too late, even if we wanted to apply for extradition."

Quarry pounced. "Why is it too late?" he asked quickly.

A look of discomfort flooded again over Yates' patrician face. "Well, if you must know, it'll be in the press soon, I expect. We can't keep anything quiet these days. They've been released. The Greeks freed the terrorists—well, guerrillas—three days ago. They flew out the same day."

Simon felt the words like blows. His head jerked back in startled surprise, a flush of amazement coloring his face. "You must be joking," he said, his voice choking. "Released? What do you mean, released? They killed nearly three hundred people, burned them alive. They can't have been released. Good God!"

"But no Greeks," said Yates quickly. "They killed no Greeks. Apparently they were very careful about that. You see. . . ." He raised his hand to silence Quarry's interruption. "No! Please, hear me out. The Greeks felt—and you can see their point of view—that this was not really their concern. It was an act in the Arab-Israeli struggle, as they see it. The accepted convention is that all hijackers are tried in the country they finally land in, so there could be no extradition. This wasn't quite the same, but that's the accepted procedure. Now, if they hold these men, there could well be hijackings or more trouble to get them released, even more attacks perhaps, so—well—they were deported. I expect that the authorities felt it was the best thing in the circumstances."

"Deported?" queried Simon. "Where to?"

"Flown to Beirut. I only heard as I was coming here. Lord knows where they are now. So you see, Quarry, there really is nothing we can do, is there? As you say, life goes on."

Simon drove slowly down the quiet suburban road, his foot resting gently on the accelerator, studying the names and numbers on the houses as they drifted past on either side. Fieldview—21—27—Mi Amore—49—Coltsfoot—61—there it was! He looked in the mirror, put the automatic gear into reverse and slid the BMW gently back into a parking space. He sat behind the wheel for a while, suddenly tired, depressed, that familiar dead weight still there in his stomach, his head and shoulders sagging a little. Then, catching sight of his face in the mirror, he got out of the car. It was a typical Sunday in quiet South London; a curtain twitched slightly at a window across the street.

"Ah suburbia, stern and wild," he said aloud, and walked past the unkempt privet hedge and up the concrete path to ring the bell at No. 61. He heard it shrill deep in the house but no one came. He resisted the impulse to press his face against the frosted glass door panel and stare inside. Instead, he turned away to study the street, lifting his hand to wave at the watchful net curtains in the house opposite. They twitched again and Simon turned his glance away as the door opened behind him.

"Mr. Hillary?" he asked. The man on the threshold seemed much older, much greyer, than the man Simon remembered from their one brief meeting, weeks before.

"Yes?" Hillary looked defeated, his shirt grimy at the neck, his trousers unpressed, feet stuffed into flat-soled slippers. Behind him a cat jumped down from the hat stand and slithered round his legs into the garden.

"You won't remember me, Mr. Hillary. We met at Heathrow, in the arrival lounge, some weeks ago, when . . . Well, you know. . . ."

"Ah yes." A faint gleam came into Hillary's eyes. "Of course, I remember you now. It's Mr. Quarry isn't it? I saw your picture in the paper, and that terrible picture of your little girl. I'm very sorry."

"I hope you don't mind me calling like this," said Simon hurriedly. "Look, may I come in?" He gestured toward the watchful curtains across the street. "The neighbors. It won't take long, but I'd like a brief word."

"Yes, of course. Come in." Hillary came alive suddenly and shuffled back down the hallway in his slippers. The house was dusty, uncared for and smelt a little of fried food. Neglect had set in, and yet under the recent grime, Simon detected the outline of a once well-polished and comfortable home. Hillary's life, too, had fallen to pieces.

Hillary moved about the sitting room, lifting books and papers aside, offering tea, increasingly uneasy, until he finally settled into a chair and looked curiously at his visitor. Simon watched him from the doorway and then came slowly into the room.

"May I?" he asked, taking off his coat and gesturing toward a chair.

"Oh, yes," said Hillary, half rising. "I'm sorry. Please, sit down."

"Thank you," said Quarry, dropping the coat over an upright

chair and sitting down in the armchair placed neatly by the fireside, realizing just too late that he should not have chosen that particular seat.

"I'm sorry," he said, starting to get up again, not looking at Hillary's face. "I didn't think."

Hillary smiled sadly. "It's all right. I'm getting used to it being empty, that's all. We used to enjoy sitting here in the evening, Mary and I, watching TV or, well, just sitting, I suppose." He gazed sadly into the empty grate, avoiding Simon's gaze.

"Mr. Hillary," said Simon firmly, "I need your help."

Hillary looked up, spreading his hands and then resting them on his knees, the lines on his face seeming to deepen. He smiled slightly at his visitor and shook his head slowly.

"Well, Mr. Quarry, I can't think why. I've not been good for much since Mary went. I can't think what help I could be to anyone."

Hillary's apathy swept over Simon. For a moment, he felt himself sag under the additional weight of the other man's hopelessness.

"Believe me, I don't want to add to your troubles," he began. "God knows we have all had enough of that, but—excuse me—but I need to talk to someone who feels what I feel."

"I don't feel anything," said Hillary. His voice seemed stilted, wooden, his gaze fixed on the empty grate. "I kept thinking for a long time that I'd get a letter, or that she'd just walk in. I thought she'd have missed the flight, she never could be on time, we used to quarrel about it. Then I realized it was true, that she really was gone. I never saw her you know . . . they said . . . after the fire . . . it was better not to, and so it was by her teeth, the dentist said it was her . . ." Hillary's voice faded away.

"I know," said Simon, wishing he had not come. "I know about all that."

"Then, I felt . . . guilty, I suppose, for not being there."

"So did I," said Simon in a rush. "I felt that if I had been there it wouldn't have happened. Or that I should have been there and shared it. We quarreled, my wife and I, just as she left. I took her to the airport, got her a porter and went to park the car. She always took far too much luggage, and I said she would get caught for overweight but, no, she knew, she always knew better. Anyway, when I got back, there was this great long queue at the El Al desk and at the head of it there was my wife refusing to pay £70 or so for excess baggage. I said I'd told her so, and refused to pay it for her, and she stormed off through the departure gate with the kids. So I never kissed her good-bye, never said sorry, never said 'Have a good holiday.' It wasn't serious, we talked later on the phone, even laughed about it. But the last time I saw her, we quarreled. I can't forget that."

They sat together in that depressing room for a while, sharing their thoughts, until Hillary roused himself again.

"Well, Mr. Quarry," he said heavily, "what is it that I can do for you?"

"Since it happened," said Simon, "I've been trying to get something done about it. I feel that something should be done about it, but it just keeps fading away, further back, weeks, and now it's months. Most people have already forgotten."

Hillary nodded, saying nothing, his eyes gazing again into the grate. Simon wasn't sure that he was even listening.

"But it seems impossible," continued Simon. "I just get fobbed off. I'm a publisher you know, we have a good business with lots of poweful connections. I've pulled every string I can think of, but it's no good. The consensus, the overall attitude . . . I can't think what to call it . . . but the view is that I should forget it, put it behind me, and count my blessings." He looked questioningly at Hillary. "They keep saying life goes on."

"I know," said Hillary flatly. "I had the local paper round, but they weren't really interested, it was just news to them. They took a photo of Mary but they didn't use it. I had to go down there to get it back and, do you know, they made me feel like I was a nuisance, just to want my wife's picture back."

Simon nodded his head in sympathy. "I know how you feel. It's hard to realize that what you have to live with every day is yesterday's news to the rest of the world."

"I suppose so," said Hillary, "but I don't know where I can help.

What sort of help are you talking about, Mr. Quarry? I have to tell you that I have very little money."

"I want something done about the people who murdered my . . . our families," said Simon. He sat forward in the chair, leaning across to face Hillary directly, willing his host to pay attention. "I don't know how to put this, Mr. Hillary, so I'll just tell you how I feel. I loved my family. They were good people, nice to come home to. We had a home, a real home. I have a good business and I've worked hard at it for them. It was all there at last, and the future seemed secure, and now it's gone, broken all to pieces, and they, the great *They* of this world, say, well, that's life, forget it. Well, I can't. It's not that I don't want to. It's that I can't. It's no good saying I'll have to forget it, I can't. And I have tried, believe me."

Simon's emotion struck Hillary hard, sending doubt, weariness, even fear across his face. He pushed his chair back, away from the grip of Simon's gaze.

"We can't do anything, Mr. Quarry. We are little people—even you are. What good will it do to get the ones who did it hanged or whatever? I will get compensation, you know, but I can't think what to do with it. What do you want to do about it, Mr. Quarry?"

Simon hesitated, gathering his thoughts. "It's like this. If I just let life go on, I'm as bad, or at least as indifferent as those who tell me to forget it. I'm almost as bad as those who murdered my family and your wife. They didn't care who they killed, and if we let them get away with it, it's tantamount to saying at the end of the day that we don't care either. I didn't love my children and bring them up to be burned alive. Help me to make a stink about this and force someone into action. The least They owe us is to show that They care."

Hillary sat back in his chair, his face falling into the shadow, and shook his head again, as slowly as before, but more firmly.

"Please, Mr. Quarry," he said, getting up, "leave me alone. I don't want any more trouble. It won't bring my Mary back and I don't like all this excitement anyway. I'm putting this place up for sale and moving away, down to Devon. My son and his wife live in Exmouth, and I'm going to live down there. . . ." Once again his voice faded away, as if the effort of considering the future without Mary was somehow too much.

Simon stared at the empty fireplace for a few minutes, before standing up and reaching for his coat. He looked across at Hillary and held out his hand.

"I'm sorry," he said. "I didn't come here to open your wounds. It's just that those who aren't directly involved simply don't care, so—as I see it—it's down to us to get something done."

"Whatever we were to do," said Hillary, "it wouldn't bring my Mary back."

"No," said Simon heavily. "No, it wouldn't do that. Please don't bother . . ." he said as Hillary half rose from his chair. "I'll let myself out, and once again I apologize for bothering you."

Hillary sat down again and watched as Simon pulled his coat on and headed for the door.

"Mr. Quarry," he said suddenly. "Mr. Quarry, they are right, you know. Those who said let life go on. I don't know what you intend to do, but unless we . . . you . . . can live with it . . . with what happened . . . there will be more trouble. There is no end to it, no help for it but to put the past behind us."

Simon looked back into the room as he reached for the door handle. "You're right, Mr. Hillary. I know you're right. But at the end of the day it's not a question of right, is it? It's a question of love. Goodbye, Mr. Hillary. I hope you will be happy, or as happy as you can be. Goodbye."

He closed the door behind him and went down the hall, running a finger through the dust on the sideboard as he passed. It was still there, a dark smudge on his fingertip, when he reached the car, and he rubbed it off on the roof before reaching into his coat pocket for the car keys. Looking across the road he sensed the unseen watcher behind the curtains in the house across the way. On an impulse, as he opened the car door, Simon waved at the house, swinging his arms wildly over his head in greeting. The curtain jerked hurriedly, so that as he drove away, Simon could feel a small amount of satisfaction.

* * *

Simon roughed in the outline, sat back to study the effect, scowled, nodded, tore the page from the notepad, and rang for Ruth. When she came in he beckoned her toward him, and motioned her to stop behind his chair.

"What's the matter?" she asked. "What have you been up to now?"

"Just about everything," he replied, handing her the paper. "I intend to make a gesture and I can't get the words right. What do you think of this?" Ruth picked up the page. The message was stark. MURDERING WOMEN AND CHILDREN PERMITTED: OFFICIAL GOVERNMENT POLICY.

"Simon!" Ruth seemed shocked. "What is it? What on earth are you going to do with that?"

"If I have the courage to make a spectacle of myself, I'm going to walk around Parliament Square this afternoon with that statement on a placard. That should stir things up. I've tried to stir them and now I'm going to embarrass them. You get the press there as well. Ring your pals in Fleet Street."

Ruth sighed, walked round to the front of the desk, sat down in the chair, and looked straight at him. "Simon, this must stop. You'll make yourself ill if you don't try to forget this business. After three months, even you can see it's useless."

"No one ever died of frustration," replied Simon. "Not like bullets, grenades or fire for example. It's frustration that will make me ill, nothing else. And I'll never forget it, as you put it. I don't intend to let anyone else forget it either."

"I don't mean it like that," said Ruth gently. "But what good will it do, parading around Parliament Square like a . . . like a . . . student? It's childish."

"Perhaps it is childish," replied Simon frankly. "I'm coming to the end of this particular road. The road of Sweet Reason. I've tried the path of Common Decency and that's been blocked with a big sign marked Political Expedience. I've tried pulling strings—no dice there either. So now I'm going to have a go at shaming them into it. If they *have* any shame, which I rather doubt."

"Into what?" asked Ruth. "Simon, I'm sure you've heard it before, but . . . well, terrorists have killed hundreds, maybe thousands of innocent people over the last few years. Nothing is ever really done about it because nothing can be done. They can't be caught and they can't be punished."

Simon sighed, looked up at the ceiling, and shook his head at her. "I don't *want* blood, Ruth. I really don't. All I want is all those decent people we keep hearing about, or at least their elected representatives, to get up and say, 'This is *wrong.*' Not, as they find much easier, to say, 'This is the way it is.' Do you see the difference? It's not that they—my family—are dead—it's that nobody *cares* that they are dead. That's the point."

"Yes, I think I understand," said Ruth doubtfully. "But . . ."

"No buts," cut in Simon. "Now, please get the art department to bring me a nice big piece of white cardboard and a selection of flowpens. And I'll need a broom handle."

It was over rather quickly. Simon's first circuit of Parliament Square produced little reaction. Most people either failed to read the notice or simply looked puzzled. One or two seemed a little embarrassed. Whatever their reaction, they hurried past. A taxi hooted and the driver waved, a man on a bicycle shouted something Simon didn't quite catch. A photographer arrived, asked Simon to stop with the Parliament buildings at his back, took a few shots, said "Good luck, mate" and went away. Simon stopped in front of Churchill's statue, looking up at Big Ben, and wondered whether it was all for nothing. Well, a few more circuits and then he'd try and get into the House. That might stir things up a little.

"Excuse me, sir," said a voice. Simon looked round and found two policemen standing at his elbow.

"Yes?" he queried. "Can I help you?"

"That notice," said the taller one, nodding at the placard, "it's not allowed. I shall have to ask you to move on."

"Ask away," said Simon. "I'm making a legitimate protest, and let me assure you that against accusations of libel, if that is what's bothering you, the truth is a perfect defense, and a civil matter anyway.

So I suggest you let me get on with my business. I'm sure you have other things to do."

The constables exchanged glances, but it was the taller one who spoke again. The other moved away and began to mutter into his radio.

"We don't want to be difficult, sir. It's Mr. Quarry, isn't it? I thought so. I recognized your picture from the papers. No demonstrations are allowed here, sir, not while Parliament is sitting. That's the law I'm afraid. So I must ask you to take that notice down and move on."

"Excuse me for saying so, constable, but screw the law. I've been trying to get the law to do something about the people who murdered my family for the last four months, and They—that lot over there in the Houses of Parliament—have done damn-all. So I'm not moving on."

The constable stepped up to Simon and reached a long arm out for the signboard. "I don't know about that, sir, but I must ask you to hand over that notice and go home. I shan't warn you again, Mr. Quarry."

"You can go to hell!" said Simon, pulling the placard away.

"Very likely, sir," said the constable, "but not today. In the meantime you're nicked. Whistle up a wagon, Mike. Let's get this gentleman down to the station."

At eleven o'clock the following day, Simon Quarry, publisher, widower, of Manchester Square, London W1, was fined £25 for obstruction in Parliament Square. Two surety bonds were found for his good behavior and the accused was silenced abruptly by the magistrate when he attempted to speak out on some subject from the dock. It made a few lines in London's only evening paper, which also reported that a lady paid the fine and escorted Mr. Quarry from the courtroom and into a waiting taxi. Had the reporter been more observant, he would have seen the taxi stop on the first corner, where the passengers climbed out and disappeared into a café.

"Is this the end of it, Simon?" asked Ruth. "Or have you some other crazy idea up your sleeve? That last one really didn't do anyone much good."

Simon put the teacups down on the table and slid along the bench opposite her. "Don't nag me, Ruth," he said, beginning to draw with his fingertip on the steam covering the window. "I know it looks silly from where you are, and it didn't work, but don't say I haven't tried. I've tried every trick in the book, haven't I? I've done my best."

"You have," she agreed, "and now that it's all come to nothing, won't you see sense and come back to work?"

"I shall come back to work," said Simon firmly, "with all my faculties intact, when I have got what I want for my family."

For the first time Ruth felt tired and defeated. "Oh, Simon!" she cried. "When will all this stop? What on earth can you do now? Won't you see that it's useless."

Simon took a gulp of the tea, shuddered, and then smiled across at her. "*Lear*," he said, "I think it's *Lear*. Think of *Lear*."

"What is?" she asked. "I'm not a big Shakespeare buff like you are. What about *Lear*?"

"The quotation I keep thinking of, more every day. 'I shall do those things, what they are as yet I know not, yet they shall be the terror of the earth.' That's in *Lear*. But not quite yet."

"Good," said Ruth, "because you are getting out of London until this latest nonsense of yours is forgotten."

"I am?"

"You are, and don't argue. Clissold is due to go on a sales trip to Israel, but you're going instead."

"I am?" said Simon again. "Why?"

"Firstly, because I want you to get away from here and clear your head. Secondly, I want your good friends, the Grossots, to talk some sense into you. God knows I've tried, but they might do better. Last, but by no means least, Martin Clissold needs to know who's in charge around here. Israel used to be *your* market, your personal area, so why should he horn in on it? So, you're going to take the trip away from him and go yourself. Show him that you're still the boss. OK?"

"If you say so," said Simon.

THREE

 Seven days later Simon walked slowly down the airplane steps at Tel Aviv, looking back thoughtfully at the long bulk of the big jet, his eyes narrowing against the glare, feeling in his top pocket for his sunglasses. The heat came bouncing up from the concrete of the ramp as he walked toward the terminal building, the hurrying forms of the other passengers passing him by, noisy and excited at their first contact with Israel.

"Young man! Young man!" A voice made him turn, shading his eyes against the sun. The plump form of a woman came hurrying up to him, holding out the plastic bag containing his duty-free drinks.

"You left this under the seat," she said. "It's very heavy . . . but then I guess you must have your mind on other things."

"I do indeed," answered Simon with a smile, taking the bag from her. He turned to walk with her toward the shade of the terminal building, slowing his pace to hers as the main throng of passengers billowed into a crowd around the doors.

"Do you believe in the true nature of Zionism?" asked the woman suddenly, looking up at him from over her wide sunglasses. Simon noticed her Star of David brooch, the glinting diamonds, and her bright, curious eyes.

"I don't really know much about it," admitted Simon. "I think my wife did though. Zionism wasn't much of an issue in our home. I'm not Jewish, you see, although my wife was, and therefore our kids were."

There was a slight and doubtful pause while the woman digested this information. If she had noticed the past tense, she gave no sign of it.

"Is she here with you?" she asked, looking around. "Or are you here on your own?"

"No, she's not with me," replied Simon shortly.

"My husband and I always wanted to make this trip," the woman went on, "but he died, so I came alone. I think he'd have liked it. Thirty years in the garment business and he drops dead two days after he retires. Isn't that terrible?" She didn't sound as if she thought it was terrible. She sounded like it had come as a relief.

"My wife died too," said Simon flatly, as they came to a halt at the back of the queue. He was tired of her inquisitiveness, suddenly weary of making small talk.

"Oh, dear, I am sorry. I thought you said . . ." She looked up at him doubtfully and let the words trail away.

"I'm like you," said Simon. "I'm making the trip for both of us. Thank you for remembering my parcel."

"You're welcome," she said, keeping close. "How many children do you have?"

"Two girls," said Simon, edging forward in the crowd, but the woman came after him, pressing at his back.

"That's something," she said, "and they'll be Jewish, of course."

"They are dead too," said Simon flatly.

"My God! How awful," she said, shocked, looking round anxiously at the other passengers as if suddenly in need of support. Simon noted with some amusement that she had started to edge away from him and, bloody-minded, he edged after her through the throng.

"Where are you from?" he asked, taking her elbow.

"From New York—well, White Plains," she replied haltingly, turning her back.

"A lovely city," said Simon, leaning forward over her shoulder. "Well, have a nice time." She walked away from him quickly, to join the queue at the immigration desk, leaving Simon smiling ironically at her rereating back.

Within ten minutes he was in a taxi. As it crossed the main road the driver braked, went down through the gears and swerved away from under the wheels of a truck. Simon lurched across toward the driver, regained his seat, braced his feet against the floor, and held out a restraining hand.

"Try to oblige me," he said, "by driving a little slower. You will make more money and I will have less to worry about."

The driver nodded agreement, but without speaking or slackening pace, and delivered Simon rapidly to the doorstep of the Dan Hotel, cutting through the evening traffic pouring out of Tel Aviv as if driving a knife. As the taxi braked to a hard halt, Simon felt a strong flood of relief.

"How much?" he asked, stepping out quickly onto the pavement and handing his case to the waiting porter.

"Twenty-four pounds," replied the driver, leaning across the front seat and holding out his hand.

Simon blinked. "How much?" he gasped, looking back up the road in amazement. "That's a terrible price for a little trip like that."

The driver grinned at him. "You're English, eh? That's *Israeli* pounds, you see. We got inflation you wouldn't believe. That makes like six in your money. We have shekels nowadays, but that's Arab crap . . . after all these years I still think in pounds."

"Oh, I see. That's better," said Simon, taking the money from his wallet and handing it over. "You had me worried there."

"Plus my tip," added the driver, his hand still open. "The percentage I leave to you. Shalom. Welcome to Israel."

"Thank you." Simon smiled wryly before adding a substantial tip. He watched the taxi drive off, braking hurriedly behind a bus, to swerve and cut around it across the road and disappear round the corner. Shaking his head, smiling slightly, he walked up the steps and into the hotel.

Up in his room Simon unpacked unhurriedly, then sat on the bed, consulted his diary and dialed a number, holding on until the ringing tone abruptly stopped.

"Grossot Agencies," said a familiar voice.

"Ari? It's Simon, Simon Quarry. I've just got in. How are you and why are you answering the phone yourself?"

"Hello Simon." The voice sounded pleased. "Shalom, welcome, and why shouldn't I answer my own phone? I'm sorry I didn't meet you at the airport, but you know how it is, I got busy. Forgive, eh? Anyway, you are here, good. Are you OK?"

"More or less. I'm here at the Dan. Come over and I'll tell you all about it."

"I'll come over right away—or do you want to come here? I have father's office now, it's very private."

Simon pondered for a second or so, still holding the receiver to his ear. "No . . . it's personal and I know your office phone never stops. Do you mind coming over? We can have a drink."

"Give me half an hour. By the way, remember tomorrow is Shabbath, so you are invited to dinner tonight—just family. Also my father wants to have lunch with you tomorrow. Just you and him. I'm not invited; you know how he is. Three days like this though and you'll get fat."

"No chance, even with your hospitality," replied Simon. "How are they all, anyway? How are the sisters?"

"They're fine. We often talk about you. Well, take it easy. I'll be there soon," and he hung up.

Simon had done business with the Grossots, father, son and family, for many years. They had published books together, exchanged their children for holiday visits, shared good times and thin times. A man of many acquaintances, Simon had few close friends, but Ari and his family were closer than most, and they knew each other well. When the house phone rang Simon poured out two whiskies, added the right amount of ice, and was ready to hand one to Ari as he opened the door. A small man, squat, hairy, usually cheerful, wearing the Israeli business suit of open-necked shirt and yarmulke, Ari, as usual, looked harassed. He nodded at Simon and clutched the glass.

"Ah! You haven't turned teetotal, I see," said Simon. "This is your favorite brew, so enjoy, enjoy."

"Teetotal! That will never happen, never!" said Ari, sniffing the glass and sitting down on the bed. "Glenfiddich . . . good. This stuff is terribly expensive here, thank goodness you remembered the duty-frees."

"Only just. I nearly lost it. I forgot all about it in the plane, but a very nice, if rather earnest Zionist lady brought it back to me."

"I'm glad to hear it. You look well, Simon. Yes, in spite of all the stories, you look well. In fact you have lost weight—or do I just think so?"

"I hope not," replied Simon. "I go out running in the park almost every evening, and I don't seem to eat like I used to. Also I get out into the hills at weekends and do a lot of hard walking. I try to keep busy."

Ari smiled a little carefully. "Don't tell me you've become a jogger?"

"God forbid," said Simon. "I run faster than that—a mile in ten minutes is my mark, and that makes me a runner. You could do with a little exercise yourself."

Ari patted his sagging waistline heavily, than abruptly changed the subject. "Yes . . . well . . look Simon, I know we wrote a letter, the family and all, but . . . we are all very sorry about what happened, about Eleana and the children. It was a terrible thing. My mother was with them at Eilat and you know how she loved the girls. We all loved Eleana. Look, there is nothing to say, but I wanted to say that. OK? Enough! So, no more. Finish!" He drank again from his glass.

There was a little silence, a little clinking of ice cubes as they swirled about in the glasses. Simon rose, tipped a small measure into each glass, and sat down on the chair by the window.

"Thanks," he said finally. "I mean it, and I know you mean it.

Not everyone does—well, no that's not fair. Everybody's sorry, God knows, but that's as far as it goes. The question is, what are we going to do about it?"

Ari looked down at his glass, his face doubtful. "Do? What do you mean? What can we do about it? What can anyone do? It's a tragedy."

"Ari," said Simon firmly, "don't be like the rest. I need to do something. Something has to be done about the Athens business, let's face it. Hundreds were killed there—murdered rather."

"Nothing will be done, Simon. I know how you feel. We hear things, even here, about what you have been doing. Ruth phoned my father, you know? That's why he wants to speak with you, to tell you that nothing will be done . . . believe me . . . or believe him."

Simon shook his head slowly, shaking away Ari's words. "I can't accept that, Ari. Let me explain what has happened these past few months. My family died. All right, it happens. It's terrible, but it has happened to others. But that's not all of it . . . let's see." Simon thought for a second, then began ticking off the items on his fingers. "One of my directors, Clissold, is trying to arrange a buy-out on the grounds that I'm not capable of running my own company, that I'm a broken man, if not actually demented. An old friend invited me to dinner within a month of my wife's death, and fixed me up with the local merry divorcee. According to him sex is the answer to everything. My letters to the Prime Minister demanding action against the terrorists get fobbed off, and those to the press were not even published. My main government contact tells me that making a fuss is a waste of time. The photographer who took a picture of my child running down the airplane wing with her hair on fire won the News Photographer of the Year award; I saw him acclaimed on television. I made a small demonstration outside the Houses of Parliament and I got arrested. When I tried to state my case from the dock I was threatened with imprisonment for contempt. I'm here because Ruth thinks I'm making a fool of myself, and you and your father are to talk some sense into me. The plain truth is that not one single person in my country gives a damn about what happened to my family, and they all wish I would shut up about it. It's politically, and even worse, emotionally, embarrassing for them. I think I've heard every cliché in the book. Time, you will be pleased to know, is the great healer. Old friends of my wife assure me that I will forget, even that I should marry again because Eleana would want me to. How's that for an idea? They add that those who live by the sword will perish by the sword, et cetera, et cetera, and so on and so forth . . ." his voice petered out. "I'm exhausted with excuses for doing damn all."

"But what is it that you want?" asked Ari, leaning forward urgently. "Nothing you, nor I, nor anyone can do, will bring them back, Simon. Why go on torturing yourself with what you must see now is a pointless task. You say that no one cares, and I have to tell you that is true. Or they may care a little, but not enough. So, what do you want? What do you expect to happen?"

"I expect nothing, not any more. At the start, being a decent middle-aged, law-abiding tax payer, I hoped for a little justice, but I've learned a lot in the last few months. Now I expect damn all."

"So?"

Simon sighed, heaved himself out of his chair and poured another measure into his glass. He raised an eyebrow at Ari. "Yes?"

"No, no more. And no more for you either."

"Don't fret. I'm not on the booze if that's what's worrying you. I'm just . . . confused."

"About what?"

"Ari, don't be dim; it's not your style. I don't know what to do, dammit. I feel . . . terrible. I can't leave it be, but I don't know what to do."

Ari nodded heavily, and set down his glass on the table. "Then I am glad you are here. I think you must talk to my father. He knows about this and, I must tell you, he is worried about you; he told me so. If you had not come here, I think he would even have gone to London, old as he is. He has lots of time for you, you know. You must talk to my father before you do anything foolish. He will know what to do."

Simon shook his head doubtfully. "I'm sorry to trouble you with all this, Ari. I'd like to talk to Fritz though. He always says something worth hearing, and maybe he can think of what can be done.

Otherwise . . . I don't know what I'll do. It's not that I don't want to let it alone, it's just that I can't."

"Be patient, Simon," said Ari softly. "Don't do anything foolish."

"I've been patient," replied Simon. "I've been patient for a long time, and I'm tired of being patient. But before I do anything at all, I'll talk to your father."

Sitting back in his chair, hardly eating, Simon studied his host. By any calculation, Fritz Grossot had to be well over seventy, but he didn't look it. He didn't look Jewish either, or even a bit like his eldest son, Ari. He looks, thought Simon, like a Prussian cavalry officer ought to look; thin face, aquiline features, snow-white hair just over regulation length, slim body, and immaculate turnout. Simon stopped these thoughts when he realized that Fritz's clear blue eyes were fixed on his face.

"So," said Fritz, "what is all this I hear? You look quite well. I said to Muddel last night, 'The boy looks well,' and she agreed with me."

"Fritz, when are you going to stop regarding me as a long-lost son? I'm pushing middle-age—quite hard, and I feel every day of it."

Fritz flapped his hands impatiently, waving his fork in Simon's face, and pointing around the restaurant. Outside, sharply etched against the blue sea, the old walls of the Crusader port of Jaffa stood out clearly in the mid-day sun, but here in the restaurant it was cool, quiet, relaxed. Waiters hovered about, voices murmured.

"Look at the world and see how you talk rubbish," snapped Fritz. "I have known you for years. I told you to work for yourself. I introduced you to your wife. I am your old, old friend. This gives me rights, and so when I talk you will listen. Agreed?"

Simon shook his head and smiled slightly. "So, talk, and I'll listen."

"Once again I am going to tell you what to do," said Fritz, "and you will listen, and do as you are told. Agreed?"

"I've said that I will listen," conceded Simon, "but then we will see. Times have changed for me."

"All right. First, a little thing. This director of yours, the one who was coming here, this man Clissold? You must get rid of him. He is not your friend."

"He's my sales director, and he's efficient. I don't need him as a friend."

"I tell you, get rid of him. You know he is trying to steal your business? You know he talks to your competitors, to your agents, to your authors? You know he delays deals so that, perhaps, he can do them for himself when you have gone?"

"I know all that," said Simon abruptly. "I'm not daft."

"Then so? Why don't you sack him?"

"I'll fix Martin Clissold's wagon, don't worry. I've just been busy. I have all the problems I can handle right now, and as I say, he's efficient."

Fritz took another forkful of food and shook his head. "You will have another problem if you keep this shmuck in your employ . . . but I have told you what to do. Now the other business."

"What other business?"

"This business of the way you are behaving, writing letters to the newspapers, parading in public with a banner like a student, getting arrested. Are you an idiot? At your age, it's ridiculous. You are acting like a child."

Simon sat up in his chair impatiently. "So what do you advise? Do you *know* what I've been trying to do? Can you imagine what it's like?"

Fritz looked at Simon, a long hard look. Then he put down his fork and without taking his eyes from Simon's face rolled up his sleeve. He looked down at the number tattooed on his forearm, and showed it to Simon.

"Auschwitz," he said. "Believe me, I know all about Hell. I've been there." He rolled down his sleeve again, picked up his fork and began to eat.

"I'm sorry," said Simon.

"Don't be sorry. You feel guilty, that's the problem. You think you should have been with your family, that you would have saved them . . . I know. But you are wrong. I felt like that after I got out of the camps, after I came here. I lost my first wife and my first family back there, all of them. So I fight back, I build a new life, and you must do the same. Be a man."

"How? I've tried to live with it and I can't. I sometimes think I'm going crazy."

"Ari told me all about it. Don't go over it again. I told you I know."

"So?"

Fritz put down his fork, drank some water, patted his lips, and leaned across the table, his face close to Simon's. "Use your brains, and hit them," he said fiercely. "Hit them hard. Hit them as hard as they hit you. That will cure your pain and guilt. And maybe it will do a little good."

"I've been trying to hit them. I've pulled every string I have. As you know, I even got arrested. Result? Zilch. I hoped that you Israelis might be about to clout them. You don't usually let such atrocities go unpunished."

"Times have changed, as you have noticed," said Fritz. "You know important people in England. I know important people here. After all, it's a small country. We try diplomacy, the soft touch. We turn the other cheek, we give a little ground." He shrugged. "Maybe after three wars, another way is needed. Anyway, no reprisals."

"Even so," said Simon, "normally your jets would have been pounding the PLO camps half an hour after the attack."

"Times change," said Fritz, patiently, "and besides, after the Lebanon invasion we are not so keen to bomb the Palestinians. Anyway, it was not the Palestinians who killed your family."

"It was a terrorist group," said Simon shortly.

"Not all terrorist groups are Palestinian," said Fritz. "This group we know well here. They call themselves the Green Jihad. They create riots, throw grenades at buses. The Athens business was their biggest coup. They are quite small, very vicious, and funded by Libya. But you should know this—they have an office in London."

"In London!" exclaimed Simon incredulously.

"Why not in London?" replied Fritz, his mouth giving a small twisted smile. "Doesn't every group of . . . freedom fighters . . . have an office in London? They claimed responsibility for the Athens massacre from their London propaganda center. How do you not know this? It was just a day or so after the attack. They stood out on the steps and boasted of it."

Simon shook his head. "I didn't know," he said vaguely. "I went to Athens as soon as I heard. Maybe I just missed it, and terrorist is one of those words, like wife, child and daughter, that people don't use much in my hearing any more. But are you sure?"

"Oh yes, quite sure," said Fritz briskly. "They have an office in St. James's Square, right in the middle of London, near the place they used before your people threw them out. I could even find out where they are now."

"I didn't know," said Simon slowly, "and you say they are Libyans. That's interesting. How do you know all this?"

Fritz smiled at him. "You are not the only publisher with contacts, my boy. Anyway, you shall hear all this for yourself. I am arranging for you to meet some people, some very special people, in a day or so. But it will do no good. They will only tell you what I have told you."

Simon was hardly listening, his eyes now gazing thoughtfully out of the window, fingers tapping lightly on the table. "Yes, good. I'd like to do that," he said vaguely. "But not Palestinians . . . Libyans . . . really?"

"Libyans, Iranians, who knows. They are a little group of terrorists who try to make trouble, and they do it very well, if that is the right word. You are not eating. Do you want coffee?"

Simon was still deep in thought. "No, no . . . I mean yes, lots of it. I thought it was a big thing, and they are a little thing."

"So you see what you must do?" said Fritz, raising his hand to a waiter.

"Not exactly," said Simon. "Tell me. Be more specific."

Fritz ordered their coffee and sent the waiter away. Then he looked directly at Simon. "I know you better than you think. I know what you are. Sometimes you are not a nice man, Simon, but then I like that. At least you are not one of those terribly nice, well-brought up Englishmen who come to my office and think they are liberals because they are polite to the old Jew. I too am a good hater."

"So?"

"So, let the hate and the guilt out against these people. They are nothing if you stand up to them. You have a brain; use it. You have money, time, influence even. These can be powerful weapons, especially the brain. Don't waste your time writing to the newspapers. Think what you can do, you alone, and do it."

"I see," said Simon, blankly. "All right, I'll hit them as hard as I can. I'll stop trying to stir up political people who don't care, and I'll do it myself somehow . . . directly. Is that what I should do?"

"You must do what you must do," said Fritz, "but it is my belief that if we had stood up against the Nazis in Germany during the Hitler time, there might be six million more Jews alive in Europe today. That's why it is sometimes good to be a hater. Just be sure to hate the things that are wrong. Do you follow me?"

"Exactly," said Simon.

Three days later Simon, as instructed, left his hotel just before eleven in the morning. Keeping to the shady side of the street, he walked slowly toward his appointment, glancing at his watch every few minutes, fighting his impatience. It was a warm day and he felt it important to arrive cool. After crossing a few roads and turning down several streets, he consulted the directions on a list he took from his shirt pocket, and found the house without difficulty. Seen from across the road, above a fringe of palms, it looked much like any other house in Tel Aviv, except perhaps for the number of radio aerials which sprouted from the roof. He crossed over to the iron gates, and at exactly eleven o'clock, he pressed the small bell in the wall. A man appeared from a hut on the other side of the gates, and looked at him stonily through the bars.

"I'm Simon Quarry," said Simon briefly. "I'm expected. I have an appointment. At eleven o'clock precisely."

"Passport," demanded the man curtly, putting out his hand through the iron bars of the gates.

Simon handed over his passport and waited while the man returned to the small gatekeeper's office, examined the passport and checked something against a list. After a few words on the telephone he came out again and unlocked the gates, ushering Simon through, then locking the gates behind them.

"Go straight up to the house," he said, returning the passport. "Don't leave the drive. Stop in the open, ten meters or so from the door and wait for a count of twenty. Count slowly. Then enter the front door. You're expected."

Simon nodded, pocketed the passport and walked on up the drive, the gravel crunching under his feet. It was only a few yards before the house came fully into view, a double-storied whitewashed building, heavily shuttered. The garden leading up to it on either side of the drive was a mass of shrubbery, tall palms and green orange trees screening an open courtyard before the door. Simon halted in front of the steps and waited, looking up at the building, the sun now hot upon his head. Somewhere, hidden cameras were scanning him closely, as he counted to twenty. Then he continued slowly on up the steps, and put out his hand toward the door. Before he could touch it, it opened.

A woman stood in the entrance, smiling at him. She was dark, thirty-ish, cool in a crisp, pale linen dress. She looked pleasant and efficient, but her eyes were watchful, and behind the smile her gaze was steady.

"Mr. Quarry," she said. It was a statement, not a question. "Do come in."

Her English was the impeccable English of the educated Southern English counties, her tone as cool as her looks. Simon entered the hall, unable to see clearly at first after the glare outside, his shirt sticking to his back in the sudden chill of the house. There was no furniture in the hall except a desk by the stairway, which climbed up to the left. A man sat behind the desk, facing a bank of monitors, all relaying now familiar scenes. Simon saw the street outside, the gates, the area immediately outside the front door.

"Come this way please," said the woman, touching him lightly on the arm. Simon followed her through a door on the left into a waiting room. A tall, fit-looking young man rose from a chair as they entered and came toward them.

"Yashpal must search you," said the woman firmly. "Please take off your jacket."

Simon removed his jacket, raised his arms and submitted to a close combing of his person, first by hand and then with an electronic scanner. His pockets were emptied and the contents of his wallet turned out onto the table. Even his signet ring was removed and inspected.

"For microphones or tape-recorders," the woman explained, sensing his surprise. "They are miniaturized now, and this will be a confidential meeting. I believe that has been explained to you. There must be no notes, and we assume that you will say nothing of what occurs."

"May I be permitted to know who I am to see?" asked Simon, exchanging friendly nods with Yashpal, and replacing his possessions in his pockets. "My contact, our mutual friend, has been very discreet."

"I am afraid not. However, I can tell you that the gentleman you will meet has a senior position in the organization in question, and can answer any of your queries, if he sees fit."

With that Simon had to be content. The woman left him with another of those slight, cool smiles and he sat under the watchful eye of Yashpal, until the far door clicked open. Yashpal rose, ushered Simon into another, larger room, closing the door behind him with another smooth, firm click.

The man who came from behind the desk to greet him had obviously been a military man. Simon recognized the type immediately. He was middle-aged but looked very fit and alert, with close-cropped greying hair, tanned skin, and that direct military look. His eyes raked his visitor from head to toe but gave nothing away in return. The room itself was light and airy, a breeze ruffling the curtains at the window which, Simon noted, were covered with a thin wire mesh. There was a sofa along one wall, a metal filing cabinet with a combination lock, a few rugs on the tiled red floor, and a large desk on which rested a thin, green paper file. Before the desk stood a wooden armchair. Simon's host waved him into it, then returned to the desk and sat down behind it, resting his elbows on the top. They studied each other silently for a few moments before the man spoke.

"Well, Mr. Quarry," he said briskly, "you come strongly recommended. You must have powerful friends here, good connections. I can't say that I am pleased to see you, but, well, here you are." His English was fluent, but here there was a trace of an accent, guttural, Central European, perhaps Polish.

"Thank you for seeing me," said Simon, "even if you don't want to. I'm grateful for your time."

The man ignored this. "I have been asked to see you concerning what action, if any, my department may or may not take concerning the recent atrocity at Athens. You will appreciate that any information I can give will be only in the most general terms and strictly confidential. Even that is highly irregular and will depend far too much on your discretion for my liking."

Simon nodded. "Perhaps you already know what I have been doing in the last months," he began. "I have been trying, in various ways, to extract some positive action from my government over the death of my family. The result has been, in a word, zero. So, anything you can tell me will be something more than that. You can rely on my discretion. I hope you can accept that."

The man smiled slightly, relaxing, nodding in his turn. "Your reaction," he said, "is quite understandable. It is only unusual in the degree to which you have pursued your aim. Many people, once they get over the initial shock, are eager for revenge, or justice, as you call it, but most people, however aggrieved and outraged they may be, would have given up by now, or have been worn down by the general indifference. But then, your contacts and resources are—as I have already observed—more extensive than most."

"But no more effective," put in Simon. "You are, almost, the last resort. Can you tell me if any action is planned over this tragedy? Or is it, here too, just one of those things the families of the victims must learn to live with?"

The man studied Simon briefly across the desk and rubbed his nose reflectively. "It was your Mr. Churchill who remarked that nations do not have friends, only interests. I gather that you are a friend of this country, Mr. Quarry, but it is not in our interests to avenge your family, or our people. Not this time." He watched as Simon sagged a little in his chair, swept with a sudden sense of weariness and hopelessness. "I'm sorry, but that is the situation."

"But why?" asked Simon, sitting forward in his chair. "Israel has always struck back after an attack. That's been your instant response. Look at the Entebbe raid. Look how your organization hunted down the terrorists after the Olympic killings in Munich, not to mention a score, maybe hundreds of assassinations of terrorists who attacked your people. Normally your jets would have been over the Palestinian camps an hour after the attack. Why should this latest dreadful business go unnoticed?"

"Times change, Mr. Quarry," replied the man gently. "We are seeking an accommodation with the Arabs, even with the Palestinians—and, incidentally—the men who attacked the aircraft in Athens were not Palestinians."

Simon nodded. "I know that," he said. "Even so, your jets have the range to reach Libya, and I am sure you have other resources, some contingency plans."

"Air strikes tend to hit the wrong people, however well directed," said the man, opening the file on the desk. He looked at the file for a moment, then looked up at Simon. "And this group is too small for that. It was carried out by a two-man team from an organization called the Green Jihad. Green, as you may know, is the Islamic Holy Color, Jihad a holy war, and they were Libyans. Such people like glamorous names for their squalid little groups. They are now back in Libya, at a small town called Tarhuna, some fifty miles south of Tripoli, no doubt planning further attacks. We know all about them."

The man closed the file again and looked calmly across the desk at Simon.

"I still don't understand," Simon said quietly, shaking his head. "I don't understand why no action is planned against them. You know what they are like. They will do it again, or something very similar. Surely they have to be dealt with. Isn't that why you always respond to such attacks?"

The man leaned back in his chair, folded his arms and looked up, across Simon's head to the ceiling.

"Mr. Quarry, let me explain. We have had a number of wars since this nation was founded, always with victory, but never with peace. We have, as you say, pursued these terrorists, or guerrillas, call them what you will, relentlessly but not always with success. Counterterrorism has its risks as well as its satisfactions. It provides our opponents with the excuse to say that we are no better than they are, and there are those who, for political reasons of their own, would like to believe that. So, we have tried other methods, notably prevention, which is always better than cure. Our security is good, our airports protected. We have armored the luggage holds of our jets and no bomb small enough to smuggle aboard could do substantial damage. If a jet is hijacked today, the hijackers know that they will be ferried around the world into a rendezvous arranged with our commandos, or such groups as your own S.A.S. That is why hijacking has declined in popularity. There is only death at the end of it. Terrorists want other people to die. They are not keen on dying themselves. Hijacking has become unfashionable among terrorist groups, so now they attack aircraft on the ground. Your family and the others were victims of a new type of attack for which we were unprepared, and Athens is, anyway, notoriously insecure. Indeed, after the Entebbe business, one of our leaders remarked that a terrorist could get a tank onto an aircraft there and no one would notice. So perhaps we should not have been surprised at this new technique."

"I'm not concerned with their techniques," retorted Simon savagely. "I want some action. I wanted my country to extradite those bastards, then try, convict, and put them away for a very long time. That's what ought to happen to criminals. Instead, they were released. Now I want them dead. That's what I'm left with, and what it's come down to. That's been your method too, so here I am to see if you will use it this time. And now you tell me, just like everyone else, to forget it, that nothing will be done."

"No, Mr. Quarry, I do not tell you to forget it. I tell you simply that we are attempting to reach a peaceful accommodation with our Arab neighbours, including the Palestinians, and killing terrorists is not in our program. That is what the Libyans want us to do, to stir up the reasonable Arab nations against us yet again, and we will not oblige them. Not this time."

Simon looked suddenly stricken. "I just don't know what to say," he began slowly. "I've spent months looking for someone, some official body to show that liberty and justice and care for the victim— the things that democracy is said to be all about—actually mean something. From my closest acquaintances to people like you, I get the same answer; the individual is just a pawn, a voter, useful at elections if he votes the right way, but not otherwise. They wrap it up in various ways, but that is what it amounts to. People like my family simply don't matter, and it's all a sham . . . it always has been."

"You are an idealist, Mr. Quarry," replied the man softly. "Nations have broader interests today. We may not like it but we must accept it. Rage for revenge is no substitute for a policy leading to peace."

"I think you're wrong," said Simon shortly. "Deny justice to those who have suffered and you leave nothing but revenge."

"Go home, Mr. Quarry," said the man flatly. "Take up your life, which is not a bad one, and try to be happy. The course you are on will destroy you if you don't give it up. I have seen that happen, many times."

Simon sighed heavily and shook his head. "I talk, people agree, but no one listens. There are some things, and God knows this must be one of them, which just can't be fobbed off. Don't you *see* that? I don't *want* to forget my wife and children. I want their deaths to matter to somebody, just like it matters to me."

"It won't," said the man bluntly. "Don't delude yourself. The kind of action you seek went out with gunboats. Terror is what rules the world today, and the fear of terror. Justice and the rule of law have very little to do with modern politics. It's a pity, but that is the truth."

"We shall see," replied Simon slowly, shaking his head. "We shall have to see about that. In my business, attracting somebody's attention is all part of the job. I'll just have to see about that."

"Mr. Quarry," said the man, leaning toward Simon across the desk, "I gather you like Shakespeare. You have published critiques on his work and go to all the plays performed at Stratford-upon-Avon. Is that not so?"

Simon nodded, half smiling. "You are well informed. I do, yes. You seem to know more about me than I expected."

"Then," the man continued, ignoring Simon's last remark, "why not remember the Duke of Burgundy's speech in *Henry V*? Do you recall what he said would happen to people who 'nothing do but meditate on blood'? They become savages, Mr. Quarry. Don't let that happen to you. You seem to be a cultured man, and this Athens business has already done you enough harm. Don't let bitterness sour your life. There is also another point. The people you pursue are dangerous. If you should ever be able to threaten them, which I doubt, they will strike at you. Don't doubt that. Don't make yourself a target, as you are already in danger of doing. Leave it alone, please."

"Thank you," said Simon, rising to his feet. "I've taken enough of your time, but I won't take your advice. The biggest shock in these last months has been the discovery that everything I thought worthwhile is meaningless. I'm getting over that now, thank God. There is freedom in the wild after all. Now, I must go. Thank you again for your time."

From the wire-mesh-covered window the man watched Simon walk out into the sunshine and then down the driveway out of sight. He sensed the woman coming to stand at his elbow, and they looked out of the window together for a moment.

"Did you get it all?" he asked her, without turning his head.

"Yes, I'm running the tape back now," she replied. "What do you think? Is it just hot air? He sounded very upset. Will it go any further, or will he give up, poor man?"

"I don't know," replied the man. "I don't think so. He's working something out in his head. Put a note in the London bag, and have them keep light tabs on Mr. Quarry. He has come to the end of his search for justice and now he may go looking for something else."

Simon hardly stirred as the aircraft flew across the sea to Athens. He sat in his wide, first-class window seat, gazing down to the blue sea far below, deep in thought. A procession of stewardesses offered him the usual champagne, earplugs and travel slippers, but he waved them away without speaking. Eventually they left him alone.

The voice of the captain announcing their descent into Athens roused him from his thoughts and he peered down anxiously out of the window, palms wet, stomach empty, mentally reliving that day, five months before, when he had been led into that hangar full of coffins and been assured that three of them, the larger one with two smaller ones, belonged to him.

As they taxied in, he saw the burnt-out aircraft still there on the edge of the airfield, the top of the fuselage cut clear away, broad splashes of whitewash obscuring the tail markings.

The plane stopped. Simon sat on for a moment, looking out at the passengers already streaming past the wing, then got up, smiled at the stewardess and asked, "How long will we be on the ground?"

"About an hour. They will call the transit passengers first, but you can put a reserved card on your seat. You can go into the transit lounge if you like, or go right through. They have a very good duty-free shop here—marvelous prices."

Simon nodded again and she watched him go down the airplane steps and follow the crowd across the concrete toward the terminal building. Once inside the terminal, pocketing his passport, Simon wandered about, at a loss. He bought some Scotch; jostled by the crowd and deafened by regular announcements blaring from the loudspeakers, he was about to return to the departure lounge when he saw the notice on the door of an office on the landing above the hall. Even from down below, among the crowd, he could read it clearly—*Chief Security Officer.*

A sudden pulse throbbed uncontrollably inside Simon's head. He pushed his way through the crowd, turning often to look up and back at the doorway, until he found a staircase. He stepped over the guard-chain and slowly mounted the steps to the upper landing which ran right around the booking hall, high above the crowded floor. No one paid any attention to him, no faces upturned, and here, above the crowd, the noise if anything was even louder. Paneled walls, half glassed-in, gave views into the various offices. All were empty and a glance at the clock hanging above the hall reminded Simon that it was lunchtime. His knock on the Security Officer's door was drowned by another unintelligible blast of noise from the loudspeakers so, knocking again, he turned the handle and walked straight in.

The room was large, uncarpeted and very, very warm. Large, high windows gave out onto the forecourt and a big jet was lumbering past, the tail just visible above the frosted glass of the window, sending another roar of noise and a blast of jet fumes through the open window above.

Under the window, on the far side of the room, a man sat behind a desk, a sandwich in one hand, a half-empty bottle of white wine at his elbow. He was looking at Simon inquiringly, chewing on a mouthful, a big, dark, bulky, uniformed man, dark sweat patches showing on his stiffly ironed shirt.

Simon smiled at him and walked across the room toward the desk. "Excuse me for interrupting," he said, raising his voice above the noise. "I hope you speak English."

The man nodded, took a gulp from the bottle and swallowed. "Andreas Stavropopolos," he said, wiping his mouth with the back of his hand. "I lived in London many years. Do you know the Tottenham Court Road? I lived near there."

"I know it well," said Simon. "My offices are near there. May I sit down?"

"Have some wine," said Stavropopolos, producing a plastic cup from a drawer. "It is Demestica, Greek wine, very good." He poured the cup full to the brim and pushed it across the desk.

"Thank you," said Simon, taking a sip and replacing the cup on the desk. "Yes, it is very good." He looked again across the desk, and waited.

"Well," said Stavropopolos, putting down the bottle. "What can I do for you, Mr. . . . er . . . Mr. . . . ?"

"Are you what it says on the door?" asked Simon, ignoring the question. "Are you the Chief Security Officer for this airport?"

"Yes, I am," replied Stavropopolos. "That's why I'm here now. Lunchtime for all the others, but me, the boss, I stay here and . . . what's the saying? . . . hold the fort."

"Were you the Chief Security Officer last year, when that plane out there was attacked?" interrupted Simon.

"Yes, I was. A terrible thing, Mr. . . . er . . . Ah! All those people . . ."

"Then you are the stupid, incompetent bastard," snarled Simon bitterly, the rage he had contained till now suddenly breaking through, "who got my family killed."

Stavropopolos' face paled. Noticeably startled, his eyes widened before this outburst. "Your family?" he cried. "I don't understand. Were your family on that plane? Who are you, and what do you want here? This is private . . ."

"My family and lots of other families," said Simon. "And you . . . you clown! You allowed two gunmen to come into this airport, of which you are Chief Security Officer, for Christ's sake, and murder them. How many of your men were killed? How many, eh?"

"None," replied Stavropopolos. "The gunmen stopped when my men appeared."

"None. Exactly! How many rounds did your men fire at the terrorists?" asked Simon, biting down hard on his words. "How many rounds; precisely?"

"None," said Stavropopolos again. "They surrendered and we arrested them," he added. "We took them away, and did what we could."

"You arrested them," mused Simon. "Why didn't you stop them? Why—and how—did they get onto the airfield?"

Stavropopolos shook his head, recovering a little, "Please, I must ask you to leave. These are private quarters, official. I do not have to talk to you. Please go now, at once, or I will have to call for the police."

Simon couldn't stop now. Waves of fury kept sweeping through him. All the pent-up frustration of the past months poured out, shaking him, making his hands and voice tremble.

"You will answer me," he shouted at Stavropopolos. "How did they get onto the airfield in the first place? Whose fault was that, eh? Yours, wasn't it?"

"There was a lapse," said Stavropopolos angrily. "It should never happen, but a gate was left open in the security fence. I reprimanded my men. I can't be everywhere."

Simon stood up slowly. "So there was a lapse, and you reprimanded your men. And you can't be everywhere. And I lost my family. And that's the end of it?"

"Yes," yelled Stavropopolos, rising to his feet and shouting back into Simon's face. "Yes, and now get out. Get out or I will have you put out."

"Why didn't you attack the terrorists?" asked Simon flatly, his face flushed. He felt calmer now, but as his anger subsided and simmered, so Stavropopolos grew angry in his turn.

"What with?" he shouted. "With pistols? We have only pistols. They had machine-guns. Uzis, Kalashnikovs—we have only these." He dragged a drawer open and flung a holstered pistol onto the desk between them. "You see that?" he said. "You know what that is?"

"It's a Webley .38," said Simon, leaning over the desk, looking down at the weapon. "A British Army pistol."

"Yes," sneered Stavropopolos, as if that proved something. "A British pistol, and they have machine-guns, so what do we do?"

"You could have used it," said Simon desperately. "You could have done *something*. You could have *tried*. You could have tried to do your job." Simon picked up the holster and pulled the pistol from its case. "If I had been you, I would at least have tried."

"I could have used it?" laughed Stavropopolos. "Against men with machine-guns? No, no, not me. And please put it down."

"It's loaded," said Simon, "Why do you have a loaded pistol if you don't intend to use it? A few shots would have scared them off, even fired into the air. It's one thing to shoot at unarmed people, but if people are shooting at you at the same time, it's not so easy. Believe me, I know. But you did nothing, did you . . . you . . . you bastard."

Simon stepped back from the desk, leveling the weapon at Stavropopolos' chest, thumbing back the hammer. "Sit down!" he said, his voice steady. "I have to think. Let me think."

"Put that down," said Stavropopolos carefully, falling back into his chair. "Please—be careful what you do . . ."

"Sit down," said Simon again. "I must get this clear. You are the Chief Security Officer here? Yes? That's what you are?"

"Yes," said Stavropopolos. "Please be careful with that pistol. Never do that with a loaded gun, never. This is not amusing."

"Sit still," said Simon sharply. "You are *still* the Chief Security Officer here, even after you let an airplane full of people die and you did damn-all about it? You haven't suffered at all, have you? Life goes on, right?"

Stavropopolos' nerve snapped. "Right," he yelled, raising his voice shrilly against the roar of the jets outside. "What could I do? What do you think I am? Who are you, to tell me what to do? What would you have done?"

"But *you* were the Chief Security Officer," said Simon flatly, "and you were no good at it . . ."

The pistol in Simon's hand thundered. The bullet's impact hurled Stavropopolos back against the wall. Simon hesitated for a second, then thumbed back the hammer and fired twice more, putting two bullets neatly into the lefthand pocket of Stavropopolos' shirt. Simon walked slowly round the desk and looked down at him.

"Chief Security Officer, God help us!" he murmured to himself. "And they didn't even sack you." He took aim carefully and put another bullet into the security officer's head. Then he tossed the pistol onto the desk where it lay, next to the half-eaten sandwich, smoke wafting gently from the muzzle.

Suddenly exhausted, drained of all energy, Simon sank down in a chair. "Well, you bloody fool, you've done it now," he said aloud. The jet outside was taxiing away now, the noise level receding, taking with it all Simon's anger. He waited, quite relaxed, for someone—the police—to come bursting through the door, but nothing happened. A minute passed, then another, and still nobody came. He looked down at the pistol, and seeing a box of cartridges in the open drawer picked it up, broke the cylinder from the weapon and reloaded it, tipping the empty cartridges into his pocket. Another jet roared past, shaking the room with noise, the noise that had drowned the gunfire. Simon took out his handkerchief, smiling to himself, and wiped the pistol carefully, replacing it in the holster and putting it back in the drawer. He tipped the wine from the plastic cup down his throat and walked away toward the door, crumpling the plastic cup in his hand as he went. When he reached the door he paused and looked back at the room.

From the doorway there was no sign of Stavropopolos' body and, but for his absence, the room looked as it had when Simon first entered it a few minutes before. He closed the door quietly and walked along the landing toward the stairs. Nobody noticed him. The crowd below still milled and chattered, the loudspeakers still boomed, the offices he passed were still empty. No one had heard the shots, those shots which still rang loudly in Simon's ears. He passed quickly back through Immigration to a seating section, a slight smile playing on his lips. And still nothing happened. Ten minutes later he was in the air again, heading out over the Mediterranean. After a few minutes Simon turned his eyes away from the sea far below and spoke to the passenger sitting beside him.

"Have you ever done a parachute jump?" he asked.

"What?" asked the man, surprised. "No, never."

"I have," said Simon, "a hundred and thirty of them to be exact, and I was thinking, looking down, how one comes to do it. It's quite unnatural, jumping out into thousands of feet of damn-all."

"It must be." The man sounded puzzled.

"So you do it a step at a time. You decide to do it, you put on the chute, you get in the plane, it takes off . . . that's easy, but you have started a train of events and there is only one way out. So you take it. You either take it or you are . . . what? Do you see what I'm getting at?"

"Not really," replied the man.

"Well, never mind," said Simon. "It doesn't really matter. It's done now."

He fell silent, and they stayed like that, all the way to London.

FOUR

Simon came through the front door quickly, bursting into the hall and catching the receptionist hurriedly disconnecting a telephone call to her boyfriend.

"Oh . . . Good morning Mr. Quarry. Nice to see you again. Did you have a nice time in Israel . . . you're quite brown."

"Good morning, Maureen," replied Simon cheerfully. "Yes, I had a very nice time, thank you. A few days in the sun there, and back here it's suddenly spring. Isn't it a beautiful day?" He leaned on the reception counter and smiled down at her broadly. "And tell me, how are you?"

Maureen looked surprised. "I'm fine thanks, really." She turned to watch him bound up the stairs and disappear around the bend and out of sight. "Well," she wondered aloud, "whatever's happened to him?" She picked up the telephone and got back to her boyfriend.

Ten minutes later a similar thought went through Ruth's mind as she came into Simon's office carrying coffee, the morning post tucked under her arm. He was already busy, leafing through the folders in front of him, reading memos, scribbling comments on the bottom of each piece of paper, sorting out those which he considered needed a more detailed reply and placing them onto a rapidly growing pile at his elbow.

Ruth placed his coffee on the desk before him and started to open the post, glancing across the desk from time to time. He looked well, she thought, much better than he'd looked over the past months. Surely that was a new suit. That apart, he looked brisk; slimmer, less tired and more alive than he had looked for ages. Ten days in Israel had clearly done the trick.

"Is that a new suit?" she asked. Simon looked up at her, smiling, and then looked down at his jacket, smoothing the lapels with a swift movement of his hand. He looked even a little smug.

"Ah, you noticed. Good. I bought it on Saturday," he said. "Do you like it? It cost a fortune, even off-the-peg."

"Mmm, I suppose so," answered Ruth. "It looks very smart, not like you at all. Frankly, you usually look a bit, well, comfortable. Scruffy actually. That's a new tie, too, isn't it? At least I don't recall having seen it before . . . No, I like it . . . you should take more care of yourself. Heavens! . . . you've had a haircut."

Simon swung his feet up onto the desk, presenting to her the clean yellow insteps and the lightly scuffed soles of new shoes, and swept a hand over his newly bought splendour.

"Regard," he said. "All new. I went out last weekend and bought myself some new threads, as the Americans are said to say. They go with my new flat, and by the way, thank you for organizing that. You chose well and I'm sorry for having to lumber you with all that extra work, particularly when I was away. As you can see, I have pulled myself together. Say hello to the whole new Simon."

"I'm glad you like your flat, Simon. You didn't give me a lot to go on, but I thought that it's miserable to have something poky and stupid to have something too big. I kept some of the personal items because, in spite of what you said, they make the flat more home-like and, well, I'm pleased you're pleased. You look really different."

"You got it just right," said Simon, "and I even like your choice of furniture. How much did it all cost?"

Ruth looked surprised. "Don't you know?" she asked curiously.

"You are a strange man. I left all the receipts and accounts in the folder. It came to rather a lot. Well, over a hundred thousand pounds anyway. I've quite enjoyed spending that sort of money. I could get used to it."

It was Simon's turn to look surprised, even alarmed. "Can I afford that?" he asked, a little worried. "Lord knows I'm not mad about money, but is it all right?"

"According to your solicitor you can afford that and very much more if you want to. We are doing quite well here, and with Eleana's money, even after death duties, and the money from the sale of the other house, you are, well, more than comfortably off. Besides, the bulk of the money went on the flat, so you can look on it as an investment. I got it for a very good price, considering the area."

Simon had lost interest. "Good. I said I would leave it to you, but I do apologize for all the extra work. If I knew what to give you I'd buy you a present, but since I don't, write yourself a cheque and I'll sign it. Look on it as commission."

Ruth shook her head at him. "You don't have to do that, Simon. I was happy to help."

"I know I don't have to," interrupted Simon, "but I want to. You could use the money for a holiday, but I need you here, as I won't be around too much for the next month or so. I have a few things to sort out."

"Oh dear!" murmured Ruth. "You aren't going off again, are you Simon? You *are* the managing director of this company, and we do need to see you occasionally. When you came in this morning looking so different, I thought you were better, and had pulled yourself out of it, if you know what I mean. Israel must have agreed with you. Incidentally, exactly what happened out there? Did you do any business? Was it worthwhile?"

Simon nodded, a little smile flickering over his lips. "One of the few blessings of publishing is that we work so far ahead. We have enough in hand to keep this business rattling away for several years, and you are more than capable of signing for me on any issues that come up. They call it delegation. As to Israel, nothing firm but plenty of interest. I have it all here in various memos, so all it needs is a follow-up. It should more than cover the cost of the trip, and you won't need me here under your feet for a bit."

"Rubbish!" said Ruth abruptly. "If you have lost interest in this company, then why not sell it? Don't just let it wither away. A business needs a boss, and you are it. Take an interest or we may end up with a new one. Martin Clissold tried to chair the last board meeting in your absence, incidentally."

"Did he, indeed . . . how did he manage to do that?"

"By the simple expedient of getting there first and grabbing the top chair. You know what he's up to?"

"I do," said Simon, with a smile. "Leave him to me and all in good time, I'll step on him."

"You might remind him that I'm the deputy MD before that, will you? I don't like scenes, and I don't want a repetition of the board room incident, but he's becoming a little too smooth for me to pin down."

"Oh come now, Ruth," said Simon gently. "You can handle Clissold. Anyway, are we not doing well? You just said so. I have the computer print-outs and the profit and loss figures for the last quarter, and we look very healthy and deeply in the black. Not every firm can say that, not in this business. I don't intend to sell, and I am still interested. I just need some time to settle some unfinished personal business."

"What business?" asked Ruth bluntly. "Simon, I have to tell you that you have moped and mourned long enough. It's been over six months now, and it really is time to get up and do something positive with your life. I hoped the trip to Israel was a step on the road back, but if not, what else can any of us do?"

"There is nothing you can do, and as to Israel, I quite agree," said Simon lightly, "and in the end it was. A step back, that is. You know, I've always thought Fritz Grossot was a wise old owl, but I was wrong. He's really a fierce old hawk. He showed me what has to be done."

Something in Simon's tone caught Ruth's attention. He was sitting back in his chair, the light from the window slanting across his face, his eyes in shadow, and her lively mood suddenly evaporated.

"I see," she said slowly, doubtfully. "Well, in that case, you can start by having lunch with your girlfriend."

Simon's eyebrows rose, his smile broadening and becoming more genuine as he leaned foward toward her. "My what?" he asked. "I mean, who? I wasn't aware that I had a girlfriend. Who is she?"

"Miss Winter is in town," said Ruth. "The lovely, if over-aggressive Clio. She has been in London for a week and rings me every day to see if you are back. By now she will have off-loaded anything decent onto our competitors, so don't buy anything. On the other hand, as she scouts for several big American houses, you can try and sell her some of our spring list."

Simon shook his head and looked doubtful. "I can't do business with Clio," he said. "Tough American ladies scare me to death. Besides, selling US rights or co-editions is an editorial matter. If I start interfering in contracts no one will know what's going on. Get me out of it, will you? Say I'm still away."

"I've told her that," said Ruth, "but she insists on dealing with you, personally. I suspect that she fancies you. Half London would agree with me. She's had her eye on you for years, since before her divorce."

Simon laughed. "I doubt it. She makes me laugh though, I'll say that. She's not dull. You may not like her but she's an entertaining lady."

Ruth glanced at her watch. "She's at the Connaught and will be there till ten o'clock. Then she goes out man-eating. Shall I say you'll be there around one o'clock? Just to keep the facts straight, I do like her. I just think she can twirl you round her little finger."

"The Connaught, eh!" murmured Simon thoughtfully. "She must be doing well to stay there. Is she paying for this lunch or am I?"

"I think the invitation is hers," said Ruth smoothly. "But in any case, as I told you, money is the least of your worries. I should just concentrate on Miss Winter. Concentrate on saying no to anything she asks, and don't be distracted by the bill. Now, here's your post. And by the way, when I say *anything*, that covers *everything*. All right? Now, do some work."

Simon was still staring after her, his hand full of the letters which she had thrust upon him, when she reached the door and went out.

"Cheers," said Clio sipping and licking her lips with one quick ripple of her tongue.

"And cheers to you," replied Simon, sniffing doubtfully at the contents of his glass.

They paused, placed their glasses on the bar counter, looked at each other and smiled. Simon turned on his stool, propped his elbow on the bar, and leaned his chin in one hand, regarding her calmly.

"Do you know why I stay here?" asked Clio, biting an olive off a cocktail stick and snapping the stick in half. "Any idea?"

Simon shook his head. "None," he replied. "I expect it's for some reason I couldn't begin to imagine. Perhaps it pushes the commissions up? Outward and visible signs of success. Is that it?"

Clio shook her head. "No, it's because they serve the best dry Martini in London," she replied, "and us New Yorkers just love Martinis, as all Britishers should know."

"Really?" said Simon. "I rarely drink Martinis. I drink Scotch in the winter, gin in the summer, and wine all the time. Mixed drinks make me indiscreet and give me a headache. Especially drinks at lunchtime."

Clio indicated his glass with one long, elegant forefinger. "You are drinking a real Martini right there, my friend," she pointed out, "and let me tell you, as an expert, that it's a good one."

"Ah, but that's in your honor," replied Simon with a grin. "I don't actually like it. I'm actually forcing myself. I shudder at every sip."

"Actually, actually," mimicked Clio. "Why do all you British say actually all the time?"

"Well, actually we don't," said Simon, sparring. "You Yanks just think we do. It's another of your delusions, like the idea that London is foggy. It's just an idea you have."

"Have we?" she said dryly.

"Yes, you have," he replied, grinning at her.

"Actually," they said together, raising their glasses and clinking the rims, then draining them to the last drop.

"All right," said Clio, raising a finger to beckon the barman, "let's stop shadow-boxing and look at the menu."

Simon sipped his fresh drink and slipped a discreet look at his companion. Clio Winter was, by any standards, a beautiful lady, very intelligent, very attractive, also very demanding, a highly successful literary agent from New York. She looked up from the menu and caught his eye.

"What are you looking at?" she asked, leaning toward him, placing one long, red fingernail gently on his wrist.

"At you, who else?" he said. "It's really no hardship, looking at you, Clio. I was thinking that you are, as we British would say, quite well favored."

"Well, thank you," she said, smiling. "A compliment, no less. You are looking quite good yourself. I had heard in New York that you were looking terrible, or had taken to drink, or were about to kill yourself. Then I heard nothing."

"I thought of those things," he admitted, "and in that order. Somehow, I never got around to them, and now it's too late. I'm full of fresh resolve, full of pep . . . that good old get-up-and-go."

"Well," she said briskly, "then that's fine, and you know how I feel. I wrote and told you how sorry I was, but I'm not here to pull at the stitches and open old wounds. You look just fine and I'm happy to see you looking that way." For a second she looked at him directly, letting their eyes meet, not looking away and not letting Simon look away.

"I'm happy to see you, too," said Simon, breaking the silence, "but why, exactly, are you here?"

"Three reasons," answered Clio, twirling the cocktail stick rapidly in her glass. "To sell my list to you deadbeats over here and so make some money. To go to Paris and maybe to Rome for more selling and some shopping. . . ." Then she paused. "And. . . ."

"Well, go on," said Simon, urging her, "that's only two reasons, what's the third? Do drop the other shoe."

"If you must know now," said Clio, "I thought I might ask you to marry me."

Simon's surprise was genuine. "I beg your pardon," he said, putting down his glass and shooting a quick glance across at the amused face of the barman. "Why on earth would you want to do that?"

"Why not?" she said, sliding down from the stool and offering him her hand. "I'm perfect for you. Can't you see that? Everybody I've spoken to thinks we'd be ideal. Come and have some lunch and I'll tell you all about it."

"I think the right remark to make at this moment," said Simon, handing the wine list back to the waiter, "is 'Darling, this is so sudden.' "

Clio laughed and smiled at him across the table. "I didn't think you published romantic novels," she said, "but I think you must have been reading one. That's exactly what you ought to say. Is this a new area?"

"I haven't and it isn't," said Simon, "and if you are trying to soften me up for some list you are peddling, with all this luxury, good food, and the offer of your hand, forget it. Behind my flinty exterior there beats a heart of stone. The 'everybody' you have been listening to should have added that."

Clio lit a cigarette, waved away the smoke with one hand, and shook her head at him. "I'm serious," she said. "Consider the facts. Here am I, thirty-seven, rich, beautiful, well—quite well favored—intelligent, and you like bright girls, Simon. I'm divorced, yes, and who isn't, but with no noticeable hang-ups. Finally, I'm very sexy . . . and highly available. I'm a gift. Then, there's you."

Simon held up a defensive hand. "Please leave me out of it," he said. "I can't compete with such a long list of attractions."

"Not at all," said Clio. "You are rich, mature—which means only attractively wrinkled—and as yet with no paunch. In fact, you look very good. You're usually funny and, for reasons I won't go into, available. Besides, we're in the same line of business, and we like each other. What a team we'd make. Besides, everyone has to be married. We're too old to stay single. Right? As a clincher, I make you laugh, Simon, and you make me laugh. You could use a laugh, Simon. That's not bad for a start. True?"

"True," said Simon, nodding. "This is not the sort of offer a man gets every day but, and I hate to be negative at such a moment, thanks a lot, but no thanks. I don't want to get married again."

"I bet you say that to all the girls," said Clio. "Permit me to talk you into it. I can be very persuasive, but I don't want to be pushy, so I'll just plant the seed and wait for it to grow. You'll come around in time."

"Not a chance," said Simon firmly. "I have my own plans and marriage is not in the cards. Not now, not ever, not again. Neither do I wish to discuss it."

"Think about it," said Clio blandly. "Don't be nervous, you're protesting too much. Relax and stay cool."

"Let's eat," said Simon.

They enjoyed their meal. They chatted about business, looked around the room and discussed the finer points of the other diners; it was all very pleasant. Plates cleared away, brandy refused, and coffee on the table, Clio lit another cigarette and returned to the attack.

"Face it, Simon. You aren't cut out to stay single for the rest of your life. No man is. God knows, I'm sorry about what happened, but you . . ." Something in Simon's expression, a hardening of his mouth, brought her flow to a halt.

"Now, look Clio, I like you," said Simon evenly, his eyes fixed directly on her face. "I more than like you. You're a good friend, but don't push it. Not this matter of all matters. Is that clear?"

Clio looked out of the window, until the silence between them began to drag. The clatter of plates and cutlery, the conversation from other tables swamped the space between them, and the pleasure of their meeting seeped away.

"I'm sorry," she said at last, putting out her hand and touching his wrist again with her finger. "I don't want to push."

Simon smiled gently, and relaxed. "I'm sorry too," he said. "I didn't mean to be so—so final. I just can't cope with more people trying to wipe my slate clean. And I don't want any misconceptions about the future. I . . . God, how I hate the word 'I' . . . have things to do, that's all."

Clio drew in a deep breath. "Well," she said, looking at him directly, "you've been blunt, so now it's my turn. I can hardly bring myself to say it, but I love you, Simon, it's just that simple. It's not hard to do, you're a very lovable guy. I think that you and I would be nice for each other. So, can we call that a bid and leave it on the table? Until you feel like playing? Win, lose or draw? I promise not to cry if I lose." She grinned at him. It was a big smile, but her eyes were serious. Simon smiled back and suddenly, nodded.

"Why not," he said, his shoulders slumping, "but don't hold your breath. You could end up an old maid."

"Great!" enthused Clio with relief, waving to attract the waiter. "White hair suits me. More coffee, please. And now, my friend, you owe me."

"What for?" cried Simon. "Don't tell me that I've somehow taken on a commitment. I've just rejected one, flat. So, what do I owe you for?"

"For being so nice," replied Clio. "You owe me a favor."

"Do I hell!" said Simon, shaking his head. "I have strict instructions from Ruth to say no to anything you have to offer."

"Sure you do, but don't worry. You'll enjoy it," she said, grinning. "And Ruth need never know. It can be our secret."

"I will?" asked Simon doubtfully. "She won't?"

"Sure. I want you to come with me to Paris." She raised her eyebrows and closed one eye in a long, slow wink, nudging his knee with hers under the table. "Gay Paree. What do you say?"

"All right," said Simon abruptly. "When? Soon, I hope."

Clio was surprised. "That's it?" she asked, eyebrows rising again. "You agree? No contest? No arguments? No fears for your virtue? No ifs or buts?"

Simon shook his head. "None. I like Paris. I'll come with you. You can do your shopping and I'll do mine. We can go on Friday."

Clio saw that smile return, the slow thoughtful one, the one she didn't quite care for, but she held her thoughts and let it go. So far, so good.

"What are you going to buy?" she asked him, resting her chin in her cupped hands. "Anything special?"

"I'll think of something," he replied slowly, his eyes fixed somewhere beyond her head. "Don't worry about it. If you are very good I may even buy something for you."

"That'll cost you," she promised. "I have very expensive tastes, but you'll need to get used to that."

"Just one thing," Simon said, interrupting her suddenly. "We go over in my car and you come back to London with me afterward. In fact, that's a condition. No car, no go."

"But why?" she cried. "I mean, I'd love to, but I have a through ticket to Rome, and anyway it's quicker by air. Besides, I want to go on to Rome directly and I could do it from Paris, and then come by and see you on my way back home. You'll be pining for me by then, I promise."

"My car, out and back, or no deal," said Simon firmly. "Never mind why. Let's say I hate flying. I want to go by car and I don't want you bailing out halfway."

Clio practically pouted, then shrugged her elegant shoulders. "All right," she said, "but you make all the arrangements, book the hotel in Paris and . . ." She smiled at him wickedly and gave him another nudge under the table.

"Yes?" inquired Simon. "What else?"

"You pick up the check," she said, and handed him the bill.

They came into Paris as they had left London, driving against the rush-hour traffic, then turned off the *periferique* and arrived at their hotel on the Île St. Louis just as dusk was falling. Clio uttering delighted cries at the views as Simon cursed other drivers racing along the river bank, and found somewhere to park. Simon conferred with the desk clerk and saw their luggage into the old creaking lift. As it vanished from sight above the stairs, he turned to hand Clio her key.

"Your key, Madame, Room 27," he said. "Chilled chapagne will be served in my room . . . in Room 49 . . . in. . . ." he consulted his watch, "forty-five minutes precisely. Don't be late."

Clio waved the key at him. "What's all this? *My* key, *your* key? Aren't we sharing a room? Hell, Simon, where's your sense of adventure? I thought you had dragged me over to Paris to have your evil way with me. That was the whole idea."

"Was it?" asked Simon blandly, "I thought it was the other way round. Anyway, I'm playing hard to get, at least for the moment, so shall we say my place at seven? Dress formal . . . so have your clothes on."

Clio raised her eyebrows. "That's another thing I'll have to talk you out of. We American girls have our methods, and the night is young."

Simon opened the door, kissed her on the check, approved her perfume, admired her dress and handed her a glass. His room was large, well-furnished, quiet, the traffic noise only a distant roar from the streets below.

"Do you like your room?" he asked, leading her over to the window and putting an arm around her waist.

"No," she said abruptly. "Not one bit. Not that you care."

"Oh, dear me, why ever not?" he asked with assumed concern. "Something wrong with your view of Notre Dame? I ordered it specially. It cost a fortune. And you don't like it? Oh, dear!"

Clio pointed up at the ceiling. "I had that in mind as the view, not the local tourist trap," she said tartly. "Look Simon, I don't want to come on strong, but nice guys don't play games. So, something serious is out. All right, but if you don't want to know, then say so. Don't just be indifferent and cruel. It makes me feel stupid."

Simon peered at her over the edge of his glass and put it down on the table. "Come here," he said softly, putting his arm around her shoulders and turning her toward the window. "Now, look at this." The evening light outside had faded to a deep purple. Across the river, lights were glinting along the *quais*, casting deep yellow shadows on the sides of the houses which ran in a long sweep round to the point where Notre Dame, floodlit and splendid, reared up above the rooftops, magnificent against the deep blue, star-studded sky.

"There," said Simon, "isn't that nice?"

"You have no soul," said Clio, "only a cold-blooded Englishman could call that view 'nice.' It's beautiful. It's, hell . . . it's romantic. I just wish you were, you cold-hearted swine."

"Quite, but why not wait and see," said Simon. "Let's not spoil this evening by quarreling about who sleeps where, before it begins. We'll have a drink, go to dinner, and then. . . ."

"And then what?" she demanded.

"And then we'll see what happens." He held her at arm's length and looked at her hard. "It's been a long time, you know. A lot has happened to me in the last year. It's not easy to be bright."

"Let's go to dinner," said Clio, "and then we'll see."

"You've never smoked, have you?" asked Clio, rolling over onto her back. The cigarette end glowed in the dark and a long, slow cloud of smoke curled away toward the open window.

"Never," said Simon, absently looking up at the ceiling. "It stunts your growth."

"You don't know what you're missing," she said smugly. "Right now, a cigarette is just perfect."

"So I've heard," he said. "My spies have always told me that the best cigarette is the one with the breakfast cup of coffee."

"That's the second-best cigarette," said Clio. "This one is the very best. I know. Where's the sheet, I'm chilly." They lay together comfortably in the darkened room. The breeze from the river was ruffling the curtains, the late-night traffic had dimmed to a distant drone, and the air felt fresh and cool. Somewhere a clock whirred alive and struck three.

"You were right," said Simon suddenly, rolling over and leaning up on one elbow to look down at her.

"I always am," said Clio, "but what am I right about this time?"

"Your view." He pointed up at the ceiling. "It beats Notre Dame every time. How can you *bear* being right all the time? That's a great view."

"Only when you're lazy," she said silkily, running her knuckles gently along his jaw. "You're a very lazy person, do you know that?"

"Or you're just being aggressive," he countered, twirling a strand of her hair around his forefinger. "We can't both be tigers."

"I'm never aggressive," said Clio. "It's just that, right now, if I hadn't made the running in this affair, we wouldn't have reached first base. And we are having an affair, aren't we? What else can we do in Paris?"

"Heavens!" exclaimed Simon, falling back against the pillow. "You Americans actually use that phrase! I never really believed it. First base—my God!"

Clio rolled over onto her side and looked closely into his face. "Sure we do," she said, "but we Americans never say 'There dear, better now?' just like they say English women do."

"My God!" said Simon feebly, sliding one arm around her and pulling her close to him. "You are impossible, but I could get to like it."

"Well, do you?" she asked, her voice muffled against his shoulder. "I have to know."

"Do I what?" he asked.

"Feel better now?"

Simon thought for a moment, looking up, unblinking, into the darkness, stroking her back gently. "Yes, I suppose I do. No, it's more than that. I definitely do. Very therapeutic."

Clio pushed her hair away from her face, laid her cheek upon his shoulder and asked, "You don't feel . . . guilty? No regrets? None of that postcoital *tristesse*—really?"

"No, no, not guilty," said Simon thoughtfully. "No regrets at all. Funny, but true. I don't know how I feel, but I feel good."

"But that was the problem, right?" Clio pressed. "You were afraid you'd feel guilty if we got together? That you would feel guilty about your wife? Like you . . ."

"Please," Simon interrupted her. "But yes, I thought I'd feel guilty. I thought if I went to bed with you I'd be just like all the others . . . not caring. To be equally honest, sex hasn't interested me much in the last few months. You're a perceptive woman, Clio."

"I love you, Simon," she said simply. "You don't believe me yet but you will. I actually like saying I love you. Me! The Iron Agent, in love with a Limey. Shock! Horror! But then you don't believe me?"

Simon shook his head. "You're wrong. I do believe you, or at least I'd like to believe you, but it takes time. I'm not ready to love or be loved, and I'm not even sure I ever will be. It takes two, Clio, you can't do it on your own. I don't know if we have enough time."

Clio sighed. "Yes, you have. I'll talk you into that, like I did into bed." She stretched out luxuriously. "Hell, it wasn't all that difficult."

"Maybe, but I have things to do," said Simon. "Important, necessary things to do. I don't have the time for you."

"What things?" she asked curiously. "You keep talking about 'things.' What sort of things?" She tried to make out his face in the darkness, wanting him to look at her, anxious to see his expression. The pause before he replied was just a shade too long, and the answer avoided the question. "Well," he said at last, "if you'll just put that cigarette out, I think you can take your turn at looking at the ceiling."

"You've got it," said Clio.

They breakfasted together at the table by the window, looking out at the river, enjoying the sparkling air of a spring morning in Paris, watching the barges and *bateaux-mouches* plough past against the flooding stream.

"What plans do you have for today?" asked Simon, pushing away his coffee cup and tossing his napkin onto the table. "Do you want lunch?"

"I have a lunch date at Hachette from noon to, say, three. Before then I'm going to get on the phone and make appointments all over for tomorrow. Then, after lunch, a little visit to the rue St. Honoré to see the fashions, but from about five o'clock I'm all yours. What about you? Want to come shopping with me? You can carry my checkbook, or bring yours."

Simon shook his head, smiling, "I don't think so, if you'll excuse me. I'll just look around and do a little shopping of my own."

"What are you going to get me?" she asked. "Anything will do, provided it's marvelous. I'll always settle for the best."

"I'm quite useless at buying presents," he replied, "but if you'll spare me an hour tomorrow, we might just find you a little something to remember this trip by."

"I already have something to remember this trip by," she said, "but diamonds are *still* a girl's best friend. Come on, I'm a working girl, remember."

Simon parked his car by the most distant pillar at the back of the St. Lazare carpark, reversing into the corner, then checking and locking all the doors. He consulted the list in his diary, then, after walking to street level, took the Metro to the Palais-Royal. On reaching the street again, he walked directly to the gunsmith's. There he spent several minutes outside examining the contents of the windows, the racks of shotguns and rifles, the display cases of pistols, revolvers, knives and hunting equipment. At last he saw what he wanted and went into the shop, the bell clanging loudly as he closed the door behind him. The shop was empty and smelled pleasantly of oil and leather, dim lights glinting on the glass cases and the dark shining barrels of the guns. Simon walked slowly around the cases, touching the gun barrels reflectively, waiting for someone to appear.

"*M'sieu?*" said a voice behind him. Simon turned to study the man, a white-haired, slightly stooping figure, wearing a brown overall, well dabbed with oil. Simon smiled. "*Bonjour,*" he replied, continuing in French. "I want to buy a shotgun, a good one. I don't know the correct word in French, a *canon* perhaps?"

"*Oui, M'sieu, un canon,*" said the gunsmith. "Which type do you want? We have a good selection, the finest in Paris."

"I have an English twelve-bore double-barreled shotgun," said Simon, "but I want to go big game hunting, for boar—*sanglier?*—down in Morocco. What about that repeater over there?" Simon did not have a shotgun and had no knowledge of such weapons, but the one in the window attracted him. He knew about weapons like that.

The gunsmith went to the window, taking a bunch of keys on a long chain from his pocket. He unlocked a padlock, slid back the interior glass and ran another longer chain out through the trigger guards, before handing the indicated weapon to Simon. A cold sensation ran down Simon's back as he felt the weight of the shotgun settle in his hand. It was a forbidding, single-barreled gun, the metal a dull black, a dark, menacing weapon relieved only by the light wood housing of the butt and the sliding action. Simon swung the weapon up across his body and worked the ejector, hearing the oily clash of the mechanism, feeling the balance. "It feels good," he said. "Very light, very well balanced. Is it accurate?"

"It's a riot gun," said the gunsmith. "Not for hunting. An American Winchester twelve-gauge, what you English—*M'sieu* is English, *oui?*—call twelve bore. It is very accurate up to, say, fifty metres. It will take up to seven cartidges, and as you can see, the reload is also the ejector."

Simon took the weapon from his shoulder and lowered the muzzle, cradling the butt under his armpit, noting that the barrel reached from there down only as far as his thigh.

"It's short," he said, thoughtfully. "In my country, shotguns have to be a certain length. Is one of this length legal? Do I need a license?"

"Not in France," said the gunsmith. "There are no police regulations for *canons*, no forms. We are not such a disciplined country as yours. That weapon is not the best for game, but then, it depends on the game. Can I show you some of the other weapons?"

Their eyes met briefly. "No, I think this will suit me perfectly," said Simon. "Can I pay you the money and take it away? Without delay?"

"Of course, *M'sieu*. At once if you wish. May I suggest you also buy some cartridges, some cleaning material, and a case? *Bon!* If you would care to come to the counter . . ."

Ten minutes later Quarry was crossing the rue de Rivoli, the guncase dangling from his hand. In a side street he found an electrical shop, where he bought some strong wire and some insulating tape. Then, hurrying now, he piled into a taxi, getting out at St. Lazare station and returning to his car in the dark shadowed corner of the carpark. There, undisturbed, he wired the shotgun into place, under the rear parcel rack inside the boot, taping the boxes of cartridges high inside the glove compartment. That done, he slammed the passenger door and trunk lid shut several times. The shotgun and ammunition stayed secure and out of sight. They were still securely in place when he returned to the hotel. He tried slamming the doors again, and failed to disturb the weapon, so, satisfied at last, he went in to wait for Clio.

For the next two days he devoted his time to Clio and allowed himself to be happy. They wandered about, shopped, dined, went to shows, and the weapon and its purpose were almost forgotten until they were on the ferry, bound again for Dover.

"When we arrive," said Simon, as they had a drink at the bar on board, "can you help me in the Customs shed? They may get difficult over that bootful of wine we bought at Amiens, so lay on the charm, will you? I've got your allowance and you're not a resident. Keep their minds off the contents of the boot—or trunk, as you call it."

"Sure," said Clio, leaning against his arm. "Anything for you, lover. I'll even show them my legs. That'll blow their minds."

"Anything to declare?" asked the Customs officer, peering through the nearside window and glancing at Clio.

"Some shopping, mostly the lady's," said Simon, getting out, "and large amounts of wine. I have a list here."

"I see," said the officer, taking Simon's note, his eyes still watching Clio as she uncoiled herself fromt he passenger seat. "Well, we'd better look at it. Could you open the boot, please?"

Clio came with them and chatted animatedly to the officer as Simon raised the lid of the boot and opened up several of the cartons of wine. "As you can see," said Simon, "I've got forty-eight bottles, at around thirty-five francs a bottle. Less our allowance—well—my allowance. The lady is American and all her purchases will be on their way to America in a couple of days. Anyway, there will be some duty to pay."

"No tobacco or spirits?" asked the officer. "No other purchases?"

"I have two hundred cigarettes," said Clio. "And I did get a very nice present, but I left it in Paris." She smiled slowly and winked an eye.

"I see," said the officer. "Well, let me work this out and I'll try not to overcharge you for the wine." He walked off, winking at his colleagues, and began to punch out the amount of duty on his till. "Let's call it eleven pounds forty-five," he said on his return. "Thank you," said Simon, "you've been really kind."

"Thank you, sir," said the officer, hurrying round to hold open the door as Clio swung her legs into the car, and he was rewarded with a great big smile.

"How do I get a woman like that?" asked his colleague as they stood watching Simon's car move through the entrance doors and out of sight.

"You start by getting a car like that," said his friend. "No, no . . . first you start by having the money to get a car, to get a woman like that. That'll be the next lifetime, for you and me."

"He's a lucky bastard, anyway, that . . ." he glanced down at the name on the check, "that Simon Quarry. I hope he knows it. Some blokes don't even know they've been born."

FIVE

 Alone in his kitchen, all the doors locked and the blinds down, Simon sat perched on a stool by the worktop, a glass of Scotch in his hand, and contemplated the shotgun. It lay on the table, squat, black and powerful, glinting dully in the light. Beside it, spread on the newspaper, stood a small can of oil, a pair of pliers, a long brass cleaning rod, and a box of cartridges. In a saucer close by, a handful of ball-bearings lay sparkling brightly.

Simon looked at it all, rubbing his forehead with his fingers, thinking. He sighed heavily, sipped a little whisky from his glass, then put the glass down and, slipping off the stool, he picked up the shotgun from the table, and began to clean it. He stripped the shotgun down, carefully laying the parts out across the table, prodding the heavy packing wax loose from the inner parts with the screwdriver, working oil deep into the weapon to loosen up the mechanism. He wore thin surgical gloves and stopped from time to time to wipe them clean on some cotton. Slowly, the weapon emerged from its protective skin of grease.

When he was satisfied that the gun was clean, he wiped it dry and oiled it again, spreading a thin film from a can across the working parts, then reassembled the weapon piece by piece, until it again lay complete upon the table. That done, he climbed back onto the stool, refilled his glass from the bottle and nodded half-contentedly to himself. He sat like that for some time.

After a while, he threw the remaining contents of the glass into the sink and ran hot water from the tap over his gloved hands. When they were clean he went back and, picking up the shotgun from the table, worked the action savagely several times, head cocked, listening intently to the oiled clashing of the mechanism. Satisfied, he opened the box of cartridges, and turning the gun over, fed seven rounds into the charger. Then, jerking the gun into his shoulder and without pulling the trigger, he worked the ejector again rapidly, sending cartridges arcing out across the floor; the fifth one jammed.

Simon cursed, and used the screwdriver to prize the cartridge free. He examined the deep groove scored across the case carefully, and placed that cartridge on one side. Those who knew the smiling, amiable Simon Quarry well would not have recognized this grim, thoughtful figure. Simon shook his head slowly and reloaded the weapon with care. Then, more slowly this time, he worked the action again and the seven cartridges leaped out to roll across the floor. Simon nodded to himself, picked them up and stood them upright one by one across the table.

"So far, so good," he said aloud. "Christ! I must stop this talking to myself. I must. I must."

He poured another drink, added more ice, topped up the glass to the brim with water from the tap, and returned again to the table. Picking up the pliers and one of the cartridges, he removed the cardboard disc and wadding from the top and tipped the lead shot out onto the table. Slowly, one pellet at a time, he squeezed the shot between the jaws of the pliers, flattening the ends, dropping them, one by one, back inside the cartridge case, a grim smile fixed on his mouth. "Wait till I empty that lot into you, you bastards," he said aloud, again.

When it was half full, he picked up one of the ball-bearings and dropped that inside, and then continued filling in the space around it with more flattened shot until the cartridge was full. Then he replaced the wadding and the sealing disc, and refolded the lips of the cartridge down to hold the contents secure. When he had repeated this process with three cartridges, he reloaded the shotgun and ejected the cartridges again, nodding to himself with satisfaction as they spun neatly out of the weapon and rolled across the floor, clashing the action shut smoothly at the end, and placing the weapon back on the table.

It was nearly midnight by the time he had finished. The shotgun, cleaned and now fully loaded, stood by the door. The oil had been returned to a cupboard under the sink where it joined his collection of household cleaners. The pliers lay with some fuse wire and a spare lamp bulb in the hall cupboard, and the stiff cleaning rod went into hiding below the sink. He gathered up the cotton and the stained oily paper from the table and, stripping off the gloves, added them to the pile. Tomorrow that would all disappear into the furnace which warmed the apartment block. He washed his hands, dried them on a kitchen towel, and went contentedly to bed.

"You're late," remarked Ruth, looking up from her typewriter as Simon came hurrying through the door.

"I'm the boss," said Simon lightly. "Bosses are entitled to be late sometimes, it's a perk of office and, incidentally, I was here until after nine last night. Everyone notices when I come in late, but there is never anyone here to see me leave. So stop complaining. I haven't been idle."

"I know," said Ruth, indicating the pile of paper and memos on her desk. "I can see you've been busy. It'll take me most of the day to clear this lot, so you might as well go home again."

Simon hitched a leg over the corner of her desk and craned round the typewriter to read the letter in it. He looked and felt remarkably cheerful.

"No thanks," he said, "but it's still true though, isn't it?"

"What is?"

"I was here late last night, clearing my desk, and no one will know but you. Yet, right now, half the firm are looking at the clock and saying how lazy I am." He turned over a set of galleys on her desk, glanced at the host of correction marks, shuddered, and put it down again.

"Clearing your desk, as you call it, is easy," Ruth pointed out. "You just scribble on your papers and then dump the lot on me. Look at all this, piles of it."

Simon brooded, shaking his head from side to side. "Even so, you could get killed in the rush if you're standing in the front hall here at five-thirty," he said. "Do you remember the old days, Ruth? Everyone stayed on and worked till all hours and then we all went down to the pub and got plastered. Ah! Those were the days. It was fun then."

Ruth raised her eyes to the ceiling. "Heaven help us," she said. "Please, Simon, no dreaming about the good old days, *please*. The old days were hell and you know it. The old days were long hours, hard work and no money. Now we're successful, established, and profitable, which is very rare in this business. So thank God for it and stop complaining."

Simon got up, spreading his hands defensively. "All right, all right," he said hastily. "Put me to work and stop me thinking. What am I doing today?"

Ruth opened her desk diary and ran her finger down a page. "Not much, as it happens," she said. "Promotion meeting at 10:30, the usual row about white dust-jackets, I suppose. Then lunch with Lord Strathlairig, and that's it—unless you want me to set something up for this afternoon. There is plenty of routine stuff you could help with, and it wouldn't hurt if you went round the offices just chatting to the staff. You've been away too much and there are those who get delusions of grandeur unless the boss puts in an appearance from time to time—and don't be too friendly while you are at it, find a little fault here and there. Straighten paper clips, things like that. The best fiction in London is found in their expense accounts."

Simon nodded. "Who is Lord Strathlairig?" he asked, drifting toward his office door.

"Last of his line and a rare breed," said Ruth. "Normally the peerage breed like rabbits. He is also the editorial department's latest find. Hereditary peer, Scottish Nationalist, very vocal on the Scottish oil question, panel show regular—and I'm amazed you haven't heard of him."

Simon shrugged. "I don't watch the box much these days, or even read the papers, come to that. Why am I seeing him? Can't the editors butter up their own conquests? I'm off noble lords. They were no help to me."

"This noble lord may be awkward," said Ruth. "Besides, if you cast your mind back, any author who gets a four-figure advance or more has to be seen by you before we part with the check."

"I'd forgotten that," said Simon, half-surprised, "but it's still a good idea. I can tell them the real facts of life in case four-figure sums delude them into thinking they're clever. What's his book supposed to be about? Note my air of doubt."

"Broadly, it's a review of Scottish political history since the 'forty-five rebellion. If he can write it, it should be very interesting. Besides, the sales people are always complaining that our list is weak on Scottish titles."

"That's because Scotland is weak on decent bookshops," replied Simon. "We can publish books but who will buy them? However, where do I meet the noble lord?"

"At The Empress. I've reserved a table, twelve forty-five for one o'clock, and he'll meet you at the bar. I hear he is partial to single malt."

"I've never met a Scot who isn't, but could you change the restaurant? Make it Wiltons—same time. That would suit me better."

"But you don't like seafood," protested Ruth. "You've always said so."

"I'm not mad about it," admitted Simon, "but I want to go to the London Library first and it's nearer. If we have lunch at Wiltons I can go to the library first and walk to the restaurant without getting wet."

"Why are you going to the library?" asked Ruth. "You haven't been there in years."

"Well, we do have corporate membership. Anyway, if I am going to discuss Scottish politics, a subject on which my ignorance is profound, then a browse through the Scottish titles in the London Library may come in useful. Anyway, can you change it?"

Ruth nodded and picked up the phone briskly. "Leave it to me," she said. "His Lordship probably likes salmon and Chablis."

The London Library, a tall, grey-fronted building, stands tucked into a corner of St. James's Square, lights shining out across the wet streets from the tall windows to the gardens in the center of the square. Simon stood against the garden railings, studying the library and the other houses thoughtfully, before dodging through the circling cars, up the steps and through the swing doors. Nodding at the staff, he made his way firmly round the counter toward the glass doors in the far corner.

"Excuse me, sir!"

Simon stopped, hesitated and turned. "Yes?"

The counter clerk smiled apologetically. "Could I ask you to leave the briefcase down here, sir? It's a rule now, I'm afraid, and we have to insist. It will be perfectly safe in the corner."

"Of course," said Simon understandingly. "Even here, eh?"

"I'm afraid so," said the clerk sadly. "Times have changed."

Simon placed his briefcase in the corner by the hatstand, then leaned on the counter. "Tell me, do you lose many books?"

"Well, no, not a lot, not too many really," said the clerk reflectively, "but then a lot of our books are difficult to obtain and often out of print so, well, we can't afford to lose any."

"Of course not," said Simon agreeably.

"You can leave your raincoat, too," said the clerk.

"It's just a short visit," said Simon. "Unless I must. . . ?"

"No, no, not at all," replied the clerk. "It's just the bags and briefcases. But there is a rack . . ."

"Tell me," said Simon, "what is the least popular subject in the library?"

"The *least* popular?" replied the clerk, surprised, rubing his chin. "Well, the *most* popular must be biography. The *least*, hmmm, I suppose—well—religion isn't what it was."

"No, I suppose it isn't," said Simon, and left. He went through the glass doors and up the carpeted stairs to the reading room on the first floor.

It was, as usual, quiet and peaceful. A handful of people were working away at one or another of the desks which dotted the floor, or seated in the comfort of the deep leather armchairs, reading books and magazines. Simon picked his way across the room to the big windows which looked across to the far corner of the square. There, above the lines of cars, a plain green flag marked the portico of the Green Jihad press office. As he had hoped, the view from the reading room was perfect; smiling slightly, he nodded contentedly to himself and turned away.

Two floors higher, the religious books section was empty of people. Simon walked slowly round the room, looking under the shelves, pondering, standing back to study the layout of the room, listening carefully. No visitors, no sound, all was quiet. Even the highest shelves were visible from where he stood, and removing a book from a shelf at chest level, he examined the shallow inverted tray made above the books by the shelf above, but shook his head, worried. The rows farther along produced what he was looking for, at a place where several of the lower shelves were missing and the lowest shelf was knee high from the ground. He stopped, listened carefully again, then knelt down to look under the shelf, examining the flat green metal surface carefully. He touched it lightly, and studied the dust that came away on his fingertips.

"Mmmm, then I'll need a duster," he said aloud, ". . . some insulating tape . . . and a rainy day."

Three days later the sound of the weather forecast on his radio-alarm woke Simon early. The overnight rain, it said, would continue all morning, dying out slowly from the west. Simon lay against the pillow, looking at the ceiling, listening until the end of the forecast, then threw back the covers and strode swiftly across to the window and pulled up the blind. Blinking in the grey light, he looked down through the raindrop-flecked glass to the wet streets below. A taxi swished past, the tires leaving a wide swath along the rain-pocked road. A few people, crossing the street on their way to work early, were huddled under their umbrellas, tilting them against the rain which sheeted down from the sky. Simon looked up at the grey clouds, at the rain slanting down across the rooftops, and smiled slightly. "Perfect," he said, and headed for the bathroom.

Half an hour later he was ready, sitting by the kitchen table, taking gulps from a mug of coffee, checking off items against a list. He touched each article on the table, then ticked it off from his list with a pencil.

"Shotgun—insulating tape—duster—gloves—strap. Right!" He picked up the thin leather gloves and put them on. Then, taking the duster, he wiped the shotgun carefully, rubbing every part to a fine dull shine. He paused and thought for a moment before turning the weapon over onto its side, and ejecting the cartridges onto the table-top. Laying the weapon down, he picked them up in his gloved hands, one by one, and wiped each one carefully before pushing it back through the loading gate into the magazine. Then, with a rapid, well-oiled clash of parts, he worked the action and fed a round into the breech, his thoughtful face suddenly grim.

Next, and again after giving it a thorough wipe, he fitted the long leather strap to the shotgun and, hanging it from his left shoulder, picked up his raincoat from the chair and put it on. With the coat buttoned and the shotgun held close against his side, he went through into the bedroom and looked at himself in the dressing mirror. It looked fine. The short-barreled riot gun made no outline under his coat, and a few strides to and fro across the room showed nothing either.

Simon nodded to his reflection in the mirror, gave a grunt of satisfaction, picked up his car keys and left the flat.

The trial run worked well. At a little after nine o'clock there were plenty of empty parking spaces in St. James's Square and Simon had to circle the square only once before reversing into a slot on the far side. Across the road lay the former People's Bureau of the Libyan Republic, now the London office of the Green Jihad movement. Even as he watched, a man came along the pavement, turned into the doorway and rang the bell. Almost immediately the door opened and the man stepped inside, pulling off his raincoat as he entered. Simon caught a glimpse of a long, dimly-lit corridor before the door closed again. He sat there, thinking, then opened the car door and, holding the barrel of the shotgun carefully, slid out onto the road, closing the door behind him.

The London Library had just opened as he arrived. One or two of the staff were still arriving, so no one paid any attention as he came in, said "Good Morning" and left his briefcase with the clerk by the door, before going into the lift. He pressed the fourth floor button and, as before, found the section empty. It took only a couple of minutes to unbuckle the strap, wipe the fine dust from the underside of the shelf and, cutting strips of insulating tape from the reel he took from his pocket, fix the weapon securely under the bottom shelf, well out of sight. Simon stood up, dusting his hands and knees, then gave the shelf a sharp kick. Nothing happened. He stepped back and bent down. Nothing in sight. Unless someone got down on hands and knees as he had done, and peered up under the shelf, the weapon was invisible.

Simon folded the strap against his knuckles and placed it in his pocket, then stripped off his gloves and removed the raincoat while walking down the stairs to the reading room. A girl was there, rearranging the magazines on their racks, but she took no notice of him as he went over to the window and looked out toward the Jihad office. As he watched, two men arrived, loitered briefly on the doorstep, and passed swiftly inside.

Simon left his viewpoint at the window, put on his raincoat again and, collecting his briefcase, left the library. Head bowed against the rain, he walked slowly across the square for a closer look. He had to walk past the entrance twice before a small dark man overtook him, hurrying against the rain, but Simon stayed close on his heels, until this man too turned into the doorway and rang the bell. Again it opened instantly. Simon caught a glimpse of another Arab face, another brief view down a long corridor, before the door closed again. He walked away thoughtfully and found breakfast in a small café in St. James's Street. He sat by the steamed-up windows amid the bustling office staff grabbing a sandwich on their way to work, thinking, considering the next move, the unavoidable step on the path he had chosen to follow. And he couldn't stop now.

He had moved the weapon closer to his chosen target, and glimpsed inside the building. As far as possible all was set. Beyond that, he had no plans, no clear idea of what he would actually do. He would simply wait for another rainy day, then go inside the building and kill them all. The cost of killing his family was going to be high. That decided, he got up and went to work.

"I don't know why it is," said Ruth, who was standing by the window as he came in, "but whenever it rains in London the traffic just stops."

"You mean half the staff were late in this morning?" inquired Simon lightly, pouring coffee into a mug. "I'll circulate a stiff memo on time-keeping to one and all. Just to show that there's a firm hand on the tiller."

"No, I didn't mean that," Ruth replied, looking over toward him. "It was just a comment, that's all. You'd think that we would be used to rain in England by now, and able to cope with it. It's the same every winter when it snows. Everything simply stops. Look here now, the street outside is absolutely blocked. It's quite amazing."

"It doesn't snow every winter," Simon pointed out. "That's why we don't have the equipment to cope when it does. Even if we did. . ." he continued over her attempted interruption, ". . .you'd be the first to complain about expensive snow-clearing equipment standing idle year after year."

"No, I wouldn't," said Ruth firmly. "I'd be amazed at the foresight shown by the authorities, that's all."

"Would you?" said Simon doubtfully. "Mmmm . . . well, if you say so. Anyway, let me get to work, or to be more exact, leave me in peace to drink my coffee and read the papers. It's Thursday you know, review day. Let's see if our PR people are earning their keep."

They were. Simon read half-a-dozen reviews of various Quarry Press titles in the main national papers, and tempered his satisfaction with the thought that the length of a review in the newspapers was no real indication of eventual sales. Still, it kept the authors happy. He was scanning the news pages briefly when a small item caught his eye. He read it carefully, then called Ruth into the room.

"Read that," he said, tapping the paper and handing it to her. She did so, glanced at him, then read it again.

"Well?" she said, handing the paper back. "What about it?"

Simon frowned. "You do understand?" he went on, taking the paper. "Reading between the lines it means that our precious Foreign Secretary, while touring the Middle East at the taxpayer's expense, probably to avoid our shocking winter weather, has invited the leader of the group that murdered my family to come to London for talks! And did you know that their political office here in London actually issued the statement claiming responsibility for the attack, and one of their people stood on the steps and handed the release to the press. No one even punched him in the mouth. Unfortunately I was in Athens myself at the time."

Ruth abruptly pulled up a chair and sat down, slamming the paper down onto the desk. "Simon. . ." she began firmly, then stopped and sighed deeply.

"Please listen . . . Don't start again. There is nothing you can do about it, and after a year nothing is going to be done. You know the politicians are trying to patch up some kind of durable peace in the Middle East. Those Jihad people spoiled the last attempt by attacking the aircraft, so it's sensible to talk to them in case they try to ruin another one. Surely you can see why we—well, they—have to talk. Anyway, this man is the spokesman, the leader of the group. He's no gunman. Simon, it's been going on for years; surely trying to stop it, once and for all, is worthwhile."

Simon grunted and shook his head. "He's the head of that mob, whatever his title. At the end of the day, he gave the orders, that's certain. I don't give a damn about their peace talks. What sort of world is this anyway? Can people kill when they want and talk when they want? It's too late for that. Far too late."

"Simon. . ." implored Ruth, but he wasn't listening. He had risen from his desk and had stridden across the room toward the window.

Outside the rain had finally stopped and the streets were drying. He turned toward Ruth, his face a shadow against the light, his body silhouetted against the window.

"Will you contact Yates again, that fellow we know at the Foreign Office. He was involved in the Libyan Bureau siege, when we first threw them out. He's on our authors' list. He seems to know a lot, so let's ask him to lunch."

"But why?" asked Ruth, bewildered. "Why should. . ."

"Never mind why," said Simon abruptly, "just do it . . . please."

"Very well," replied Ruth doubtfully, getting up, her notepad, as ever, tucked under her arm. "When for? Will some time next week be all right?"

"Yes . . . no . . . you'd better make it for the end of the week after. I have a lot to do first," he said. "And don't worry, Ruth, everything will be fine."

"All right," said Ruth, resigned, heading for the door. "Anything else?"

"Yes. Get me the London Weather Center on the phone."

"The what?" Ruth looked at him in surprise, but he had turned away again and was gazing out of the window, his eyes raised to the cloudy sky.

It was almost as before. The morning was chill, grey, depressing. The heavy rain was back, glistening on the road, sluicing in streams down the gutters. Simon circled the square once, then parked across Pall Mall, well away from the library and the Jihad office. He walked back toward the library, collar turned up, hands deep in his pockets, shoulders hunched against the rain. It was only a little after nine o'clock and as he neared the library steps he realized he was far too early, and turned away for another circuit of the square. What time did it open? What time did the officials arrive at the Jihad office? He didn't know, but at a guess, not too early. It would be useless to get inside when nobody who mattered was there, but the waiting was terrible.

He turned away, suddenly nervous, and walked back across the square, past the Jihad office once again and along to Haymarket, through the hurrying office workers, the rain spattering hard against his shoulders and running even faster from his hair. He found a café and went in, drying his face with a handkerchief, squeezing the water from his hair. He bought a sandwich and ate it slowly, standing at the counter, his mouth dry, his throat tight. At ten minutes to ten he could wait no longer. He felt suddenly old and tired, too old anyway to be here among this crowd of damp young people. He walked slowly back to the square, and his feet were wet by the time he reached the library, but he felt calmer now, his nervousness disappearing as he began to move in on his target. He felt almost normal, controlled, and that same feeling which had overwhelmed him at Athens began to seep into his joints, spurring him on. The library was open and by the time he reached the fourth floor he was totally in command of his emotions, everything running smoothly and under control.

Simon glanced again about the shelves. The shotgun was where he had left it, and he tore it from the tapes and half-opened the breech. With that deep-oiled click, half a red cartridge slipped into view. Smiling slightly now, Simon eased the chamber shut. The shotgun slid under his coat and he went down the stairs two at a time, the clatter of his feet echoing along the shelves, then out onto the carpeted main stairs and down across the library floor, past the clerks and the waiting borrowers and into the street. Outside the rain beat into his face, harder than before, but he hardly felt it, his attention fixed on the door ahead, as he hurried along the pavement, crossed the road and came at last to the Jihad door.

Under the portico, out of the rain, he stopped, just for a second, to wipe the rain from his eyes and look about him. Apart from some hurrying umbrella-draped figures and the cars across the way, the square was deserted. It didn't matter now anyway. He unbuttoned his coat, pulled the shotgun clear with his gloved hand and, holding it against his side, rang the bell.

As he expected, the door opened immediately. As it began to swing ajar, Simon flung his weight against it and burst through into the corridor, hurling the porter aside, against the wall.

When Simon kicked the front door shut behind him it was dark in the hallway. The slam of the door almost drowned the porter's angry shout, but he hurled himself forward, not noticing the shotgun in Simon's hands until his own hands were on it. They wrestled briefly, Simon snatching the weapon free as the man jumped back with a yell of alarm and turned to run down the corridor. He barely made three paces.

Simon swung the barrel up and fired full into his back. The noise was tremendous. The world dissolved in a roar as the blast boomed off the walls, the packed shot hurling the man forward, into and through the glass doors ahead. The glass rained down in a shower of splinters as the doors burst open and swung hard on their hinges. Simon ran through, his feet crunching over the splintered glass, jumping over the porter's body. He moved on quickly, working another cartridge into the breech, and then sprang through the first door to appear in front of a man half-rising from his desk, his mouth open, his face pale with shock and surprise. Simon fired, directly into the man's chest, half seeing the shot plough up deep furrows and splinters from the desk top as the man cartwheeled backward in a spray of blood, to thud heavily against the wall. Simon chambered another round, his ears ringing from the blast, and ran around the desk toward the inner door.

As he reached for it, the door at the side of the room was slamming shut, but Simon, coming on hard, fired again into the woodwork by the lock, blasting it open, and shouldered his way through, chambering another round and firing at a third man who was turning toward him from a cupboard across the room, clutching a pistol in his hand. The shot caught the man and threw him back, but he was still on his feet, still raising the pistol as Simon fired again, blowing open his chest, hurling him round and back, leaving a red smear down the wall as he sank to the floor.

Simon turned and ran back through the outer office, out into the main corridor, bumping hard into a dim figure which ran toward him, trying to scramble past, making towards the front door. It was a woman, but Simon was too close to turn the barrel, too close to fire. He struck her hard on the side of the head with the barrel and knocked her sprawling across the floor, before he turned and moved on down the corridor, heading at a trot through the door at the far end. So far, only seconds had passed.

Two men were inside the room, a big, well-furnished room, more than a simple office. One of the men was fumbling with a weapon taken from a cupboard, the other ran screaming, straight at Simon as he came through the doorway. Simon halted, jerked the shotgun up to his shoulder and blew the man's face away. As he slipped into the room and slammed his back against the wall, the second man whipped around toward him, raising a pistol, but Simon worked the action again, raised the shotgun and fired full into him.

Suddenly it was over. Simon knew that. Apart from the ringing in his ears, it was over. The building was silent. He walked quickly across the room and looked down at the last man, sprawled against the wall. He was finished, cut to pieces by the charge of buckshot. Simon realized that he had fired his last cartridge and the shotgun in his hand was empty. He reached into his raincoat pocket and took out fresh cartridges, turning the weapon over and reloading the magazine as he walked back toward the front door, his feet crunching on the broken glass shards, stepping round the pool of blood from the porter's body lying in the hall. The woman lay still against the wall, pressing herself back against it as Simon walked past, his wet coat flapping over her. He ignored her and tucked the weapon out of sight under his raincoat as he heaved open the door and went out. The slam of the door loosened glass splinters from the inner doors, and they fell, tinkling, onto the tiled floor. Then, apart from the woman's sobbing, there was silence.

Outside, Simon found everything in the street quite normal. That struck him as odd. His ears still rang and he could hardly hear the swish of tires as the rain still fell and the cars still circled the square looking for a place to park. No one even looked at him as he walked the few short steps to the library and made his way yet again into the lift. Within a few minutes he had replaced the shotgun in its hiding place and stripped off his wet raincoat. He went into the lavatory, washed his hands, and regarded his face in the mirror. He saw with surprise that there was no change in it. He had killed maybe five people in . . . he looked at his watch . . . the last six minutes, and nothing showed on his face. He found that amazing. He was tired though. Suddenly his legs felt weak and it was an effort to climb up the stairs to the reading room, take a magazine and collapse into a chair by the window.

Outside, the square still looked the same, no alarm yet, no cars, no police, no excitement. Simon noticed his shoes, the welt encrusted with splinters of glass, the uppers with dark, congealing spots of blood, and for the first time felt a sense of pursuit. He rose and quickly ran downstairs to the lavatory, to wash his shoes in the sink, picking out the glass shards and poking them through the grille. It was while he was in there, rubbing his shoes clean with toilet paper, that he dimly heard the first approaching siren. In the reading room, back in his chair by the window, he watched the scene outside develop, the arrival of the police cars, the circle of ambulances, the erection of tape barriers, the arrival of the press, the slow collection of a small crowd. Through it all, the rain beat steadily down.

SIX

Commander Wintle stepped out of his car before it stopped, letting the last braking momentum swing him up onto his feet, slamming the door shut behind him. He acknowledged the hurried salute of the police constable with a brief nod, ducked under the tapes and dived through the doorway, without waiting for his deputy, John Catton, to join him.

It was dim and dusty inside the hall, the only light coming through the doors on either side of the corridor. Catton arrived on his heels and they stopped, bumping together, letting their eyes take in the scene.

"My God!" Wintle murmured, peering around at the litter of glass and blood that lay the length of the hall. The two policemen walked slowly down the corridor, their shoes crunching on the glass shards, past the shattered glass doors still hanging on their hinges in the center, almost colliding with a man who came hurrying out from one of the side rooms.

"Who the hell are you?" the man began, abruptly. "What are. . ."

"Commander Wintle, Special Branch," said Wintle briefly, flipping open his identity card and holding it up to the light. He jerked his head toward Catton. "This is my deputy, Detective Chief Inspector Catton. And who are you?"

"I'm sorry, sir," said the other, half straightening. "The name's Ames. Inspector Ames, from the Savile Row station. We got the call first and came straight over." He gestured at the scene. "It's a shambles, isn't it?"

Wintle nodded heavily. "What's the form?"

Ames spread his arms and swung around, indicating the scene. "It's as you see it. There are five dead and whoever did this used a shotgun. There's a young woman here too, the one who raised the alarm. She's not hurt though. There's a woman police constable in there with her now, but she can't get much out of her. Shock." He nodded toward the door opposite, from which Wintle could hear a murmur of voices and the occasional sob. "We'll talk to her later, I think. Let her calm down a bit. She's foreign."

"Start at the beginning," said Wintle. "Tell us what you know."

Ames shook his head again. "There isn't much to tell," he said. "We got the call, a 999, about nine o'clock. Some gentleman had found the young lady—the one in there—hanging onto the railings outside. He couldn't get much sense out of her, so he stuck his head round the door and saw all this. It gave him a bit of a shock, I'll bet, and he gave us a call."

"Did you get him?" asked Catton sharply. "Is he all right?"

"Not a scratch on him, or on her," said Ames. "Oh, I see what you mean. No, he's got nothing to do with this. He's just a passerby, a journalist, or a writer, just someone going to the library over the way. He's in there, talking to my sergeant. He didn't see anything, or anyone, except the girl. Didn't hear anything either. It was all over well before he pitched up, so he's not a lot of help. I've sent for forensic, and the usual crowd, and they're on their way now. I expect you got the same call." He looked up at them, a small rumpled man, blinking the dust out of his eyes.

"Let's have a look round," suggested Catton to Wintle, "before a mob arrives and their boots get over everything."

They moved together into the first office and looked quickly at the scarred desk and the body sprawled on the floor behind it.

"That's Ahmed something-or-other," said Ames. "He's the press officer of this lot. I've met him before. He used to come round to the station now and then and strafe us about parking tickets—not that they ever paid them. Claimed diplomatic privilege, the cheeky bugger. Can you tell me why there wasn't a copper on the door? Shouldn't the embassy guard have kept an eye on this place after that bad business when the Libyans were here? At least this time *they* copped it, and not one of our girls."

"It's not an embassy," explained Catton briefly. "It's called the Jihad Press Office and Information Center. Basically, they spread propaganda about the Arab cause. We know all about them, but they reckoned they didn't need our protection. It looks as if they weren't quite right, for once."

"Almost right though," said Ames. "Look under the desk." The three crouched down and regarded the pistol indicated by Ames. "We haven't touched it," Ames went on, "but it's a 7.65 Walther. I've seen one before. It's a nasty weapon. And look in here." He led them through into the far office, stepping deliberately around the large spreading bloodstain, pointing to the man huddled in the far corner. Wintle and Catton exchanged glances and looked again at Ames.

"That cove was about to use a machine pistol when our chum nailed him," said Ames. "My sergeant, he knows all about guns, says it's a Steyr. He's lying on top of it, but you can see the butt."

"It didn't do them much good here, by the look of it," remarked Catton. He knelt down, took a pencil from his pocket and scooped up a cartridge case from the floor, letting it slide off the pencil onto the splintered desk top. "Shotgun," he said. "Look, sir, a shotgun cartridge."

"We've got several," said Ames. "The bloke who did all this used a shotgun all right, probably a repeater. That's what tore the place up—all the pellets."

"Mmmm. . ." said Wintle, brooding. "Let me see that." He took the pencil from Catton, picked up the cartridge case and spun it round on the end, peering closely at the writing on the bottom, pulling his glasses down onto the end of his nose. "Twelve-bore—Gevelot—Paris," he read. "French . . . that's interesting. Why not Eley, or some British make?"

The three men stood looking about the room until the sound of voices outside announced the arrival of the forensic and technical people, a trampling of feet, a loud laugh suddenly stilled.

"I think we'll leave you to it for the moment, inspector," said Wintle. "This looks like a political job to me, and if so, it'll be our pigeon, but I'd be grateful if, just for now, you could regard it as a straight crime. Give it the usual works, and let me have a copy of your report as soon as possible."

Outside on the doorstep Wintle paused, looking out on the street. He offered a cigarette to Catton and took one himself, sharing a light, puffing smoke into the rain, hardly noticing the crowd of pressmen and photographers who were gathering at the barrier, shoving through the small crowd behind.

"Well," he said at last. "What do you think? We've had our moments in the last few years, but this is a big one. That's a real bloodbath in there, and there is going to be one hell of a stink."

Catton shrugged. "It's early days, sir. We'll know more when we get the reports in, but if this sort of thing runs true to form, someone will soon be phoning that gentry," he jerked his head towards the press, "and claiming the credit. It looks like a typical—no, well—not typical . . . terrorist caper. You know what they're like. What can you do? That's life."

"Yes," said Wintle thoughtfully. "You may be right. It's curious, though. Not quite to form, is it? Why use a shotgun? Usually these people use handguns or machine-pistols, even grenades. And then think . . . the Libyans back more terrorist groups than any other country in the world, except the Russians, or Cuba. It's not usual for one of their groups to be hit. Why would one of their clients do this to them—assuming that one has, of course."

"Maybe it's the Israelis?" suggested Catton. "They do tend to get a trifle direct, if provoked. Perhaps they are behind this? It's an idea, anyway."

"Hardly their style, though," said Wintle slowly. "Very messy."

"Yes, that's true," brooded Catton. "I haven't seen so much blood since the IRA pub bombings of a few years back. Whoever did this wasn't mucking about though. This is a really professional job."

"Yet whoever did it didn't kill the girl," went on Wintle. "No professional terrorist out for a clean hit would let a witness live like that. Another little point of difference, perhaps. It's interesting."

Catton shrugged his shoulders again and threw his cigarette into the street. "Well, as I say sir, we'll know more about it later. Maybe we'd better get back to the Yard and start to look in the files."

"Yes," agreed Wintle, leading the way toward their car, "and John, phone Paris. Tell them what we've got here. Ask if anyone they have over there uses a shotgun."

"Paris?" inquired Catton, surprised. "Just because of that cartridge? It's a bit thin, sir. You know the French. . ."

"That cartridge," agreed Wintle quietly, as he stepped over the tape into the crowd of pressmen. "Excuse me, please, gentlemen. No, no statement yet. No comment. No. When we have something to say you'll have it. Not before. Excuse me, please. Thank you. No, no statement."

They had to elbow their way into the car, and said nothing until it had backed out and turned off toward Westminster.

"It may be thin," said Wintle suddenly, "but it's a start. Anyway, John, never let us neglect the obvious. That's why it's there, after all."

Simon strode across Ruth's office with hardly a glance at her startled face, walked through the door into his own office and collpased into the chair behind his desk, without a word. He looked up to see Ruth standing in the doorway, staring at him.

"Whatever's the matter?" she asked with concern. "You look terrible, and you're soaking wet. Whatever have you been doing?"

"Nothing," said Simon abruptly. "Nothing. Why?"

"Don't tell me 'nothing,'" replied Ruth sharply. "You look like death. You're shaking like a leaf. Are you getting a cold?"

Simon laughed harshly. "Probably. I've been walking in the rain."

"I can see that," said Ruth. "I'll get you a towel and you can at least dry your hair. Look at your new suit, even the shoulders are soaked."

"Wait," said Simon, holding up his hands. "Can I have a drink first? And for God's sake stop clucking."

"Coffee? Tea?" suggested Ruth, turning to go.

"No, Ruth, not coffee. I mean a real drink. Scotch or brandy. Something with some bite in it."

"Good Lord, Simon, it's barely twelve o'clock!"

"All right," Simon sighed, sagging in his chair. "Coffee then, but put a brandy in it. And tell me what's new. No bad news though, please."

When Ruth returned with coffee and notebook, he was patting his hair dry with a handkerchief, and looked a little better.

"No brandy," she said. "Be your age."

"Thanks," he said, taking the cup and the towel she offered. He put the cup on the desk and began to towel the rain from his face and neck.

"All right," he said, "so what is happening in the real world today?"

"I ought to ask *you* that," replied Ruth, "but the answer is, nothing much. Your lunch appointment with Alex Yates, the man from the Foreign and Commonwealth Office, has been canceled. His secretary rang a little while ago, full of apologies, but they have some sort of flap on. I've rearranged it for next Tuesday. There is nothing in the book."

"Good," said Simon heartily. "I'm not up to small talk today. And now, whatever you say, I'm going to have that drink."

Ruth watched him go to the cabinet and pour himself a large cognac, halfway up the glass. He stood for a few seconds, staring at the wall, before turning toward her. "Want one?" he asked, lifting the glass.

"No, thank you," she said primly, "but I think you've been up to something. Do you want to tell me what's going on?"

"Yes I have, and no I don't," said Simon, taking a long deep drink, then rubbing his mouth with the back of his hand. "No names, no pack drill, as we used to say in the mob."

"Well, I won't ask what," said Ruth, "but don't let Clio find out. She's just telexed that she's coming over next week, especially to see you."

Simon looked surprised. "She said that? On the telex?"

"Of course," said Ruth. "It's called tactics. I'm beginning to admire Clio. She's a very tactical lady. It'll be all over the office by now, and all over the publishing world by just after lunch. And, one thing, how about using less of that rough army jargon? I've noticed you are using it more and more recently. It's not like you. Now, you'd better look over your mail. I've got work to do, and so have you."

Wintle held a conference in his office high above Victoria Street later that night. He sat behind his desk, a tired, grey-haired man in his fifties, his alert dark eyes studying each individual as they came into the room, and waiting until they had arranged themselves onto chairs placed around the walls. When all were assembled and the door firmly closed, he nodded to Catton. "Good evening, gentlemen, and what do we have, John?"

Catton flipped open the file on his knees, looked around at the others who were all looking at him, and began the summary. "At or about nine o'clock this morning, a person or persons unknown, but believed to be a white male, entered the former Libyan People's Bureau in St. James's Square, now the offices of the political wing of the Islamic Green Jihad movement, which we all know about. He was armed with a weapon, believed to be a Remington or Winchester twelve-gauge pump shotgun or riot gun, loaded with doctored cartridges of French manufacture." Catton looked up. "The autopsy found a large ball-bearing in one of the victims," he added. "The normal twelve-gauge load is bird-shot or buck-shot, so ball-bearings beef up the weapon considerably." Catton returned to his report. "With this weapon the assailant killed five members of the staff—a guard, the head of the office, the chief press officer, a gentleman described as a political attaché, and a chauffeur. The chauffeur was found to be armed with a 7.65 automatic. Another 7.65 automatic was found near the body of the press attaché and a Steyr machine-pistol was in the hands of the chief. Another member of the staff, a Miss . . . I can't pronounce this but it looks like Ran-ad-hark, saw the attacker, who struck her with his shotgun. She has slight bruising and is now in Guy's Hospital in a state of shock. The doctor says she will be all right. Apart from her, we have no witnesses. Investigations continue."

Catton closed the file and looked up at his chief. "That's about it so far."

"Forensic?" asked Wintle.

A man stirred in the corner. "We have no prints. The main physical evidence we have so far is four shotgun cartridges of the French Gevelot brand, twelve-bore. That's how we know it was a pump."

"Twelve-bore? What's the difference?" asked Wintle, making a note on the pad before him. "Twelve-bore, or twelve-gauge?"

"None," said forensic. "The Americans call it a twelve-gauge, that's all. As I say, the indications are that this was an American pump shotgun. They are very fast, and can hold five or seven shots. The killer used at least five shots to judge from the dead and damage, and since the others had weapons but no time to use them, either the killer was Wyatt Earp or he used a pump. He might be American."

"We only have four cartridge cases," pointed out Wintle.

"They don't always eject automatically. You have to work the action, like so," explained forensic, demonstrating with his empty hands, "so one may still be in the weapon, although normally you would reload after firing. He might have picked up one cartridge."

"I find it surprising that anyone can fire a shotgun five times in the middle of London and no one heard a sound," remarked Wintle. "It must have made a considerable noise."

"We wondered about that, but then it's an old, solid building," Ames put in from his chair by the window. "We questioned the people in nearby offices, but the walls are thick. The front door is reinforced to keep intruders out, which is a bit of a joke now, but it's heavy. Then there is a plate-glass door behind that and, as you can see from the plan here, most of the shooting was in the side offices

anyway. In addition, it was raining, there were very few people about
in the square, and there is a lot of traffic circling the square at that
time of the morning. It's not really surprising that people either
didn't hear, or didn't notice."

"One would have thought, however," said Wintle, "that someone
would have seen something. It isn't easy to carry a shotgun about in
Central London. They tend to be noticeable."

"It was raining," pointed out Ames again, "and these shotguns,
especially the pumps, are short-barreled weapons, easy to conceal
under a raincoat, say. I expect that's how our man got it in and out.
Then into a car and away."

Wintle brooded, studying the report, stroking his eyebrows with
one forefinger. "Yes, well, we shall see," he said slowly. "At the moment I'm less concerned with how it was done than as with why, and
by whom. Any suggestions, Evans? Any word from your friends in
the committed world?"

The police officer lounging in a chair opposite Wintle, straight-
ened hurriedly. "No, sir. No one has as yet contacted the press, not
even the cranks, or those groups who always get a bid in. We have
spoken informally with our contacts in various sensitive embassies
and at the FCO, but so far no news. The Americans are not interested. The French, as usual, non-committal. It's all a bit surprising really, because a big shooting like this usually sets everyone
buzzing, and we get too much information, rather than damn-all."

"What about the Israelis?"

"Well, they laughed," admitted Evans, "quite fell about, in fact. I
got the impression they were quite pleased, but also that they were
surprised. I doubt it was them, sir. It's not their style. Really, no one
seems to know."

"Well then, who? IRA? Red Brigades? ETA?" asked Wintle.
"Palestinians? The Salvation Army? Come on, gentlemen, we have
five dead people here, and Libyan money at the back of them."

"All likely," put in Catton, with a slight smile. "The Libyans are
liberal paymasters, and suppliers of weapons to all except the Salvation Army—I don't believe they export automatic tambourines. The

chief surviving Arab was screaming about capitalist killers as he threw me out the door. They want their bodies back, by the way. Pronto. I think he's one of those who can dish it out but not take it."

"Carlos?" asked Ames. "You know, that South American gunman. We have found a French cartridge case after all, and Carlos is said to work out of Paris. Is there anything in that?"

Wintle grimaced and shrugged his shoulders. "The French won't thank you for saying that," he said. "They have no love for our friend Carlos, but even so, I doubt if this is his work. As you said this morning, John, it's early days, but from what we have here, it looks like some internal quarrel or the work of a talented amateur. Otherwise we would know by now who did it."

Catton disagreed. "No amateur would stop to pick up the cartridge cases before leaving. And no amateur would have the nerve to penetrate a place like that and kill five people. It can't be easy work, after all."

Wintle shook his head. "No professional would leave even one cartridge behind, or fail to kill the only witness. That girl was very lucky, or he let her go. I favor the latter. Gentlemen, we must continue along all avenues, but I suggest we try to talk to the Libyans and see if any large sums of cash have gone missing from the till. Perhaps staff loans remain unpaid. I don't suppose they will tell us, but thieves falling out is one distinct possibility here. Then, apart from the avenues we have discussed, I want a rundown on all contract killers currently available in Europe, and information on anyone with any reason to wipe out this office in London."

Someone laughed, and Wintle looked up sharply. "Explain the joke," he said abruptly. "It had better be good."

"Sorry, sir," said a voice, apologetically, "but that list could run to thousands. The Libyans have been directly or indirectly involved in hijacking, murders and assassinations for years now. It was from this place that the then ambassador announced that any Libyan who failed to return home, if ordered to by Gadaffi, would be hunted down and killed. Bold as brass he was. Then we had the shooting of one of our WPCs, after which we turfed them out, and this Jihad lot moved in to keep the place warm. It's only a wonder that this, or something like this, hasn't happened earlier. Perhaps they threatened someone, and this was a pre-emptive strike?"

"I'm aware of that possibility," snapped Wintle, "but it's happened *now*, and on our ground. I might mention that I had the Home Secretary on the phone this afternoon. He expects us to clear this up quickly, or at least assure him that it's just a case of Arab fighting Arab. Law and order is a big public issue and we don't want the sons of the desert slaughtering each other on the streets of London. We must find out what's going on, and fast. So, on your way gentlemen, and get on with it."

The group rose and the room cleared slowly, Ames alone nodding goodnight, leaving Wintle looking directly at the one remaining figure standing by the window, looking out across the rooftops to the floodlit towers of Parliament.

"Well?" he asked.

Alec Yates came across and sat down in Catton's recently vacated chair. "Did the Home Secretary really say that?" he inquired. "Implying that if wog killed wog he wasn't worried too much. It's not like him."

"Nicely put," said Wintle, "but hardly accurate. The gist of his remarks was that he wanted no St. Valentine's Day massacres on the streets of London. That would be contrary to government policy, raise questions in the House and all that. I believe, and you will know better than I do in this instance, that everyone wants the lid on all Arab issues at the moment. Suddenly, anything involving the Middle East is very sensitive, so don't rock the boat."

Yates took out a cigarette and tapped it rapidly on the desk. "It is more complicated than that," he said slowly, groping in his pocket for a lighter. "HMG are right in the middle of very delicate negotiations with various Middle East political groups. We must avoid any more conflict in the Gulf or between Arabs and Israelis. That last war in 1973 and the oil embargo which followed damn near ruined the Western world. It's taken us years to recover. We are sure that the Arabs in general and the Israelis in particular now want peace. It's these little groups who only want peace on their terms who are rocking the boat, as you put it. They supply the muscle and the Libyans are supplying the cash. I'd suspect the Israeli Mossad, though not at the present time, but we must find out who did this before the whole mess starts to boil up again. It may sound ridiculous after God knows how many Middle East wars, but one killing at the wrong time could just upset the lot. If we don't have the man, at least we need an explanation. That will keep everyone, well, happy for the moment."

"We will have both," said Wintle, "but it may take a little time. As you heard, there are no leads, no whispers. Not yet anyway, but give it time."

"We only have a little time," said Yates. "You might as well know that we are inviting Abu Sayid over here in a couple of weeks on an official visit."

"Good God!" exclaimed Wintle, pushing his chair back. "That . . . person! Who next? Soon you'll be wining and dining the head of the Provisional IRA. That Sayid is little better than a gunman. In fact, he's worse. He's the one who plans their attacks. We have a file on him that thick." He held up a hand with widely-spaced thumb, and held it before Yates' eyes.

Yates tutted gently. "He is also head of the political faction of this Green Jihad movement, a potent force at the moment, the sword of Allah and so on. He may have been a little, well . . . direct, in his time, but HMG feel certain that this time he's willing to listen to our ideas for a peaceful settlement, on terms favorable to all parties, and he is coming over for a nice, quiet chat. We don't have a choice, man. Think about it. Every government, save perhaps Libya and Iran, wants a Middle East settlement. It's these little groups that keep the tension up."

"The best of luck to you," said Wintle. "I think it's a bummer."

"We will require your help, commander," Yates pointed out meaningly. "It won't make Sayid feel too secure or willing to talk business when he hears, as he must have done by now, that his Libyan backers in London and the staff of his private press office have been murdered. He may not even come here, and that would put our plans back months, if not years."

"Why bring him here at all?" asked Wintle sharply. "Only a year ago, his merry men burned to death over two hundred people, including several English, at Athens airport. And you are going to entertain him? Surely you could cook up your little compromises somewhere else?"

"That's politics," replied Yates, rising. "What these people want is recognition. If they get treated like statesmen by statesmen, they may start to act like statesmen themselves. Look at Arafat, for example."

"Well," said Wintle, "we always heard it was a dirty business, and it seems to be true. I wouldn't touch that animal with a ten-foot pole."

When Yates had gone, Philip Wintle sat on at his desk for a while, thinking, looking out of his window toward the towers and spires of Westminster Cathedral and the Houses of Parliament, which rose up above the flat, modern rooftops into the red sunset sky. Then he groped in his pocket for his keys, locked his desk drawers and made his way out of his own office, stopping briefly to look in on John Catton, working in the one next door.

"I'm just going down to see Seamus McGary," he said. "He's been down there all day. . . . I just rushed out and left him. Do you have any cigarettes? He's bound to want some. He smokes like a trooper."

Catton reached back into the side pocket of his jacket, which was hanging over the back of his chair, and tossed a packet across the room into Philip's hands.

"They're filter," he said, "but he won't mind. I'd forgotten all about him with all this." He gestured helplessly toward the piles of notes and paper on his desk. "I'll be here all night."

"Don't be," said Wintle. "Get some sleep, you'll think better. I'd forgotten about McGary too, but we have more on our plates than mad Arabs. He'll need to go back to Scrubs prison tonight. We can't keep him here any longer, and anyway we've got enough to put him away for years. Pity, in a way. I like Seamus."

"He's one of the old school," agreed Catton. "Not a half-crazed

Mick . . . still, a flat full of gelignite and two Armalite rifles is serious stuff."

"Quite," said Wintle. "Very serious stuff, but it will have to wait. I'll just go down and tell him so. I'll be back up in half an hour."

Wintle took the elevator down to the cells in the basement, jingling the keys in his pocket until it slid to a stop, and emerged into a bare, white-painted, brightly-lit corridor. He walked to the interrogation room at the far end, peered briefly through the porthole in the door, then turned the handle and went in.

Two men were inside. A plainclothes policeman scrambled up from his chair beside the door as Wintle entered, but the other man, seated at a table under the sharp light in the middle, simply looked up, smiling briefly when he saw who it was.

"Had your supper?" Wintle asked the constable.

"No sir, not yet, sir."

"Well, go and get it now. When you come back, bring some for our friend here. Move along now. . . . I'll stay here. You can lock the door behind you."

Wintle went over to the table as the constable left the room, pulling out a chair, sitting down and tossing the cigarettes across to McGary. Seamus McGary was a small, foxy little man, with sharp, cheerful features below his greying red hair, neat even in his shapeless prison overalls.

"I'm sorry about all this, Seamus," said Wintle apologetically. "We have a flap on. Anyway, you will find the food here an improvement on that at the Scrubs."

"That I will," said Seamus, opening the packet. "Do you have a light, sir? The food in these prisons of yours is a real crime, I'll tell you that. It's terrible, so it is." His voice was the soft brogue of the Southern Irish, not the harsh whine of Ulster. Wintle cocked his ear and listened to it with pleasure, pushing a box of matches across the table.

"Lucky for you I smoke a pipe," he said. "Listen, Seamus, can we have a word? This flap that took me away this morning, is it anything to do with you? Someone shot up the Jihad office, killed five people . . . used a shotgun, very messy. Any ideas?"

Seamus drew in a lungful of smoke deeply, and blew it out again up toward the light, his face thoughtful.

"How would I know, Mr. Wintle?" he said finally. "I've been stuck in here, or in the Scrubs, for two months or more now. It doesn't sound like us, not with a shotgun. The Army has good weapons now, it doesn't sound like us . . . no." He shook his head decisively.

"The Jihad have supplied weapons to the IRA," pointed out Wintle, "and maybe you fell out over something. Money, or deliveries, or something?"

Seamus shrugged. "Who knows . . . but I can't see one of the boyos using a shotgun. It's very unprofessional."

Wintle chuckled dryly. "You didn't see the mess in St. James's Square, or you wouldn't say that. Anyway, I tend to agree with you. I've been chasing terrorists . . ."

"Patriots," said Seamus, grinning.

"You pick your words, I'll pick mine," said Wintle, smiling back, "and I've never seen one use a shotgun. By the way," he went on, "exactly what *did* you intend to do with two Armalite rifles and all that jelly?"

"Strike a blow for the Good Old Cause," said Seamus cheerfully.

"That I know," said Wintle, "and thank God we caught you. But where?"

Seamus shook his head. "You're a good man, Mr. Wintle, and you've treated me very fair, but I can't be telling you that."

"We could do a deal," suggested Wintle. "I could drop a charge or two, save you a lot of years . . ."

Seamus shook his head again. "Don't be asking me to tout for you," he said. "That's not how it's done. You do your job and I'll serve out my time. Even in a British prison, it's the same fight."

Wintle leaned back in his chair, tilting it onto the rear legs, and swept his fingers through his hair, his face tired.

"Ah, it's the Cause," he said wearily. "Seamus, you have no idea the damage done by people with a cause. I expect our friend who has just slaughtered five people in broad daylight has a cause too."

"I expect he has," said Seamus. "Why else would he do it? A man needs a cause these days."

"Tell me," said Wintle curiously, "off the record now . . . why do you do it . . . carry bombs, shoot, maim, murder? Never mind the cause, why you, in particular?"

Seamus took another cigarette from the packet and lit it slowly, his eyes on Wintle through the smoke. "You know about me, Mr. Wintle," he said. "None better. You could ask yourself the same question. Why do you do what you do? You don't have to be a policeman if you don't want to be."

Wintle studied Seamus closely for a moment before replying, drumming his fingers loudly on the hard wooden top of the table. "Let me tell you something, off the record," he said. "I'm nearing retirement, you know, and that's the very question I've been asking myself, more and more often, for the last few years. Maybe it's time to go, once the doubts set in."

"We all have doubts," said Seamus softly.

"Do you know how I came into the police?" asked Wintle. "No? I was in Germany at the end of the war, a colonel in the Royal Artillery. I'd been a Territorial before the war anyway, and they made me Town Major in a little place called Rhinesalen, up near Hanover. It had been knocked flat, and my job was to put it back together, working with the local people, clearing the streets, opening schools, restoring light and power. It made a nice change, building things up after years of knocking them down. I really enjoyed it. So, when I was demobbed, I looked around for something worthwhile, something where authority could help people . . . and so I joined the Police."

"You've done well," said Seamus, "getting to where you are now and all."

Wintle shrugged. "It just happened. I did the usual route, two years on the streets, a spell in Traffic, into the Detective Branch, C.I.D., then to the Staff College. Eventually I came to the Special Branch, hunting down terrorists, the wild boys, people like you."

"And you don't like it?" suggested Seamus.

"I love it," said Wintle firmly. "It's very worthwhile, and people who go about shooting other people and planting bombs have to be stopped. It's just . . . I don't know why I'm telling you this, of all people . . . but I sometimes feel I'm only defending the bad against the worse. You people have a cause. Sometimes I wish to God I had, that's all."

"Ah well, there, sir," said Seamus. "You'll need to find something that needs doing, like that job in Germany, or mix with people who believe in what they are doing. Maybe it's the politicos—they're the same everywhere—there's no living with them."

Wintle chuckled, and sat up again in his chair. "You're probably right," he said, "and I only wish you were in a different line of business, but there it is. You and I are too old to change our ways."

"There it is, sir, indeed," agreed Seamus. "Maybe we should warn young Mr. Catton to get out before he gets old and cynical like us."

"Young Mr. Catton, as you call him," said Wintle, "is pushing forty, and heading for the top. He's a university man, with a degree from Cambridge, no less. He actually chose to be a policeman, when he could have done anything he wanted. I believe he tried six months as a graduate trainee with a chemical company, and then a spell in a bank before he joined the Force. He did three years on the street, walking a beat in Liverpool."

"There's dedication," said Seamus, marveling, "and him with that beautiful Oxford accent and nice suits and everything to live for."

"Cambridge accent," corrected Wintle. "He's very sensitive about that. Ah, here's your supper."

The door at the back opened, and the policeman came in, balancing a tray and holding the door open with his foot as he came through. Wintle got up and moved away from the table as the constable dumped the tray before Seamus and went back to his chair.

"I'll be going along now," said Wintle, "back to the salt mine. I've enjoyed our chat, Seamus. Take care of yourself."

"I will that, sir," said Seamus, taking the metal lid off a plate, "and you too now. I suppose I'll not be seeing you again, but you've been fair with me. I'll not forget it."

Wintle nodded and went out, closing the door behind him, leaving Seamus and the constable looking at each other across the room.

"He's a gentleman, that one," said Seamus. "One of the old school."

"Shut your mouth, Mick, and eat your dinner," said the constable, "and we'll get you back to the Scrubs where you belong."

"I do apologize for letting you down last week," said Yates, sipping his wine and nodding appreciatively. "That business with the Green Jihad really threw a spanner in the works, and I simply haven't stopped since, papering over the cracks. You know the sort of thing."

They were lunching at Simon's usual table, tucked away at the back of the restaurant, chatting amiably, pausing from time to time to study the lunchtime throng.

"I wouldn't have thought that sort of thing would be your concern," said Simon, casually. "If your literary tastes are anything to go by, I would have thought your field was purely diplomatic, far from the maddening crowd."

Yates gave a slight smile, put down his glass and tapped the side of his nose with his forefinger. "Wheels within wheels, old boy," he said. "I yearn for the days when things were purely diplomatic. That is why I enjoy writing the book, which is going well by the way. I get home, take a glass of Scotch, have dinner with my long-suffering wife, and then spend a couple of hours work back in the days of the Raj, when diplomacy was simple if not easy, and this country had some clout. It's really very relaxing."

"And now?" asked Simon, smiling, his eyes on the room around him.

"Now we play the field, have interests, take up positions, and sup with various devils using spoons of assorted lengths," replied Yates. "Principles don't count. We'd make a treaty with the Devil if there were oil fields in hell, which, to keep those fires going, is probably the case."

Simon laughed slightly, lifting his hand toward a waiter. "Surely a shooting is hardly your concern, though? There was a great flurry in the press, but it will die down quickly. These things do."

Yates took a strong swallow of his gin. "This is hardly just a shooting, dear boy," he said. "Some person or persons walk into an office in central London and murder five foreigners. Scandal, old boy, *cause célèbre*, questions in the House. Worst of all, at a 'delicate time,' and as the honorable Harold once sagely remarked, in politics time is of the essence."

Simon let the matter drop, refilled their glasses and then returned to the question.

"Why is now a 'delicate time'?" he asked. "If it's not too delicate for my ears."

"HMG are trying to negotiate a firm peace in the Middle East. The last Middle East war damned near ruined the world's economy, and with economic matters looking up at last, we don't want another one now. The key, let's face it, is the Palestinians, and more particularly their various militant arms. If we can persuade them to come to the conference table, it would be a great coup for us, and provide economic stability for the foreseeable future and . . . there's an election coming up. A nice political coup like that and the government are back in with a bigger majority. Goodies all around."

Yates paused and looked across at Simon, a slight, triumphant smile playing about his lips. Clearly he was expecting comprehension and approval, but Simon seemed unimpressed.

"And that is why Abu Sayid is coming to Britain?"

"Well, yes, old boy, that's it. Sayid is all sorts of things, but more particularly he is the power behind the most militant Palestine-Libyan terrorist group currently in the field, the Green Jihad group. The Jihad is very small but potent and vicious. Bad as they are, the political groups feel bound to support them, so their influence exceeds their size. Putting the brakes on the Jihad is essential. But I expect you know that."

Simon's gaze slipped out of focus for a moment. With bleak eyes he looked across the table at his guest. "Are you trying to tell me— me of all people—that the head of that . . . that gang, is coming to London to be wined, dined, and buttered up at the taxpayer's expense? And then the taxpayers will be expected to vote the government back in out of gratitude. You people are amazing!"

Yates looked surprised, taken aback. "Sayid's very much a backroom boy, you know."

"As you will recall," said Simon, "I have good reason to know of him. His group, or whatever you call it, murdered my family. I know all about him. I've got good cause to."

Yates shifted uncomfortably in his chair. "All sorts of terrorist groups claimed responsibility for that dreadful event. Surely the best way to stop such incidents once and for all is to persuade those involved to settle their differences peacefully. We can't carry on like this. Sooner or later they have to talk, and since he wants to talk, we're happy to meet him. Better jaw-jaw than war-war, you know."

Simon sighed. "There are other ways, as the Israelis have often demonstrated," he said. "But then, it's not our way, is it? And you really think this Sayid will listen to you? You never struck me as a fool, Yates."

An uncomfortable silence settled over their table, which even the surrounding clatter was unable to lift. Both were relieved when the waiter arrived with their order.

"By the way, Simon," said Yates suddenly, changing the subject with relief, "there is a very attractive woman over there, who keeps staring in this direction. I'd like to think it was me who intrigues her, but I suspect that she may be more interested in you."

Simon nodded, not looking up from his soup. "I know her. Her name is Clio Winter, and you ought to make her acquaintance. I saw her come in some time ago. She is lunching with one of my rivals. I was trying to be discreet."

"A business rival?" asked Yates, stealing another glance across the restaurant. "She really is most attractive. You're a lucky dog."

"Perhaps I should have said, he's a competitor," replied Simon. "Another publisher in fact."

"Well, he seems to be losing the competition. She's coming over."

Simon looked up as Clio came curving her way slowly across the room, through the tables, heads turning as she passed. Both men rose as she reached them, and looked from one to the other with a broad smile.

"Hello, Clio," said Simon, taking her outstretched hand and leaning forward to kiss her briefly on the cheek. "You are stopping the show, as usual, and I'm happy to see you."

"Hello too, you bastard," said Clio sweetly, looking expectantly over his shoulder at Yates. "Who is this gentleman you prefer to me?"

"Let me introduce Alec Yates," said Simon, hastily, "diplomat, gourmet, and about-to-be author. Alec, this is Clio Winter, an American, as you can see, or rather hear. What may be less obvious is the fact that she is a literary agent, of some renown and considerable promise, and a very dear friend of mine."

"I'm always eager to meet a promising literary agent," said Yates, smiling blandly, "and attractive as well. It's all too much."

"And I to meet a promising author," replied Clio sweetly in return. She turned her eyes on Simon. "Is he any good?"

"Possibly," said Simon lightly. "The manuscript is awaited daily, but the outline and sample chapters look very good."

"And the subject? Lots of sex and violence I hope, and not too dull."

"British diplomacy and the British Raj. It's really much lighter than it sounds. Just right for the Washington and East Coast literary markets. Plenty of sex and violence, and the Brits losing in the end. They'll love it," replied Yates.

Clio ignored this and changed the subject abruptly. "Why didn't you phone me? You've heard of telephones haven't you, Simon? They were invented by Alexander Graham Bell in . . . oh, years ago. He was an American, and his telephones work."

"I didn't know you had arrived in London. And Bell was born a Scot, just for the record."

"I meant, phone me in New York. I wouldn't be here otherwise. I just hopped on the Concorde today and came to see you. The cost was horrendous."

"Lies," said Simon, smiling. "You sent a telex to Ruth last week. We have no secrets at Schloss Quarry. But how do we come to be lunching in the same restaurant?"

"My spies are everywhere," said Clio simply. "Ruth said you were lunching here, so I rang Miles and made him bring me here too. I hope you're embarrassed. He is—terribly. Say you are, too."

"Far from it," said Simon. "I'm delighted. So is Alec. Won't you join us?"

"What?" exclaimed Clio, "and leave poor Miles over there to languish alone? You finish your lunch and we can all have coffee together." She smiled again at Yates, squeezed Simon's fingers, and walked away among the tables.

"Phew!" said Yates, sitting down, and picking up his wine glass. "I was beginning to feel a touch *de trop* there. The lady has her eye on you, old boy. I can see all the signs."

"There could be worse fates," admitted Simon, "but she can be a little overbearing at times. Another glass of wine?"

They continued their meal, chatting about Yates' book, and were approaching the coffee stage when Simon returned briefly to the subject of Abu Sayid. "What are you going to do with him?" he asked. "He's not being lunched by the Queen, I hope?"

"Good God, no!" said Yates. "Next week is not exactly an official visit. Not a secret of course, all above board, but nothing more in the press if we can help it. He's lunching with the Foreign Secretary just after he arrives, of course, and there will be a small evening reception. Then he gets shown the sights next day, and has a day in Birmingham to see a bit of British industry—hopes of investment for the new Palestine State—and so on. Just as if he were the visiting statesman we hope he'll become. Then he goes to Oxford to discuss education for his bright young hopefuls, as an alternative to that Patrice Lumumba terrorist academy they run in Moscow, stopping on the way for a performance at the Shakespeare Theatre in Stratford. We've got tickets for Scofield's *Macbeth*—have you seen it?"

"No, not yet," said Simon. "I find Scofield's delivery disturbing. Those pauses always make me fear he'll forget his lines. I hear it's very good though. I used to go to Stratford a lot, in the old days."

"Well, I don't suppose Sayid will notice his delivery. He probably won't understand a word, but at least there's plenty of action in *Macbeth*, blood, ghosts and so on. The plot should intrigue him."

"He likes blood, I believe," said Simon bitterly, "and we all have our ghosts. A very wise choice, Yates, yes indeed."

"Here comes Clio," interrupted Yates hastily. "Her escort doesn't look at all pleased."

Sitting in his flat that evening, showered, dressed, and sipping a large well-iced whisky, Simon reviewed the events of the day with considerable contentment. He had discovered some useful information from Yates, outfaced a competitor after lunch, and had done some useful business. When the doorbell rang, he rose and went to open it, looking forward to the rest of the evening with considerable pleasure.

"How do I look?" asked Clio, sweeping in, brushing his cheek with her lips, and raking the apartment with her eyes. "Who on earth chose the wallpaper?"

"You look *ravissant, comme toujours,*" replied Simon, gallantly. "You also smell intriguing. And Ruth chose the wallpaper, so watch your step."

"You say the nicest things, even in French," she replied, draping her coat over a chair and looking around again. "Anyway, what does a girl have to do to get a drink around here?"

Simon slid past her, squeezing her arm, and went over to the sideboard. "The usual?" he asked, rattling the bottles and taking the lid off the ice bucket. "Dry Martini, and lots of it?"

Clio coiled herself up on the sofa, lit a cigarette and looked directly at him for the first time. "Yes, dry Martini, but a small one. I've already had lots of it. This will be my second, or maybe my third. Your friend Alec rang me at the hotel and asked me to have a drink with him. He's gone on to Paddington Station in my taxi."

"Did he, indeed," said Simon, raising his eyebrows. "And how did he learn where you were staying?"

"He extracted the information at lunch. Over our second coffee, most diplomatically, while you were paying the bill."

"Well," Simon conceded, shrugging, "he is a diplomat, after all. Such duplicity must be second nature to him by now."

"He's very nice."

"He's very married."

"All the best men are."

"I quite agree," said Simon, "or so I've heard. There are exceptions to every rule."

"Well?"

"Well, what?"

"Well, why don't I move in here for example . . . when I come over. You'd be able to shoo away the married men, and I could play house."

Simon sighed, handed her the glass, smiled and sat down beside her. "You never give up, do you?" he said, looking up at the ceiling. "On a practical note, you wouldn't like it. No telex, no room service. I don't see you with dishpan hands."

"Do you really want to?" asked Clio. "I'm happy to wait around until you change your mind, but a little nudge now and then can't be too bad. Besides, if I stopped pushing you now, you'd miss it."

"I might," said Simon, thoughtfully. "At least . . . Yes, I might. Look Clio, you cheer me up, you make me laugh . . . I like that, but I don't want to get married. That's a fact and you ought to accept it."

"We don't have to get married right now," said Clio, "or even at all. I'd be perfectly happy to live with you. Here, or in New York, or both. You choose. We'd have a great time, and I could cheer you up all the time, not just on visits. I could move in tomorrow and we'll see how it works out."

Simon shook his head. "I don't want anyone living with me," he said firmly. "I've got things to do, and I can't cope with having someone around all the time . . . sorry."

Clio swung her legs off the sofa and stalked swiftly across the room, to glare back at him. "What things?" she cried. "That's the umpteenth time I've heard about your *things*. For God's sake, Simon, stop moping about and come back to the real world. If you want me out of the way, then say so. If you want me here, say so, but don't say maybe you do, maybe you don't. Christ!" she exclaimed savagely, grinding out her cigarette in an ashtray. "I just hate indecisive men. I thought you were different, not one of those typical, boring Englishmen this town's full of."

Simon calmly looked up at her, shaking his head slightly. "But I am indecisive," he said gently, "and I don't see the harm in it. I'm not a tycoon, I never have been. I'm not one of those ruthless, ambitious men-of-business you profess to admire so much. I'm just an ordinary person and I like to take my time before I make big decisions, particularly where they affect others. Now, it so happens that I made a personal decision a while back which doesn't concern you, let alone us, and I'm working it out. Until I have, I would be no use to you, believe me. I'm thinking of you as well. Why can't we just go on as we are, for the moment."

Clio's shoulders sagged a little. "What sort of personal decision?" she asked. "Personal about us?" She plucked another cigarette from the packet with her long red-tipped fingers, but took her time fumbling in her handbag for a lighter, while Simon sat back and watched her carefully.

"I can't tell you, and I won't tell you," he said at last. "So don't ask me. It's personal, and I don't need any help with it."

It was Clio's turn to shake her head slowly, sadly, looking at him through a small haze of cigarette smoke. "It's the same old business, isn't it? You can't forget what happened to Eleana and the kids. . . . I'm sorry. I'm sorry, I didn't mean you should forget. I mean that . . . well, things are no better . . . you haven't got over it yet, or come to terms with it even."

Simon gazed past her, looking out of the window, watching where the sun was slipping down across the evening sky, sending blocks of shadow across the walls and windows of the houses opposite, letting her questions hang in the air between them for a moment.

"To be honest, I think I have," he said slowly, "or at least, I've found a way to come to terms with it. Believe it or not, I hardly think about it any more. At first I tried to put it out of my mind, but I found that I couldn't. So then, I just thought about it. I let it hurt and hurt until it simply couldn't hurt me any more. After a while, pain gives up the struggle. It leaves you feeling exhausted, but the edge is gone and you can function again."

Clio shook her head. "I was wrong about you," she said slowly. "You're not soft at all. That's the Cold Turkey treatment. It still affects us, though."

"Everything affects us," said Simon, "but I can't help *us* at the moment. I've got . . . well, you know."

"Yes, I know," said Clio wearily. "Things."

"Yes, that's right . . . things."

Simon got up from his chair and walked across the room to take the glass from Clio's hand. He put it on the mantelpiece, looking down at her, then took her hands, pulling her up out of the chair and holding her close.

"Well?" she asked, her arms hanging close to her sides. "What happens now?"

"Well," said Simon, leaning back to look down into her face. "I had tickets for the theatre, but we'll miss the first act at least, so we could go to dinner?" He waited but there was no reply. "Would you like dinner, or . . .?" he asked.

"On balance, I prefer 'or,' " said Clio slowly, "and then dinner later, if that would be all right."

Later that night, back alone in his flat after seeing Clio to her hotel, Simon took a newspaper from his raincoat pocket and, spreading it out on the table, turned the pages until he found the "Entertainments" section. He ran his finger down the columns until he found what he wanted.

"Now," he said, talking aloud again, "let's see . . . Stratford . . . evening performances of *Macbeth* . . . hmmm . . . Friday 7:30 P.M." He stared, unseeing, out of the window, then got up to pull the blinds before turning back into the room. "I wonder what time they come out."

SEVEN

 Wintle took off his glasses, laid them carefully on the folder in front of him and leaned back in his chair, stretching his arms high above his head. He rubbed his eyes carefully with thumb and forefinger, then looked wearily across the desk at Catton. He felt tired, older, and noticed the shadows under Catton's eyes, the deep grooves around his mouth. Neither had had much rest recently.

"That's very comprehensive for a week's work," he said, tapping the folder. "But there's not a lot in it, is there? It's very thin. If that's all we have, we don't have much and, as you know, in this business with every day that passes, the trail gets colder."

Catton nodded, then shrugged. "I'm sorry, sir, but that's all there is. We have tapped every source, made every contact, pulled every string, but all we can say with any confidence is that none of the normal terrorist groups is involved. Even the nutters have failed to claim the credit and just for once we even have no suspects. It's a total blank. It seems impossible but, well, there it is."

"So?" queried Wintle, rubbing his eyes again.

"So, that leaves us with a loner." He nodded toward the folder on

Wintle's desk. "I say as much in the report. Not directly perhaps but the implication is clear. Just who did it, or why the press office was attacked, remains a mystery, though if we knew why, it might be a good indication of who. All we have at the moment is a killing, a very big killing."

"Not quite. Why? That's the big question at the moment, but it leaves us with one further unanswered question for the future, and given that the Libyans and their surrogates have no shortage of enemies, the biggest question of the lot."

Catton stiffened in his chair and looked up expectantly at Wintle. "Yes, sir," he asked, "and what might that be?"

"Will he, or she, do it again? Can we expect more attacks?"

"She!" exclaimed Catton in surprise. "I doubt if a woman could do a job like this."

Wintle laughed, waving a forefinger at Catton. "No, don't worry, we know it's a man. The woman there gave us that much, even if that's all we do know. This business of writing non-sexist confidential reports for the prime minister is habit-forming. She's very concerned with this affair, so a lot of the heat is coming from Downing Street. Notice the press articles and leaders, all planted, to show official shock and horror."

Wintle rose, pushed his chair away from the desk, and walked over to the window, looking down toward the evening crowds making their way along Victoria Street, running a forefinger slowly across his lower lip, brooding.

"We don't know what we have here," he said slowly, thinking aloud. "There isn't an obvious pattern. A man walks into an Arab office and kills five people. Is he crazy? Perhaps. Is it political, or done for revenge, or even for profit? All are sound, possible motives, even for an affair like this, given the people involved. But where did he come from? How did he get away without a trace, right here in the middle of London? Where has he gone? Probably abroad, or is that a hasty conclusion? And why? Above all, why? We have so few leads to any part of this. In fact, none."

"We have a description of the man," offered Catton, "and the French cartridges. That's a start. We can rule out the blacks, probably even Arabs. He is a European, maybe an American. We might even get more on him if we get a photofit."

"That narrows the field to about two hundred million people," Wintle pointed out ironically, "and that Miss What's-'er-name has given us at least three descriptions. Incidentally, she's gone home. Or rather has been sent home by her office. They flew her out yesterday. They are not a helpful crowd. We get the blame, but not the assistance."

"Home!" exclaimed Catton. "She's a material witness. We'll need her evidence when . . . well, if . . . no, *when* we catch up with the killer."

"I think the *if* is more honest; unless he tries again," said Wintle, turning back into the room. "And this brings me to our next problem. Will he try again?"

He walked back to his desk, unlocked a drawer and took out a folder. Removing a piece of paper, he studied it briefly, then slid the paper across the desk to his assistant.

"That is the detailed itinerary," he remarked, sitting back in his chair, "for the visit of one Abu Sayid, gunman, terrorist, political head of a notoriously militant Arab faction, funded for years by our Libyan friends and, for three days next week, the honored guest of Her Majesty's Government."

"Really?" said Catton, starting to read it, and looking up in surprise. "Why? We don't normally have much truck with such people. Is his visit really necessary?"

"You may well ask. That smoothie Yates, my contact and pressure-point from the Foreign Office, just taps his nose and mutters darkly about wheels within wheels. However, I gather that by some secret agreement between the Western countries, an effort is under way to find an enduring political settlement in the Middle East; no papering over the cracks this time. All hands are to the pumps and the government has offered to cool down this particular group. They sabotaged the last peace effort a couple of years or so ago, hence the red carpet treatment this time. Better from us then from Moscow apparently. However, our killer nearly threw a spanner in the works last week with the job at the Green Jihad office. They were organizing Sayid's visit and liaising with Yates. Did you know that this London office was a terrorist front? Did our man know? Is that why he hit them? Is there a connection?"

"Sayid is Palestinian," said Catton, "even though the Libyans have joined and support his group. It's in the files. So I expect it's no dark secret. But is this the reason for the attack?"

"I don't pretend to understand it," admitted Wintle, "but we have to guard this bloke with kid gloves, until he's safely back where he came from, full of roast beef and good fellowship for Britain. If anything happens to him there will be egg all over the government's face—and blood all over the carpet. Probably ours."

"Providing cover for this will be fairly routine," said Catton, tapping the itinerary. "Thanks to our national love of state occasions, we have the protection business down pat. This should be no problem, and anyway, there is no reason to connect the shootings with Sayid's arrival. Or is there?"

Wintle shrugged his shoulders slightly, but shook his head warningly. "It's anybody's guess," he said, "but wrap this visit up tight, Catton. Put our best men onto him, twenty-four hours, round the clock; armed of course. I'd like you to be there as well. We have a killer running loose, and until we have him in the slammer we can take no chances. On the other hand, it has to be very low profile. We don't want the press getting the idea that HMG are leaning over backwards to crawl around terrorists. Not until they have a deal. Is that clear?"

Catton took a turn or two up and down the room, reading over the program, nodding to himself, noting points. "That's very clear, sir," he said firmly. "But can I ask who knows about this itinerary? Low profile is no problem. I'll cover this myself with a good sergeant, but who's in the know?"

"So far as few people as possible," replied Wintle. "Even the directors of the desalination factory in Brum don't know who he really is, just some Arab. So keep it to yourself, other than for the briefing. Mark that I don't want the press getting onto it. I gather from Yates that this is to be regarded as a social call and two things will ruin it. The first is nasty pointed questions from the press about whether entertaining killers is a vote-catcher. The other is if our current killer uncorks his shotgun and spreads our guest's brains across the wall. Your job is to prevent both events from occurring. Clear?"

"Yes, sir," said Catton again, rather wearily. "Not quite my line of country, the first part, but I'll get to work on this and dope out a plan for you."

"Good," said Wintle, satisfied, returning to the folder in front of him. "Now, about our friend here. Widen the net. I want a list of everyone who has had access to that office—cleaners, postmen, tradesmen, the lot—and their families. Draft a report listing everyone of any significance, friend or foe, who has been in or around that place within the last, say, two years. Also, I want to see detailed reports on any capers, or any attacks their people have pulled off during the same time span. If that produces nothing we'll go back a bit further. There has to be a connection somewhere. Killing five people is not a spur-of-the-moment thing."

Catton looked doubtful again. "We'll have to shop around, sir. I doubt if we'll have that amount of stuff in our own files and, as you can see, our contacts so far have drawn a blank. We'll have to shop around."

"Well, shop around then," said Wintle, testily, "but start at the Jihad office. That's where it all began, after all, and they may have some ideas. We must come up with something soon, or the pressure will really come on."

Catton was halfway to the door when Wintle called him back. "Forget what I just said about the Green Jihad office, or information center, or whatever it's called, being where it started," he said thoughtfully, pulling again at his lower lip. "That's jumping to conclusions. I'm sorry, but I have a feeling this started somewhere else. We start with the man, not the event or place. That's the way to do it." He looked up, directly at Catton. "Find me some triggers to set of such an attack. Find me a man with a motive, the skill and the nerve to stroll into that place one wet morning and kill five people. That will narrow the field a fair bit."

After Catton had left, Wintle sat on at his desk for a while, his eyes closed, thinking, before getting up and going again to the window to look down at the evening crowds. "You're out there some-where, aren't you, my friend?" he said quietly to himself. "I wonder who you are."

On the following day Simon Quarry left his office early at lunchtime, and made his way to the map shop in Long Acre to check on an idea half-formed in his mind. He prowled among the shelves there, buy-ing large-scale maps of the Stratford-upon-Avon area, and that after-noon, after a further look at the maps, he left the office promptly at five, driving through the evening traffic up the fast motorway route to Oxford, around the ring-road and on, across the rolling, eastern edge of the Cotswolds, into Straford-upon-Avon.

He parked his car among scores of others in the Hilton Hotel parking lot and crossed the road to the Shakespeare Memorial The-atre. Unnoticed in the throng, he studied the programs and ex-changed a few words with one of the ticket sellers. Then he walked across to the Dirty Duck pub, bought a beer and walked out onto the terrace to watch the crowd flock in for the evening performance.

By seven-thirty, the theatre doors had closed for the performance and the grounds around the theatre were quiet. Simon walked back to his car, opened the boot and took out his anorak and, sitting in the driving seat, put on a pair of walking boots. He took up the large-scale map and, returning to the point where the road bridge spanned the Avon, found the footpath along the bank beside the river, and began to follow it, jogging quickly whenever he was alone, slowing to a stroll whenever a boat or another walker came into sight. The tow-path was smooth and slightly muddy, easy to follow in the evening light, and after a couple of miles he found the point where it veered away from the river and turned toward the town of Warwick. He peered closely at the map and his surroundings in the growing dusk, until, happy that the map was accurate and that he could find his way back there again without difficulty, he turned back to Stratford.

Running steadily now, his boots noiseless against the soft ground, he was back at the Avon bridge in half an hour. Panting for breath, he ran lightly up a flight of concrete steps to emerge beside the road. Cars crawled past, forming into long queues and slowed by the roundabout beyond the bridge. Simon sat on the bridge parapet watching the traffic before returning to his car, changing back into his city shoes and pulling on his jacket. Then he walked into the town to dine at a small restaurant, eating slowly, stopping from time to time to look at his watch, thinking hard, making the odd note on a piece of paper. By ten o'clock, he was again waiting on the terrace of the Dirty Duck as the crowds came flooding out of the theatre and sought their cars.

Simon noted one particular car, parked by the theatre wall, a large black Rover, similar to the type favored by his Foreign Office contacts. As it began to move from the carpark he left the pub terrace, walked quickly through the crowds and ran across the park, crossed the road again and dropped down the steps to the river towpath. He stood there, counting off the seconds, in the darkness below the bridge, before returning to the top of the steps. There, still screened by the bridge parapet, he watched the cars crawl even more slowly now, the occupants' faces lit clearly by the headlights of the cars heading into the town. There was plenty of time. Several minutes passed before his marked Rover came into view, the occupants of the rear seats craning forward talking to the people in front.

As it passed, Simon walked into the road behind it, dodged round the cars to the far side of the road, then returned through the crawling traffic to his own car, still standing in the parking lot. He could see how it might be done.

By just after midnight, Simon was letting himself into his flat in London. He felt excited, even light-hearted. If the traffic was like that after every evening performance, he could see no difficulty, no difficulty at all. He could walk it. That night, for the first time in a week, he slept like a log.

The next day he completed his plans and built up a cover story. With the map spread on his desk he rang a hotel in Warwick and booked a room. He arranged appointments with his Midlands salesman, making plans to visit bookshops in Stratford during the afternoon before the *Macbeth* performance next week, and again on the following morning. Late in the afternoon he retrieved the shotgun from the library, and that night he sat again in his flat, stripping and cleaning the shotgun, whistling contentedly as he pried open the caps of the cartridges and seeded heavy lead fishing weights in among the buckshot. When all was ready, he stowed the weapon away in a cupboard, and went out for a run. His mind felt empty as he trotted across the park. He felt fresh and fit, the action had started, and he had only to play his part.

Wintle placed Catton's proposals carefully on his desk and studied them closely, pausing from time to time to compare the protection plan with the visitor's itinerary. Finally, and to Catton's slight but concealed relief, he nodded with satisfaction, leaned back in his chair and smiled across at his assistant.

"That seems very adequate," he said. "Since we don't want a great convoy of police for obvious reasons, the way you propose looks excellent. Quite sufficient. Very well judged."

"I think so, sir," said Catton, smiling. "I'll go in the car myself, to make a party of four in all. The driver and I will be armed, so Yates can relax and entertain his guest. I've talked to him, and he seems very pleased that I'm going along incidentally. I have prepared two routes for each stage of the trip, and I'll just tell the driver which to take as the mood or traffic dictates. That way, there can be no leak, and if we have no fixed route an ambush is difficult. The local police will check out the parking lot and the hotel in Woodstock, and so to bed. At the theatre we'll leave the driver to guard the car, and I've arranged a clear space by the theatre where no one can fix a bomb to it. We have a box, and Mr. Yates has arranged for drinks to be served there, not in the bar. The theatre management have been most cooperative. Our client does drink, I hope?"

Wintle shrugged. "Heaven knows," he said indifferently, leaning forward to look at the folder again. "Now, let me see just once more. Our guest arrives from Tripoli on a scheduled flight. Usual private clearance—good. You pick him up with police car escort and an unmarked car to London, a lap of the sights and lunch with the mandarins at the FCO. Fine. Afternoon in conference, then on to Claridges, dinner with some selected MPs at the hotel—private room. Good. Next day, early start for Oxford and Birmingham, visit some factories, lunch with various discreet businessmen interested in investment, blah, blah.... I see, yes, then on to Stratford for evening performance at Shakespeare Theatre. Night at the Bear at Woodstock, and back next day to Heathrow ... and goodbye. A very typical mix. I hope he's bored to death by it. At least he's not laying a wreath at the Cenotaph. I expect he's saving that for his next visit."

Catton grinned slightly at his chief's bitter tone. "Personally I never did care much for factories. I'm quite looking forward to an evening out at the theatre. It will be the first evening off since our friend hit the Jihad office. I just hope that Mr. Yates can chat to our guest and explain the plot. Shakespeare can be obscure, even if you understand English."

Wintle smiled ironically. "The play's *Macbeth*, the murderous king, so he should have no real problem. Now, to other matters. How are we getting on with finding our killer? If we could put him away, or be sure he was elsewhere, then you could really have an evening off. And so could I, come to that."

A doubtful look spread over Catton's face. "Well, sir, in spite of Sayid's visit we are getting precious little help from the Green Jihad. They even clean the place themselves, and are very reluctant to let anyone British in through the door. I suspect they are hunting for the killer themselves. I get the impression that they believe it was one of their own people, or perhaps one of those exiles Colonel Gadaffi ordered home. Those who didn't comply were killed or threatened with death, so someone may be hitting back. The Libyan exile community here is in a high state of nerves, so they may even be right. I have a recent list of acts which their press office here has claimed the credit for, or at least put in a bid on behalf of some terrorist gangs they support. It's quite comprehensive and includes two killings of exiles here, as well as one in Paris—it's funny how Paris keeps coming up—a car bombing in Rome, against the Pan Am office and, of course, last year that airport incident in Athens, when the airliner was set on fire. Most of the passengers were burned alive. Most people would be ashamed of deeds like that, but they boast about it."

Wintle nodded grimly. "I remember it. My God! And next week

you are guarding the man who ordered it. We're all mad! Were there any survivors from the aircraft, anyone who might feel that the time has come to hit back?"

Catton shook his head. "There were only a few survivors, I believe. I'm getting a complete list, but it was a very bad affair. Even so, it was well over a year ago now, and you know how it is, memories are short. There is one curious thing, though, but probably unconnected with that aircraft incident. Someone killed the security officer at Athens airport a few months ago, the same sort of thing as the Jihad office business. Someone just walked into the security office, shot the boss dead and disappeared. I noticed it in our file of supposed terrorist acts and queried it with Athens when I was talking to them about the airplane."

Wintle's eyebrows rose abruptly. "Really? That's very curious. When was this?"

"On the first of March, to be exact," replied Catton. "I have asked for full details because this officer, the one killed, was in charge of security when the airliner was attacked and during one or two other incidents. You told me to trawl deep, so I have. Security at Athens has never been too good, and this man has had a fair amount of flak in the past about his lax methods."

"And now someone has killed him," said Wintle. "As they say," he mused, "just like our Jihad man. Do we know how?"

"He was shot. But with a pistol, not a shotgun. Different weapon entirely. In fact, that's another odd thing which caught my eye. He was killed with his own pistol. Typically, it took weeks for the Greeks to check out the officer's pistol, even though they were looking for the murder weapon. Then the new officer, the one I spoke to, decided to clean his predecessor's weapon and found it had been fired. Ballistics checked it and, lo and behold, it was the murder weapon. It's not very often that happens, I should think."

Wintle rubbed his jaw slowly. "There's probably no connection," he said, "but again, no contract killer would act on spec, just like that. It has all the marks of an opportunist, and a very lucky opportunist, so that is a connection. Check it out, Catton. It tingles."

"I could ask for the complete file," suggested Catton. "We have very few details so far. I could get it, but then it will be in Greek. Odd though, isn't it?"

"Let us not speculate," said Wintle, "but it's curious, I agree. I'd like to see full details on that case, if the Greeks will part with them. If they get too difficult, put them on to me. And add to your list of lists, a list of all the relatives of people on that airliner." He scratched his chin thoughtfully. "As I remember it, wasn't there a famous photograph of that affair, one with a child in it?"

Catton nodded grimly. "That's the one. The photo was in all the papers. We have a copy on file, showing some kid running along the wing of the aircraft with her hair on fire. God knows what that must have done to her parents."

Wintle shrugged and sighed heavily. "They were probably on the aircraft. Check it out, anyway. There may be no connection but without anything else to go on we'd be foolish to ignore it. Killing a security policeman with his own gun is novel, to say the least. If we keep in mind that we need a man with a motive, we may get somewhere, and burning their loved ones alive would provide most people with a motive, wouldn't you think? Now, about your business, young man. I have more paperwork here than you could shake a stick at, so send in my secretary on your way out."

EIGHT

Simon enjoyed visiting bookshops. Even today, with a lot on his mind, he found the time slipping quickly by and business, it seemed, was good. By the end of the afternoon he had visited four bookshops with Ron Cohen, his Midlands salesman, taken substantial orders for the titles on their autumn list from the local library supplier, arranged an exhibition on the university campus and sold a comforting amount of stock.

"I like selling stock off the back-list," Simon said to Ron Cohen as they emerged from the last call and went in search of a cup of tea. "That's where most of our profit is, tied up on the shelves of the warehouse. If we, or rather you, can shift it from our shelves onto the accounts receivable as quickly as possible, we'll have cash in the bank, and that means peace of mind to me, and more money all round."

"It always amazes me that we can still sell our sort of books at present-day prices," said Cohen. "Political and historical subjects are not exactly tits and ass, are they? Yet they still seem to go."

Simon agreed. "It's good, solid business, I suppose. We can pre-dict fairly accurately how many and how much, so we can usually make a reliable profit. You can always rely on politicians to plug their own books. Good PR is half the battle if your book is basically right. Besides, we get a good income from syndication and second rights."

"Well, it all helps," said Cohen, "and what about you, Simon? Are you all right?"

"I'm fine," replied Simon, shortly. "Don't you start."

"Sorry I spoke then. I was going to add that you look pretty good. Very fit in fact. You've lost that paunch that was starting to blossom at the sales conference."

"I feel good," admitted Simon. "I get out for a run round Hyde Park every evening, and unless there is something on, I'm off to Wales or somewhere, hillwalking every weekend. Feel that thigh, solid muscle, hard as a rock."

"I gave up feeling men's thighs when I got out of the navy—and especially marine thighs. You bootnecks never change."

"Of course not," laughed Simon. "It's the secret of our charm. But look, let me ask you something. How would you like to move to London?"

"To do what?"

"To come off the road, move up the ladder, and help Ruth and me run the firm. We could use an old friend at the top."

A cautious, guarded look drifted across Cohen's face. "What about Clissold? Isn't he a friend at the top?"

Simon smiled. "Don't fence with me," he said. "You know all about Clissold."

"Oh, I know all right," replied Cohen. "It's all over the trade. I didn't think that you knew though, because I thought if you did, he'd be out on his ear."

"Exactly," said Simon. "So if he goes, do you want the job? The terms will be favorable."

Cohen nodded slowly. "I'll have to talk to my wife, but it will be all right."

"Good," said Simon, "but until I move officially, keep your mouth shut . . . clear?"

"Very clear," said Cohen, grinning. "I know you better than our about-to-be late sales director."

John Catton knew one certain thing about police work; it wasn't dull. He had entered the police service after leaving university and trying to settle down in some more acceptable occupation. For six months he had walked the floor of a chemical factory, following the well-trodden path of the graduate management trainee. Then he had tried working in the City of London, but eight hours a day staring at a computer screen, buying and selling tin futures, had finally driven him to quit.

Industry, trade, commerce, were simply boring, and not for him, he had decided, and since the Army promised too much discipline in return for only a little more, occasional excitement, he joined the police, treading the beat in a working-class area, working his way up from the bottom. Now he was a Detective Chief Inspector, working for the Special Branch, one of the top jobs in the Service, and a day touring factories in the Midlands with Sayid and Yates simply served to remind him how right that early decision had been. The party had left London early with a police car to lead them quickly through the morning traffic out onto the M40 motorway, and by ten o'clock they were walking around the grounds of an Oxford college, Catton and Yates in the rear, Sayid talking animatedly to the escorting professor up ahead.

"Education is a big thing for these people," murmured Yates in Catton's ear. "The idea of getting an Oxbridge education is very attractive. They see education as the key to progress, or at least to power. A good degree is worth a Cabinet post almost anywhere in the Third World."

"As long as Sayid doesn't expect extramural instruction in ambush drills or weapon-handling, I expect Oxford would do them very well," replied Catton sourly, huddling deep into his overcoat against the chill air.

A slight frown eased across Yates' face. "That's rather a cynical approach even for a policeman," he said. "These people have been fighting for their future. We hope to persuade them that there are other ways to achieve their aims, apart from terrorism. Diplomacy, statesmanship, the democratic process, that's what we are selling here. That's what this visit is all about."

"And what if the other ways don't work?" asked Catton. "Will he just shrug and say, 'Well, we tried,' or will he get the guns out again? Is he armed now, by the way? His minders were, when they arrived at the airport. We took their shooters away, but Sayid's being treated as a diplomat. Has he a weapon?"

Yates looked shocked. "Dear me, I hope not. I've no idea. Are you armed?"

Catton nodded, flipping open his jacket briefly to reveal a holstered pistol clipped at his waist. "The difference is," he said, "that I have permission for it. My driver is armed as well. We have all the protection we'll need."

"Are you expecting any trouble?" asked Yates, a slightly worried note in his voice. "I have heard no rumors. Have you?"

"None at all," replied Catton, nodding to the couple ahead, "but our friend up there has plenty of enemies. We've pulled in a few unfriendly people for a chat, just to see if anything is brewing, but this visit is very private and we have heard of nothing. However, we still don't know who shot up their office, and if it is this fellow, or his group, that our killer is after, then we have to take care. Anyway, you know all that. The commander hinted that all this was your idea. We're just helping out."

Yates waved a hand at the lawns about them. "God, what a world. All this peace, the groves of academe themselves no less, and we talk about killings."

Catton shrugged and permitted himself a wry glance at Yates alongside. "We are escorting a killer after all: what do you expect us to talk about. Incidentally, we ought to hurry. The program is crowded and the schedule is tight, but I want time to change it—just in case."

From Oxford they went north to Birmingham, calling at an army munitions depot near Bicester on the way to inspect a wide range of small arms, where Catton cynically observed a surge of interest in their guest. By the time the tour was over, Catton was more than ready for the drinks they were offered in the boardroom at the end of the afternoon.

"If you gentlemen would care to save time and have a wash here, we have a private bathroom," suggested their host. "You are going on to the performance at Stratford? How nice. Are you fond of Shakespeare yourself, Mr. Sayid?"

Abu Sayid smiled pleasantly, shaking his head. "I have had few opportunities to see his work, I'm sorry to say. But to see another culture is always interesting, and I look forward to this evening." His English was good, barely accented, and he accepted the gin and tonic without hesitation, chatting easily to the various directors, resembling nothing more than the wealthy foreign buyer he was supposed to be.

Catton stood watching quietly in the corner. He had remained on edge throughout the day and he, too, was looking forward to an evening at the theatre and the chance to wind down and relax. In twelve hours Sayid would be gone, and Catton could return to his real work. "The performance starts at seven-thirty," he said, moving forward to interrupt the chatter, "and so I think we had better be moving soon. I have arranged for us to park close to the theatre entrance, but we still have to get through the traffic, and that can be heavy." Within minutes the group had broken up and they were again in the car, beginning the last part of their journey.

"That's the snag with the English theatre," Catton explained over his shoulder to Abu Sayid, as they drove out of the factory gates. "The performances begin very early, really too early to dine first, and then most restaurants stop serving by eleven o'clock. However, we will be able to eat at our hotel later. I hope that will be all right. Are you hungry?"

"I am not hungry at all," said Sayid. "We had lunch, and that was sufficient. Perhaps later . . ."

They drove to Stratford, where they edged slowly along through the streets in the theatre-going traffic, and turned towards the red brick bulk of the Memorial Theatre. After a few words with a gate-keeper they were admitted to the staff parking lot and here Catton became anxious again, hurrying the group into the theatre and leaving the driver with strict instructions to stay close to the car. This done, he hurried Sayid and Yates toward the theatre entrance, fumbling in his wallet for the tickets. If his eyes fell upon the figure of Simon Quarry, watching their arrival from the terrace of the pub across the road, his mind failed to record it.

Simon had got back to his hotel just after six o'clock. He had showered quickly, changed into cord trousers, sports jacket and a pair of light training shoes, and reflected how much pleasure he still got out of his business. This feeling of satisfaction remained with him as he ran downstairs to the reception desk.

"Can you tell me what time you close the door at night?"

The receptionist looked up. "About eleven-thirty," she replied, "after the bars shut. We have a night porter though, or I could let you have a key, if you prefer that."

"I'll take a key. I should be back much earlier, but you never know." He accepted the key with a smile, then went out to his car. By seven o'clock he had driven into Stratford, arriving just ahead of the theatre traffic, leaving his car in a side street and walking to the pub across the road from the theatre.

He had been waiting about on the terrace for twenty minutes, his eyes fixed on the arriving cars and crowds, when he saw one of those familiar Rovers arrive at the staff entrance and swing into the private parking lot. He studied the position of the passengers as they got out and stood about chatting amiably. He noticed Yates, attentive to his guest, and saw Catton round up the party and hurry them inside the theatre. Mostly, though, he concentrated his gaze on Sayid, but he felt nothing. He had thought he might have felt some emotion, but nothing came. When the doors closed, he left the terrace and returned to his car. Everything was falling into place.

Simon drove back to Warwick as the evening grew dark, and parked again behind the hotel. Then he walked down the road and ate a quick meal in a Chinese restaurant before returning to the now dark parking lot. It was empty. With a swift look in all directions, he opened the car boot, took the shotgun from the clips under the parcel rack and slid it into the gun-case. He removed his jacket and put on a dark anorak, feeling in the pocket for the jar of camouflage cream. That now familiar sense of excitement was beginning and he observed, with some contentment, that his hands were still steady.

He walked calmly out of the carpark and turned toward the river. It was dark as he reached the towpath and turned along it, past an old couple strolling along in the falling dusk, and a fisherman just packing up for the day. They took no notice of him as he ambled beside the river, the gun-case hardly visible behind his shoulder. He had plenty of time and had no wish to be early. By nine-thirty he had arrived in Stratford and hidden the gun-case in a corner below the bridge, and was sitting quietly in the Hilton coffee shop, sipping a cup of tea, watching the clock, completely composed.

As the minute hand snapped up to ten, he rose, left money on the table to settle his bill, and made his way swiftly across the parking lot toward the bridge. Here, away from the lights, it seemed even darker. There was no one about as he collected the weapon from beneath the bridge, removed the gun from its case and worked the action, loading the weapon, leaving it propped against the wall below the bridge step. The lights from passing cars on the bridge gave him just enough light to see by, and he carried the gun-case back up the towpath for a hundred yards and slid it into cover among the reeds. This done, he returned to the bridge, checked the shotgun again and then ran up the steps toward the noise and glaring headlights of the cars creeping past across the bridge. He stayed back a little on the narrow stone platform behind the wall, noting the dazzle of the lights, the even darker blackness outside their limits. It was all perfect.

He dodged through the cars and walked across the park, just as the first early leavers were beginning to trickle down the theatre steps, pulling on their coats and turning away into the darkness. Simon walked to his vantage point on the crowded pub terrace, picked out the official car in the parking lot and saw the red glow as the driver inside pulled on his cigarette.

The departing crowd grew thicker as the performance ended. As

the doors opened and closed Simon could hear the sound of ap-
plause. Then, with a sense of relief, he saw the three of them coming
down the theatre steps. He saw the driver get out of the car and the
inside lights came on as the doors were opened. He waited until the
car was pulling slowly out into the traffic, noting the shape and color
of the cars ahead. Then he was off, trotting through the park, glancing back to see where the car was, crossing the road again and running down the steps into the darkness. Suddenly he felt breathless; a
nerve in his cheek was twitching. Too late now. He pulled the jar of
camouflage cream from his pocket and, wrenching off the top,
smeared a wide, dark band across his cheekbones and nose, distorting
his features, and then, stuffing the jar away, he snatched up the shotgun, half-opened the breech and clashed it home. The cars crept
past, engines roaring, as he ran back up the steps with the weapon
held under his arm to the shadow of the trees at the top. There he
waited.

"My word, this traffic is heavy," remarked Catton, turning back in
his seat, "but we'll soon be through it. Did you enjoy the play, Mr.
Sayid?"

"Very much," replied Sayid politely. "I must thank you gentlemen for such an enjoyable day. I should add that it was most in-
structive and very interesting."

"Well, I'm sure we're all glad you enjoyed it," said Yates, sitting
forward to peer through the front window. "Personally, I'll be glad
when we're through this traffic and having a little supper at the hotel.
It's been a very long day."

Then the rear window exploded and the world fell in.

Looking back, Catton saw Abu Sayid's head dissolve. His mind
rocked with the concussion that shook the car and swept through his
ears. He felt the car swerve across the road and crunch grindingly
into an oncoming vehicle as their startled driver, raked by shot, leapt
in his seat. Catton clawed at the door handle and rolled out of the
car, sprawling in the road among the wheels, the headlights and the
blare of horns. Kneeling, he felt for his pistol as there was another

shot, a long streak of fire from somewhere behind, and then another, a great blast above the hooting horns and shouting that mounted on every side.

Catton could see the man now. He was standing in the middle of the road, a tall, dark figure, a black silhouette against the lights. Then another car rolled past, swerving up onto the pavement, blocking his view, and as Catton staggered to his feet the man disappeared. The noise was tremendous, a racket of engines, shouting, the still incessant blare of car horns. Someone came up and seized Catton roughly by the arm, shouting in his ear.

"Look at my car! Are you all drunk? What in God's name is going on?"

Catton pushed the man away and walked unsteadily over to the car, leaning forward to stare inside. The driving seat was empty, but in the back a shocked Yates still sat rigidly among the bloody remains of Sayid. He found the driver sitting huddled on the wall, clutching a bloody, mangled hand, more blood oozing from his head and shoulder.

"He came right past, sir, just as I was hopping out, and smashed my hand in the door, the bastard."

"Were you hit?"

"A bit, I think. But my hand . . . Christ! I think my fingers are broken."

"God! What a mess," exclaimed Catton. "What a bloody mess."

He turned back and was helping Yates from the car when a policeman appeared, pushing his way through the growing crowd. Catton flashed his identity card and jerked his head to indicate the contents of the car. The constable looked inside briefly, and turned to stare, eyes wide, at Catton.

"There's been a murder, right?" said Catton sharply. "So get on your radio and fetch some help down here fast. Then get me your inspector. We want roadblocks out as fast as we can. The man who did this is on the run and he can't be far away."

Simon dropped down beside the bridge and ran hard for a few hundred yards along the towpath, slowed to a walk, his legs trembling, and then sat down suddenly on the grass beside the bank. Looking back, he could hear the noise and see the lights from the bridge, but knew there would be no pursuit, at least for a while. His legs still unsteady, he levered himself up with the shotgun, the heat from the barrel warm against his hand, and began to hunt among the rushes for the gun-case, finding it easily and slipping the weapon inside. Then he slid down the bank to the river and washed the black camouflage cream from his face. Refreshed and calmed by the water, he reclimbed the bank, picked up the gun-case, and trotted swiftly away along the towpath, soon leaving the lights and confusion far behind.

An hour later, even as the first roadblocks began to ring the roads out of Stratford, he emerged onto the streets of Warwick, slipped into the parking lot and replaced the weapon in the boot of his car. The front door of the hotel was still open, and he walked calmly across the hall and went to bed. He lay for a long time, listening to the occasional siren of a police car. It was a while before he slept.

NINE

Ignoring the clamor, the passing people and the incessant ringing of the telephones in the outer room, Wintle poured two cups of coffee from the pot on the cabinet, took them across to the table, put one in front of Catton and the other before his own chair, and sat down.

"Will somebody close that door!" he snapped over his shoulder. The door connecting the room with the adjoining one, which was now established as the operations room, closed abruptly, cutting out much of the noise.

Wintle looked grimly across at his assistant. "You don't need me to tell you there will be all hell to pay over this. First things first though. Are you all right? You look like death."

Catton was sitting huddled in a chair, a blanket slung round the shoulders of his bloody shirt. He stirred his coffee awkwardly and shrugged, wincing with pain.

"A doctor from the hospital gave me a local and took four pellets out of my shoulder," he said, "but it's nothing much. The driver's worse, a clutch of shot in his shoulder and two broken fingers. They've kept him in. It's been a hell of a shock, though, and so I keep getting the shivers. It's hard to describe, sir, I've never seen anything like it."

Wintle nodded, leaning across the desk, resting on his elbows and cradling the coffee cup in his hands. "I've seen the car and what's left of our guest. Not a pretty sight, I agree. Can you tell me what happened, exactly? Did you get a look at him? Where did he come from? It's sheer chaos out there by the theatre; the roads are jammed with traffic for miles either side. Thank God there was a helicopter at Kidlington I could use."

Catton drank some more coffee and shook his head again, puzzled. "It was all so quick," he said slowly. "He must have known where Sayid was sitting, for he fired into the car at very close range. He blasted the window in and Sayid's head went with it. I think this . . ." he touched his shoulder, "was an accident. He could have killed the lot of us, quite easily. I'm sorry sir, but it was all so fast I was—well—useless. I don't really know what happened."

"But did you see him?"

"Yes, just for a second. I've worked out that after he killed Sayid, he fired another shot into our near tyre, and then one into the radiator of the cars behind. Then he blasted a car coming the other way, and it crashed into ours. That's what jammed up the whole works. Our driver was hit, like I was, but the gunman ran past as he was getting out and just slammed the door on him. I was out of our car on the other side and rolling across the road when I saw him fire once, or maybe twice. But then another idiot in a car came round the front and cut off my view, so I only saw a shape. You can't imagine the confusion out there, sir, lights, car horns, people yelling, there was a real panic. When I got up he had gone. He just disappeared. Since then, well, we've been trying to cope here, but we have put out roadblocks and we are checking the town."

"Have we any descriptions at all? Did *anyone* get a clear look at him?"

Catton nodded toward the door. "You know what it's like, sir. We have a dozen people out there, all talking their heads off, and not two of their descriptions tally. One old buffer even insists there were three gunmen, all armed with sub-machine guns. However . . ." he flicked open a notepad on the desk. "I got this down as soon as I pulled myself together. Our man is tall, at least six foot, slim build, possibly in his thirties; that's just an impression but something in the way he moved made me feel he's no kid. He's handled weapons and he's got good nerves. We *are* looking for a professional here, chief. He came out of nowhere, killed the man he wanted and no one else, created havoc on that bridge, and disappeared leaving such confusion—well—you've seen it. He created that pile-up in order to cover his escape, the crafty bugger." Catton closed the notebook and looked across at his chief. "That's all, I'm afraid."

Wintle frowned but nodded his head in approval. "All that from one glance, John. Well done, you're getting perceptive. You were right to get your impressions down quickly and, as far as they go, they are fine and very useful. You are not forgetting various other points, I hope? How did he know you were there? Who fed him the information? Why did he do this? Does it tie in with the other job at the Embassy? Should we assume it's the same man?"

Catton tipped up an envelope and two empty shotgun cartridges rolled out across the desk top. "French Gevelot twelve-bore," he said. "It's the same man. I think ballistics will confirm it, but there is really no doubt. He's a contract killer of some kind, and a good one."

Wintle shook his head doubtfully. "Don't jump to conclusions, John. I still don't think our man is a professional. I think he may have been a professional of some sort, but I think he's just an experienced opportunist. On both occasions far too much was left to chance for a professional. Moreover, on a job of this size, they don't usually work alone, but our man is experienced enough to know that confusion is his ally and usually reigns at such a time, so he uses it to get away. As you say, if it doesn't exist, he creates it. Clever, that. It's all too quick, but I think he simply has a rough plan and lets the rest go hang and plays it by ear. He could hardly plan this killing in any detail. He wanted to kill Sayid and he wasn't too much worried after that. As it turned out he had no need to." Wintle looked at the ceiling and half to himself said, "He interests me. I've never had a case like this before. . . . He's . . . different."

"He's got to be stopped," said Catton abruptly. "Do you realize he's already killed six people. Six people, in broad daylight. Well, practically. Or at night in a crowded street and we don't have a clue. We've been after him flat out for the last month, and before we get a sniff of him, he kills again."

"Police work, John," said Wintle firmly. "Police work, that's the answer. Start at the beginning, apply the routines and we'll come up with the answer. He'll tip his hand somehow. There will be too much noise over this for tongues not to wag. Start by checking out everyone who had access to your itinerary last night. Find everyone and anyone who had any reason to shoot up the Green Jihad, and then kill Sayid. Eliminate the impossible and what remains . . . well, you know the rest. Now, I'd better go and let London know the worst. Can you get someone to arrange a car for me? Then, try and get some rest."

"Sorry I'm late, Simon," said Ron Cohen, pulling out a chair and sitting down. "There are damn great traffic jams on all the roads. The police have roadblocks everywhere, looking for the gang who killed that Arab over in Stratford last night, I expect. That was a turn-up, eh? I can't say I'm knotting my hanky over what happened to him, though. From what the papers say he was a terrorist of some sort . . . a real shit."

Simon nodded toward the open paper on his breakfast table. "I've just been reading about it. A nasty business. There seems to be some doubt about how many people were involved. I wonder why our government was squiring a terrorist about the country. It seems odd to me, and it should cause quite a stir in the corridors of power. Serve them right."

Cohen poured himself a cup of coffee and began to butter a piece of toast. "I can't face food first thing in the morning, but I feel a bit peckish now," he explained. "I heard the local police chief on the car radio asking for witnesses. They're searching the hotels in Stratford and beating the bushes for the gunman, but apparently they think it's the same bloke, or blokes, who killed those Libyans in London some weeks ago. It's Arab killing Arab, if you ask me. You know how they are. I just wish they'd do it at home and not on my territory. These delays play havoc with my plans."

"Well," said Simon, dismissively, "just as long as the police don't bother us today. So, what's on? Where are we going first, and how can we get paid by that library supplier?"

That evening Simon collected his car from the hotel parking lot and drove out toward Oxford, picking his way across country on minor roads, resisting a strong urge to travel through Stratford, past the scene of the shooting. On reaching the main road he turned south, his eye caught by a sign to the Rollright Stones. He swung his car out of the traffic stream and drove up onto the ridge to the prehistoric stone circle, where he came to a stop and switched off the engine, feeling suddenly tired. Seeing another car drawn up on the verge ahead, he got out, swinging the door softly shut behind him. Leaning against the door, he gazed across the countryside below and soaked up the calm of the evening.

"Well, that's that," he said aloud. "It's hard to believe it really happened." He looked down at his hands and shook his head wonderingly. "What am I doing here? How did all this start? And stop talking to yourself, you fool!" He stirred himself away from the car and strolled up the road and through the gate into the field, walking toward the stone circle. The Rollrights swept round the field, some large, some small, grey stones as old as time, a relic from the distant past. There was another man there already, looking at the circle, smoking his pipe and flapping the smoke gently at the encircling midges. They nodded silently to each other and stood together regarding the ancient stones.

"They say," said Simon, breaking the silence, his eyes on the circle, "that you can count the Rollright Stones a hundred times and never get the same total twice."

"So I've heard," said the man. "I made it thirty-seven. I also read in some book or other, that if you can get the same total twice, it means you become King of England. That's quite an inducement."

Simon counted. "Thirty-five," he said.

"Did you count that small one? You can just see the tip of it over there. Some are probably hidden in the grass, anyway."

"Yes, that one's in," said Simon. "Now I'll try again. How about you?" They counted again, heads nodding, lips moving, until the circle was completed, once again. Then they looked at each other, smiling cheerfully.

"Thirty-six."

"Thirty-eight," said Simon.

"I give up," said the man, spreading his hands, "and now I come to think of it, I don't want to be King of England, anyway."

"Life's too short," agreed Simon, "and who wants to launch ships for a living?"

They looked again about the field, in friendly silence.

"It's a pleasant spot, this, isn't it?" said the man. "And a beautiful evening. I just felt like a breath of air. It makes a break at the end of the day."

"So did I," replied Simon. "There's too much rushing about nowadays, somehow. It's just hard to slow down."

They walked back together toward the road and down toward their cars. "Are you alone?" asked the man, looking about. "I heard your car arrive, but then I thought I heard voices."

Simon smiled apologetically. "That was me, I'm afraid. For some reason I have suddenly acquired this bad habit of talking to myself, out loud. I hardly know I'm doing it. I was just telling myself off about it, before we met—aloud of course."

"I did that for a while after my wife died," said the man. "Talking to myself, that is. I don't know why I did it, but after a while I stopped. Anyway, I don't do it now."

"Perhaps that's the reason then," said Simon. "My wife died about a year ago, and now I come to think of it, that was about the time I started the habit. Yes, you're probably right."

"I'm sorry to hear you lost your wife," said the man, tapping his pipe out against the heel of his shoe. "Well . . . must get on, I suppose." He opened the door of his car, and looked toward Simon.

"Yes, well, good night," said Simon, turning toward his own car. "Nice to have met you."

"Good night," said Philip Wintle.

Back in his flat that evening, Simon went through the now familiar routine. He pulled on the rubber gloves, took the weapon from the gun-case and stripped it down to clean it thoroughly, wiping the fouling from the barrel, unloading the unfired cartridges from the magazine. When the weapon was clean and oiled, he reassembled it, slipped a cartridge into the magazine, and worked the action a couple of times to load and unload the weapon, catching the cartridge each time as it spun out from the ejector. Then he placed the shotgun back on the kitchen table and covered it with a cloth.

"Tomorrow," he said aloud, addressing the weapon, "I'll wipe you through and get the last of that fouling out. Then it's back to the library." He shook his head, suddenly annoyed with himself. "Jesus! I really must stop talking to myself."

At the regular ten o'clock meeting three days later, Wintle expressed some satisfaction at the amount of work being done upon the killings. Two trestle tables were now lined up along the one wall of the operations room, covered with ever-fattening files. On a green baize board behind, a series of photos was going up and charts linking the various terrorist groups were being completed. From the other office, voices, the chatter of a telex and the constant ringing of the telephones marked the arrival of still more information, the constant probing for facts.

"This is the time I like on a case," Wintle told Catton, rubbing his hands enthusiastically. "When the wheels start to move, when the team starts to pull together. We'll have this one cracked before too long, and it will be by pure police work. Nothing spectacular, just solid routine, and a bit of luck, perhaps. We need a bit of luck."

"Most of this is dead ends," warned Catton, indicating the files with a wave of his hand. "We have a very thin file of hard facts, and those we have are mostly circumstantial. There's not a lot to go on, and I wonder where we will go when the leads peter out." He looked tired, still drawn from the shock of the shooting, strips of adhesive strapping bandages to his neck.

"It doesn't matter at the moment," replied Wintle soothingly. "Even a dead end is one less area to explore; it narrows our field of search. Besides, we can continue to provide our masters with plenty of paper as evidence of effort, while we hunt through the world for our man. Don't despise those files, though. He's in there somewhere, believe me. It's just a question of time."

"How are our masters?" asked Catton, with some amusement. "If the press is on their backs as hard as it's on ours, they must be having a very thin time. After all, they invited Sayid here. How do they explain that away? What is their reaction?"

"Shocked, flummoxed, embarrassed and thoroughly pissed off with us. They sit down with murderers and then they can't understand it when the murderer gets murdered. It's very difficult to explain to the press why he was here in the first place, that's their big hurdle. Fortunately, that fellow Yates was with you and got himself well splattered with Sayid's brains, so the responsibility for Sayid's death seems shared. Yates didn't get scratched, but he's livid. A bad fright has done nothing for his self-esteem. For the moment, our masters are more concerned that their policy is in ruins, at least until another leader of the pack is appointed, although I doubt if they'll risk inviting him to London, even if he was daft enough to come. Dilly-dilly-come-and-be-killed is no basis for negotiation." Wintle leaned back in his chair, laughed and clapped his hands together again.

"You seem almost pleased," said Catton, smiling at the pleasure in his chief's face.

"Well, no, not pleased. Let's say amused," said Wintle. "It all comes down to standards, changing times. I've only got a few months before retirement, remember, and to be honest I'll be glad to go. In the old days, when I was a younger copper on the beat, we played cops and robbers with clear-cut rules. There were the good guys and the villains, us and the mob. Now we have political agents about who tell us that bloody murderers like that Sayid fellow are honored guests. When I was a young copper we'd have had him in the nick the minute he arrived at Heathrow, and extradited him to some hostile country double-quick-time, and damn the political consequences. A killer was a killer, you see. Now half the people reckon they are above the law. Everyone is a special case, except the poor ordinary bastard who doesn't get a look in. You'll find a pressure group for every faction in this country, but let Joe Public get down on his luck and nobody gives a damn. But what really amuses me is that the political gents can't make it stick. They can squire killers about the country and treat them like VIPs, but killers they still are. When our friend killed him on the bridge, Sayid got what he'd been asking for these ten years or more. The pity is that it took another killer, and not the law, to sort him out. Go and read your Bible, Catton, if you have a Bible. Study those lines about what happens to those who live by the sword. There's a lot of truth in it, and it's all a matter of time."

"Then is that what will happen to our man as well?" asked Catton. "A shot in the head? If we can't catch him, and at the moment nobody even knows who he is, he'll have a fair chance of getting away with it."

"No," said Wintle firmly, "the law will take care of our friend, sooner or later. I'm not having unsolved killings on my patch. It's bad for business. We'll find him, the courts will try him and put him away for a good long spell. So, let's find him. What have we got?"

"Not a lot," said Catton honestly. "On the face of it, this is a terrorist gunman. But if so, he's not Arab, Japanese, Italian, Irish or German. All our connections in those countries tell us that the terrorist movements there are, or were, supporters of Sayid's group. It's not the IRA. We have good contacts there and they regard his death as quite a blow. They are even putting it about that the SAS killed him. It's not the Red Brigades or what's left of the Baader-Meinhof. It's not the Libyans themselves. They have sheltered Sayid's people when the rest of the world got too hot for them, and since Gadaffi controls Carlos, it's not Carlos. It's not his style anyway. So there is no political motive here, as far as we know."

"Money?" suggested Wintle. "Missing party funds from Swiss accounts? A spot of nest-feathering gone wrong? Thieves falling out? A power play within the Green Jihad?"

"We've asked about that specifically," replied Catton, "but apparently Sayid didn't care about money, he's a power freak. At the moment, I mean up to the moment he was killed, he was unchallenged in the Jihad movement. They don't even know who will replace him. His murder has caused them real problems and everything, including our government's delicate negotiations, will have to wait until they have a new leader. It's really knocked them for a loop."

"In my private capacity, I could be pleased about that," said Wintle, nodding, "but with all those avenues excluded, what are we left with?"

"It could be revenge," said Catton. "Every other avenue soon peters out, but that one's crowded." He pointed to a thick mass of files on one of the trestle tables. "Those contain facts on the victims of Sayid's hit teams, or rather their relatives. That's just the final cull, because I have eliminated the old, the sick, the children and the downright impossible. I even eliminated the Israelis, partly because they have given up their eye-for-an-eye policy in recent years, partly because I have the assurance of their man in London that this is not their work. I get the impression that they are tickled pink, incidentally, but not directly involved. Finally, as you suggested, I've only gone back two years."

"That will do for a start," said Wintle, "though if we come up with nothing there, we'll have to dig deeper, or go back further."

"Then we have the usual forensic and tracing procedures," continued Catton. "The French are trying to trace sales of shotguns over the last year or so. We think he bought the weapon in France, because of the cartridges, and also because pump-guns are hard to come by over here. The problem is that the French don't worry too much about shotguns, and so the retailers are not obliged to keep records. At best, we may get a description of who bought it. Fortunately, it's an unusual weapon, and that narrows the field a bit. So far though, we have no leads. That's the story everywhere."

"What about the backroom boys. They usually have something to help us."

"Fingerprints have the cartridges, but there are no prints. They'll be up with anything or nothing fairly soon. We are running down all the descriptions we have on Identikit likenesses, and checking out hotels and lodgings in the Stratford area. He'd have had a hard job to get away since he himself jammed up the traffic heading south, and the police in Brum had roadblocks on the northern roads within twenty minutes. So he may still be in the area, unless he slipped through the net before we could close it, which seems unlikely. Either way, we're checking and considering all angles. He must have slipped away by now, but again, we might get a lead on who he is, and how he did it."

"All right," said Wintle, heavily. "That's good solid stuff, so just keep everybody at it. Now let's have a look at your Possibility file. If we can trim that down to a Probability file, we are heading in the right direction.

Catton got up from his chair and went over to the trestle table against the wall to collect a fat brown file. He came back and placed it on the desk between them.

"We could start almost anywhere," he said, tapping the file, "but these are all men, of roughly the right age and all with good reason to hate Sayid and his gang. They all live in the US or Western Europe, so they have access. That's all we really have to go on, so that's what these people correspond to. Having said that, it still amounts to thirty or so people, and there is absolutely no other evidence against any of them. I've got all the information I can on each one. More is coming in all the time. Where possible, I've got photos, mostly taken at funerals."

"Funerals?" asked Wintle, puzzled. "Why at funerals?"

"When they were burying their relatives, killed by Sayid's group," explained Catton. "That's why the photos all look alike. They are mostly press photos, taken at funerals."

"I see," said Wintle, slowly. "Well, spread them out and let's have a look."

They were laying the photographs and files out across the desk, when a knock came at the door, and they both turned to meet the fingerprint man who came in, bearing yet another file and the tagged cartridges in a plastic bag. He waited while Wintle and Catton read his report. Wintle ringed a few words in pencil, then asked, "If there are no prints, have you any ideas about the latents referred to here?"

The fingerprint man slowly lifted his eyes from the photos on the desk. "No, sir, not much. The cove was probably wearing rubber gloves, but we wouldn't get much from just the end of a cartridge case anyway. We dusted all the cars in case he put a hand on one, but we got nothing there, except an awful lot of work. This isn't going to help you much, I'm afraid."

"Well, never mind," said Wintle. "It was too much to hope that he had left a nice set of prints and you had him on file. He's a lucky man, this one."

The fingerprint man's eyes strayed down again to the pictures on the desk. "One thing, though," he remarked suddenly, tapping one of the photos, "it's not this one anyway. I know him. He's an old mate of mine. This is a funny place to see a friend's photo."

Wintle smiled, and reached across the desk to pick up the indicated photo and glance at it. He frowned briefly, switched on the desk light, and studied the photo more closely, turning it to read the details on the back. He studied the photograph again, then looked at the fingerprint man.

"You say you know this man?" he asked. "How do you know him?"

"We were in the services together. Years ago. In the Royal Marines. We served together for years. I haven't seen him recently, mind."

"It's curious, all the same because I know him too," said Wintle, chewing his lip. "For I met him just the other night, near Oxford. Sit down Mr. . . . er . . . what is your name?"

"Rivers, sir, Jake Rivers," said the fingerprint man uneasily. "But I really ought to . . ."

"This won't take a minute, Mr. Rivers, please sit down," interrupted Wintle. "Mr. Catton, do you think we can find a cup of coffee for Mr. Rivers?"

Catton got up and drifted gently over to the door, putting his head round the corner to speak to someone, then strolled gently back to slide into his chair. They both looked steadily at Rivers, their eyes alert. Wintle looked at the photo again and then smiled across the desk at Rivers. He turned the picture over again and studied the name on the back, nodding his head gently, as if thinking something to himself.

"Now, Mr. Rivers," he said, waving his hand casually at the files and photos spread out across the desk, "you know what we are doing here. It's just routine, but we have to start somewhere. So, can you tell me something about the mutual friend we have here, Mr. Simon Quarry?"

TEN

 Wintle rearranged the files on his desk, placed Quarry's photograph on the top, and then looked expectantly across at Jake Rivers, who sat uneasily in the chair opposite, nervously stirring his coffee. This sudden transition from messenger to witness was clearly less than welcome, so Wintle attempted to lighten the atmosphere before asking any further questions.

"How long have you been at the Yard, Mr. Rivers?"

"Almost twenty-three years, sir."

"As long as that? Well, then, you know what we're about?"

"No sir, not really. I just do my job, sir."

Wintle nodded sympathetically, and gave Rivers a cheerful smile, waving his hand across the crowded desk, indicating the files. "We have a stack of files here, almost forty in fact. It is most unlikely that Simon Quarry, whom I gather from this brief note is a person of some consequence in the community, has anything to do with this business. On the other hand, to stumble on a personal friend, actually in-house as it were, is a real piece of luck for us. We have a lot to do, and if you can help us eliminate Mr. Quarry from our into do, and if you can help us eliminate Mr. Quarry from our inquiries it will save us a lot of trouble. And, of course, we won't need to bother him at all. So you can help everyone, and Mr. Catton and I will be most grateful."

Rivers sipped his coffee and looked doubtful. "I haven't seen Si Quarry for, well, let me see, three years," he said, his mouth setting stubbornly, "so what can I know?"

"But once you knew him well?"

"We were in the mob together. We soldiered on and off for years."

"The mob?"

"The services. That's what we call the mob; the Royal Marines. He was my section corporal in 45 Commando for two years, maybe more. In Egypt, Cyprus, Suez, Aden, lots of places. Then I was his corporal later, when he was a sergeant after that."

Wintle ceased doodling on his notepad and slid a glance gently across the room at Catton, who sat at the far side of the room now, listening to the conversation.

"Mr. Quarry was in the marine commandos?" inquired Wintle, casually. "I didn't know that. When was this? It must have been a long while ago."

Rivers thought for a moment, and scratched his nose reflectively. "That'd be from about 1953 to 1960. He was in for a long hitch but he got left some money and bought himself out. We still meet at reunions and that, and he's still a bit of a mate. You know how it is, once you've soldiered with someone. Of course, I only see him on and off nowadays." Rivers was clearly unwilling to get involved.

"You liked him, I can see," put in Catton, smiling in a comradely way from across the room. "He wasn't the sort to crawl behind the officers, or anything like that?"

Rivers looked round at Catton, glancing sharply across his shoulder, then back to Wintle. "He's a good bloke and a bloody good soldier. We were up the sharp end a couple of times and, well, you get to be pally after that. You don't make good mates sitting on your arse in the Officer's Club."

"So it wasn't just peaceful soldiering?" asked Catton, sounding interested. "You saw some action? You and Simon Quarry together?"

"A bit," admitted Rivers, reluntantly, turning back to Wintle, "but like you said, sir, it was all a long time ago. We were all good kids once, but it was years back."

"But could you tell us something about it?" asked Wintle persuasively. "I know you old soldiers don't like telling war stories, but as you can imagine, it helps fill in the picture."

"Well," said Rivers doubtfully, "like I said, it was a long time ago—over twenty years now. I was talking about it to Si last time we met. He just laughed and changed the subject. But he never was keen on thumping people. I'll tell you this," he threw in sharply, as if daring Wintle to argue, "Si Quarry never lifted his hand against anyone who wasn't bloody well begging for it. Holding off when he shouldn't have nearly got him killed once."

"Really? When was this? Where?"

"At a place called Lapithos, in the north of Cyprus, during the Emergency. It's on the coast, near Kyrenia, quite a pretty place, or it was then. The Turks hold it now."

"What happened?" asked Catton. "You fellows had a rough time there, I remember."

Rivers was warming up now and ready to reminisce, and Catton sat back in his chair as if ready to share a story. "We had a bit of trouble there from time to time. Nothing like Ireland, but it got warm sometimes," began Rivers. "The Greek Cypriots had a terrorist movement in the late fifties, called EOKA, and they were trying to kick us out. It was the usual campaign, a few riots in towns, a bit of ambushing in the country, a string of murders, and us in the middle. Nothing much really. We were at this police station doing the Aid to Civil Power bit . . . dead boring it was."

"Who is this *we?*" asked Wintle. "Who was there exactly?"

"Our section. Well, Si's section, that is. About eight of us. I was the bren-gunner, he was the corporal. He got made sergeant later. We were on our own though, and Si was in charge. We didn't have an officer."

"I see," said Wintle. "And . . ."

Rivers looked reflectively over Wintle's shoulder, out into space beyond the window, thinking back twenty years. "We usually went out on patrol twice a night, once before midnight and once after. Always at different times and on different routes. Si was a good soldier, like I said, and he was careful. The village was mostly Greek and pretty hostile, but nothing ever happened, not until this night. We went out, just Si and me, about two in the morning. Si took my pistol and I had one of the police riot guns, a Greener shotgun. Si used to say that shotguns were the best for night work. He always carried one if he could wangle it off the local coppers."

Wintle kept his eyes fixed on Rivers, and said nothing, avoiding Catton's glances, and ignoring the quick notes which he made from time to time on the scratch pad.

"We started to pick up leaflets soon after we left the station, first a couple, then one in every doorway, then handfuls of them. Leaflets from EOKA were forbidden, so we thought we might try and nab the blokes distributing them. When we came drifting quietly into the town square, there they were, two blokes under a lamp, cutting the string off bundles of leaflets, chatting to each other without a care in the world. Si gave me a nudge to stay where I was and cover him. Then he went forward, very quiet, to pick them up. He could move like a cat when he wanted to and he'd got quite close before he challenged them. Then it all went wrong. They were off like a couple of hares. They nipped off across the square, but we were blocking the only way out. One went dashing into a doorway, and then the other turned and came running right at us. Well, right at Si that is. I still don't reckon he saw me. He had a pistol." Rivers shook his head suddenly and looked directly at Wintle. Suddenly he was alert, knowledgeable, and Wintle caught a glimpse of the infantry soldier that Rivers had been, all those years ago.

"It all happened very quick; it always does. Si was still in his way, just under the light, holding his arms up, and this bloke fired straight at him, twice. I couldn't use the shotgun because Si was in the line of fire, so I yelled 'Lie down' at him, but he wouldn't. He just stood there. The bloke ran past Si and fired at him again, real close, and missed again. God knows how. He was a lousy shot, that kid. Do you know, Si said to him, 'Be careful'—I ask you, at a time like that, 'Be careful!' " Rivers shook his head, marveling at the memory, but his smile faded. "When the lad ran at me, Si shot him. If he hadn't. I don't know what we'd have done. I couldn't fire. If I'd uncorked the shotgun I would have hit them both. He couldn't go on missing, so I expect he would have got me. I had a right good row with Si about it afterward. I reckon he should have fired sooner. He said it was only a kid and he didn't think it right. Silly bugger. I always reckon that if they're big enough, they're old enough."

Rivers fell silent, stirring his now cold coffee again, thinking about the past. A silence fell in the room, and Wintle and Catton exchanged glances.

"How old was this gunman?" asked Catton curiously.

"About seventeen, maybe eighteen. A lot of them were kids in those days. We had a few kids in our unit who would've shot their own mothers. Si let that lad get off three shots before he fired back. It wasn't his fault, even then. He had to shoot him, for my sake."

"Did the lad die?" asked Wintle.

Rivers shook his head. "Not at the time. We got a doc to him, but he snuffed it on the way to hospital. I think Si was pretty upset but he never talked about it afterward, and I never asked him how he felt. The MPs pulled him in and questioned him, but not for long. Like I say, the kid was begging for it."

"Was Quarry a good shot?" put in Catton, tapping the pad with the end of his pencil.

Rivers shook his head. "No, not as I remember, only fair. He was all right with a pistol, but he wasn't interested in weapons. He always said that he'd choose a shotgun for serious stuff so that even if he got nervous he couldn't miss. He never got nervous, though. He's a cool bugger when the shit starts flying."

Suddenly the sense of what he had said struck Rivers, and he looked directly across the desk at Wintle. "I know this bloke the other night used a shotgun, but Si's not like that. Look, all this was a long time ago. We were just kids ourselves. Anyway, I had the shotgun that time."

"Of course, of course," said Wintle soothingly, raising his hand calmly. "Nevertheless, it helps to fill in the picture. I know it was all a long time ago, but was Mr. Quarry ever in action again?"

"I don't know," said Rivers shortly, shrugging his shoulders. "Why ask me? I can't remember."

"But you were together throughout the Cyprus campaign and then again at the Suez landings. Did you see more action there?"

"A bit, not much. It didn't last long, you know. They packed it in, or we did. I don't know."

"Did Quarry ever kill or shoot anyone else?" pressed Catton. "At Suez, or elsewhere during his service career?"

"I don't know. I don't remember," said Rivers again, rising hurriedly from his chair and knocking it over. "Look, I've got to be getting back, so if you'll excuse me . . ." He turned to pick up the chair, and placed it firmly against the desk, his mouth set. There were going to be no more revelations from that quarter for a while, so they thanked him and let him go.

Catton finally broke the silence. "Well?" he asked. "What do you think?"

Wintle got up from the desk and stretched, walking slowly over to the window. "I think we could be jumping to conclusions," he said reflectively, "and I'm always wary of coincidences. It could be just a coincidence, or even luck that I met Quarry last night near Stratford, and that our Mr. Rivers, from this very building, had served with him in a commando unit some twenty years ago. It was even luckier that his photo was lying on the desk here, but it'll take more than luck to solve this case. On the other hand . . ." he paused.

"Without a bit of luck I doubt if we'll ever crack it, as you said," continued Catton, "and besides, what we heard from Rivers helps fill in the picture, as you say. We know now that Quarry can handle firearms, and has killed before. You can swear he was at least in the area, and he has a motive—what a motive!"

"But the killing was twenty-four hours before we met," pointed out Wintle, "and he might have a dozen excellent reasons for being up there. As for the killing described by Rivers, it was as a serving soldier, during an emergency, clearly in self-defense, after provocation, and last but not least, half a lifetime ago. We also have plenty of other possibilities, so let us not leap to conclusions." He stabbed a finger at Catton's notes. "What we have there isn't evidence."

"So you think it's a bust?" asked Catton. "We give up and look elsewhere?"

"Not at all," said Wintle, shaking his head firmly. "I'm not averse to a little luck. Find out everything you can about Quarry. Go back twenty years. Find out about his movements over the last few months. See if he went to Athens, and above all, find out why he went to the Midlands two or three days ago. But don't neglect the others. Now hop it. I have to read through these files and think out a report for the minister."

Ruth looked up from her typewriter as Simon returned from lunch, handing him some papers and a bundle of telephone call slips from the pile on her desk. Every inch was covered with paper and she looked mildly harassed.

"If I give you a line, could you ring these people yourself?" she pleaded. "Do you mind? I'm in the middle of a very complicated contract, and I want to finish it this afternoon. The phone hasn't stopped."

"Sure," said Simon, glancing at the papers and moving toward his door. "Leave them to me and I'll clear this lot and let you know what happens."

"There has also been one somewhat mysterious call," she said, catching him in mid-stride. "Someone rang who wouldn't give his name, but I don't think he's a would-be author. I know you hate people who won't leave a name, but he said he was an old friend of yours and wants you to meet him tonight. Usual time, he said, at Harry's Club. It all sounds rather sordid."

Simon turned in his doorway and looked surprised. "At Harry's?" he asked, his voice rising. "Is that what he said? Harry's? Good Lord!"

"That's what he said. Is he a friend of yours? He sounded very cagey on the phone."

Simon grinned at her suddenly. "If he's a member of Harry's Club he's a very old friend indeed. I haven't been to Harry's in years."

"Where is Harry's Club?" asked Ruth, turning to her typewriter. "I thought you belonged to the Savile. I've never even *heard* of Harry's."

This time Simon chuckled, his smile even broader. "Harry's Club is *much* more exclusive than the Savile. A very select bunch meet at Harry's. A hand-picked clientèle in fact."

"Well, it still all sounds rather sordid to me," said Ruth primly.

"It's that too," replied Simon, winking. "I wonder who it can be. Now, if you'll give me that line . . ." and he went into his office and closed the door. Ruth looked after him for a moment, shook her head, then switched the phone to his extension and began to type hard and fast.

At home that evening, Simon closed his book just after eleven, switched off the record player and carried the empty coffee cup through to the kitchen. Rinsing it at the sink, he glanced out of the window, down through the rain-flecked pane and watched a car swish past in the street below. Simon grunted softly at the sight and, going through into the bedroom, opened a cupboard and dug out some heavy walking shoes and a rain-proof poncho, even contemplating a pair of waterproof overtrousers before rejecting them. Changing into the shoes, he pulled on the poncho and left the flat, running down the stairs to the street.

The rain rattled down on his shoulders as he set off through the silent streets where the few latecomers hurrying home from the pub were hunched against the rain. Simon looked around and shivered before he pulled up the hood of the poncho and set off briskly toward the river, cutting down to Piccadilly, across the grass of Green Park, and along The Mall to Trafalgar Square, empty even of pigeons at that late hour.

He reached the Embankment just as the hands on Big Ben moved toward midnight, and the first booming notes of the hour reached him as he turned under Hungerford Bridge and arrived at the all-night coffee stall. This was Harry's Club, the ancient rendezvous for Simon's marines on their way back to barracks, and there, sheltering under the arch, biting moodily into a pie, stood one of the founder members.

"Hello, you bugger," said Simon warmly, walking over to him. "Is this the best you can do? To think I left a good book and a warm flat for this! We could have met at my place."

Rivers ignored him, nodding his head at the coffee stall. "Do you want a wad and some char?" he asked bluntly.

"Why not?" said Simon genially. "I haven't had a char and wad in years."

"You get it then," said Rivers abruptly. "You've got more money than I have. I'll see you across the road. Get a move on. I haven't got all night."

Simon ordered a bun and a mug of tea from the man behind the counter, and peered across the road to where Rivers stood, leaning on the parapet, gazing out across the river. Cursing as the hot liquid splashed over his fingers, he hurried across to join him, and they stood side by side for a moment, staring at the rain-flecked water, drinking their tea.

"Do you ever see anything of Harry these days?" asked Rivers, resting the mug on the parapet and wiping his mouth with the back of his hand.

"Not for years," replied Simon. "Not since his wife died, anyway. I don't see many of the old bunch, not these days."

"Your wife died, too, didn't she?" said Rivers.

"Yes," said Simon flatly. "She died. So did the kids, as you well know. Now, what's all this about? Are you in some sort of trouble?"

Rivers sighed, threw the remains of his pie into the river, and turned toward Simon. "No, I'm not in bloody trouble, you are. They're on to you. If you did it, that is. Anyway, you're on their list."

"What?" said Simon sharply. "What *are* you on about? What list?"

Rivers' finger prodded Simon hard in the chest. "Did you kill that wog up in Stratford a couple of nights ago?" he asked. "Did you? Out with it, you bloody fool. Because the bloody Special Branch think you did."

Simon laughed softly, shaking his head. "My gunning days are over, Jake. I never did care for it, if you remember. We're getting too old for dramas, both of us, and a good thing too. Now, what's this all about?"

"Don't bullshit me, Simon," said Rivers swiftly. "Not me. I know you well enough to know you could have nailed him if you'd wanted to. God knows the bastard asked for it, if it's true what they say about him in the papers. So, did you do it?"

Simon threw back the hood of the poncho and drank deeply from his mug, his eyes staring at Rivers across the rim. "Why don't you stop getting so excited," he said, "and tell me what this is all about?"

"I *am* telling you," stressed Rivers patiently. "I work at the Yard, in the fingerprint department. You know that. I've been there for twenty years, ever since I got out of the mob. I took up the dabs on the shotgun cartridges left at the shooting, to the chief of the Special Branch, and there was your photo, as large as life, lying on his desk. I was so surprised I just gawped at it. Anyway, they dug it out of me, about you, about me, about the old days. I told them about Lapithos."

"What was my picture doing there?" asked Simon. "And what dabs . . . do you mean prints?"

"I dunno. There were no prints, anyway. It's not that. They're looking for anyone who had a reason to rub out that wog and, God knows, you've got a reason. Snag is, there's more than that." He paused. "Well, there is now. And it's my fault in a way."

"Really? Go on," urged Simon, still half amused. "Tell me more. What's your fault. Your only fault is that you talk too much."

"Well, me indicating you like that. I just said, 'It's not him,' or something like that, and he, the big chief, had a gander at your picture and suddenly, out comes the red carpet treatment. They sat me down, gave me coffee, and asked how we met, about the mob and . . . the lot."

"And so you told them," said Simon. "What, exactly, have you been saying?"

"It just came out. Look, Si, if this means trouble for you, I'm sorry. I'm taking a risk coming here, remember, ringing your office and that. That's why I asked you to meet me at Harry's. I knew you'd come, and that it wouldn't give the game away even if they had a tap on your line. I just hope you weren't followed."

Simon's eyebrows rose in his rain-soaked face. "A line tap? Can they do that, without a warrant or something? Don't we have laws in this country anymore?"

"They can do what they want, Si. This is the heavy mob. There was a real big flap on last week, like the other time, a few weeks back when the wog's building got shot up." Rivers' head jerked suddenly, and he slapped his hand to his brow. "Jesus Christ! Was that you, too? Bloody hell, you have been busy."

Simon looked back at Rivers impassively, the rain plastering his hair and beginning to run in streaks down his face. "What do you expect me to say?" he asked. "If I say no, will it change anything? But if I say yes, you're involved."

Rivers shook his head sadly. "If it's true then you're a bloody fool, Simon. You were a real good mate to me. When those wogs did that to your wife and kids, I felt so sick. I could have killed them myself. I went babbling on to the brass today, because I was, well, proud that you and I were mates. You went your way and know all the knobs, but we were in the mob together and, well, it still means something. Anyway, it does to me."

"It does to me, too," said Simon, slapping Rivers gently on the shoulder. "I never had friends like I did then. Listen, Jake, stay out of this."

"Well," said Rivers, "you know how it is. I have to know. Did you do it or not?"

Simon gazed at him. "I can't lie to you," he said. "I'm sick of lies."

"So? So? So what?"

"So, don't ask me," replied Simon, turning away and looking out across the river. They stood together silently for a short while, shoulder to shoulder, leaning on the parapet, listening to the rain splashing down on the river, watching the water sweep past below.

"Thanks for coming," said Simon suddenly. "Whatever happens, I won't let on about what you told me, but you'd better go now. And no more phone calls."

"They'll get you in the end, you know," said Rivers gloomily. "They'll beaver away at it and, bit by bit, they'll open it up. You won't like it in prison and you'll go down for years, mate."

"I don't think so," answered Simon. "Anyway, I haven't finished all I have to do yet. When I have, I don't really care what happens. That sounds like bullshit, but I mean it."

Rivers glanced along the empty Embankment, reached inside his raincoat and placed something on the parapet between them, something that glinted in the rain.

"If it gets rough, this may come in handy," he said. "Let's call it a present."

"What is it?" asked Simon.

"It's a nine-mil Browning. I've had it for years. I got it off a dead wog that day in Port Said. The magazine spring is new and it's fully loaded. It's a good pistol. You used to be a dab hand with a pistol."

"No thanks," said Simon. "I don't need a pistol." He jerked up the hood of his poncho, and hunched his shoulders against the rain. "I've got to go."

"No one can trace it," said Rivers persuasively, "and a handgun might come in, well, handy. Besides, I want to help. That's why I rang you, to say I'm sorry I spilled the beans, and to give you this. Take it. I'll feel better."

Simon shrugged, then picked up the weapon and slid it under his poncho, tucking it into his waistband. It felt familiar, suitable. "You might be right," he said, straightening up. "If the dogs are on to me I may need all the help I can get. Thanks anyway, and don't worry. Now push off."

Rivers turned up the collar of his raincoat, and stuck out his hand. "Good luck, Si," he said. "And look after yourself. Keep your head down. We've drifted apart over the last few years, but I don't like to see a mate in trouble."

"Just keep out of trouble yourself," said Simon, shaking Rivers' hand firmly.

"I'll be all right," replied Rivers. "I've only got ten more years to pension. I'd like to see old Harry again, and all the others. Just once, for old times' sake."

"So would I, but, well, things are different now," said Simon, turning to go. "You start something new and you can't go back. Good luck Jake, take care."

Rivers stayed, watching until Simon had passed out of sight, and then faded away himself into the rain and the night.

ELEVEN

 As the weeks passed, the pieces came together. Wintle sat on at his desk until far into the night, sifting the information his staff brought to him, spending long hours on the telephone, and more with the door closed, thinking. One by one the Possible Suspect files were closed, but the one on Simon Quarry continued to grow. Photographs came in from his demonstration in Parliament Square, from Athens, press cuttings, reports of conversations, opinions, letters he had written, speeches he had made, copies of books he had published. A small team worked on him full time, filling in the picture, seeking for clues. From the Admiralty came his service record and a yellowed report of the shooting in Lapithos, together with reports of another incident when Simon Quarry had shot and killed yet another terrorist. Among the papers was a statement on this later affair from a Marine J. C. Rivers.

"Our friend from fingerprints has told us less than he knows," said Catton, digesting this information a month after the Stratford shooting. "He told us that Quarry is a pussy-cat unless provoked. On the other hand he clammed up about the fact that Quarry doesn't mess about if and when provoked."

"He likes Quarry," said Wintle. "Most people seem to. Read the files. He's well connected and very well liked. We had better bear that in mind when we have to put all this together and present our findings. People are going to find it very hard to believe that the successful, amusing, articulate Simon Quarry is our latest assassin. And not just ordinary people either. He knows MPs, people in society, members of the government, journalists—it's a good place to meet people, is publishing. We must be very careful to keep our investigations quiet, not only from Quarry, but also from those we talk to. Tell the others to mention him, if they must, but keep it discreet. I don't want a leak tipping him off until we're ready. And I want more facts. That's what will nail him. Solid, hard facts."

Catton brought in the next piece of useful information by the simple trick of walking into the Quarry Press office and talking to Maureen at reception.

"I'm sorry to bother you," he said, breathlessly, "but I'm trying to find a good travel agent. Would you happen to know of one nearby? I'm in something of a hurry."

"Well," said Maureen, helpfully, "we use Taskers Travel in Baker Street. That's just round the corner."

"Are they any good?" asked Catton, leaning on the counter and switching on the charm. "I mean, do they handle long trips, not just . . ."

"Oh yes, I think so. My boss uses them, and has done for years. He goes abroad often, to America and places like that."

"I have to go to Bahrain you know, the Middle East."

"I don't think he's been there, but he went to Israel not long ago. Anyway, I'm sure if he likes them, they're all right."

"Demanding, is he?" smiled Catton, turning to go.

"No," said Maureen, thoughtfully, "but he likes the best."

Two hours later Catton walked back into Wintle's office and placed two pieces of paper on the desk, with a small air of triumph.

"What's this?" asked Wintle, replacing the telephone on its hook. "You're looking very pleased with yourself."

"Two more pieces of the Quarry jigsaw," replied Catton. "Last spring, Quarry went to Israel. That's just after he was fined for demonstrating in Parliament Square. His last appeal for action to the established order, you remember. He had an open-date return, but I've checked the ticket with the airline and he returned on the 21st, on Flight BA192. That stops at Athens, arriving 12:05, departing 13:00. According to the Athens police, the Chief Security Officer was killed around 12:30, when Quarry was in the same building. How about that! That's the second killing we can tie him to."

"Go on," said Wintle. "More, more. This is solid information. If we can once again link him close to a killing, he has something to explain away."

"Second item," said Catton, "is that a week later, Quarry and a young lady went to Paris, Dover to Galais on Sealink. He took his car, and that's curious, because the young lady had an air ticket to Paris. Quarry's travel agent canceled one flight and re-booked her on another, back again to Paris, after they got back. Why? She could have stayed on in Paris. Then I rang the French police. Only two Winchester pumps were sold in Paris this year. It's not a popular model. One was sold on April 8th, when—wait for it—Quarry was in Paris! My guess is that he bought it and smuggled it back into the country, hidden in his car. Anyway, a shotgun of that type, using French cartridges, was used at the Jihad office a few weeks later. It all fits. I've sent a photoprint of Quarry over to Paris and they will show it to the man who sold the shotgun. It was months ago but we could get an identification. How's that?"

Wintle nodded contentedly, and slipped the papers into Quarry's file. "Excellent work, John. It all helps to complete the picture. However, what we need now is a bit of forensic. So far, and good as it looks, it's all circumstantial. He probably has the most excellent reasons for being in Athens, Paris, or Stratford. If we can find that shotgun, or even traces of it, in Quarry's car or his flat, well, that's something else. Meanwhile, we'll put someone onto him. I'll get a warrant to go over his flat. Find someone to give his car the once over, but off the record."

Meanwhile, Simon had been covering his tracks. In spite of police pressure several people had told him that his name was coming up in police inquiries, each one swearing that they found their questions curious. Simon listened, smiled quietly, and shrugged his shoulders, giving nothing away, but taking precautions. The shotgun, cleaned and fully loaded, was back under the shelf at the London Library. The gun-case, with the spare ammunition, cleaning gear and the pistol went in a private safe deposit box a few hundred yards from Simon's office. He took his car to a specialist car cleaner who steam-cleaned and polished it inside and out. He took the outdoor clothing he had worn on that wild night at Stratford to two dry cleaners in rapid succession, and spent an entire evening scouring his flat for any conceivable trace of his recent activities. Finally, he took to wedging a small piece of camera film into the jamb of his bedroom door. When he found it lying on the floor a month after his conversation with Rivers, he smiled to himself and went carefully to the window. The blue van at the end of the mews had not been there when he arrived last night either. Perhaps the two men inside were on some private errand but Simon felt the breath of the hunt. He moved away from the window to pour himself a whisky and sit in his favorite chair. The waiting game had begun.

Police searches into Simon's car and flat were therefore inconclusive. "There's not a thing there, sir," said Catton at the morning conference a few days later, "but we think we were just a bit too late. Sergeant Curzon and Sergeant Davies can tell you what I mean. Curzon!"

"Yes, sir," began Curzon, apologetically. "I went to his flat yesterday and got in, no problem. It was like a new pin. I know Quarry is an ex-bootneck, but even so, it was immaculate, like someone had scrubbed it from top to bottom. You could eat off the ceiling. Then I found an anorak in one of the cupboards with a dry cleaner's ticket on it. Apparently, Quarry goes in for hill-walking and stuff like that. Anyway, since I had found nothing in the flat, I popped into the dry cleaners and they remembered the anorak. Not that there was anything in it, but because it had been cleaned before Quarry took it in. Now, why should he have it cleaned twice? I was going to nick it for the forensic boys to test for powder grains, but I gave them a ring and they said if it had been cleaned once with modern chemicals, never mind twice, they'd find nothing. You said to be discreet, so I left it out."

"You did right," said Wintle, nodding approval. "I don't want to tip him off just yet. What about you, Davies? You went over his car?"

"That's right, sir. It's the same story as Ted's. Normally, Quarry takes his car to the car-wash or gets the caretaker at his flat to give it a weekly once-over. However, last week he took it to one of those specialist car cleaners. They're the ones who charge £100 or more for the job and make the car look like new. It really didn't need it, so why did he do it? It's practically a new car, just over eleven thousand on the clock."

Wintle sighed and sat back in his chair, putting his fingertips together. "He did it to destroy any forensic evidence that he couldn't see himself. He's already been tipped off. He'll have the weapon stashed away somewhere, and we'll be left with a lot of circumstantial evidence that may well have no bearing on the case. We can't build a case on a man having his clothes and car cleaned. It all adds up to us, but it's not hard evidence we could use in court." He looked across at Catton. "Apart from Athens, are we any further forward in linking him to the scene of the other crimes?"

Catton shook his head. "He's a busy man, sir, in and out all the time and no one keeps track of his movements. Frankly, sir, I think it's time we pulled him in and asked him straight to account for his movements. Maybe we should turn over his office."

Wintle shook his head, "No, not with this one. If we pull him in we open this story up and then the press get involved. Then the pressure goes on and we'll never make it stick. We'll try it another way first. Ring his office. Ask his secretary for an urgent appointment, let's say at eleven-thirty, in forty-five minutes' time. A little shock treatment may jar him slightly, though I doubt if it *is* shock treatment in this case."

"How do you mean?" asked Catton, leaning on Wintle's desk as the other two got up to leave, hustling each other out.

Wintle smiled at Catton cheerfully. "How would the average middle-aged businessman feel if a police commander suddenly wanted to see him? At best, well, perhaps, concerned? 'What have I done? What can he want?' But I'll bet that Mr. Quarry will be as cool as a cucumber. He didn't just polish up his car and flat by chance. He's a clever one, our Mr. Quarry. He may even be feeling smug. Now, pass me the telephone."

Wintle found Quarry reading a manuscript when Ruth ushered him into the office. Simon looked up and smiled, then rose from behind his desk to welcome him.

"Have a chair. Have you met my co-director and right-hand lady? Can I just finish this page? The Frankfurt Book Fair is coming up and we want to complete our offer list. I read very quickly, and it won't take me a minute."

Wintle sat in the chair across the desk, accepted a cup of coffee from Ruth, who went out without looking at Simon, closing the door quietly behind her. Wintle rose again and walked slowly and softly across the room to study the photograph. He looked at it for some minutes and when he turned back to his chair, Simon had put the manuscript aside and was looking at him steadily.

"A nice photograph that, isn't it?" he said. "The man who took that picture of my child on fire won an award. Can you believe that? He became News Photographer of the Year, no less. There's glory for you. Did you know that?"

"I'm afraid not," said Wintle. "I suppose it's a good photo technically, but then I'm no judge. It must upset you all over again, seeing it everyday. I'm surprised that you should keep such a reminder. Surely you'd like to forget that business?"

"Surprised are you?" said Simon, a touch of irony in his voice. "You think I should forget the whole business? Like everyone else has, you mean?"

"No, not at all," said Wintle gently. "It's just that I wouldn't think you need any reminders. I believe you were quite a family man."

Simon's face relaxed a little. "You're right," he admitted. "To be honest, I don't really know *why* I keep that picture. It is terrible, I know that. I have others in my head, better ones. Christmas, birthday parties, family holidays. Even after what has happened, you still remember the good times." He stopped and looked closely across the desk at Wintle, his eyes wrinkled, remembering.

"We've met before," he said, thoughtfully, rubbing a finger across his lip.

"Yes, Mr. Quarry, that we have. About a month ago."

"At the Rollright Stones," put in Simon suddenly, slapping the desk top with his hand. "In Oxfordshire. I remember you now. We even talked. You didn't want to be the King of England."

"That's right sir. That was the evening after the Stratford killing. I expect you read about it in the papers. Stratford isn't too far from the Rollright Stones."

Simon chuckled and smiled broadly. "Come on—er—what do I call you? Inspector? Commissioner?"

"It's commander, but you can call me Wintle, if you prefer. I'm not much given to formality."

"Neither am I," said Simon, "and as you probably know, I'm Simon. However, and as I was about to say, you can do better than that." He laughed aloud. "Have I read it in the newspapers, indeed! You are referring, my dear Wintle, to the shooting?"

"Can I assume then," said Wintle, "that you have some more personal knowledge of the affair? More personal than you read in the newspapers?"

"It would solve all your present problems if I said yes, wouldn't it, Mr. Wintle? However, I can't be that obliging. Your assumptions are wrong."

Simon slid open a drawer and extracted a piece of paper, looked across at Wintle and smiled a cold smile. "Last Monday one of your people questioned a former Royal Marine officer of mine at his home in Hampshire. Your man was there for over an hour, and my officer phoned me the second he left. On the same day one of my authors, an MP, John Transon, was interviewed in the House of Commons by one of your inspectors and questioned concerning my political attitudes. You have also visited the travel agency we use and taken away my travel records, without a warrant or permission incidentally. I also suspect that someone searched my flat the day before yesterday. In addition you, or one of your people, have certainly searched my car and questioned the caretaker at my flat. You may have done other things. I had better tell you that unless I get a good explanation for this sudden interest now, you and I will have a jolly half hour with one of Her Majesty's ministers. I have strong strings to pull if I have to—or want to. That's the only reason I agreed to see you. It's put-up or shut-up time, Wintle."

Simon's voice had steadily chilled and sharpened during this recital. Wintle kept his expression impassive, searching his mind for some way to put the meeting back on course and regain the initiative. When he spoke, he was firm and steady.

"We are investigating the killings at the Green Jihad office in St. James's Square six weeks ago, and the one at Stratford-upon-Avon last month. These were carried out by a gunman, about six feet tall, late thirties to forties—not unlike yourself if I may say so—armed with a pump shotgun. We believe it to be the work of one man."

"If you are going to question every tall, middle-aged man in London, you'll have a lot to do," said Simon shortly. "Incidentally, I'm forty-seven."

"I know," replied Wintle. "You don't look it. But then you take lots of exercise. All that skiing and hill-walking I suppose, and you were once a marine commando . . ."

Simon leaned back in his chair and laughed, holding up his hands defensively. "All right," he said genially. "You've done your homework, I can see that. What do you want?"

"To begin with, I think we'd better be formal for a minute. I'd like an account of your movements for the night of the Stratford shooting."

Simon nodded. "I thought you might. Rather than be vague about it, I've written it out for you." He opened his desk drawer again, and pulled out a piece of paper and slid it across the desk. "That covers my two days in the Midlands with my area representative, the calls we made, customers visited, the address and telephone number of my salesman up there, my hotel bill, from Warwick please note, not Stratford, the clothes I wore, my movements during the evening in question. You'll see that during the crucial time I was either dining in a Chinese restaurant at Warwick or having a drink or two in a couple of pubs. I can't tell you their names because I don't know them, but I've put in a note of where they are. Finally, I've included a photo. I expect you have one already, but I thought I'd be as helpful as possible."

Wintle shook his head in amazement. "You're a curious man, if I may say so, Mr. Quarry. Why all this cooperation?"

Simon put his fingertips together against pursed lips. "Why not? But for various reasons," he said. "I suppose the sooner you find out the facts, the sooner you'll stop pestering my friends. Then again, it's always advisable to cooperate with the police. It could even be evidence in my favor. Anyway, I want it on record. If we do have a row, I want no excuses of my noncooperation being used to justify your illegal activities in entering my flat and car. The law can be invoked even against people like you, commander."

Wintle frowned a little. "That sounds a little like a threat, Mr. Quarry."

"Oh, it is, it is," said Simon frankly. "It's very much a threat. I do hope you don't confuse my cooperation with weakness. I'm not remotely afraid of you, commander. I know my rights to the inch and I'll invoke them in a flash if you provoke me. I don't respect the police as much as I did, and if you bend the law in any way, I'll see you regret it. If that is understood, I'll help all I can. I don't wish to be difficult. I actually believe in the law, commander."

Wintle thought it over for a minute, fighting the urge to argue his point, realizing that, for the moment, Quarry held all the cards, cursing whatever carelessness had tipped him off about the searches. Finally, he nodded.

"That seems fair enough," he said, relaxing. "I'm glad you believe in the law. Might I have another cup of coffee?"

"Of course," said Simon gladly, pushing the tray across his desk. "And if you want to search these offices, feel free. You won't even need a warrant." He smiled at Wintle. "I'm sorry, I'm not being prickly. I mean you can bash on without one if you want to. I suppose you are looking for a weapon? A shotgun, it said in the papers. Nasty."

Wintle nodded. "That's correct. The killer has used one twice, so he probably prefers it. Therefore there is a good chance he's stashed it away somewhere, in case he wants to use it again."

"Well, look away then," said Simon cheerfully. "We also have a warehouse at Basingstoke, but we share that and anyway, I haven't been there in weeks."

"I don't think searching either place will be necessary, or useful," said Wintle, "in view of your attitude, that is. However, there are a couple of other points. You went to Israel earlier this year; could you tell me why?"

"Business," said Simon briefly.

"But you have a sales director? Couldn't he have gone?"

"He could, and often does. However, I have friends there and I wanted to discuss some co-editions—that's a joint publication of a book—with an Israeli publisher, and it involves considerable investment. You can check it out."

"We shall," said Wintle evenly. "Then on the way back you stopped in Athens."

"No, I didn't. The plane stopped in Athens for nearly an hour," replied Simon, "but then that flight always does. That has nothing to do with me."

"I see," said Wintle. "And?"

"You tell me," continued Simon. "What about Athens?"

"You stayed on the plane all the time?"

Simon seemed to ponder for a moment. "No, come to think of it, we all had to get off. They clean the airplane or something. Athens, as you might imagine, is not my favorite place. We went into the transit lounge. But I didn't leave the flight or go into the city. I just mooched about until the flight was re-called. Why do you ask?"

"Did you know, that about the time you were there, someone killed the airport security officer?" asked Wintle. "The same officer who was responsible for security when the airliner was attacked and your family killed."

Simon looked at him steadily, unblinking. "With a shotgun?" he asked. "Is that the point you are getting to?"

"No, as it happens, with a pistol. The security officer's own pistol, as a matter of fact. It was weeks before his successor decided to clean it, and he found it had been fired."

"What sloppy care of arms," Simon remarked, carelessly. "But what has all that got to do with me?"

"Probably nothing. I note that as an ex-marine you deplore an uncleaned weapon. How do you feel about his death?" Wintle was watching Simon's face closely.

Simon was silent for a moment, deep in thought, his eyes fixed on Wintle. "I didn't know the man. He was nothing to me. I have other deaths in Athens to think about."

"We think the two killings might be linked," said Wintle.

"Then think away," said Simon dismissively. "Your thoughts don't disturb me."

Wintle turned his notepad over and studied his notes for a moment, before looking up again at Simon, and moving on to the next question.

"Shortly after your return, you went to Paris."

"That's right."

"Business?"

"Not at all. I went with a lady."

"Yes, we know that too, a Miss Winter. An American lady. Can I ask why you went by car? Surely it would be quicker to fly?"

"I wanted to bring back some wine. I always do. I brought back four cases of excellent Burgundy. I paid the duty on it. Time was not important, it was a little holiday."

"Did you also bring back a Winchester twelve-hundred pump shotgun?"

"That's a quantum leap from wine," replied Simon. "Why should I do that? What do I want with a shotgun? The short answer is no, but what's the connection?"

"Because one was sold by a central Paris gunsmith to a foreigner answering to your description during the time of your visit, and used a week after your return to murder five people in St. James's Square."

Simon said nothing to this, and they sat looking at each other for several seconds, each waiting for the other to speak.

"Well?" said Wintle eventually.

"What do you want me to say?" asked Simon. "If you have evidence, produce it. You say someone answering to my description. Has this gunsmith identified me positively? Obviously not, or you'd arrest me. I don't have your shotgun, commander. I have nothing to do with any murders."

"You don't flinch from the word," said Wintle bluntly. "You accept that this man would be a murderer. He has killed six people, perhaps seven."

"Why should I flinch? I might say, from personal experience, that those murdered were the sort of people who'd be none the worse for a hanging but no, I don't flinch from the word. They are dead after all, and beyond words. Now, do you have any more questions? I do have work to do." Simon seemed suddenly a little tired, a little less sharp.

Wintle closed his notebook and slipped his pen into his pocket. "No, I don't think so, not for the moment. We'll check these movements of yours and if they are as you say, I don't suppose you will hear from us again. I'm sorry to have troubled you. Thank you for your cooperation."

Simon got up and came round the desk, offering his hand. Wintle shook it with only the slightest hesitation and they walked together toward the door.

"Listen," said Simon suddenly, "why don't you have dinner with me some time? When all this is over? I nearly asked you to come for a drink up on the Rollright Stones. When you drove off, I thought to myself, I'd like a chat that fellow."

Wintle smiled at last. "That's funny, I thought much the same thing. Yes, thank you. Dinner and a chat would be most pleasant, but not about business, I hope. We do share some other interests, you know. I'm a bit of a walker myself, and I enjoy the hills."

"Fine," said Simon. "At the moment you know more about me than I do about you, so when you are free, you will give me a ring?"

"I will with pleasure," replied Wintle, "and, just one word of advice . . ."

"Yes?" asked Simon, guardedly.

Wintle nodded toward the stark, glossy photo on the wall. "Get rid of that. It does you no good. No good at all."

TWELVE

Three days later Wintle and Catton, both dog tired, worked late trying to close the file on the Quarry inquiry. Afterward they dined together in a small restaurant, saying nothing until they had ordered, received a bottle of wine, and watched the waiter go off out of earshot. Catton filled the glasses, then raised his, and looked inquiringly at Wintle, who picked up his glass wearily and nodded at Catton.

"Well, tell me," he said, as he took a sip of wine and put the glass back on the table, "does that wrap it up?"

"I think so, as far as it goes. It has to be him," said Catton positively. "There can be no doubt about that . . . but enough to prosecute? I'm not sure. You agree it's him though?"

"Oh, I'm quite sure it is. But, as you say, proving it is something else. We have almost a classic case here. There's enough background and circumstantial evidence to be certain who the killer is, but probably not enough to prove it in court. I've sent the papers through to the Home Secretary and the Director of Public Prosecutions. The DPP will decide if we have enough for a case, although I can tell you now that we haven't. This is a very sensitive matter. I know that the

Home Secretary is constantly in touch with the Foreign Secretary and even the Prime Minister on this one."

Catton whistled softly. "That's heavy stuff," he said, topping up their glasses. "Does Quarry really merit all this attention? We've had multiple killers before."

"If he didn't, the CID or the beat bobbies would be handling it. John, you must realize that our friend Quarry is a very different kind of killer. Even if we got him to court, he'd make one hell of a scene before they sent him down. He's rich, articulate and has one hell of a motive. If someone burned your wife and kids alive, and no one in authority did anything about it, what would you do? Think about that. The press will love him and Joe Public will be with him to a man. There's an election coming up, and while a nice Middle East agreement would have won it for the government, a merry brawl with Quarry, pointing out just how little the powers that be really care for British people, will cost them millions of votes. They're still wriggling around the fact that they invited Sayid here in the first place. A trial will be very unwelcome."

"But the man's a cold-blooded killer," said Catton, hotly. "He's killed six people that we know of, maybe more."

"True, but then none of them was exactly a decent citizen," said Wintle. "He didn't kill you, or that girl at the Jihad office. He's a killer all right, but he picks his victims with care. He's not like those he kills, who will kill hundreds of innocent people just to make a political point. Morally, Quarry will have a good case, and he'll play it for all he's worth."

"He killed that copper at the airport in Athens. What was the point of that?"

"Yes," mused Wintle, sipping his wine thoughtfully. "So he did. I wonder why. It's not like him at all."

Catton chuckled. "You sound as if you like him."

"I do," said Wintle. "You haven't met him, have you? Well, not socially. He's a nice man. Not the sort one would willingly get into a scuffle with perhaps, but a nice man for all that. He's even asked me to dinner."

"Will you go?"

"Who knows?"

"Well," said John Catton candidly, "you know the rules. Mixing socially with a known suspect is bound to raise eyebrows, and if it came out in court, his lawyer might make a lot more of it than it's worth. Even a murmur of entrapment could damage our case."

"Maybe you're right," said Wintle, "but we haven't charged him yet, and I'm not at all sure we'll be able to. Besides, we do have a certain discretion at this level."

"At your level, maybe," put in Catton.

Wintle laughed gently. "It will soon be your level. I'm on the way out, and in a month or two you'll be sitting behind my desk. At least you will if I have anything to do with it. So start getting used to the idea."

"I am. I mean I'm trying to," said Catton, smiling now. "And ... look ... I expect we'll all give you a clock or something, but I'd like you to know how grateful I am, personally."

"Come on," said Wintle, dismissively. "It takes two. I've done nothing for you that you couldn't have done on your own. Don't turn modest."

"You've been a good boss," said Catton firmly, "and you've taught me a lot. Especially the things that aren't in the book. I'm grateful, and I want you to know it. That's all."

"Thank you," said Wintle, "and the feeling is mutual."

"So ... ?" said Catton.

"Yes?" asked Wintle.

"So, I think you should stay away from Quarry."

"Why?"

"All sorts of reasons. You know why. Besides, he's dangerous."

"Rubbish!" said Wintle, half laughing. "Quarry isn't dangerous. At least, not to you or me. He's not like most of the scum we deal with, the bombers and the shooters."

"Well, there's another example," said Catton. "Look how friendly you were with that IRA man, Seamus McGary. You were always talking to him, laughing away. People notice, you know. And they talk."

"Let them," said Wintle. "And being friendly with McGary

didn't stop him getting twenty years for possession of firearms and explosives with intent. That was business. On a personal level, McGary, like Quarry, in a way, was an interesting human being. I learned something from him."

"I'd hate to think what," said Catton.

"Well, John, let me tell you one last thing, and try to remember it. You can learn worthwhile things in the most unexpected places, even from killers. Don't ever close your mind to that, or you may miss a great deal that really matters. We can even learn something from Quarry. We'll soon see."

"Meanwhile, what are we going to do about him?" asked Catton bluntly. His eyes were bloodshot and red-rimmed. The grooves around his mouth had deepened in the last weeks. "What happens now?"

"That's up to the DPP. We'll keep tabs on him, of course. I just hope that he leads us to the shotgun. Perhaps we can get some positive ID and tie him into one or other of the killings. He must make a mistake, sooner or later, and then we'll nab him."

"What if he kills again?" asked Catton. "Have you considered that? He could be mad, you know."

"So far he has only attacked those involved with the airplane, who were responsible directly or indirectly for killing his family. It depends how wide he swings his net. Once he goes outside the UK it's not our problem anyway, and I fancy he'll have to do that to reach more of Sayid's group. I can't see any more Arabs coming here with a hit-man on the loose, and I gather Sayid's death has put a real spanner in the works, with any Middle East agreement once more up for grabs. Anyway, that's for the powers that be to decide. There will be a meeting at the DPP's office tomorrow. All interested parties will be there, including myself, and we'll see what happens after that."

The waiter brought their order and a couple came to sit at a nearby table, so they turned their conversation to other matters.

"Come in, Wintle," said the DPP, holding out his hand. "I think you know everyone here. It was suggested that we meet here rather than at the Home Office. The fewer people who know about this affair the better and, as I am constantly complaining, I have very few staff to interrupt us."

Wintle found a chair, noting with some surprise the presence in the room of two government ministers, Harland and Willoughby. There was also Yates from the FCO, and Collins, Wintle's opposite number at the Yard, the head of the CID; all waited until the DPP returned to his desk and sat down.

"Well, gentlemen," he began, tapping the folder on his desk, "You have now all read through the report on the St. James's Square and Stratford shootings. Before we discuss the astounding conclusions to this report, may I say how much we are all indebted to Commander Wintle and his staff for finding our man so quickly. I must add though, as DPP, that there is not enough here to arrest, charge and try the man named. I want at least a fifty-one percent chance of conviction, and this evidence, good as it is, falls a long way short of that."

Yates rose suddenly and took a rapid pace across the room. "I don't believe it at all," he said sharply. "The idea that Simon Quarry, of all people, is a . . . terrorist . . . is just ludicrous. I know him well. So do you, minister. He's known to half the people in Parliament. I don't care how the conclusion was arrived at, it's wrong. It is all simply conjecture. There isn't a shred of positive proof."

All eyes turned on Wintle. "You've read the report," he said heavily. "I agree, the evidence is circumstantial, but overwhelmingly conclusive. Quarry has the motive, means, opportunity and ability to carry out these attacks. We can place him in the area of each attack and at a time when he could have carried them out."

"Rubbish," spat Yates. "It's just conjecture."

"With respect," said Wintle evenly, "it's not rubbish."

"When we were attacked at Stratford, Quarry was miles away, dining in a Chinese restaurant. It says so in the report, in your own report."

"That's what Quarry says," conceded Wintle, "and we are unable to prove otherwise. He has a bill, and describes the restaurant accurately. So I accept that he was there. But when? The waiters do not recall him. You know that to us all Chinese waiters look alike? Well, it works for us with them. All European males look the same. I suspect Quarry knows that they would be unable to confirm if he was there or not, let alone at what time. You might also consider that Warwick is not all that far from Stratford. Incidentally, Mr. Yates, I gather you dined with Quarry about a week before the Stratford attack?"

"Yes. We had lunch," said Yates aggressively. "What of it? I lunch with him quite often. He's my publisher as well as my friend. I'm writing a book for him. The minister here is already one of his authors."

"Did you by any chance mention the visit of Sayid on that occasion?"

"Certainly not," snapped Yates. "I don't discuss departmental matters with anyone."

"Why not?" prodded Wintle mildly. "You were involved in the first shooting, and fixing up Sayid's visit. I'd like to know how Quarry knew when Sayid would be in Stratford. Quarry is a big Shakespeare fan, so if you were going there it would be natural to mention the fact to him. It is also curious that while Quarry was staying in Warwick, he didn't try and see a performance at Stratford. It's out of character."

"I can tell you why," said Yates. "He doesn't see Scofield in the role of Macbeth. He told me he finds his delivery distracting."

"Did he tell you this at lunch?" asked Wintle, taking a quick glance at the other listening faces around the desk.

Yates hesitated. "I suppose he must have done. All right, yes, he did."

"So you were discussing, however distantly, your intention to visit Stratford and see *Macbeth?*"

"Yes," admitted Yates reluctantly, "I suppose we were, but I never mentioned Sayid."

Wintle sighed, and settled back in his chair, looking around at the others. "Well, there we have another small piece of the jigsaw. There are two evening performances of *Macbeth* each week. It wouldn't be hard to guess which one we were taking Sayid to. I'm afraid your friend Quarry pumped you, Mr. Yates. I wonder what he would have done if you had recognized him on the bridge? You may be luckier than you know."

"Gentlemen," said Harland, "I have read this report and hard as it is to believe, I accept the commander's conclusion. I also accept the DPP's conclusion that we can't bring Quarry to court at the moment. Frankly, I'm not too sorry about that because—let me put my government's cards on the table—we need two things at the moment, or rather we need one thing, a successful treaty to solve the Middle East situation. What we don't need, with an election coming up, is a martyr made of Simon Quarry, publisher, widower, and archetypal Englishman, for taking his revenge on a group of terrorists."

"I don't follow you, minister," interrupted the DPP. "Could you explain what the government's problems have to do with this situation? We have a criminal here. He has killed six, perhaps seven, people."

The minister leaned forward in his chair, placing his elbows on his knees and the tips of his fingers together. "Let me explain," he said. "To us, in this room, to the police and to the law, Quarry is a criminal, I agree. He's a killer, a man outside the law. We can't prove it, but we know it. However, get him into open court, where he has every right to state his case, and what is he going to say? He will say that he is a citizen of this country, as were his family. I see you are nodding, commander ... that is his argument, is it not? He will maintain, correctly, that the first rule, the first obligation of a citizen is to obey the laws of his country, but that—and this is the crux of the matter—in return, that country must provide protection and justice within the law. Am I not right? That is why we have, and enforce, laws to prevent people carrying arms and defending themselves. Now in Quarry's case, he will say we failed to provide protection, but even worse, we failed to give him justice. I have studied many other files of letters, newspaper clippings, and so on, about the Athens affair, and Quarry, with the support of several editorial leaders might I add, made that point again and again at the time. There is a contract between the citizen and society and we, the elected guardians of that society, broke it. Quarry wanted those criminals who murdered his family arrested, tried and jailed. That's all he asked for and we didn't do it. He wanted something and we did nothing. So the contract is broken, and the right in this matter rests with Quarry. That will be his argument. Legally it's nonsense, a recipe for anarchy, but think what the press will make of it. He will be a hero."

"The original attack took place in a foreign airplane in a foreign country," pointed out the DPP. "It was outside our jurisdiction. What could we do? It was up to the Greeks."

"They did nothing either," said the minister, with a shrug. "Anyway, let us not quibble. Bring Quarry to court and he'll be a national hero. Worse, he'll spawn imitators, vigilantes. Even if he goes to prison he'll be out in no time."

"He'll get life," said the DPP. "If we can prove he killed all those people, a life sentence is inevitable."

"And how long is that?" asked Wintle. "Nine years for a real villain. No judge would recommend a maximum term, or even a twenty-year stretch. With Quarry's money and a good counsel, public sympathy and so on, he might get six years, and he'll be out in two. Then he'll have more people on his hit list. The man's unstoppable."

A silence settled over the room, with no one willing to speak. In the interval Yates rose to his feet and walked over to the window, his back turned to the room.

"He's got to be stopped," said Willoughby, abruptly. "The man's an anarchist. We can't have people taking the law into their own hands. He has already destroyed a possible chance for peace in the Middle East by killing the one man who could help us cobble an agreement together. Quarry isn't outside the law. No one is."

The DPP smiled at this. "Really? On the evidence we have here, he is quite beyond our reach. So are lots of other people. Strikers, many trade unionists, most terrorists, media people, some minority groups, all get special treatment under the law. The law is selective these days, I'm sorry to say, and not the even-handed instrument we say it is."

"It's not really our problem," grumbled Commander Collins.

"It's those bloody Arabs who started this. If Quarry had killed them off our patch, I'd cheer him on."

"What if he kills again?" asked Wintle. "On our patch. Who's to say that he won't?"

"He mustn't," put in Yates from the window. "You must stop him."

"How are we to stop him?" asked Wintle. "He's rich, well connected, has perfect cover. He's also getting very good at it. He was a good soldier, and he's remembered all he was ever taught about killing."

"Warn him off then," said Yates. "Tell him what we know. I'll see to it that his official contacts dry up for a start. He won't find it so easy to kill people if he's out in the open. He'll have a hard enough job to make a living."

"I'd be very careful with Mr. Quarry if I were you," said Harland. "He has more guns than you have, and I don't just mean that weapon he uses with such ability. Slander him and he'll slaughter you. A career diplomat can't afford to be called a liar in open court. But I agree with the commander, I want him off our patch and out of our hair. One way or another, this affair has to end."

"I have warned him, sir," said Wintle. "He knows perfectly well we are on to him and he hasn't turned a hair. You won't frighten him, and if what I hear today is true, we have no powers to stop him."

"Let the bloody Arabs know about him," said Collins. "They started all this, let them finish it. Tell them what we know about Quarry, and leave it to them. That Gadaffi fellow has gunmen on tap, better men than Quarry."

Harland broke the silence that followed, while the others were still digesting that remark.

"Now that seems to be a most sensible suggestion," he said smoothly.

"Rubbish," snapped his colleague. "They will kill him in a week—shoot him down in the street."

"Then it's definitely worth thinking about," said Yates bitterly. "It would serve him bloody right."

"I thought you didn't want trouble on our patch," said Wintle, "and I won't have more Arab terrorists coming to London to murder anyone, let alone British citizens. It's what I'm supposed to prevent. Tell the Arabs about Quarry and we'll have gunfights in Central London. That apart, I think it's a despicable suggestion."

"Why in London?" asked the minister blandly. "Quarry travels a great deal, and once he's abroad he's out of our hands. Surely these matters can be left to the Libyans or what is left of the Jihad. They have more experience of these matters, and we don't have to get directly involved. A word to the press should be sufficient to put the finger on Quarry."

"I can't believe I'm hearing this," said Wintle, amazed. "You are seriously suggesting that we set Quarry up for assassination?"

"I'm quite certain that I should not be hearing this," said the DPP sharply. "You are free to use my office, gentlemen, but I'm afraid this conversation is not to my liking." He got up, pushing back his chair and gathering some papers from the desk, and left the room without looking back. After a few seconds Willoughby rose, nodded stiffly to the others and left the room, followed by the CID commander.

Wintle looked from the minister to Yates, still waiting by the window, nodding slowly to himself.

"You two discussed this before I got here," he said. "You prepared the ground," he said to Yates, "and you, sir, authorized it and presented the proposal. That was a good act you put on, Yates. You'd already worked out how Quarry found out about Sayid."

"That's not the point. The point we are at now was initiated by your own report," said Yates. "Be sensible, we either put a stop to Quarry legally, or we let the Arabs do it, any way they choose. If you and the law can't stop him, something else must."

"I don't think you can realize just what a mess Quarry is causing," said the minister gently. "Today, we have to negotiate on a basis of trust. This country doesn't have power or much influence, so we have to cajole and persuade and get people to trust us and see our point of view. All was going well until this madman with a shotgun quite literally blasted a hole in the Middle East peace talks. Thousands more will die because of what Quarry has done."

"And you need a successful treaty to win the next election?" snorted Wintle. "Or had you forgotten that? You don't want Quarry caught and tried. You want him dead, and want him shopped to the Arabs as evidence of our goodwill—right?"

"It would help," admitted the minister, candidly, "but we want a treaty for its own sake, for peace in the Middle East, to stabilize the world economy, for a host of reasons. We can't let one criminal stand in the way forever."

"Anyway," said Yates, "you see the dilemma. Quarry did as we are doing. He followed the law until it failed him and then he took more direct methods. We are doing the same. Without more evidence or a confession, there is nothing more you can do, Wintle. Besides, once the Arabs discover Quarry's identity, by a press leak, or if it becomes public knowledge in some way, they may kill him anyway. If we offer them our information he is no worse off, and we gain credibility with them at a very sensitive time. His death will be quite useful."

"I won't do it," said Wintle flatly. "To hell with you. My files remain closed, and only a madman would leak this information without proof. Who would publish it and expect anyone to believe it? Your scheme won't work."

Yates looked at the minister, who was studying the toecaps of his shoes. "Wintle, you are due to retire in a few months I believe, at the end of the year. If you would like to retire a little early, I'm sure we would understand. If not, and you find this task distasteful, we do have other resources. You and your department need not be concerned at all. But this last service would be appreciated."

There was a long pause, running into minutes, while Yates and the minister waited for a reply. Finally, Wintle rubbed his hand across his face and looked at them dourly. "All right," he grunted. "What do you want me to do? But only because, as I told you, I want no more half-crazed Arabs killing on my patch. I'll keep it clean. So what now?"

"I have already had some discussions with my Arab contacts," said Yates. "Just calming them down a little, assuring them that the assassin would be found, and so on. I shall tell them that we have identified the man and refer them to you, without explaining why, of course. Simply as an act of cooperation."

"And what then?"

"You suggest we cooperate, aid them in the hunt a little, and nudge matters ahead. You have Quarry under surveillance, I suppose?"

"Not all the time," admitted Wintle, "but he can't go far without us knowing."

"Good," said Yates. "He will certainly be going to the Frankfurt Book Fair in a couple of weeks. Suggest that the Arabs might find that information useful. They will have good contacts with extremist groups in Germany, I'm sure, and something can be . . . well, arranged there."

"Since you know so much, why don't you handle this?" asked Wintle sourly. "You have all the facts. You might enjoy it. He gave you quite a fright the other night, didn't he?"

"I have other roles to play at the moment," replied Yates smoothly, "and setting up Quarry is not one I relish. Just so long as he is removed from the game, that will be sufficient."

"I see," said Wintle. "The police get the dirty end of it, as usual. Well, it's all been very interesting. I will await their call, Yates. Good day to you, and to you, minister."

Catton entered the office and sat down opposite Wintle without invitation. "How did it go?" he asked.

Wintle waved his hand about vaguely. "So-so," he replied. "Not quite what I expected, I'm afraid."

"You were there a long time," said Catton curiously. "What did they say?"

"I was only there for about an hour. I've been walking in the park all afternoon, thinking. The DPP agrees with us. We don't have enough, and unless Quarry makes a bad mistake, we can't touch him. If we do, he'd scream the government down, and the very thought of that scares them to death."

"So, what now?"

Wintle ignored that question and asked another. "Have you ever noticed how we are getting as bad as the rest?" he said. "All of us. Some ministers lie in Parliament, others get caught with their trousers down. There's a war in Ireland. Coppers carry guns. When I joined the force—it wasn't called the police *service* then—you might see a gun once in your entire career. Do you know that last year six hundred coppers in the Met alone were eased out for aiding and abetting criminals, or actually committing crimes? We can't prove it, mind, so we let them resign, but six hundred coppers! My God, what's the world coming to?"

"Nobody likes a bent copper," said Catton sturdily, "let alone another copper. What on earth happened over there? What's the matter, Philip?" It was the first time he had ever called Wintle by his Christian name.

"No, we don't like them, but we tolerate them and we can't clean up the mess because, as I've just realized, it goes right to the top. I found that out today. That's what's the matter."

"What's got into you? Come on, tell me, what went on over there this morning?"

Wintle sighed and shrugged. "Pragmatism. That's the in thing. Not decency, not justice, not honor. None of that stuff we ought to belive in. It's not what you ought to do, but what's expedient, what you can get away with."

"What has all this got to do with Quarry?" asked Catton.

"Everything," replied Wintle, shaking his head. "They want to stop him uncorking his shotgun again and spoiling their little schemes. Since we can't stop him legally, they want to throw him to the wolves."

"The wolves? What wolves?"

"They want me to hand the file to the Libyans."

"Jesus Christ!" exploded Catton, looking round worriedly toward the door. "Hand one of our confidential files to the Libyans! They'll kill him."

"Exactly," replied Wintle, nodding. "We've become an assassination bureau. Marvelous, isn't it? We've come to this."

"Did you agree?" asked Catton curiously, his eyes fixed on Wintle's face. "No, I'm sorry, I didn't mean that. Of course you didn't."

"That's what I was thinking about in the park," said Wintle. "They pointed out that I was due to retire in a couple of months, that they had other sources, hint, hint. So I agreed. Only to give me time to think. If I don't play ball, they do it themselves. But this way, they will have clean hands if anything goes wrong. I've got to find a way of keeping Quarry alive. That's the problem now."

"Can I help?" asked Catton. "I'll do anything I can, you know that. Believe me."

"No," said Wintle. "In a couple of months you'll be sitting here and this particular business will be over. Keep out of it, and keep your hands clean. Just learn about the sort of people you'll be working for. I don't want you shunted out, this office needs a decent man in charge of it. And I think you are a thoroughly decent man, John. What a pity you don't have decent masters."

The silence that fell between them was heavy, but friendly. "I appreciate that, but I'd still like to help," said Catton. "Really."

"You can't," said Wintle, bleakly. "And that's final. It's in my lap. You could do one small thing though."

"Name it," said Catton, rising to his feet, slipping his chair back, close to the desk. "Anything."

"Get me a pot of coffee sent in, and see that I'm not disturbed for a while. I've got more thinking to do."

When Catton had gone, Wintle sat on at his desk in the darkening room, brooding. He drank the coffee and heard the noises outside gradually subside as one by one his staff went home. He watched the clock on the wall crawl past the half hour before he consulted a folder, picked up his telephone and dialed a number.

"Mr. Quarry please," he said and waited. "Ah, Simon, it's Philip Wintle here; from the Yard. I hoped you might still be there. Are you free this evening? I think it's about time we had that dinner."

THIRTEEN

Wintle took care to arrive at the restaurant early. He was sitting at the back, watching the door as Simon entered, looking sharply around the dimly lit room. Wintle raised his hand and watched him make his way across the floor, pulling off his raincoat, skirting the empty tables, stopping for a few words with one of the waiters as he handed over his coat. Wintle smiled as he came up and indicated the chair opposite.

"It's a filthy night to be out," Simon remarked cheerfully, pulling out the chair and sitting down, "but at least you have saved me from a dull evening, grinding my way through yet another urgent and utterly ghastly manuscript. I don't imagine this will be a dull evening."

Wintle ignored the ironic glint in Simon's eye, raised the wine bottle and gave Simon a questioning look. Simon passed over his glass and they watched in silence as Wintle filled it almost to the brim.

"Steady," said Simon, sliding the glass back across the cloth, and leaning forward to sip a little from the rim. "Mmmm, that's very good. What is it?"

"It's called Est-Est-Est," replied Wintle. "I know very little about wine, but it's the one I usually drink here. I've never actually seen it anywhere else. Incidentally, I didn't know you spoke Italian. That was Italian you were talking to the waiter?"

"Spanish," said Simon briefly. "Most Italian waiters are Spanish. In fact, and to be quite accurate, most waiters are Galician. Waiters are the principal export of Galicia."

"I see," said Wintle, nodding his head slowly. "I should have known that, but then, I learn something new about you every day. Tonight, nothing is as it seems."

"Really?" said Simon.

Silence fell as the waiter came with the menu. "Wait," said Wintle, keeping him at the table, and they studied the list for a brief moment.

"Personally," said Wintle, "I'd like minestrone, grilled fegato with a mixed salad . . . and then I'll see."

"That's a quick choice," said Simon, his eyes still brooding over the menu. "I'll have the same but with some zucchine." He handed the menu back to the waiter and picked up his glass again. "Are you usually so quick and decisive?"

"It's not really so quick," said Wintle. "It's what I always have here. I like liver but I can't abide cooking it at my flat, so I eat it whenever I come here, and I come here quite a lot. It's handy for the office and close to my flat."

"You live alone?"

Wintle took a drink and nodded, replacing the wine glass on the table. "For the last few years, since my wife died. I have a daughter but she's married to a naval man. They live down in Dorset, and when I retire at the end of the year I shall move down there—not in with them, of course, but somewhere nearby, and see a little of my grandchildren."

"That sounds nice," said Simon tonelessly, glancing about the room, "but I imagine this is not just a casual meeting?" He looked directly at Wintle. "Having dinner with a . . . suspect, shall I say, can't be a common event?"

"It's not actually forbidden, but it is strongly discouraged," replied Wintle. "At our last meeting, I recall you told me you were a quick reader."

"In my profession, you have to be," said Simon.

"I assume you mean your publishing profession," said Wintle with a thin smile, reaching into the briefcase by his chair. "Then read this and be quick. Put it away if the waiter comes back." He produced a file and passed it across the table, then picked up his glass again and sat back to observe his guest. Simon read the title, gave Wintle a wry look, then opened the folder and began to read.

He went through the close-typed pages with surprising speed, his face expressionless, turning back once or twice to read a section again, but he had handed the folder back to Wintle before the waiter returned with their soup, and said nothing until he had gone away again and left them alone. Then he looked across the table at Wintle, his gaze direct.

"Thank you for letting me see that. I can't imagine why you did so, but there is nothing in that file to frighten me, not one bit. I'm not afraid, you know," he added, his voice rising a little. "Not of you, of your department, the government, the whole damned lot of you."

"Then try being afraid of this," said Wintle evenly. "They are planning to kill you. Or rather, to have you killed."

Simon blinked, surprised, and spread his hands. "Who are? Who is this *they*, exactly?"

"*They?* Surely you, of all people, know who *they* are. They're the *they* people are always talking about, the *they* who are going to do something about you. Not directly, of course. In a day or so I shall be instructed to meet a gentleman from the organization whose ranks you are thinning with such rapidity, and hand him that file. The rest is up to them, but I have no doubt they will try to kill you. They have little choice. You have overplayed your hand, Quarry. That's why I'm here."

Simon shook his head, smiled, picked up his soup spoon and waved it casually at Wintle. "I don't believe all this," he said. "For a start, you are assuming that I am the killer. If I may say so, that's a very pretty story you have there. It hangs together very well, and if we went in for fiction at the Quarry Press, I'd offer to publish it, but the snag is that it doesn't stand up. Not enough facts. It's all conjecture. You can't prove anything, and I'm admitting nothing."

Wintle nodded in agreement. "Precisely the words of my masters. We have enough to know you did it. I know you did it Quarry. It was a real stroke of luck meeting you at the Rollright Stones, but after that it all snapped together so quickly, you wouldn't believe it. You may be a good gunfighter, Quarry, but your luck has run out. We haven't enough to arrest, try and convict you, that I admit, but I *know*. So please, don't let us waste time beating about the bush."

"So . . . " said Simon, "while admitting nothing, what happens now?"

"The situation is complicated," said Wintle candidly. "We need something definite to tie you into the killings. The shotgun with your prints on it would probably do. An eyewitness, or better still two, would help. A confession from you would be ideal. That's why I'm here. I want you to confess to both the St. James's Square and Stratford shootings. I'd like it in writing, and I want the weapon."

Simon's laughter was genuine, surprised, and loud enough to turn heads at nearby tables. "My dear fellow," he said, "you can't be serious. Even allowing that all your theories are correct—which, of course, I deny—do you seriously expect me, or the killer, whoever he is, to hand himself to you on a plate?"

"Why not?" said Wintle evenly, filling up their glasses. "Look, what choice do you have? You'll be watched now and you won't find it so easy to go about this business. Besides, you have had your revenge, so why not stop now? If you come in we can protect you. With a good lawyer presenting your case, and given that you have surrendered voluntarily, I doubt if you'll get a full sentence, and at worse you'll get life. That means you'll go down for seven years and be out in, say, four. Maybe parole before that. Four years in an open prison is better than being shot down by terrorists like—well—like your family was. That's the alternative option. In four years all this will be water under the bridge, but you've got to be stopped now. Also, unless you come in, I can't protect you."

Simon drew in his breath again, shaking his head. "I say again, are you serious? I have no intention of being treated like a criminal. I simply don't feel like a criminal."

"But you *are* a criminal," said Wintle. "You have shot people down in cold blood, not once, but several times. What else can you be but a criminal? You have broken the law."

"I have killed people who either let my family die, boasted of killing them, or ordered them dead. You and your masters as you call them, the guardians of the people, did sweet damn-all. Your precious law didn't help my family, or even attempt to punish their murderers."

"I have my confession," said Wintle contentedly, picking up his glass.

"And much good will it do you," said Simon, shrugging. "All right, dammit, I'm your man. I'll deny it, of course, any time I have to, and you can't prove any of this without hard evidence."

Wintle sighed heavily. "If you don't come in, they'll have you killed," he urged. "Can't you see that? Anarchy cuts both ways. They—that *they* again—say that you are now outside the law, and therefore anyone's game. You are making the whole system look sick and they can't allow that. As they think more about it, they don't even want you arrested. The press and TV will be on your side at the trial, and so will the public. There's an election coming up. No doubt your brief will make a great play of how this government fails to protect its citizens. That dreadful photograph over that headline will lose this government a million votes. You've already screwed up their entire foreign policy and they were relying on a Middle East treaty to swing the electors their way. You have also made powerful and vindictive enemies."

"Well then," said Simon flatly, "meet your friendly foreign killers and hand over the file. They might find nailing me more difficult than killing defenseless women and children."

"I can't," said Wintle, firmly. "I can't do that."

"Why not?" asked Simon. "You'll have to. You're in their pay. I might almost say that doing the nation's dirty work is what we pay the police for."

"Good God!" exclaimed Wintle, amazed. "You are an arrogant bastard. Do you think you're the only one with principles? I've been a policeman most of my life, for thirty years, and I'm a good policeman. I tracked you down, which wasn't too difficult. Now I'm advised, oh-so-gently I admit, to set you up. I really believed in the law, in justice, just like you did, until this. If I pull you in with what I've got now, you'll deny it. You'll go free, but once all this is known, the Arabs may kill you anyway. It's a total mess. How does that strike you for a moral dilemma?"

Simon chuckled and leaned across the table to take up the bottle and refill their glasses. "My dear Wintle, you do have a problem. A two-bottle problem. Let's have another one. What do you propose to do?"

"I don't know," replied Wintle slowly, attracting the attention of the waiter and pointing to the empty bottle on the table. "That's the point. It isn't only me. You may think your friend Yates is just a Foreign Office stooge, but you're quite wrong there. He's a leg man for the Cabinet between all sorts of agencies. Security and intelligence work are his special provinces and he has many other means to stop you, apart from me. We do have a secret service, though you might never think it, and if pushed they can play dirty tricks with the best of them. Besides, you scared the hell out of Yates up at Stratford and he's a mean bastard at heart. He'll enjoy seeing you get chopped."

"I say again," said Simon, ignoring all this, "what are you going to do? You are already out of order in telling me this much and showing me that file. Your masters would not be pleased."

"*You* tell *me*," said Wintle shortly. "I want you to stop. I don't want you dead. I thought you might have some ideas. I don't know what to do."

Simon pulled at his lower lip reflectively. "Let's be logical," he suggested. "I can tell you, from personal experience, that there comes a time when you can't sit on the fence. To bring me to that point, they had to kill my whole family. Now you have to turn your back while someone kills me, and you can't do that, it goes against the grain—right? But you can't protect me and you can't stop them. Agreed? Yes?"

"Yes. So?"

"Then, just like me, you have a choice. You can turn your back and forget it, letting what will happen, happen, or you can help me."

"How?"

"I don't know yet. All this is still a surprise. But do I clarify the problem?"

Wintle said nothing for several minutes, his eyes fixed on the table, the tired lines deepening on his face. Finally, he looked across at Simon, their eyes meeting, and nodded. "It's been coming to this for years," he said slowly, "and you are probably right. So, what do we do now?"

"First, welcome to the club. I think we have just joined forces. How would you like to sort out a group of terrorists? That's your real job, the one you enjoy—and that's all I've done. Look on me as a freelance. Once that is done, I could stop, if they'll let me. Will you help me?"

Wintle felt a sudden surge of relief, enthusiasm, almost of pleasure."

"I'd love to," he said, smiling grimly. "At least I'll know who the enemies are. Putting that bastard yates' nose out of joint will be a pleasure as well. Any ideas where we might start?"

"The idea has only just come to me," said Simon, slowly, "but the two people I still want are the ones who actually attacked the aircraft. They need killing but I can't get at them where they are."

"Where are they?" asked Wintle softly, as the waiter came up with another bottle of wine. They let him fill their glasses and returned to the subject as he went away.

"They're in Libya, of course, that great holiday camp for the misbegotten. Probably at a place called Tarhuna, a town in the desert about eighty miles south of Triploi."

"How on earth do you know that?" asked Wintle curiously. "You must have some excellent contacts. Not that that's too surprising, I suppose. Your powerful connections are one reason the powers that be are afraid of you."

"I looked into it while I was in Israel. That's where I learned about

their office in St. James's Square. The Israelis keep close tabs on
groups like the Jihad, and so should you. That's where they are, believe me. Now the ones I want, the gunmen, are just a little group
. . . Sayid's muscle, a few men at most. If we play our cards right, we
can lure them out to where I can get at them. I've been thinking
about it for some time, but until now I couldn't think of the right
bait."

"And you have now?"

"And I have now."

"And what is it?"

"Me," said Simon.

Forty-eight hours later, in the kitchen of Simon's flat, the two men
were talking again, their heads close together across the table.

"So he bought it?" asked Simon. "Hook, line and sinker?"

"Only just," said Wintle, frowning, "and I nearly lost him at one
point, for Yates is no fool. Curiously enough it was the demand for a
knighthood that threw him. A brilliant touch that, Simon—congrat-
ulations! He offered me a CBE but I pointed out that I already was
one."

"Are you?" said Simon in surprise.

"It goes with the job, eventually. Anyway, he now has me tabbed
as one of his own kind, someone on the make. I pointed out that
otherwise there was nothing for me in all this, and the thought that
your certain demise might be in my personal interest finally clinched
it. I fancy he'll have more than a little difficulty actually persuading
them to give me a knighthood, but then that will keep him busy
until I am firmly in charge of your—well—assassination. I told him I
won't budge until I have it in writing, and now he's stuck with me."

Simon laughed and leaned across the table to clap Wintle on the
shoulder. "Relax, Philip," he said. "I find a certain humor in all this.
Here we are, discussing my murder, and be honest, the thought that
you'll end up kneeling before the Queen for fixing it does add a certain spice to the whole affair. Look on the funny side, for God's sake.
Life's too short for worries."

Wintle smiled back, slowly. "It may be a curious thing to say, but I am actually enjoying this. However, let's get on. Have you any ideas on how I should play things when I meet Yates' contacts?"

"Not a lot," said Simon frankly. "As you know, I've tended to create confusion first, using surprise to get me started, then exploited the situation as matters developed. If they are the ones coming after me, then they will have the initiative, and that's the snag. They get first strike but I must retain the initiative in order to survive. That's your task, Philip. It's not supposed to be a suicide mission."

Wintle frowned and scratched his chin, pondering. "That's not going to be easy. We'll have to play the they-know-we-know-they-know game, and hope for no wild cards. The problem is that I don't know as yet just how cooperative Yates' contacts will be. Once I tell them who you are they may take the matter into their own hands, and come straight at you. Incidentally, we should be careful how we meet or what you do from now on. Yates might put some of his own people on to you. As I'm in charge of the affair, our meeting and my detailed knowledge of your doings will come as no surprise, but be careful on the phone. And be discreet, always."

Simon nodded in agreement, leaning forward to pour more Scotch into their glasses. "You must control the game," he said, "and I think you can. For a start, the Arabs must be aware how much they can lose by more bloodshed in London. Some big deal is cooking and they won't want to blow it. Point out that you can and will protect me here, and keep their people out, or at least closely watched. Check my mail, will you? I don't want any bombs arriving at the office. See that they know that. Make *your* cooperation dependent upon *their* cooperation, and by the time they are able to strike at me, you'll be hand in glove. The first point you must insist on is that the job is done by the old Athens team. You might explain that by saying that if there is a slip-up, or when I'm dead, the leaked story will be that I have been pursuing a personal vendetta—which is true—and overreached myself. The second point is that you need to know where they intend to hit me, in order to guide me there. That's only half true, but it's plausible. Remember that in many countries the police either cooperate with terrorists and death squads, or actually provide terrorists or death squads. They won't find your involvement as strange as you do. For our part, it would be much better if you actually set up the hit yourself. You will, of course, find me very cooperative."

"Of course. May I say how I admire your grasp of the phraseology," said Wintle, ironically. "I intended, with or without your permission, to go further. I don't think they will tell me their actual plans. They will never trust me that much, so I think we will have to go the whole hog and set you up. Then all they have to do is provide the gunmen. In other words, Simon, you work out a feasible plan for your own murder, and I'll try and see that they use it. If the plan covers all points, why shouldn't they use it? I'll feed it to them a bit at a time, and let it seem to be their idea."

"Why not?" agreed Simon. "I'll enjoy that. If it works, I'll at least have the satisfaction of knowing they'd never have managed it without me."

"Yates tells me that you are going to the Frankfurt Book Fair at the end of the month," said Wintle. "That's outside my bailiwick, but might that do? I'm not for it, myself. These Arab groups have good contacts with German terrorist organizations such as the Baader-Meinhof and the Red Army Faction; the temptation to employ local contacts might prove too tempting, and I would have no control over anything in that area. I'd rather not reveal anything to the German police, and they are very shrewd."

"I'm not for it, either," said Simon. "I have no wish to tangle with the German police. I want to knock these people over but I also want to stay free. Anyway, I don't always go to Frankfurt—it's really an editorial swap-shop, so if I don't go it will cause no great surprise. I'd rather have our affair on ground of my own choosing, where the odds are less one-sided. At the same time, our opponents must feel they can get away with it and be off home free, before the police can interfere. And I think I have the answer."

"And where might that be?" asked Wintle. "Anywhere but in the UK, I beg you."

"I'll need your help to arrange it, but we have a good cover," said Simon. "As you know, I'm fond of hill-walking, and I think we can finish this matter somewhere in the mountains of Spain. Somewhere remote, wild and open, not the sort of place where these gentry usually operate. I'll go up there and pull them after me, onto my ground. If you'll just wait here a minute, I'll get a map and show you."

FOURTEEN

 From his seat by the window at the London Library, Simon could keep the Jihad office door in plain sight. He saw Wintle arrive, walking slowly round the corner from Jermyn Street, and throw a swift glance up toward the library window before walking on to the door. Once there, he pressed the bell and looked again toward the window, sending Simon back deep into his chair. He knew that he could not be seen from the road below, that Wintle could not even be sure he was up there, though they had both chosen the time and place of the appointment.

As the door opened, Simon sat upright again. He caught a brief glimpse of a head, saw Wintle pass through and out of sight. Simon sat back, a weight settling steadily into the pit of his stomach. This was it. In a few moments the opposition would know his identity. How long he lived after that depended entirely on whether Wintle could persuade them to accept their plan, and keep to it. There was nothing to do now but wait.

Simon sat on in his chair, the newspaper resting in his lap, looking out into the square, thinking long and hard about Wintle. They seemed to be friends. He knew that Wintle liked and trusted him, that they were now in this together. He felt the warmth of Philip's friendship all the more because he seemed to have been without friends for a long time. The evenings they spent talking, sharing a drink at Simon's apartment or a meal in some quiet restaurant helped Simon to relax, at the same time reminding him how much pressure he was under. He began to understand why people talked to the police and the press, how much relief there could be in confession.

In spite of their growing friendship, Wintle continued to pressure Simon to give it all up. This only cleared Simon's mind and hardened his resolve to continue. He said as much to Philip, often.

"I know you mean well, Philip, but really, you're wasting your time," he had told Wintle one evening. "I know from my own experience how hard it is to cross the line, to take on new values. You are still looking for a legal way out, and there isn't one. Even if I wanted to, which I don't, it's much too late to stop now. Look, you are due to retire soon, and when all this is over, you must see a few plays. I can recommend some that will make my point, far better than I can."

"More of your precious Shakespeare, I suppose," grunted Wintle, heaving himself out of his chair and plodding over to the drinks cabinet. "I always forget that you're the educated type. You usually seem far too practical. I'm afraid I shall never feel the same about the Bard of Stratford-upon-Avon after your last exploit up there."

Simon shook his head, smiling. "No, it's not Shakespeare, not this time. I was thinking of Ibsen. When all this is over, go and see Ibsen's *An Enemy of the People*. It's bound to be on somewhere in London. It's not an easy play, but it will make my point, and you'll probably enjoy it."

"What's it about?" asked Wintle, raising the bottle invitingly. "I don't care much for those gloomy Swedish dramas, not that I've ever seen any."

Simon waved away the offered refill, and thought for a moment. "Hmmm, well, like most good plays, there are several sides to it, but you could say it's about a man against the establishment. He's a chemist I think, but anyway he fights, on behalf of ordinary decent people who, needless to say, would prefer not to be troubled.

"Do you see yourself like that?" asked Wintle curiously. "If so, it sounds a bit pretentious to me; saying they are acting for the general good is the excuse politicians trot out every time they want to grind their own axe."

Simon shook his head again. "No, let me finish. In this play, the aforesaid ordinary decent people turn against him as well. They much prefer to believe what they're told by the officials, by the time servers, rather than accept unpleasant facts. They smash his windows, call him a liar and drive him out of business, but he's driven too, so he won't stop. The line which comes to my mind quite often is right at the end of the play, when the man's daughter tells him he is beaten, that the forces against him are too strong, that it's a waste of time anyway. Even that he is wrong. Just like you do to me, actually," Simon finished ironically, looking up at Philip as he walked back across the room.

"And what is his reply?" asked Wintle, slumping back into his chair.

"He disagrees with her, of course. He says he can't really be beaten. He says, 'The most powerful man in the world is the man with nothing to lose.' "

A little pool of silence had fallen across the room. Wintle looked thoughtful and said, "The analogy isn't quite correct. You have a lot to lose. Your business, a very pretty woman who could, I gather, make you happy again. Probably even your life. Losing all that won't change anything you know, not a bit. A few more dead Arabs or one dead Englishman won't change the world one jot. The people in power will win. They always do, and survival is their first requirement. You will hardly ruffle their hair and you can hurt a lot of your real friends trying to do even that much."

"I don't want to hurt Clio, or good people like Ruth, but none of that matters now," said Simon, "and I don't want to change the world. It's just something I have to do. They, that famous *they* of yours, just can't get away with it all the time. Time hasn't changed my mind on that."

Wintle tugged his earlobe thoughtfully, and looked skeptical. "That's easy to say," he said, "but I can't think it's easy to do. However it turns out, you lose everything."

Simon shrugged. "You *do* understand what I'm getting at, otherwise you'd stop me, even now. You've just forgotten the things that really matter. It's a question of justice, not the law. There shouldn't be a difference, but there is. Look, all I really cared about, all that really mattered to me was burned away at Athens. Then afterward, all the rest was spoiled. That sounds dramatic, overemotional, but think about it. The family I loved was burned alive, the country I respected let me down. That's not something one can simply overlook, and fortunately I don't have to. I can hit back, unlike most people, who can't, but when did we start to accept things like that? How did we ever sink so low? Accepting cold-blooded murder can't be right. And what isn't right, shouldn't *be*. I can't accept that it simply has to be forgotten, and believe me, I've tried. And then, finally, there's another thing . . ."

There was a silence between them. Simon's voice petered out, his eyes staring out unblinking into the room. Wintle looked down into his glass, keeping his eyes away from the pain in Simon's face. Eventually he spoke, "What's the other thing?" he asked quietly. "Now you've started this, you had better tell me the lot."

Simon's voice was thick and slow. "Well, it's like this, or I think it is. Sometimes, I think that if I die doing this thing, then I'll see my children again. I know that's nonsense, but even so, I believe it. Either way, it'll be worth it. Doing this is a way of saying how much I loved them. I told someone else this, months ago, and it still sums it up. It's the little things that you remember, that still hurt so much. When I took them to the airport, Eleana's luggage was overweight. I told her it would be, but she wouldn't listen. Then we had a row about it, at the check-in desk. I refused to pay for the overweight, and we had a row, with the kids listening, staring up at the pair of us. They were quite upset. I can't forget that the last time they saw Eleana and me together, we quarreled. When they were alive, I was always working. I worked all the hours God sent, just to build up the business, so I never had enough time to play with them or tell them I loved them, or simply just listen to them. I don't think I realized how much I loved them until they were gone, and then it was too late. Some advice, Philip—never wait to tell someone that you love them. The chance may pass and never come back."

Listening to Simon's quiet voice, Wintle felt his own throat tightening. "Is it still that bad? It's been nearly two years now, and a lot has happened since then."

"It's been one year, eight months, eleven days, to be exact," said Simon, "but it will soon all be over, one way or another. It depends on you, really." He looked directly across the table at Wintle. "Don't let me down."

"I won't," said Philip Wintle. "I won't let you down."

Simon thought about this, waiting in his chair in the library, wondering what was going on across the way at the Jihad office.

"Come in, commander," said the Libyan, half rising from behind his desk. "Please sit down. Will you take coffee?" His English was pure, almost accentless, his voice friendly, an open hand indicating the chair beside the desk.

"Thank you, but no coffee," said Wintle, accepting the chair as the door closed softly behind him. He looked around the room carefully, noting that very little had changed since his last, memorable visit. A new desk had replaced the one behind which the previous attaché had been found, but that desk was still in the room. It stood against the far wall, the white splinters on the torn top still standing up jaggedly. Behind his host, a wide brown splatter of dried blood marked the shot-pitted wall. Even in the dim light of the desk lamp Wintle could see that, apart from a little clearing up, nothing much had altered.

"We are not concerned with appearances here," said the man, reading his thoughts. "We only do work here. Our money goes to other, more important things. More important than thick carpets, potted plants and other Western status symbols." There was an edge in his voice.

Wintle shrugged his shoulders. "It's all one to me how you spend your money. Unless it's for guns or gunmen to kill people in the streets of London. Then I become very concerned indeed."

The man leaned forward, his hands together on the desk top, the fingertips touching, pointing toward Wintle. "Ay, yes, that," he said. "Let me be frank with you on that point, commander. Our leader made it very clear years ago, to certain of our countrymen, that they should return to Libya or face the consequences. Coming from our President, that was not a request, nor a suggestion, but an order. Those who disobey our President's orders are traitors. And we all know what happens to traitors, they . . ."

Wintle held up his hand to stem the flow before it swamped him. "I'm not here to debate your internal policies," he interrupted harshly. "I just wish to point out, not for the first time, that it doesn't sit well with us when you, or rather your late predecessor, go out onto the doorstep and tell the British press and television that you have destroyed an airplane with all the passengers aboard or that you intend to murder—yes, murder—any Libyan in Britain who doesn't wish to obey Colonel Gadaffi. Nor do we permit the firing of automatic weapons on peaceful demonstrations, the murder of policewomen, or a good many other things you seem to find normal. That's why we threw you lot out last time. So, we'll have a little less lip this time. You have no status here as far as I'm aware, so watch your language. If you didn't know that before, you know it now. Right?" Wintle's voice was harsh, his anger visible.

The man sat back in his chair, eyes on Wintle's determined face, his mouth twisted bitterly. "As you say, commander, you are not here to debate my country's policies. You are here to tell me the name of an English murderer who, in this very room, shot to death the head of the Jihad press office and several members of his staff." He held out his hand across the desk. "The Incident file, please, commander."

Wintle found himself surprised at the man's grasp of police phraseology. "You are well informed," he said, eyebrows raised. "Who told you about the Incident file?"

"Your superior, Mr. Yates, has been very helpful to us," said the man smoothly. "But then, he wants something. We only want the

Incident file, so . . . please?" He held out his hand again impatiently.

"He wants something, does he? Then so do I," said Wintle, "and if I let you see the file . . ."

"If?" queried the Libyan. "There can be no if, commander. You have your instructions, or you would not be here. So, please?"

"I said if," said Wintle firmly, his hands grasping the briefcase on his lap, "and I mean if. Don't try to bully me, Mr. Whatever-your-name-is. There are conditions. Yates told you that too. These conditions form part of the deal, and there will be repercussions, at the highest level, if these conditions are not met to the letter. So, let us just take the matter gently, in order. There is no rush."

"Mr. Yates made no mention of conditions," said the man, flaring. "I recognize no conditions."

"I think he did," replied Wintle positively. "Yates—and he is not my superior, incidentally—Yates is far too much of a politician to part with any information without insisting on something in return. I, too, have my price and I assure you, again, that you will not see this file until you agree to my terms. They are to your advantage anyway so why not listen to what I have to say?"

"Very well," said the Libyan again, holding out his hand. "The file though, first, please. Now!"

Wintle chuckled and shook his head, keeping the briefcase firmly in his lap. "Come now," he said, "that's too easy. Once you know the killer, I lose my lever, and this interview is over. Who are you anyway? What is your status here? I don't want to waste time talking to someone without authority."

"Then what do you want?" snapped the man irritably. "I am a special envoy from my government, a political attaché, though we have no representation here. I am not interested in these childish games. I want . . . I want . . . What is it that you want? Get to the point."

"I want guarantees of cooperation. So pick up a pen," said Wintle, "and find some official notepaper. Then write as I dictate."

"I have no official notepaper. This is an information center for a resistance movement."

"Very well, write on their notepaper. I want a letter, in English, stating that this office, or center, contains arms. We saw them after the shooting so don't quibble on that point. Name, type, calibre, the lot. You will also provide a list of the people, here and elsewhere, whom your people intend to kill. I want that firstly so that we can warn and protect them. Secondly, if anything does happen to any one of them, we will release the letter and the list to the world's press. It should cause quite a stir. Your precious colonel will not enjoy being directly fingered as some kind of Muslim Mafioso, even though that is exactly what he his."

"I cannot do it," said the man. "I won't. It is more than I am permitted to do. It's impossible."

"Of course you can," replied Wintle, smoothly, firmly. "You say that you're not an office boy. If you were, you would not be handling this affair. Without such a letter I will leave with the file, and unless you know who he is, how can you stop him? It's a fair exchange. It may be you next time, for he's getting very good at it. We can't stop him." Wintle looked directly at the man and let his smile broaden. "It's nothing to me," he added, "but if we come to an agreement and you keep to it, we have a stalemate. If we use what we have on you, you use what you have on us. Namely, the Incident file. First, the letter."

It took nearly an hour to write the letter. Wintle insisted on specifics; on names, dates, and places. Negotiations faltered when he produced a camera and took several close-up photographs of the man at work on the letter, but eventually the deed was done. Winkle took the letter, read it several times and placed it carefully in his pocket.

"Good," said the Libyan. "I trust you are satisfied. Now, give me the file."

"Oh no," said Wintle. "Not yet. First the conditions."

"What conditions? You have your conditions."

"No, I only have the lever which will keep you to them. The conditions are as follows." Wintle began to strike them off, one by one, on his fingers. "Firstly, our man is to be attacked and eliminated by the same team who attacked and set alight the Israeli airliner in Athens last year. Secondly . . ."

A sudden light dawned in the man's eyes. "Ah, it goes back to that," he cried, interrupting. "It's the Jews. I knew they would be in-volved. So it goes back to our attack . . . well!" He sat back, his hands spread.

"It does," said Wintle. "Your people started this. For reasons I won't go into at the moment, the same team must finish it if, of course, they have the competence. Do you accept this first condition?"

"Very well. Why not? It has a logic."

"And do you have the power to implement it? We feel this to be most important, so if you need higher authority, get it. In writing."

"You have the letter," said the Libyan pointedly. "We must agree, but as I say, it seems logical. I do not know where these men are, but I will find out."

"I can tell you where they are," said Wintle, grinning. "They are living in a small town called Tarhuna, south of Tripoli. They are currently unemployed." He smiled at the look of surprise on the man's face. "Do not think we are totally without knowledge of what you do." He leaned over and tapped his forefinger sharply on the desk top. "Look, I told you, we are going to help. There is no need for such grudging agreement. Secondly, your men will work to a plan I shall present. Our plan will work, all you have to do is produce the gunmen and make sure they follow it. Agreed?"

The man stared across the desk top at Wintle. At this close range Wintle noticed the blood-flecked yellow of his eyes, the pent-up dis-like behind the smooth smile. He began to enjoy himself.

"Tell us your plan," said the man dismissively. "We will consider it. But you ask a lot."

"First the conditions," said Wintle, smoothly. "You agree that the task of eliminating our man is carried out according to our plan, and reserved for the Athens people? Good. Then thirdly, the opera-tion is to take place outside the United Kingdom. There is to be no killing on my patch. He's our man and we want no slip-ups, no mas-sacres of innocent bystanders, no bombs, no booby traps under his car. Do you understand that?"

"I am not stupid, commander. Not being stupid I find your eager-ness for involvement curious. If you just tell us the name of this assassin, I assure you we can deal with him. We have some little practice in these matters. You are, after all, a policeman, who upholds your English justice. This is a new role you play here. It is not quite correct."

Wintle leaned back in his chair and laughed harshly. "That's rich," he said. "*You* lecturing *me* about justice. You have murdered your way around the world for years. I'm involved because your people are a bunch of clowns, and this man is too good for you. You are giving up the gun for the moment to try diplomacy, but there is a spanner in the works—our man with the shotgun. So we will help you dispose of him, without diplomacy but without a bloodbath either. Anyway, he leaves us no choice. He has to be stopped."

The man pursed his lips. "I assume your plan will work?" he said, doubtfully. "About our men, they are not clowns."

"As yet, I have no firm plan," said Wintle, relaxing a little. "What I am offering you, and we insist you accept, are the services of my department. We, or rather I, will report on the target's movements, and tell you where and when to strike. Your people are not excluded. We will work on this together. *How* is up to you; *where* is up to us; *who* we have already agreed. This is no planeload of unarmed women and children. It may not be that easy. Do you accept these terms?"

The Libyan shook his head, suddenly. "It's too thin, commander. I can't accept this idea. What is behind this offer of cooperation? From you, a policeman of long standing, high in your profession, to be involved in this business is truly incredible to me."

Wintle studied the attaché for a moment, letting the urgency seep from his voice, and allowing tiredness to creep in. "It's very simple," he said openly. "You'll understand, when you see who it is. This man is a rogue, an anarchist, but a person well connected in English society, in political circles, respected by the press. We cannot touch him without a huge scandal. We can't stop him. He's killing your people because you killed his family. When he's finished with you he'll turn to those of us who did nothing about it. My masters say he has to go, and go quietly. Do you accept these terms and do you want the file?"

The attaché studied Wintle's face and at last nodded slowly. "So, a madman is loose," he said carefully. "I can see—yes—he has to go, as you say. We will accept your terms, and we will carry out your plan. I understand now what Mr. Yates wants, and why we must do your dirty work—a typical British trick. He is not just helpful to us, as he pretends."

"Don't foul it up," warned Wintle, closely. "It could prove fatal for us both if your team fails. Our man will know who set him up."

"We won't," said the man, firmly. "We dare not. As you say, this man is a very efficient killer." He gestured toward the desk against the wall. "We have felt his hand already."

"Very well," said Wintle at last, giving the man a friendly smile and opening up the briefcase. "Then here is the file."

Simon swung open the door of his flat quickly, and urged Wintle inside. Then he locked and chained the door behind them before leading the way through into the sitting room and heading toward the drinks cupboard at a fast pace.

"Did he buy it?" he asked, turning to face Wintle across the room. "Come on, out with it. I'm dying to know what happened."

Wintle was stripping off his overcoat and hurling it onto a chair. Then he shrugged his jacket back into position and collapsed into another chair.

"Who?" he asked, stretching his arms and legs out.

"Whoever you spoke to. The Green Jihad. My God, you were in there for ages, over two hours! I was going frantic sitting in that damned library. Did they buy it?"

"Only just," said Wintle, wearily. "It was touch and go for a while. He was harder to convince than Yates, funnily enough. Look, could I have a drink? Dealing with such people is just a little wearing and I need a drink like never before. Where's your hospitality? Then I'll tell you the lot."

Simon opened the cupboard, took out a bottle and glasses, splashing Scotch into one of them and holding it toward Wintle. "Never mind all that," he said. "Just put me out of my misery. Did they bite or not?"

"Yes, damn you, they did. They have the file on you and I have their letter admitting to their possession of arms and all that. They ought to play ball. When he realized who it was, and it all suddenly clicked, I thought he'd have a heart attack. Apparently he knows you. You met at some diplomatic do or other. He was practically biting the carpet with fury when I left. I'll keep an eye on them for a day or two, just in case."

"I thought he might be upset," said Simon with satisfaction, "though I don't remember meeting any Libyan. What do they have to lose anyway, bumping me off? It ought to be a piece of cake with their hit teams roaming about the world."

"It wasn't just you, or the pressure I could put on them which sold our plan though," said Wintle, gulping his drink in quick swallows. "They wouldn't have bought that. What sold it was the idea that we, the Brits, want you killed as well. They like that. It makes them feel cozy, almost back in the human club. You were quite right on one thing though. They don't find the idea of policemen setting up a murder too difficult to swallow."

Simon nodded. "I told you that. Very early on in this business I realized that people can only see a problem from their own point of view. That's the way it is with people. Self-interest is universal."

"How do you mean?" asked Wintle. "I don't quite see the point."

"Well, for example, if a friend rang your office to ask you to dinner and was told that you had been run over, his first thought might be, 'Oh dear, poor fellow, how dreadful,' but his next one would be 'Blast! Now who can I get to make up the numbers?' "

"You're a cynical swine," said Wintle soberly. "Don't you ever think well of anyone?"

"Not often," said Simon frankly. "Well, perhaps; sometimes. But no one ever went far wrong overestimating the self-interest of the human race. Our Libyan friends identify with you in setting me up. It gives them a warm glow and saves them the trouble. The thought that you think you are doing *them* a favor is just cream in their coffee. So, what's the deal?"

Wintle shrugged. "It's as we agreed. I am to have you watched, find out your travel plans, and tell them where and how you are to be hit. I have stressed that it must be somewhere remote, and not involve other police or intelligence forces, lest their investigators are uncooperative, discover what's going on between us and blow the whole story. Since you are planning your own assassination, my role so far is fairly simple. Thank God, I actually can have you protected, and help you, without going out of character. It all fits the story very well."

"I have the plan all worked out," said Simon, "but there is a snag, perhaps two."

"Really? As many as that?" asked Wintle ironically. "What are they?"

Simon took a strong pull at his drink and looked thoughtful. "First, can you guarantee strict adherence to the plan? For it to work I have to lead them on for half a day at least and they have to lay off until they are on my chosen ground. If they have a go at me before I get there, I am dead, quite literally."

"Guarantee is a big word, Simon, but I think that will be all right," replied Wintle. "They are keen to cooperate and I do have a lever. If you don't give the game away, or panic them, it should be all right. What's the other snag?"

"The second snag is that I have to trust you."

"I thought you already did," said Wintle. "This is one terrible time to have second thoughts, Simon. You have to trust me, don't you?"

"Not a lot," said Simon, smiling. "However this turns out, you are setting up a killing. I don't think you like it. It sticks in your throat."

"Get to the point," said Wintle shortly. "I'm tired of people either prodding my conscience or assuming I don't have one. What's the snag?"

Simon scratched his chin slowly, his eyes steady on Wintle's face. "Look, see this from my side," he said. "When you've been living like I have for the past year or so, it's hard to relax."

"I asked you to get to the point."

"The point is that you don't really have to do anything now, do you? I could say . . . Fine, I give up . . . and you could take me in, and you win. Now the Jihad know who I am, they could come at me and again, you win. Blood on your patch, of course, but you win. Or when I have explained how we do it, you let me do my part and sit on your hands, and again you win. And all you have to do now is nothing. Do you see what I mean?"

"All I can see is that this is one hell of a time to have doubts," said Wintle. "And I can't help you there. You either trust me or you don't."

"That's the snag," admitted Simon. "I have to trust you, and I'll only find out if I've made a mistake when—sorry, *if*—you let me down."

"I'm grateful for the 'if,' " said Wintle harshly. "But there's nothing I can do about your problem. What do you actually want me to do now?"

"I need the shotgun taken abroad and I need your help to move it," said Simon, "but the minute you have the shotgun you have the evidence to arrest me."

"Why do you need the shotgun? And why can't you smuggle it out by car, the way you brought it in?"

"I'm going to fly out to Spain. It's quicker and safer, but I can't conceal a shotgun on that sort of journey. It's too long to pack and it won't break down. Besides, I have to appear unarmed, but I'm not sure of myself with anything else but that weapon. Can I trust you to get it to me and not call the boys in blue when you have it? Then we meet, you hand over the weapon, and I give our friends a nasty surprise."

Wintle got up, walked across to the cabinet and refilled his glass, adding ice and soda. Then he turned to look directly at Simon. "It's too late to turn you in," he said. "Everyone wants you dead. Everyone wants an end to this affair, and you're the one they want. Now I've shopped you to the Libyans, there is a chance you'll get your wish. So don't worry about my turning you in. You lost that option this morning."

Simon nodded, brooding, his face dark against the chair covering, expressionless. "I don't really care," he said at last. "I told you, after I settle with these people, it's finally over."

"You really think so?" said Wintle, a slight smile at the corners of his mouth. "Well, we shall see. Anyway, we've talked enough, Simon. I'll help you, whatever it takes. Tell me what you want."

"You have to collect the shotgun and get it down to me in Spain. I appear to be unarmed, walking about the city of Barcelona, that is until you hand me the weapon. Surprise is all I have on my side, and if timings are right I'll have that, and that's enough. I have it all worked out."

"I bet you have," said Wintle. "What do I have to do? Why Spain, anyway?"

"Various reasons, mostly tactical, but they may help you sell the plan to set this caper in Spain. Unlike the Greeks, the Spaniards are tough on terrorists, having plenty of their own; ETA and so on. They even shoot them if they catch them. If our friends bump me off and get caught, there will be no mercy for them, so they will probably do as you tell them. It gives us a little edge. Then again, I speak Spanish, and I know the area I have in mind well. That's two more edges."

Simon rose from his chair and turned toward Wintle. "You start you retirement soon, don't you?"

"As soon as you are dead," said Wintle, smoothly. "That's the tacit assumption anyway."

"Well, it will have to be a little sooner than that. Come into the kitchen and I'll show you what we're going to do."

They were half way across the room when the doorbell rang. They both stopped in mid-stride and exchanged startled looks.

"Who on earth is that?" asked Wintle. "Are you expecting anyone tonight?"

The bell shrilled again, impatiently, and went on ringing. Simon hesitated, looked at Wintle, and then moved toward the door.

"Wait," said Wintle cautiously. "It could be your friends from the Jihad. I don't think it's likely, but it just could be. Better let me answer it."

"I thought you had them sold," hissed Simon, his lips tight. "If this is them, we have a problem. I'll have to take a look, though."

"Don't risk it," said Wintle, grasping Simon by the arm. "Let me go."

Simon shook his hand off. "Stay out of it. Go into the kitchen and close the door. Put the light out and get down on the floor."

The bell shrilled again, on and on, resounding throughout the flat.

"Impatient bastards, aren't they?" snapped Simon. He went back toward the drinks cupboard, reached up inside and ripped loose the Browning pistol, cocking the action in one swift movement, easing off the safety catch. Then he turned to leave the room, the weapon large in his fist.

"Good God!" exclaimed Wintle in surprise, "where did that come from? My men didn't find it."

"When they were looking, it wasn't here," replied Simon briefly. "Now, go into the kitchen and keep out of sight."

Keeping close to the wall, he eased down the corridor, keeping away from the security peephole, that bright eye of light in the door. The bell still rang, drowning the swift turning of the lock as he reached the door and jerked it suddenly open. The ringing stopped abruptly and he stood in the doorway, stunned.

"Surprise, darling!" cried Clio. "Surprise! Can I come in?"

FIFTEEN

"Who was that very nice man?" asked Clio. A drink in her hand, she sat curled up on the sofa, her eyes bright with curiosity, looking up as Simon returned from closing the front door and made his way steadily across the room and over to the drinks cupboard.

"A friend," said Simon shortly, rattling the bottles, hurling ice cubes viciously into his glass, his back toward her.

"He's very distinguished," Clio went on approvingly, "but obviously not a publisher. He's far too well dressed for that. He might be a doctor. What *does* he do?"

Simon ignored the invitingly empty half of the sofa, flung himself into an armchair and glared at Clio impatiently. "When I consider that you have spent the last half hour doing nothing but grill the man yourself, I'm surprised that you don't already know," he snapped. "Look, what the hell are you doing here?"

"He was rather evasive, that's all," said Clio, "but I think he said he was retired. And I'm here to see you. Why not?"

"He's not retired. Not yet. He's going to retire," said Simon.

"He's a policeman, if you must know, a very senior policeman. He's not exactly a friend, either. More of a partner. How long are you thinking of staying?"

Clio raised an eyebrow. "Put another question like that, darling, and I shall start to feel unwelcome. The pair of you looked like two kids caught with their hands in the cookie jar. But what, I ask myself now, are you doing spending social evenings with a policeman?"

Simon looked at her bleakly. He felt suddenly tired of all the evasion, and furious that yet another element had come to intrude on his plans.

"It wasn't a social call. He thinks I'm the man who murdered that Libyan terrorist leader in Stratford last month." He took a deep drink from his glass and watched Clio closely over the rim. "I think it made even the U.S. papers."

Clio laughed. "Yes, I read all about it. But *you* couldn't have killed him." She rattled her glass at him for a refill. "It wasn't you, was it?" she joked. "Did you kill him?"

"Yes," said Simon flatly. "I fired a shotgun into his head."

Clio's smile slipped and she stared wildly at him, her face puzzled, worried. She hesitated, becoming less sure of herself, "You . . . you *are* joking, aren't you?" she asked. "Tell me you're just kidding."

"Not at all," replied Simon calmly, swirling the ice cubes around his glass. "I've been at it for, well, it seems like ages. A few weeks before that, I got into the office of a terrorist group in St. James's Square and killed five of the people there. That was just after you and I had returned from Paris. You didn't know it, but I bought the shotgun in Paris and we smuggled it through in the car. Before that I shot the security chief at Athens airport. That was an accident . . . well . . . perhaps that's not the word . . . it wasn't planned, I did it on impulse. I've become a quite efficient killer since then, though. And with the assistance of that distinguished gentleman who has just left, I'm going to kill a couple more people in the next week or two. That means I'm rather preoccupied at the moment. So you must excuse me if I'm a trifle . . . abrupt."

Clio looked at him during this recital, her face becoming set and pale. Simon could see a nerve flickering along her jawline as she took in what he had told her, mulling it over in her mind, and then rejecting it."

"No ... No, you're putting me on," she said, shaking her head positively. "But even so, it's not funny, Simon. You're not the type. But I still don't like it. Don't make sick jokes."

Simon rose abruptly from the chair to walk in swift strides over to the drinks cabinet, jerk open the door and reach inside to where he had hastily replaced the Browning pistol. He held the black bulk of the automatic out toward her, and let it spin on the trigger guard, swinging to and fro before her eyes.

"You see?" he said. "It's a pistol. But I don't use this. I use a heavy-calibre shotgun, with special loads. I make the loads up myself, here in the kitchen. I'm not joking, Clio."

They stared at each other silently across the slowly swinging pistol. Very slowly, tears brimmed from the corners of Clio's eyes and began to spill steadily down her cheeks. As Simon watched, her face crumpled. She changed from being the cool, sharp, self-possessed lady he knew into a crushed, crumpled woman. He put the pistol back inside the cabinet and walked toward the sofa, sitting down beside her and letting her head fall against his shoulder. They sat there quietly, his elbows resting on his knees, until she recovered herself a little and sat up, sniffing, leaning across to take the handkerchief from his top pocket. She uncoiled herself, wiped her eyes, grabbed her handbag and half-ran from the room. Simon heard the taps running in the bathroom and the snap of her handbag as she repaired her makeup. In a few minutes she returned, still pale, but now calm, to sit in the chair opposite. She lit a cigarette, avoiding his eyes, then blew a large cloud of smoke into the air and looked directly across at him.

"All right, I'm a big girl again. What the hell have you been playing at?" she asked sharply. "Don't sit there looking like some kid who's just broken a window, Simon. Are you mad, or what? Jesus Christ, Simon—you! Of all people. Christ!" She took another savage drag on her cigarette and waved the smoke away impatiently.

"You believe me, then?" he said. "You're not hard to convince. Most people would find it amazing, but you don't. I'm not sure how I feel about that."

"Sure I believe you. It all clicks. It's Eleana and the kids again, isn't it? That's the explanation of the way you've been behaving this last year. That's why you're so bright, you've got an aim in life again. You bloody fool! They'll catch you and you'll go to jail for years, unless someone kills you. You've ruined your life—and mine!"

"I don't think so," said Simon simply. "It isn't going to end like that—not at all. I'm not going to let it."

"Oh yes? And why not?" demanded Clio, dragging again on her cigarette and then stubbing it out, half-smoked, in an ashtray. "I can see you're crazy, but how will it end?"

Simon told her everything. He told her, step by step, how he had drifted into this affair, about Yates and Wintle, about the Libyans and Stratford, and what must happen now. He poured it all out in detail, while she sat listening, her eyes fixed on his face, putting in the odd question. When he had finished, she got up silently, and went into the kitchen, coming back after a little while with two cups of coffee. She handed one to Simon and sat down opposite him again, her eyes resting on him thoughtfully.

"I'm sorry I had to tell you all this," he began, "but you had better know how things stand."

"Jesus Christ!" she exclaimed. "I'm still sitting here, and even now I don't believe it. It's true—and it's impossible. Listen, what about us in all this?"

"What do you mean, what about us?" asked Simon, blankly. "You aren't involved at all. God knows why I told you, but I just couldn't help myself. I want you on the next flight out, before you get involved any more."

"Oh, but I am involved," replied Clio. "I'm in, brother, up to my neck. First, I love you. I don't much feel like I love you very much at this moment, but when I get over the shock, I'll still love you. So, I don't want you dead. So, how can I stop this? Just two questions, OK?"

"Yes?"

"OK. Question one—can you get away with it? Question two—then what happens to us?"

Simon pondered, stroking his lips with a forefinger, "It's hard to think past question number one," he said. "I think I can get away with it. I'm in charge of the game, or I will be if Wintle can sell my plan to the opposition. What happens after that, I just don't know."

"But will it be over?" she asked him urgently, leaning forward. "Or will it go on? After this last time, what happens then? Can you call if off?"

"I don't know," he said simply. "When I realized what I had to do, I thought I'd hit them so hard they'd never forget it—and I have. If I can finish the pair who actually attacked the airplane, that will do me. After all, I can't punish the whole world."

"Then why do it?" she persisted, leaning toward him again. "Why else would you do these things? What's the real reason?"

"I need to settle this for Eleana and the kids. Had I been in Athens when they died, and done nothing about it, what would you have thought? People like me have been taking stick from people like them for as long as I can remember. Just once, just this time, they aren't going to get away with it. That's it."

Clio heaved a deep, heavy sigh. "I can't feel it like you do, but I guess you're right." She shook her head at him sadly, "It's still very primitive, Simon."

Simon shrugged. "You want words?" he asked. "I'm completely out of words."

Clio bit her lip, then looked up at him decisively. "I've been thinking about that. I'm going to trust you, and I'm going to help you," she said. "You're not the only person in the world with feelings. I'm in."

"Oh no you're not," said Simon firmly. "You're leaving here tomorrow. Go about your own business until this business of mine is over. You are going to Frankfurt to wheel and deal. And that's final."

For the first time Clio smiled, a slow, warm smile. "Go to hell!" she said cheefully. "Now we are going to bed. I've had all I can take for one night and we'll both feel a lot better in the morning."

She rose from her chair and held out her hand. "Come on, you crazy man," she said. "Do as you're told, for once in your life."

Almost with relief, Simon got up and followed her into the bedroom.

"It's impossible," said Simon. "Surely you can see that, Philip, make her see it too, for heaven's sake. I've got enough to worry about without a woman round my neck."

Wintle and Clio exchanged a friendly glance and then both looked cheerfully at Simon's frowning face. The three of them were sitting around the kitchen table at Simon's flat, the top littered with cups, maps, timetables and a host of scribbled notes. They had been talking for hours.

"Well, let's not be hasty," said Wintle. "I can see your objections, but Clio has her points too. Go over the plan again, Simon," he urged. "We can't afford to have any slipups."

"And don't be such a chauvinist pig," added Clio.

Simon glared at them both, sighed heavily, then picked up a pencil and began to run over his proposals again, ticking off the items on the list before him.

"Basically, it works like this. I fly to Barcelona and stay there for a few days, ostensibly on business. You see to it that the opposition arrives just before I leave again, this tme by train, for a few days' walking in the Pyrenees. Hill-walking is my hobby and they can check it out in *Who's Who*. Anyway, it's plausible. Now, see the timings here. They are to follow me by train to this little station here." He tapped the map. "It's called Nuria. It's very small, just a few houses and a station. I've been there before and it's perfect for us, and for them. It's high in the hills, and from there a path leads over into France. They follow me into the hills and once we are out of sight and earshot of the village, they kill me, hide the body, go back on the train and away. It's neat, and simple. English walker disappears in mountains. It happens all the time. No fuss, no scandal, and no body till the spring. OK? It's tailor-made for them. They ought to jump at it."

"That's what I will tell the opposition," agreed Wintle, nodding. "With all the relevant details, timings, and so on. It sounds good to me. Now, what *actually* happens?"

Simon scrabbled among the papers on the tabletop and picked up another list. "This is where I need your help, and the timings are crucial. Once I have left London for Barcelona, you go on pre-retirement leave. I suggest you express disgust at what you have done, and walk out. Don't just fade away, we don't want anyone nosey-parkering about. You travel out by car, with the gun hidden inside, which should be a snip for you to handle. To be exact, you travel in my car down to Perpignan, and then up to here." Simon traced a road on the map. "Font-Romeu, on the French side of the frontier. The path I shall follow from Nuria leads over to there. You climb to meet me, bringing the weapons, hand them over, fade into the mist, and the rest you can leave to me. What do you think?"

Wintle shook his head. "It's risky," he said. "Too many loose ends."

Simon disagreed. "No, it's not," he said firmly. "It's very simple, and simple plans work. It also gives me the one thing I must have—surprise. The only thing that can go wrong is if you prang my car or break down on the motorway. If so, you must ring me at the hotel in Barcelona and we put everything back twenty-four hours until you are in position at Font-Romeu. You ring me when you arrive at Font-Romeu—here's the number—and if all is well, we go. Build some doubts into the story you tell the opposition . . . say that the dates of the walking holiday are still a little fluid. It will look suspicious if you know my movements too exactly. If you are waiting up on the col, here," he tapped the map, "with the shotgun, I'll be fine. If you don't turn up, then I'll simply run away from them in the mountains. I'm not an easy man to catch in the hills."

"What if they don't wait?" asked Clio. "What if they attack you in Barcelona or hit you on the train? You won't be able to run away from them there."

Simon nodded at Wintle. "It's up to him to sell this plan to the enemy and see they stick to it, but I think they'll buy it. You don't know all the background to this, Clio, but it will be much better for all concerned if I seem to meet with an accident. I'm sure running me down with a car or pushing me under a train has already been considered, but my habit of going for walks in the hills is a golden opportunity. They won't pass it up, and if the plan works, they'll be home free, as you say in the States."

Clio shook her head. "Let me come with you to Barcelona, even to Nuria. With someone there beside you, they will hesitate to attack. Dammit Simon, I'm coming."

"Dammit, you're not," snapped Simon, slamming his hand on the table. "How many more times, Clio?" His voice softened. "I know you want to help, but can't you see you'll be just another problem. Besides, it's dangerous."

"Wait a minute, Simon," interrupted Wintle quietly, "Clio may be useful cover. She has a good point here, and you ought to consider it. And your whole plan depends on them attempting nothing in Barcelona, so it shouldn't be dangerous."

"But I don't want her involved," said Simon. "Never mind the danger."

"She is involved," said Wintle firmly. "You involved her. Let her go with you to Barcelona. It will look natural, having a woman along. It's a reason for you to be there, rather than in Frankfurt with the other publishers where you ought to be, and as Clio says, with her around they have a strong reason to hold their hand. Also it will help me sell this story to the people at the Jihad."

Simon hesitated, shaking his head and pursing his lips. "I don't like it," he said. "It's just something else to think about, something to complicate matters." He looked at both of them, sighed heavily, and shrugged. "Oh, all right, but you are definitely not coming to Nuria, Clio. When I leave Barcelona, you go on to Frankfurt."

"Not a chance," said Clio firmly. "I'm not leaving. The waiting would kill me, if you'll excuse the expression."

"Why not take the train and go over into France? Wait for us in Perpignan," suggested Wintle. "It will only be a day, then we can come back together, or decide what to do next."

Simon nodded thoughtfully. "That just might be useful. I'll take nothing with me up to Nuria, so Clio could bring my stuff out of Barcelona. If it goes as planned it will be their bodies up in the hills until spring, and I don't think anyone will connect an Englishman and his lady on holiday in Barcelona with two dead Arabs. Even so, I don't want my gear in Barcelona triggering off anyone's memory. Yes, I'll buy it."

"Good," said Wintle, shooting a quick conspiratorial smile at Clio. "Now, let's go over this yet again. This time give me all the timings, Simon, yours, mine, and Clio's . . ."

"There is still one other snag," said Simon thoughtfully, sorting the maps and papers into neat piles. "I don't know what the bastards look like, and I have to. I don't want to cut down the wrong people by mistake, and I'd like to know when they pick me up. I'd hate them to lose me and go all that way for nothing. Besides, knowing who they are and what they look like gives me another edge."

"I expect they'll look like Arabs," shrugged Wintle. "There won't be that many Arabs in a little Pyrenean resort like Nuria during October, let alone following you up into the hills. Finding them is the least of your worries. They will find you."

"Not so," said Simon. "This is Spain. Most Spaniards look a bit like Arabs, small, dark, and so on. For most of history half of them even *were* Arabs. Can you get me a photo of these people?"

Wintle looked thoughtful, then doubtful, and shook his head slowly. "I'm sure we haven't got one at the Yard," he said, "and I can't think of a reason to go around asking after one from our contacts abroad; even if they have one, which I doubt. Such people as the Jihad are careful about that. I'll hunt around certainly, but I don't even know their names, let alone their faces."

"The Greeks might have one," said Clio. "They must have photographed the killers after they surrendered at the airport, and there must be something on file, somewhere."

"You're right!" said Simon, smacking a fist into his palm, "but not just the Greeks. That bloody photographer will certainly have something, and he's probably right here in London."

"Which photographer?" asked Clio sharply. Then she clapped

her hand to her mouth. "Oh! *That* photographer . . . of course . . . him."

"Yes, that one," said Simon nodding. "The one who got an award for photographing my kid on fire. He's bound to have kept a set of prints. He's going to come in useful to me after all."

"It's a thought," agreed Wintle, nodding. "Do you want us to get them through our channels? It should only take a phone call."

"Good God, no!" exclaimed Simon hurriedly. "Let the Fleet Street reporters even suspect that your office is still interested in the Athens killing, and we'll be knee-deep in the bastards. Leave it to me. Publishers have their little ways of getting what we want, you know. Now, let's go over this plan one more time—or maybe twice."

Simon watched him come into the bar, a small, stocky figure with a big, stiff envelope tucked under his arm, eyes darting about, searching around the room. As their eyes met, Simon raised his hand, half smiling, and the man came across, staring down at him across the table.

"Mr. Evans, is it?" he asked. "The gentleman who called and wants a few good action snaps?"

"That's me," said Simon blandly. "You'll be Mr. Brice, right? Mr. Andy Brice? Good of you to come." Simon found it difficult to shake Brice's hand.

"Well," said Brice, pulling out a chair and sitting down across the table, "it's just up the road really, and you said there might be some cash in it."

"There might," conceded Simon cautiously, "but, before we go into that, what would you like to drink?"

"Well," said Brice, grinning, "seeing as you're paying, and you *are* paying, aren't you? . . . why don't we have a spot of champagne? They do a nice spot of that here, not too pricey."

Simon smiled thinly. "Why not?" he said evenly. "Just wait here a minute." Crossing back from the bar with bottle and glasses, he carefully avoided the glances of some Fleet Street acquaintances, among the crowd now assembling for their lunchtime drink, hoping that no one would feel obliged to come over to the table and spoil his story. He set down the glasses, filled them carefully, until the rising bubbles stopped short of the rim, and looked across at the photographer.

"Cheers," said Brice, picking up his glass and raising it toward Simon. "Here's to crime."

"Cheers to you," echoed Simon, pulling his chair closer to the table and leaning across it confidentially. "Now, as I explained to you on the phone, my company are book packagers. Do you know what that is—No? Well, we sell ideas to publishers, ideas for books, and if they buy it, then we put the package together, words, pictures, the lot. We are currently working on a big idea, an international edition of a book on illustrated news stories. You know the sort of thing. How they happened; the best pictures taken at the time; how the story developed at home and abroad. That sort of thing—dramatic stuff. We have to consider stories that people will remember over, say, the last five years. It has to be up-to-date . . . memories are short." The lies slipped smoothly from Simon's lips and he looked frankly into Brice's face, playing lightly with the stem of his glass.

"I see," said Brice, nodding his head firmly. "Well, I'm your man—that's why we're here, right? My work at Athens last year won the News Photographer of the Year Award, you know. They don't give that away. That's a real classy award, d'you know that?"

"So I believe," said Simon smoothly. "You took a remarkable series of pictures, if I remember correctly, and that, of course, is why we contacted you. We need to have some first-class material now to set up the deal and get the cash in, but of course, we don't want to tip our hand to the competitors."

"It was bloody fantastic," went on Brice, only half listening. "Those pics I took made *Paris Match, Time, Der Speigel, Hola*—you name it, they bought it. They made a bloody fortune."

"Did they? Well, you see," said Simon, putting a note of alarm into his voice, "perhaps any offer we could make would not interest you? I'm afraid we could only offer a small amount at the moment."

"No, no," said Brice, hurriedly. "Hang about a bit, you don't get me. I didn't make anything much out of it. Of course, the agency I work for made a packet, and I got a good bonus," he added grudgingly, "and the award. I screwed them for a fat raise after that, and they came across. But nothing big, nothing heavy . . . and a few notes on the side are always welcome."

"Then perhaps," said Simon delicately, "I could see the prints?"

Brice looked round the room, then took the brown envelope from beside his chair and slid it across the table. "I brought the negs, like you asked," he said, "and a set of full-plate glossies. You can see that the focus is spot-on, just like you wanted. Don't flash them about though, not in here."

After a swift glance around the room, Simon slid the sheaf of photographs out into his hand. Sarah's small, agonised face leaped out at him again. Her eyes were like black pits in that contorted face, her mouth a scream. He put that photograph aside and focused with difficulty on the others. Here it all was, the whole story, frame by frame, the men firing at the aircraft, one crouching halfway up the steps. Here again, running off as a grenade exploded in the aircraft door. The whole attack unrolled before him as he sifted through the prints. He turned the pictures over one by one onto the chair beside him, until at last he saw the one he wanted, a close-up of the two gunmen being led across the ramp toward the airport building, surrounded by police, their hands clasped on their heads, faces raised toward the camera and the watching crowds on the balcony above. They were smiling.

"They're excellent," agreed Simon slowly. "It's all there, isn't it? You did a great job here. Yes, certainly you did a great job."

"Bloody right I did," said Brice, draining his glass and filling it up again, until it overflowed across the table. "Those are magic. Did you see the one of the kid? That's the one I got the prize for. Now you've got to have a good look at that, it's a winner." He tugged the print from the pile and thrust it before Simon's face, tapping it with his forefinger. "Now, look at the detail," he went on. "It's not easy to get something like that. She was moving you know, running like hell. She ran right off the end of the wing. Pity I couldn't snap her in mid-air, but you can't have everything, can you? See? I saw her hit the ground, a hell of a thump, but I couldn't really snap her under there either, too much contrast, with the sunlight off the concrete and all. But this one—see? It really gets into her face, doesn't it? Bloody fantastic shot. Luck really, but well, you need a bit of luck to get a pic like that."

Simon let him talk on, the voice becoming a roar in his ears, the photo blurring before his eyes. Sweat began to gather on his back, sticking his shirt to his skin.

"Here," said Brice suddenly, sounding alarmed. "Are you all right?"

"I'm fine, just thinking," said Simon, breathing in deeply. "It's nothing."

"You looked right peaky there for a minute. Drinking at this hour doesn't agree with you, then?" asked Brice. "You'd soon get used to it on my job. It's all the hanging about. That reminds me, I've got to get back to the office. You did mention some money. Cash?"

Simon took an envelope out of his pocket and handed it over. "I'd rather you didn't count it in here," he said, jerking his head at the crowded bar, "but you'll find the fifty pounds in there, in cash, just as asked. That's a deposit, of course." His voice was steady now. "We'll take these prints to the Book Fair at Frankfurt next month and tout them around the publishers. It we do a deal we'll pay your agency the usual fees and you'll get a royalty on top of that. It may not be much . . . but we are grateful for your help."

"Never mind that," said Brice genially, stuffing the envelope into his jacket. "You help me, I'll help you. One hand washes the other—you know what I mean?"

"I really would like to keep this matter confidential for the moment," stressed Simon. "I'd hate to see the idea get to someone else. It wouldn't do either of us any good, and it could blow the whole deal."

"You can trust me, Mr. Evans," said Brice. "Anyway, borrowing prints from the office is not approved of, so I've got my own neck to think about. No one will hear anything from me, and you'll keep your head down about where you got them from—right?"

"Right," agreed Simon, rising to his feet. "Well now, if you'll excuse me. . . ."

"Don't you want another glass of this?" asked Brice, holding up the half-empty bottle. "Good stuff, isn't it? It's a pity to waste it."

"Thank you, but no," replied Simon. "As you say, it doesn't agree with me this early in the day."

"All the more for me then," said Brice, filling his glass. "But don't forget what I said. Use the one with the kiddie. If they don't buy that one, they don't know a good photograph when they see one. It's a real winner."

"I wanted to kill him," said Simon over his shoulder, staring down into the street from the window of his apartment. "I wanted to put him on the list, the callous bastard, I wanted to kill him so much, I still don't know how I made it out of the bar. When I got to the street, I started to shake all over."

Wintle shot him a quick, hard glance from the sofa, leaning forward to tap out his pipe in the ashtray. "There will be no killings on my patch, Simon. Besides, he's not involved. Forget him. People like that aren't worth it."

Simon sighed and turned away from the window, moving out into the room. "Oh, I don't really mean it. I just get tired, I suppose. He's just like all the rest. He profited by what happened, and my Sarah was nothing to him. He didn't have a clue who I was, or might have been. I bet he's never even thought about the people involved. He just took that marvelous, terrible photograph and it meant nothing to him but prestige and money—a quick buck. That's what my daughter's death added up to, a bit of personal profit. It makes me sick."

"The world's full of people like him," said Wintle soothingly. "You can't get rid of them all, they breed like flies."

"Maybe not," said Simon, "but I can deal with those I can reach . . . and I'm going to swat another tomorrow, just as soon as I get to work."

Simon came to the door of his office and stopped there, looking down at Ruth's bent head. As usual she was working busily, her fingers flying over the keys, plowing her way throught the work, as active as a dynamo.

"Hey," he said, "stop that a minute."

Ruth's fingers hesitated over the keyboard, tapped once again, and she swore. "Damn! Look what you've made me do. Why do you have to creep up on me like that? What did you want anyway; I'm very busy."

"Then stop being busy," said Simon, "and come in here, I want to talk to you."

She followed him into his office, noting the cardboard box on his desk full of the contents of the desk drawers, but she said nothing until they were seated, and looking at each other across the desk.

"Well?"

"I'm going away for a while," said Simon, "and I want you to take over while I'm gone."

"I always do," said Ruth, shortly.

"Also, it's time you had some reward for your efforts," he went on, pushing some papers toward her over the desk. "Sign here . . . here . . . and here."

"Why? What is it?"

"It's forty-one percent of the company. With the ten percent you already own that gives you control . . . and don't argue."

"But Simon, you're mad! I don't want . . . you can't give me control of the company."

"I'm not giving you anything," said Simon, smiling. "When you read the small print you will find I get ten percent of the gross for the next four years. That's my payment for forty percent, and I still hold forty-nine percent, but you run the Quarry Press. What's it like to be the boss?"

Ruth sat back in her chair, rubbed her eyes and then looked back at him, her lips a firm line, thinking.

"It's the old business, isn't it?" she asked. "Is it never going to stop?"

"This is the end of it," said Simon. "I don't know what the end will be exactly, so I'm putting my affairs in order. Even if all works out well, I'm going to retire to somewhere remote for a few months—or go to the USA. I don't know yet. All I ask is that you don't argue about it. Just sign, without another word, please."

Ruth picked up the pen and signed, took the envelope Simon offered and slipped the contract inside.

"The solicitors know all about it," he said. "So does the bank. I'm off tomorrow, but I'll keep in touch. There are one or two little things I still want you to do."

"Anything you want," said Ruth, wearily.

"When we're finished, send Clissold in here, I want to see him. Then, in about a week, I want you to send a telex message to old Fritz in Israel. Just one line. Say 'I hit them as hard as I could'—that's all."

"And he will understand that, will he?" asked Ruth.

"He will. I expect he already does. One final thing, on your way out . . ."

"Yes?"

"Take down that awful photograph. I never want to see it again."

When Ruth had gone, closing the door quietly behind her, Simon took the boxes off his desk, put them on the floor out of sight, and was seated again comfortably, leafing through a folder, when Martin Clissold came tapping on the door.

"Come in Martin. Sit down."

"Thanks."

Simon smiled across the desk at Clissold, nodding his head slightly, then tossed the folder onto the top, and swung his feet up beside it.

"Tell me Martin, how long have you been with us?"

"Just over four years—nearly five."

"As long as that? Well, I must say you've done a grand job. You've been a real help . . ."

"Thank you."

" . . . and I'm really almost sorry we shall have to let you go," continued Simon.

"What?" said Clissold, startled.

"That's a popular way to put it," said Simon. "It means you're fired."

"What?" said Clissold again, looking shocked. "But why?"

"Because you're a shit," said Simon, pleasantly.

"Now look here, Quarry," burst out Clissold, suddenly aggressive, half rising.

Simon swung his feet off the desk, and leaned forward to face his opponent.

"No, you look here. You're a good lad, Clissold, efficient, ambitious—well, that's all right, but you are no good with people. Like I say, you're a shit. No, I haven't finished. For the last year you've been conniving against me, spreading tales, delaying deals, playing politics all round the office. Rule One here is No Politics. I told you that the day you joined, remember?"

"But . . ."

"I still haven't finished. If you want a business, why not start your own? Why consort with my competitors and try to steal mine? You know what you've been doing." Simon slipped an envelope from the folder. "Here's your check, dismissal letter, etc. Leave your keys at reception. I want you gone within the hour. Now get out."

Clissold, shaken, rose to his feet, picking up the envelope, and then he rallied. "You can't just kick me out like that, Quarry. I've got a contract, and rights. I'll take you to an industrial court—I'll sue you for wrongful dismissal."

"Sue away," said Simon. "You'll find the check in there is for twice what you are entitled to. You should take it and count yourself lucky. But if you want a fight I'll give you one." He flipped open and spread out the papers on his desk. "I've been keeping an eye on you for months. There are agency agreements here, still unsigned, letters about your projected takeover of this company, spare copies of internal financial memos you supplied to my competitors; if you must act like an industrial spy, why use my staff to do it? They report to me. Don't try and deny any of this. At this moment your files are being locked. I expect to find plenty more dirt when we go through them. So you go ahead and sue, and I'll spread those facts around the trade; you'll never work again if I do that. So, why don't you just stop whining and get out? If you are still here in fifty-nine minutes, I'll throw you out myself."

* * *

Simon was back in his usual position, feet on the desk, with a glass of Scotch at his elbow, when Ruth came into the room, a worried look on her face.

"What on earth have you done to Martin? He came out looking as white as a sheet, and he says he's resigned."

"He would," said Simon. "I've given him the push—and don't say you don't know why. If he turns nasty later, when I'm not here, you'll find everything you need to squash him in this file. A clerk from the solicitors has the key to his office files; have them go through his papers for more dirt, just in case."

"Good God!" said Ruth. "Well—that's sudden."

"Sit down, get yourself a drink," said Simon, "and no crocodile tears; the bastard asked for it. Anyway, if you approve, boss, I suggest you write to Ron Cohen, offering him the post of sales director. I've already sounded him out, and he'll be happy to accept. He's efficient, and he's loyal."

"Yes," said Ruth, nodding. "I like Ron. I'll write to him today . . . or I'll call him."

Simon took a key from his pocket and pushed it toward her. "Tell him he can stay at my flat until he finds a house for the family. Then you could move in here, and he could have your office. And you'll need to get yourself a secretary."

Ruth shrugged her shoulders and sighed, shaking her head at him wonderingly. "You have been busy, haven't you?"

"Just clearing the decks," said Simon. "I don't want to leave you with all the dirty work to do."

"Hence removing the photo?"

"Yes, hence the photo. The time has come for a fresh start. I'm almost looking forward to it."

"It won't be the same, Simon."

Simon looked at her, smiling slightly. "All in all, we can say thank God for that."

That night, sending Clio out to the theatre, Simon had a last meeting with Wintle. They sat facing each other, as so often before, across the kitchen table, the top a litter of maps and pencils, timetable, glasses, their usual malt whisky in a half-empty bottle.

"I think that's everything," said Simon. "At least, I can't think of anything else. If all goes as we expect, I'll clear off for a year or two and let the dust settle on your files."

"I think that would be best," agreed Wintle. "The way things are, we will soon have more to worry about than a few unsolved killings."

Simon picked up a pencil from the map on the table and rattled it briefly against his teeth before speaking, his eyes resting thoughtfully on Wintle's face.

"There is one last problem," he said. "The shotgun. If I tell you where it is, and you go and get it, you will have all you need to tie me into those shootings. So, do I trust you?"

"We've been into all this before," said Wintle. "But yes, you can trust me. Otherwise you're a dead man. Anyway, even if I take you in, I doubt if you'll ever make it to court, and I can't back out now either. No doubt a careful record of all that has happened between us, with as much detail as you can command, is in some safe place? Am I right?"

"No, you're not," said Simon. "But you are, well, half right. Clio has all the background. She would be the perfect witness to your . . . well, my entrapment."

Wintle nodded approvingly. "I told you that lady would be useful. She's a great girl," he said, "and I like your caution. Where do I go to get the weapon?"

Simon felt his pocket and pulled out a small key. "It's in the Baker Street Vaults," he said. "The box number is on the key. If you screw the clip which you'll find with the shotgun into the underside of the parcel rack in my car, you'll find it fits. The Customs won't look there. It's fully loaded, so don't fiddle with it, but I'd appreciate the box of cartridges as well. You'd better take the car with you tonight. I won't be needing it again." He placed the car keys alongside the vault key and watched as Wintle put them carefully into his waistcoat pocket.

"When do you meet the opposition again?" Simon asked.

"I don't," said Wintle. "I have a number to ring. It's already set up. All I really need is the date you go to Barcelona. Allow three days to get the terrorists there, and myself to the col, before you move. When do we start?"

"It's October already," said Simon reflectively. "It will be getting cold up in the mountains, there may even be some snow." He looked hard at Wintle. "Did anyone ever tell you that the waiting is the worst part?" he asked.

Wintle nodded. "Lots of people."

"Well, it's true," said Simon. "So let's get this show on the road. Clio and I leave for Barcelona tomorrow night. I'll head for the hills on Saturday morning, and Heaven help us all!"

SIXTEEN

Clio was standing by the window when she saw them. She had either been standing there smoking nervously, looking down at the crowds hurrying past along the Ramblas, or pacing up and down the room, since they arrived.

"Oh my God! There they are," she cried sharply, stepping back suddenly from the window.

"Who?" asked Simon, looking up from his book.

"Your friends, who else?" said Clio tensely. Simon swung his legs from the bed and moved across to join her by the window, slipping an arm around her waist, resting his cheek against her hair. "Where are they?" he asked, looking over her shoulder, down into the street.

"Down there. Across the way, at the table on the side," she said. "I wouldn't have noticed, but they keep looking over here. Then it just kind of clicked. God! Keep back. Don't let them see you looking out."

Simon said nothing. Standing to the side of the curtain, his eyes searched among the tables of the café opposite, beyond the heads of people hurrying up and down the street. Finally, he fixed his gaze on one particular table, but after a few moments he shook his head doubtfully.

"Are you sure?" he asked, frowning. "It's hard to pick out faces from over here."

"Quite sure," said Clio. "Check the photos, if you don't believe me. Only thing is, there are three of them."

Simon picked up the glossy newspaper photos from the bed, held them to the light, and compared them, as best he could, with the men across the way.

"Mmmm," he murmured. "All right, I believe you, but where's the third one you're talking about? I only see two. But that's them."

He threw the photos onto the table, and smiled at her.

"The third one went inside," replied Clio. "No, look, here he comes now. Do you recognize him?"

Simon shook his head, turning again to peep out of the window. "I've never seen any of them before. Not for real. God, he's so young, that third one. I suppose this is a trial run for him. A little something to show him the ropes. He is about to take part in the last stand of the Green Jihad. That young man is going to have a very short career." Simon smiled bleakly to himself, and kissed Clio softly on the cheek. She broke away from him, turning away to curl up in her usual position in a chair, watching Simon as he continued to study the men below, keeping half-hidden behind the curtain. She lit another cigarette, puffed on it once, and then crushed it out hard in the ashtray.

Simon stayed at the window for a while, then shrugged his shoulders slightly and, turning away, joined Clio, and settling himself into a chair opposite her looked at her impassively.

"May I see them again?" he asked, holding out his hand for the photographs spread out on the table by her side. Clio gathered them up wordlessly, and passed them over to him, then reached for another cigarette and her lighter.

"It is them, isn't it?" she asked, snapping the flint and puffing on the cigarette. "The bad guys. The opposition, as you and Philip call them."

Simon nodded, without looking up at her, his eyes studying the pictures. "Yes, that's them. You're right about that. The one on the left, here," he tapped the photo, "he's grown a moustache, but it's them all right. That's good, that's very good." He nodded with satisfaction, half to himself, smiling at Clio, and sank back into the chair, linking his hands behind his head.

"Why good?" cried Clio. "What, in the name of Christ, is good about it?" She stabbed her cigarette in the direction of the window. "There are three killers sitting right across the street, and you're their target, lover. They are going to try and kill you."

Simon looked at her patiently. "It's good because it means that they are following the plan, and that means the plan is working. They are on the trail, just as we agreed, and that's great stuff." He got up and took a turn about the room, rubbing his hands with satisfaction, grinning at her contentedly.

"There's three of them," said Clio solemnly. "You didn't agree to that. You bargained for only two. That's a fify percent overload. What do you do about that?"

Simon shrugged, flapping his hand about vaguely. "It's a snag, but so what? Philip only suggested that those involved in the original killings should finish the job. He could hardly exclude them from bringing along the odd trainee. It might have looked odd if he had. The idea we are fostering is that this is something personal, between them and me. No; so far, so good. I'm pleased. Tonight we'll have a quiet dinner and tomorrow we'll get our act on the road. Later on we'll go out for a drink somewhere down the Ramblas, and let the dogs see the rabbit. I want to keep them interested because they will be happier and more relaxed if the plan seems to be working."

Clio shook her head sadly, sighing. "I don't follow you," she said, "not any more. How do you feel about all this?" She waved a long-fingered hand towards the window. "There they are, just a few feet away, the guys who murdered your wife and kids. Don't you feel like charging out there and blitzing them? Or just giving up and running away? To be honest, I didn't believe this would really happen. Not really. It's a nightmare."

Simon thought for a moment, sitting forward on the edge of the chair, elbows on knees, his chin resting on folded hands. He looked at her thoughtfully. "No, I don't want to hit or run, not yet," he said slowly. "Not really. It's curious, but I don't feel anything. I have thought I might want to reach out and strangle them with my bare hands, but somehow ... nothing." He shrugged his shoulders slightly, and smiled faintly, "Odd, isn't it?"

"But you'll go through with it?" she asked. "Is it still on?"

"Of course," he replied, jerking his head toward the window. "Do I have a choice? It's been coming to this for over a year now. I'm only glad that it will soon be over. If I feel anything at all right now, I feel—tired."

It was Clio's turn to smile, a slightly bitter smile which curved across her mouth. "Over?" she asked. "Do you believe that? Whatever happens, unless you die out there, it won't be *over*. It won't ever be over. You'll have killed three men, or five, or six, however many it is. You can't just shrug it off." She shook her head decisively.

"That's a rational argument from someone on the outside, perhaps," said Simon. "There is no such relationship here, far from it. In a normal world, your world, people don't go around setting fire to airliners. But *they* do. So we, the killers and the victims, live in a different world from you and Philip. There is dirt between these people and me. Those men are my enemies. They chose to kill my family and when I have killed them I won't lose a night's sleep over it. I shall return to my life without a second's thought. When they are gone, the shooting stops and everything can return to normal."

"But what if nothing happens?" asked Clio urgently. "What if Philip fails to turn up? What if this bad dream just ends, and they back off from you. It could happen. It all seems unreal, sitting here talking like this."

"Philip will turn up," said Simon firmly, "and don't think this is a work of fiction. It will all happen, just as we planned." Simon smiled at her, shaking his head gently. "You can't believe I know what I'm doing, can you? It's a scam, all of it; the whole thing is a set-up. Listen, George Orwell stayed here, during the Civil War, maybe in this very room. It's a publisher's pub, the natural place for me to stay.

Then, the bar's on the first floor, so there is no foyer, no way for them to get in and prowl around unseen. The thing is, sweetie, I'm a professional. I'm maybe the first one they've met. I hope they don't know that, any more than you seem to do, because it gives me a little edge. That's more important than anything in this game, except the weapons. And they will be there, trust Philip."

"But what if they aren't?" stressed Clio again. "What will you do?"

"Then I'll run away from them," said Simon, "but don't even think about it. I don't. I know Philip and he'll turn up. Now, why not make yourself look glamorous and we'll go out and get that drink?"

"Is it safe?" asked Clio, glancing anxiously out of the window. "What will they do when they see you?"

Simon shrugged and got up. "Nothing," he said, reaching for his jacket. "Nothing at all. We're waiting for Philip, all of us. The difference between us is that those three down there don't know it. Now, get your face on, I'm hungry."

At about the same time, a hundred miles away, to the north of the Pyrenees, Philip Wintle was turning Simon's car off the autoroute, and bumping gently through the streets of Perpignan, leaning forward in his seat to study the road signs. Eventually, he pulled over to the side and parked, opening the glove compartment to pull out a map, pushing the box of shotgun cartridges back out of sight with his fingers. He switched on the overhead light and studied the map for a while, thoughtfully. Then he snapped the light off and swung the car away from the curb, following the road along beside the river, past Villefranche and up the sheer-sided valley to the plateau of the Cerdagne.

As the car wove its way higher, in third gear now, the headlights sweeping across the rock walls as Wintle spun the car round the bends, it began to rain, long drops lancing down in the beam of the headlights, the rain then turning to sleet and snow, spattering across the windscreen, blurring the view. When Wintle turned on the wipers they gathered up the ice and snow, piling it in a thick bar at the bottom of the screen, falling ever thicker, as he came out of the gorge and up onto the open plateau. In the headlights the road ran ahead, black against the light, with the mountain peaks dim against the sky far behind, set against a mass of billowing cloud. The wind was gusting strongly now, buffeting the car as Wintle drove under the wires of the ski lifts and into the resort of Font-Romeu. He found the hotel, the neon sign bright against the black sky, and drove into the courtyard, stepping out into the chill air, the wind whipping his hair, sending a spatter of snowflakes into his face. Snatching his case from the back seat, he ran up the steps swiftly and disappeared inside, shoulders hunched against the rising wind.

"Where are they?" asked Clio, anxiously. "What's happening?"

Simon sighed, put the menu down on the table, and looked across at her, patiently. "Please," he said, "stop worrying. What would you like to eat?"

"It's all right for you," snapped Clio, "sitting there with your back to the wall. You can see what's going on. I'm going mad here. Can't you see that?"

Simon smiled. "I'm sorry about that," he said, "but if you sat here, where you can see, you would have blown our cover in five minutes, just by staring at them. We're supposed to be all unawares, remember. For your information, one, the young one, is sitting at the bar, struggling manfully against the urge to stare at me, and the other two are about to start their dinner at a table by the door. They don't appear to speak much Spanish. It has taken them ages to order, but they haven't looked over here once. A very professional pair, those two."

There was a tinge of admiration in Simon's voice, almost a note of respect. He turned again to the menu and concentrated on choosing a meal. Clio lit another cigarette, blew smoke into the air over his head, and tossed the lighter down on the table.

"You are quite amazing," she said. "You sound almost like a fan. You really go for them, don't you? This really is turning you on."

"Oh, hardly that," replied Simon, "but I respect professionalism, wherever it is. It makes things easier all around." he raised his hand and a waiter appeared at Clio's elbow.

"What will you have?"

"You choose," she said. "I don't have much of an appetite. In fact, I think I'd like to throw up."

Simon's face softened, a smile curving at the corners of his mouth. "You ought to eat," he urged. "It will all help to keep up appearances. But take something light."

"You choose," she said.

Simon looked up at the waiter, slipped into Spanish and ordered gazpacho, calamares, roast chicken with a salad, and flan. "That ought to do it," he said, "with a bottle of Torres."

"What are calamares?" asked Clio, searching in her handbag for another cigarette. "It sounds foreign. What is it?"

"Squid," said Simon, winking at her.

"And flan?"

"Custard."

"Yuk," said Clio, shuddering. "Squid and custard, that's all I need."

After dinner Wintle picked up his wine glass from the table, tucked the map under his arm, and wandered through into the bar. A line of locals were standing along the zinc-topped counter, glasses of pastis before them on the bar, eyes fixed on the television screen fixed high in the corner, where footballers moved about in a silver drift of static and a gabble of sound.

He found a table and sat down, placing the ashtray on a chair and spreading out the map. On it he marked his present location and then traced the path he must follow in the morning over it, nodding to himself as he picked out the landmarks. Presently he became aware of a man watching him from the bar, and as their eyes met the man slid off his stool and came over to the table.

"You are going across the mountains?" he asked in French, craning his head round to look at the map. "It is late in the year for the mountains."

"I'm sorry," said Wintle, "but I don't speak French."

"That is all right," said the man, switching into English. "I speak good English. In summer I am mountain guide, in winter ski teacher. We have many English here, all through the year."

"Your English is very good," said Wintle, offering the man a chair with a gesture of his hand. "Better than my French."

"I have some words only," said the man. "Put the foots here, so, bend the knees, like this, it is easy." He pulled out the chair and sat down, twisting his head again to study Wintle's map.

"Ah!" he said, suddenly understanding. "You are walking into Spain, across to Nuria. A good *randonnée* this, but it is very late in the year for that journey. We may have snow. Up on the col, here, certainly."

"Snow? When?" asked Wintle worriedly, looking down at the map. "Not now, I hope. The path is still open, isn't it? It's only October."

"Oh yes, it's open," said the man. "But it will not be open much longer, a few days only. In summer many walkers cross the ridge, over the col and down into Nuria, but now it is late. You should not go alone, for it is far. You are in *plein form?*" he asked.

"I beg your pardon?" said Wintle. "I'm afraid I don't . . ."

"You are fit?" asked the man, flexing his arm. "You are—I have to say it—not a young man, and this," he tapped the map, "this is not an easy walk. Not an English . . . stroll. You could go somewhere else. There are many walks near here."

"I won't go all the way," said Wintle. "Perhaps just to here, to the col, and then come back. That won't be too difficult, will it?"

The man looked at him reflectively, his lips pursed. "I can come with you," he proposed. "I am the local mountain guide. One hundred francs only, one day. I bring lunch, and wine."

"Oh thank you, but no," said Wintle hurriedly. "I prefer to walk alone, really. Very kind of you, but no. Thank you." His voice was firm, definite.

The man ignored him, pulling out a chair and sitting down suddenly, leaning across the table, his face close to Wintle's, his voice soft.

"It's late for walking . . . too late. What are you really doing, eh?

You tell me . . . I help." This close, Wintle could see the red veins in his eyes, the short stubble on his chin. He sat back a little and began to fold the map.

"I don't understand you," he said, "and I don't want any help. So perhaps you will excuse me . . ."

The man seized Wintle firmly by the forearm. "Come on," he said. "What you want? You have a big car, expensive car. Why are you here, eh? Walking across to Spain . . . the summer is over, M'sieu, and winter is coming. Is it something political? Drugs? This is a good place . . . no guards, no frontier posts . . . we have lots of people come here, on private business. I help them . . . not expensive."

Wintle sat still, held by the hard grip on his forearm, silent, letting the seconds tick away. From the corner of his eye he could see the group by the bar, watching them closely. "Damm," he thought, "not this, not now."

The man released Wintle's arm, shrugged and sat back in his chair, jerking a thumb at the men behind. "We have to live, right? We make a little living, this and that. You sleep here, in the morning we have a little talk. Maybe there is something you will want us to do . . . is possible."

"No," said Wintle. "I don't think so. I just want to go walking. That's all there is to it. Believe me."

The man shrugged and got up. "Very well," he said, "but M'sieu, if you go even to the col, leave early, get back early. If it snows turn back. It will take you all day to get there and back. If it snows it will not be safe up there tomorrow on the frontier."

"No," said Wintle, thoughtfully. "No, I don't suppose it will. And, one last thing, where is the telephone?"

Next morning, just after nine, Simon and Clio followed the porter across the platform of Barcelona's main station. The trolley ahead was piled high with Clio's suitcases, Simon's small rucksack resting lightly on the top. He was already dressed for walking, in anorak, breeches and boots, and they stepped out quickly, forcing their way through the morning rush.

"What have you got in there?" asked Clio, nodding toward the rucksack, hugging close to his arm.

"A pillow," he said grinning. "I stole it from the hotel his morning, but I left a thousand pesetas to pay for it in the wardrobe."

"What do you want a pillow for?" she asked. "Don't you have anything else to carry?"

"I want the rucksack to look full," he replied, "but the less weight I have in it the better, in case I have to outrun our little chums up the mountain. I may be fitter but they seem to be younger than I am."

"Are they here?" she asked, looking around. "God, what a crowd! What if they don't follow, or lose you?"

"They are sure to be here. The young dogsbody was outside the hotel all night," said Simon as they got to his platform. "Maybe they are already on the train. Why not? They know where I'm going. Thank God these little trains have no corridors. I shall find a compartment full of peasants and make myself agreeable, all the way to the end of the line. Just in case the opposition feel like getting it over with quickly."

"Please, Simon," said Clio, "don't talk like that, not now."

They stopped halfway along the platform, and turned to face each other, Simon reaching out to lift the rucksack from the trolley and swing it over one shoulder. Clio looked up at him, suddenly pale, uncertain.

"Now listen," he said, "I'll be fine, but are you all right?" He took her hands in his. "You know what to do now, don't you?"

Clio nodded, swallowing hard. "I take the train for Perpignan, get off there, and go to the first hotel listed in the Michelin guide. If that is full, I go to the next, and so on, till I find a room. I book two rooms and wait. Tonight you turn up with Philip . . ." Her voice trailed away, and she leaned forward to rest her head against his shoulder.

"Don't worry," he urged again. "It will be all right. I do know what I'm doing. And you've been a great help."

"Let me worry," she said. "You won't let me do anything else, so let me at least do that. Hell! What else is there to do?"

He took her by the arm, just above the elbow, and held her away from him, smiling down gently into her face. "It's not necessary to worry," he said. "It will be all right. It's just a game, you see, and I'm a very old dog at it."

"Go on then," she said, putting her hands against his chest and pushing him gently away with the flat palms. "For God's sake, go, and do what you have to do."

Simon nodded, his mouth set hard. "I will," he said, "and I'll see you tonight. Goodbye."

"Goodbye," she said, and turned suddenly away.

Wintle woke to the silence. He lay there for a moment, half-buried under the duvet, then poked an arm out from the covers, looking at his watch in the dim grey light that seeped through the curtains. It was eight-thirty, plenty of time. He rolled over onto his back and stretched, his feet emerging at the bottom of the bed into the cold air of the room. He pulled them back into the warmth and listened again to the silence. There was not a sound from outside, no sighing of the wind, no noise of cars, or voices, or distant trains. Suddenly worried, Wintle flung back the bedclothes, put his feet onto the cold wooden planks of the floor, went hurriedly to the window and jerked back the curtains.

"Jesus Christ!" he exclaimed.

Outside, over the road and rooftops, as far as the eye could see, the high plateau of the Cerdagne and the mountains that lay beyond it to the south were deeply covered with snow.

Five minutes later, having hurriedly thrown on his clothes, Wintle went leaping down the stairs into the hall. The reception desk was empty, no one stood behind the bar. He found the proprietor in the kitchen, crumbling a roll into his coffee.

"Quick," said Wintle, "I need to make a phone call. Can you help me? It's urgent. The same number as last night."

The man shook his head and made no effort to get out of his chair. "No use, M'sieu," he jerked his head at the window. "*Trop de neige* . . . too much snow. The phones are not working. Maybe later."

Wintle could have shaken him. "Christ! All right . . . where is the post office?"

"Pardon?"

"The Post Office. *La Poste,* the P.T.T . . . ?"

Wheels spinning in the snow, Wintle reversed the car back out of its slot, slammed it into forward drive and shot out of the parking lot and down the road into the village, coming to a long, sliding stop in front of the Post, Telegraph and Telephone Office, leaping out to bound up the steps. The booths were empty, the clerk helpful and the lines working. Three minutes later he was speaking to the hotel in Barcelona.

"*Digame?*"

"Do you speak English?" asked Wintle urgently.

"*Si, Señor.*"

"Señor Quarry's room, quickly."

"Señor Quarry has gone, señor . . . he just left."

"Damn, Damn, Damn!" Wintle leaned his forehead against the front of the booth. "Listen . . . when did he leave?"

"Just now . . . five minutes."

"And the lady, the señora?"

"She too, with Señor Quarry . . . *momentito Señor.*"

"Wait . . . Wait! Don't go," pleaded Wintle. "Listen . . ."

"Si, Señor . . . but are many peoples here."

"Now listen," said Wintle. "This is urgent. If you want to earn some money, good money, get a taxi, go to the station and find Señor Quarry. He's catching a train to a place called Nuria . . . Nuria . . . can you remember that?"

"But . . ."

"Listen! Find him. Tell him it's snowing there. He's not to go. Tell him he's not to go . . . and say you are to have . . . I don't know, ten thousand pesetas . . . twenty thousand . . . he'll give you a big tip. Will you do that?"

"*Si Señor,*" said the voice, resigned.

"You'll go now? At once? Now?"

"*Si, Señor.*"

"Thank God," said Wintle. "On your way. Be quick."

He put the phone back on the hook slowly, noticing as he did so that sweat was shining on his unshaven face, and that his legs were suddenly weak. He pushed his way through the door of the booth, and walked slowly over to the counter, feeling for his wallet.

"How much do I owe you?" he asked.

In the hotel in Barcelona, the clerk shook his head, listened to the dial tone and replaced the handset on the hook before looking across the counter at the group of tourists, standing there among their suitcases.

"*Buenos dias,*" he said smiling. "Welcome to our hotel, to Barcelona. Now, who is first?"

Simon crammed himself into an already overcrowded carriage, exchanging hearty *Buenos Dias* with all the other passengers, and was deep in conversation before the train pulled out. The journey went on for hours, the little train climbing into the foothills, halting at small stations, picking up passengers as others got out. At one of the longer halts, Simon went for a stroll along the platform, pausing within a few feet of the carriage containing his three followers, feeling their eyes on his back, sensing their stares being hurriedly averted as he walked back to his seat farther down the train. The whole journey was lasting too long and feeling unreal, a far too ordinary beginning for such an inevitable conclusion.

"Nuria!" said one of the passengers at last, pointing out of the window and nudging Simon in the ribs with his elbow.

Simon craned across and saw the rail track curving away around the side of the valley to a small cluster of grey buildings huddled against the high rearing walls of the Pyrenees behind. He stood up and swung his rucksack down from the rack, slipped it on, and climbed over the feet and legs of his companions to take a place by the door. This, he knew, would be the tricky part.

"The path to the frontier is to the right of the *monasterio,*" said an old man. "You will see it easily when you leave the station. *Buena Suerte.*"

"*Gracias,*" said Simon, smiling his thanks. He had the door half open as the train pulled into the station, and dropped off onto the platform as the train slowed to a halt. Behind him, other doors swung open and a small crowd followed him to the barrier, blocking the path of his pursuers. He was fifty yards ahead when they reached the barrier, and out of sight behind the monastery when the three broke through the scattering passengers and came after him at a hard walk.

Back at the hotel again, Wintle hurried to his room. He stripped off the garments he had pulled on half an hour before, and dressed again, in outdoor clothing, pulling on breeches and thick stockings, stamping his feet into boots, zipping up a quilted anorak. Within ten minutes he was downstairs again, to find the manager behind the reception desk, totting up bills.

"My account please," said Wintle. "Quickly!"

The manager looked up, took in Wintle's clothing and looked concerned. "You should stay here for a few hours," he said, worried. "The road down has not yet been cleared, and with this snow it is not safe. . . ."

"Look," put in Wintle firmly, "just give me my bill. If I want advice, I'll ask for it . . . and if that friend of yours from the bar last night comes looking for me, tell him the same thing. I'm simply moving on. Now, where's my bill?"

Getting across to the south of the plateau was difficult. Without chains on the wheels or studded tires, Quarry's car slid wildly on the snow-caked road, but at least the snow had stopped. After a few miles Wintle fitted the car in behind a snow plow and followed that across to Saillagouse, slowing every so often to peer at the map on the seat beside him. Eventually he found the place he wanted, forced the car off the road, wheels spinning, into a space out of sight behind a barn and got out. It was warmer now, the clouds shredding away overhead, with big drops from the melting snow pattering down from the eaves of the barn.

Wintle stamped across the tire tracks to a snow-caked signpost, reached up and struck it sharply. The snow fell off, and the lettering "Nuria" stood out sharp against the wet wood. Behind him a large section of melted snow slid noisily off the roof of the barn and thudded onto the roof of Quarry's car.

Wintle leaned his shoulder against the signpost, looking up the snowy track that it indicated, leading ever higher into the hills. Looking down, he saw that the snow reached almost to his knees, and he knew that the higher he went, the deeper it would get.

He trod his way back to the car, looking around the white vastness of the plateau, dotted here and there with the half-hidden shape of a farmhouse, then sweeping the snow from the car with one gloved hand, he heaved up the lid of the trunk and pulled out the rucksack and Simon's shotgun.

"We've got to give it a go," he said aloud. "We can't take the chance and not try it." He slammed the lid shut, stepped back hurriedly as another section of snow slid off the roof of the barn, and began to plow up the track toward the frontier.

Simon was wasting no time. Walking fast but without undue haste, he hurried across the open ground toward the mound that marked the start of the hill path, beside the whitewashed signpost with the word "*Francia*," and began to climb steadily. Forcing the pace now, he ran to where the trees hid him from view, gaining ground, hoping that his followers, now seen from time to time through the trees, would not attempt to close the distance to him until the monastery and any witnesses had been left far behind out of sight and earshot. Pressing on hard, he pulled steadily away from them. An hour later he was out above the treeline, marching steadily for the distant snow-tipped line of the col above, waiting briefly to watch his three followers emerge from the trees below, still on his path, perhaps a mile behind now but coming on steadily.

"And now," he said aloud, "we start the cat and mouse game, out of gunshot but never out of sight . . . and hold them at a distance until Philip turns up." He sat on a rock, and noticed that they had stopped too, huddled together below, their faces lighter blobs against the rocks and tussocks of grass, looking up at him. He raised his hand in greeting, but they made no answering move, just waiting until he got up to move before they turned to follow again up the path. Simon smiled grimly and began to climb.

* * *

Shaking the water from his cuff, Wintle pulled up his sleeve, looked at his watch and grunted with satisfaction. It was raining now, a soft, warm rain from the south, beating down on the path and into his face, melting the snow swiftly into water that rushed down among the ruts of the track, an ankle-deep torrent flowing over his boots, soaking his feet. Wintle didn't care. He was out of the snow now and making good time up toward the frontier. He moved off the path and sat down heavily on a rock, groping in a pocket for his handkerchief, mopping the rain and sweat from his face, shivering as the wind, sweeping down the gulley, struck through his garments. The rucksack pulled back heavily on his shoulders, so he slipped it off and placed it on the ground at his side, glancing again at his watch. Then he consulted the map.

The tumbledown hut across the stream was clearly marked on it, and so after three hours' walking he could fix his position quite accurately, tracing the path with his forefinger, his lips moving silently as he calculated the distance covered and the distance still to go. He had perhaps three more hours before he reached the col, and maybe six hours left of daylight. He wondered vaguely what Simon was doing. He must be drawing nearer now, somewhere over there, beyond the crest of the mountains, but there was nothing to be done about it. Wintle mopped his face again, took a long drink from the water bottle and, tucking it away in the rucksack, began to climb again toward the col.

It was raining hard by the time Simon came up out of the treeline onto the open rock, a hard rain beating on his back and driving him forward, half scrambling where he could, even breaking into a trot when the slope permitted, and he was even briefly out of sight of the group behind. He had gained a little distance on them, but they were moving fast, and by now they must at least guess that he knew, or suspected, who they were. Simon stopped, panting, on a little knoll beside the track, and looked back again, wondering how much he dared to force the pace, and deciding that it didn't matter. They knew he wasn't armed, and therefore running away from them was only natural. Sooner or later they would expect to run him down, and if Wintle didn't turn up soon, he would have to make a break for it across the mountains and take his chance on getting away from his pursuers. They were in plain sight now, half a mile away on the track below, their features visible even through the rain, but they made no response to Simon's ironic wave.

"Miserable, unsociable bastards, aren't you?" he said to himself. "But still, if that's the way you want it, that's fine with me."

He pressed on up the path, his shoulders hunched against the wind, warm from the effort of walking, ignoring the odd flurry of snow which burst over the ridge ahead and rattled down onto his windproofs. Low clouds began to rush across the crest above, mist settling, smoothing out the harsh contours of the rock.

"Better and better," he said, and bent again into the climb, taking the odd glance backward, slowing his pace to let the Arabs gain on him a little, keeping in touch, his breath coming evenly, looking ahead now, a trifle concerned, searching for the top of the col. Several times he thought he had reached it, coming to false crest after false crest. Now he ignored his pursuers, the pulse beating in his ears, raking every rock and patch of cover, his anxious eyes searching for Wintle. Wintle had to be there, but doubts had sifted into his head, and Simon never saw him until he spoke.

"Over here," said a voice suddenly.

Simon's heart lurched. "Christ!" he exclaimed, jumping, half turning from the path. "You gave me a turn . . . I didn't see you there."

Wintle sat carefully in the lee of a rock just above the path, his rucksack and the gun-case set beside him, a pair of binoculars resting on his lap. He looked cold and drawn, as he rose stiffly to pick up the gun and to clatter over the loose shingle down onto the path and join Simon.

"You're lucky to see me at all," said Philip. "I've been wading through snow to get up here. I even rang your hotel to call it all off, but you'd already left. But never mind that, is everything OK?" he asked. "How do you feel?"

"Now that you are here, I feel fine," said Simon, puffing. "Just let me catch my breath. How about you?"

Wintle shrugged, lifted the gun-case from his shoulder and held it out toward Simon. His face was set and worried, his grey hair plastered down by the rain and mist. "Well, I can't say I haven't had problems, but that doesn't matter. Have you seen them? There are three of them behind you," he said, "which is more than we bargained for. I wasn't expecting such odds."

"I know," said Simon, unstrapping the case, pulling out the shotgun by the butt and checking it over. "But don't worry about it. I can cope now I have this."

"That's not the worst," said Wintle. "One of them has a sub-machine gun."

His head bent, checking over the shotgun, Simon hesitated. "Are you sure?" he asked. "Quite sure?"

"I'm positive," said Wintle firmly. "I've been watching you through the glasses for half an hour. They are maybe fifteen minutes behind you, because they stopped to tool up, and one has an automatic weapon. The others seem to have pistols, but it's hard to be sure. Anyway, there is one automatic weapon down there at least, and now they are coming on fast."

Simon turned the shotgun over, groped in his pocket and began to thumb more cartridges into the magazine.

"I don't care," he said, "but it's worth a few extra loads. Don't worry, I can cope. Anyway, it's too late to fret about it now. It's time you left . . . thanks for coming . . . now clear off."

"We didn't bargain for long odds *and* automatic weapons," said Wintle. "The odds are too long, Simon. Why don't we just fade away up the path and try another day?"

Simon shook his head, working the action to drive a cartridge into the chamber. "What's all this 'we'?" he asked. "This is my show. Now, clear off and let met get on with it." He held out his hand. "Goodbye, Philip. Thanks for all your help. Now, clear off. Go to Perpignan and see Clio. With luck, I'll join up with you in an hour. But now scram before you make me nervous." There was a slight tremor in his voice and Wintle caught it.

"They'll kill you, Simon," he said flatly. "You'll never manage it. They'll cut you to pieces."

Simon smiled briefly, the rain and sweat glistening brightly on his face, water plastering his hair down thickly. "They will if I'm not ready when they arrive," he said. "I must find a place to make a stand, so please . . . go."

Wintle shook his head slowly, put out his arm to pat Simon briefly on the sleeve, then turned away up the path.

"Goodbye, Simon," he said.

Looking around, Simon followed Wintle slowly up the path for a few metres and then turned off and found his spot, an overhang of rock just by the path, with a gap which looked out across the hills. Kneeling down, he could see back down the path but the mist was thicker now, the rain sweeping in gusts across the crest. He wondered how much time he had, and turned again to study the path, seeing the rain splash into the growing puddles among the stones. Suddenly, he had an idea. Picking up his rucksack he threw it out of his hiding place, and sent it rolling down the path ahead to stop some twenty yards on, a vivid blue splash against the wet, grey stones.

Then he leaned back, waiting, bracing his shoulders against the rock, easing the action of the shotgun open until the red body of the cartridge came comfortingly into view. He slipped the action forward, listening to the oily click as the breech went home, and then he waited. Unexpectedly, he began to tremble. His cheek trembled, his legs suddenly felt weak. "Not nerves," he thought, "not now. Just let them come . . . quickly."

Then they were there, suddenly, passing by his left side in a tight group, the rain thudding onto their backs, weapons in their hands, a pistol, black in one brown fist, and not one but two machine-pistols. The leader saw the rucksack and stopped, the others bumping into him, banding together into a group. As they did so, Simon hunched his back hard against the rocks, pulled the shotgun butt into is shoulder, and opened fire.

That first shot was good. It smashed into the last man's back, hurling him forward into the others, blood spurting high into the rain. The impact knocked him down, but the others split, quickly, too quick for a second shot, diving off the path, turning fast, shooting back. A burst of fire lashed at Simon, spraying splinters from the rock beside his head. A pistol boomed in the mist and shot a red flame across the slope. The two men were moving back, scrambling across the hillside, cutting in toward him and dividing his attention.

Simon fired again, twice, to the left and right, once at each rolling figure. He saw one, the wrong one, the one with the pistol, hurled back against the ground. He worked the action again, chambered a load, and fired at the blurred fast-moving shape of the machine-gunner.

Then the bullet knocked him down. It didn't hurt. He felt only a great force, flinging him back. Splinters flew from the shotgun as the bullet plowed through the wood of the butt, smashing the weapon into his chest, driving the breath from his body. He saw the man, rising up unhurt, the pistol huge in his fist as he came scrambling toward him. Another burst of automatic fire came slashing across the rocks, whining off into the mist as the one with the pistol staggered up and aimed down at Simon's head.

Simon fired, his finger squeezing hard on the trigger as the pistol came into line. The shotgun boomed, a blast of sound, and the man disappeared, swept back and away by the hail of shot.

The sound of the shot echoed off the hills, bouncing from side to side and fading away. Simon fell back against the ground, gasping for breath, his strength suddenly gone. He looked down slowly at his hands, at the blood flowing out, dark red across his chest, at the white fleck of bone where his broken forefinger still gripped the trigger, and saw that his right hand was furred with bloody splinters from the shattered butt. He only half saw the last man rise and come slowly toward him, changing the magazine on his weapon as he picked his way across the broken ground. It was the young one.

Simon shrank back against the rocks, working with his heels and elbows, hiding as best he could under the overhang. The boy came on toward him, slowly, steadily, cocking the weapon, tucking the butt into his shoulder, crouching down, taking careful aim. Their eyes met over the barrel, unwavering. Simon noticed the boy's eyes, a dark, deep unwavering brown. Suddenly, with a rush, his nerve ran out. "Fuck you," Simon said, sobbing. "Get on with it."

From his place above the path, Wintle fired. He held the pistol in both hands, copybook fashion, swinging onto his target, and squeezed the trigger twice. He saw the gush of blood as the bullets bit into the boy's back. Then the boy was gone, spinning down the slope, the weapon flying from his hands, sliding and scraping away over the stones. The echo of the shots bounced again around the hills, and then it was silent once more, except for the patter of the rain. Wintle climbed back down to the path, stepping over the first man, around the widening pool of blood, then across toward Simon, the Browning pistol still held tightly in both hands, falling onto his knees in front of Simon's lair, his legs weak, the rain beating down on his back.

"My God!" exclaimed Simon, his voice shaking, gazing up at him, his face stark and pale against the rock. "Was that you? I thought I was dead."

"I ought to kill you," cried Wintle wildly, shaking the pistol in his face. Simon watched him carefully, squinting into the rain, lying back on one elbow, holding up his shattered, bleeding hand, before him.

"Then get on with it," he said, wearily. "I can't stop you, can I?"

The pistol muzzle wavered and dropped away. Wintle craned forward, looking at Simon closely, the pistol dangling from his hands as Simon began to inch his way out from under the rock, rolling over the shattered shotgun, wincing from the pain in his hand.

"I suppose I ought to say thanks," he said. "So, thanks. You should have stayed out of it, though. This was my fight."

"Just shut up," said Wintle wearily. "I'm tired of your voice. Are you badly hurt? You look a bloody mess . . . like the rest of it."

"It doesn't hurt much—not yet," answered Simon, "but it soon will, when the shock wears off. I'll need some help, my hand's broken, look. We must clear up this mess. It will snow soon and cover all this, but we must get well away. Now that it's over, that's all we have to do. Just get away, and it's all over." He fell back on the ground and looked up at Wintle, the rain running in streams down his face.

"Over?" Wintle laughed harshly, lifting his face again to the grey sky. "Over? This sort of thing is never over. What made you think it's over?"

"It's over," said Simon, staggering to his feet, leaning back against the wet rock. "They are dead, the Jihad is finished. This time they haven't got away with it and it's over because I say so. And I'm going home. Maybe to a new home, but home."

"Home!" cried Wintle. "You can't have a home, Simon. Homes are not for the likes of you. You can't do all this and expect to go home! They are all dead, but what have you done to yourself. Think about it, man."

Simon stared at him, at the bloody corpses lying about them in the rain, letting the shotgun drop from his hand to the ground. His body sagged suddenly, then he, too, turned his face up into the rain. "You may be right," he said wearily, "but for the moment, let's just go home."